THE HALFBLOOD KING

"I believe we are over nine hundred feet above the level of the sea. As to your second question, we are about a day from Freemarket, the last settlement of men before we reach the Southern Kingdom." Just then, an arrow flew from the dark forest, straight at Aleron. He barely raised his buckler in time to block and the bodkin neatly pierced the shield, vambrace and forearm together. He froze, momentarily, at the sight of the bloody arrowhead sticking two inches through his inner forearm. "Goblins!" Hadaras shouted. His sword was already out, and he chopped the black-fletched shaft from the boy's buckler. "Draw your blade, lad and be at the ready!" He gestured and raised a dome of shimmering blue around them. More arrows rained down upon them but were incinerated upon contact with the dome of magical energy, as was the first goblin warrior to charge the pair. The momentum of his charge carried him headlong into the blue light and they witnessed his body dissolve into gray ash, from front to back. This stopped the others from charging, and they surrounded the pair instead, shooting the occasional arrow and hurling the odd spear, only to watch them flare against the dome. "Leave the arrow in for now, boy; it plugs the hole. Are you well enough to shoot your bow?"

"I think so, Grandfather," Aleron answered. "It really doesn't hurt." At the moment, his wound was numb more than painful. He moved to retrieve his bow from his saddle, the quiver already on his hip. The goblins had them completely encircled now. There were nineteen in all, along with a half dozen of their half-tame wolf dogs.

"They know I can only maintain this for a little while and they will wait until I tire and falter. Take out as many as you can before then."

"I'll do my best," Aleron replied, as he dismounted with bow in hand. He winced as the bow forced his forearm to twist against the shaft piercing it, bringing pain at last. *I'll have to remember not to do that again.* Luckily, he was wearing a Chebek forearm buckler, with an arrow pass cutout, so he did not need to remove it to shoot.

The goblins jeered at him, one yelling, "What you gonna do, man-child, kill us all with your little bow." That one died with an arrow up one apelike nostril and a second one went down with a shaft through the eye.

"As a matter of fact, yes," he replied, as a third took an arrow through the heart.

THE HALFBLOOD KING

Book 1 of the Chronicles of Aertu

By Julian E. Benoit

THE BARDICHE PRESS

2023

This is a work of fiction. Any resemblance of characters in this work to actual persons, living or dead is purely coincidental and is likely the product of an overactive imagination. But hey, without overactive imaginations, what would we have for stories?

To Dawnna, Lucas, Tristan and Ethan
Your love and support mean everything to me.

And, to the Puppies,
who love us unconditionally,
and warn us of all intruders.

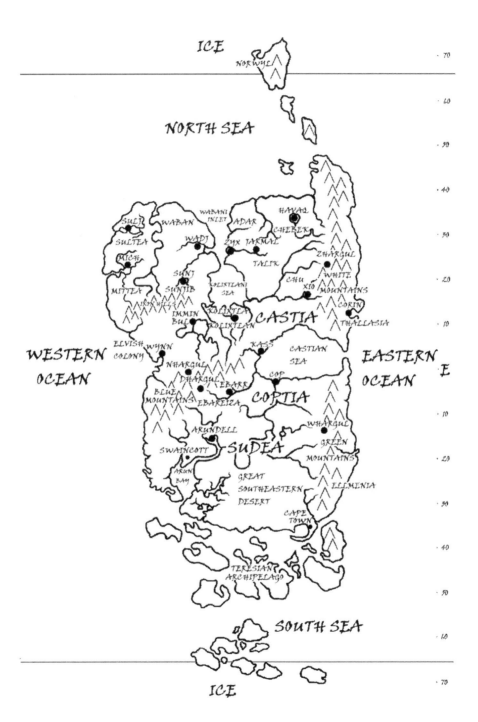

MAP OF AERTU MAIN CONTINENT

Prologue

Gurlachday, Day 7, Harvest Moon, 8747 Sudean Calendar

Valgier couldn't imagine being more content than he was at this time of his life. His occupation as a woodsman and primarily, his charcoal making business, were providing well for his young family. He built them a modest home in the foothills of the Southwestern Blue Mountains, managing to finish it shortly before the birth of their son Aleron. His customers included not only the men of the local villages, but also the dwarvish smiths of the mountains, who preferred charcoal to the rock coal they mined for the forging of their finest blades. They claimed rock coal would make the steel brittle, but charcoal was cleaner. It made for a booming business and Valgier put aside most of his other activities to devote enough time to keep up with the orders. He was happy that he could provide a good living for his wife and son.

The boy was growing well and at two years was handsome and tall for his age. In a few years, he would be able to help his father in the forest. The boy's mother, Audina, insisted on the name Aleron for their son. Valgier, at first, thought it a bit pretentious to name their son after the ancient king of Sudea, but the name grew on him, and it seemed to fit the boy well. His wife had a very persuasive way about her, as well as being the most beautiful woman he had ever seen. He could never tell her "No," but in return, she never asked for anything unreasonable. The name was a common enough one and had been for the millennia since the King gave his life in the final battle against the Nameless One. He was greatest of all the rulers of Sudea, bringing the kingdom to its pinnacle of power and influence. The trend may have continued indefinitely, if not for the decimation of the noble households from that brutal war. His thoughts wandered back to Audina, as his footsteps followed the familiar path to their home. He remembered how they had met:

He just returned to the village from a fortnight working in the forest, filthy from the baker's dozen charcoal heaps he left smoldering behind him. He brought his mule to the stables and carried his bag to the room he maintained above the tavern, requesting a couple pails of hot water from the publicans prior to climbing the stairs. Two years before, he sold his family's homestead to the south after they, along with his betrothed, died of plague. At twenty years of age, he had nothing but the money from the farm and headed north to begin anew.

About a half bell after entering his room, he heard a knock at the door. He opened it to the sight of the most stunningly beautiful woman he had ever laid eyes upon, her lustrous golden-brown hair framing features almost too perfect to be real. In her hands were two steaming pails of water. He stammered a thank you, as he quickly moved to relieve her of her burden. She smiled at that, and it seemed as if the heavens opened up before him, so beautiful she was. In the days to follow, he learned that she also lost her family in the plague and moved here from the northwest coast, bordering the Elvish Colony. He sometimes suspected that she had some elvish blood in her veins, not unheard of in the border country, though she always denied it. They had been together nearly three years now and she was still as lovely as the day they met.

As he entered the house, he set his broadax by the door and called out to his wife; there was no answer. "Aleron!" he called to his son next, with still no answer. He could smell supper cooking and wondered if they might be out behind the house. The assassin's blade slashed through his throat as he made his way past the kitchen, to the back door. His last vision was of oddly slanted eyes, so dark no pupils were visible, staring at him from a darkly tanned face. The assailant's straight black hair was tied back, out of his face. He slumped to the floor, vision dimming as his life's blood flowed across the front of his jerkin and realized in despair, that his family was most likely dead as well. Just like last time, he was powerless to save the ones he loved. It was with profound sadness that he slipped into unconsciousness and the life left his body.

The foreign killer left the man in the center hall, along with the dead woman in the kitchen and made his way to the bedroom, where the young boy lay drugged and unconscious. He picked the toddler up and slung him over his shoulder. His Master had been very clear in his instructions, that this boy would come to no harm, physically, or emotionally. The assassin made sure to render the lad unconscious before killing the parents. He had a good idea why this boy was important; his mother's elvish features became apparent as whatever sorcery she used to conceal them died along with her. This child was likely one of the few half-elves alive and potentially of great value to the Master.

THE HALFBLOOD KING

✳✳✳

Hadaras rode hard down the wooded trail, the high peaks of the Blue Mountains occasionally visible through the trees over his left shoulder. The non-descript brown mare he rode was capable of impressive speed, as befitted its lineage of elvish warhorses. He rode since late morning, as soon as he sensed the malevolent presence closing upon his daughter's family. He rarely strayed far from the family he secretly watched over. He sensed too, that he was too late to save her, or her human husband, but the boy still lived. He was close now. He slowed the mare to a trot and cast out with his senses.

✳✳✳

The assassin rode northwest, a packhorse trailing behind with a small limp bundle secured across its back. The boy shouldn't come around until well after he set camp for the night. Then he would tell the boy of the fire (he did set the house ablaze upon departing) and how he was too late to save the boy's parents. He would explain to the child how he would take him to a place where he would be cared for, just like his real parents would have. Some trauma was inevitable, but the boy was young enough that it wouldn't cause any lasting damage. He was mulling over these thoughts when he came upon the lone horseman on the trail ahead. It was a swivin elf, with no business in this territory other than with the assassin himself. Warded against elvish sorcery, he was confident in his ability in any one-on-one fight with conventional weapons.

"Give up the child and I may let you live Kolixtlani," the old elf called out.

"Let me pass unhindered old man and I may allow you to live. I do not fear your elf magic," the assassin replied, concealing his consternation at the elf's knowledge of his nationality.

"Very well, have it your way," the rider answered back. With a lazy wave of his fingers, a sliver of blue light projected from the elf's hand and neatly sliced through the other's neck. There was a look of shocked disbelief in the assassin's eyes, right before his head toppled from his shoulders. The hands still gripped the reins tightly, as the body slowly slumped from the saddle, no blood flowing from the cauterized stump of the man's neck.

Hadaras dismounted and made his way to the pair of horses. He recognized the pack animal as the horse belonging to his daughter's mate. He laid a hand on the bundle that contained his grandson and sensed that the boy was unharmed. He then turned his attention to the other horse and its rider, prying the dead fingers from the reins and laying the body on its back. He picked up the head by its hair and looked into the still open eyes, saying, "whoever you are, that sent this man, you have failed again." He then threw the head to the side of the path. Examining the body revealed the warded sigils the killer assumed would fend off Hadaras' sorcery. The sigils still glowed faintly red with the unsavory magic of the Adversary, activated by the touch of elvish magic. There was powerful magic invested in these, but a simple bend of his will dispelled it back to the source. *That will make someone flinch,* he thought to himself. Those wards must have been the reason the assassin was able to catch Audina at unawares. She had some mastery of sorcery, but not on par with her father's.

He led the horses to his own, tied the reins together and then returned to the corpse on the path. Grabbing one wrist and one ankle, he lightly flung the body to the side, to join its head. The blue flame he conjured burned with fierce intensity, consuming all, including the teeth. All he left behind was a dusting of fine gray ash. Returning to the horses, he hooked the reins of the assassin's horse to his mare's saddle and untied Aleron, removing the bag covering him. The little boy's face held a placid expression, as Hadaras carried him back to the lead horse. Resting the child on his shoulder, he remounted and then coaxed the animals forward, past the patch of ash, toward the house of his own child.

As they rounded a bend in the trail, Hadaras could see the still burning wreckage of the house and knew that the child's parents were both within. He dismounted and found a patch of soft grass, away from the wreckage, to lay his grandson. He made his way closer to the house and its attached stable. The heat was intense, but the blue nimbus enveloping the elf protected him from the brunt of it. There would be nothing salvageable now, he determined. He stepped back and raising his arms, he added his own blue fire to that of the blazing home. There would be no charred remains for the villagers to find, no bodies to count. It was in keeping with the funerary practices of his people as well and he voiced a prayer to speed their souls' return to the Allfather.

Hadaras collected his grandson and remounted the mare. Turning the train back up the path, they made their way towards the border with elvish territory. The thoughts going through his head were much like those of the assassin as he made his way up the same path. How would he explain the loss of the child's parents and everything he ever knew, without traumatizing the boy? He could feel Aleron stirring against his shoulder and knew he would awaken from his stupor before long.

A bell or more passed before they came upon the glade where he intended them to camp. Hadaras wrapped the small child in a blanket and laid him down near the well-used fire ring. Picketing the horses nearby, he went through the assassin's bags and found, surprisingly, a collection of Aleron's toys and some extra bedding, indicative of an intention to keep the boy comfortable. He chose a well-worn stuffed doll and brought it to where the little boy lay. Then he proceeded to build a fire. He would hide the lad in elvish territory for a time, safe there, even as he himself hid from his own people. He needed time to prepare this boy for a future that would be anything but uneventful. As well, he needed to figure out how the assassin made his way through elvish, or dwarvish lands, in order to attack this family. It was highly unlikely for the Kolixtlani to choose the southern route, through the heavily populated lands of men. He heard Aleron whimper and looked over to see him clutching the toy tightly to himself. Hadaras felt for the boy's mind and sensed that it was troubled. The boy knew something was amiss, though he could not comprehend what.

Chapter 1

Carpathday, Day 4, Sowing Moon, 8757 Sudean Calendar

Aleron sat with legs dangling over the side of the wooden bridge. His friends Barathol and Geldun were there beside him. All three had their fishing poles in-hand, lines dangling into the languid flow of the river below them. Cork bobbers tugged at the ends of the lines, attempting to follow the current out to sea. Steel hooks lurked inside balls of dough, infused with bacon grease, several inches below the surface, as the boys attempted to lure the local river carp to their demise. If they caught anything, the boys' mothers would complement them upon their triumphant return. The other two, that is, Aleron barely remembered his parents. He lived with his grandfather and cousin, and they were the only family he had in the world. His cousin Jessamine was much older, in her twenties in fact and had lost her parents during the plague, before Aleron was born. His grandfather Hadaras was old, maybe sixty or so, but had an ageless quality that was difficult to define.

Of the three boys, Aleron was the youngest, not quite past his twelfth year, but he was the tallest, as well as the brightest, of the three. His friends usually cast him as the ringleader for their endeavors, both legitimate and not. The exception being when they fell into trouble with the older boys in the village, then Barathol took over. Though not as tall as Aleron, he was much stouter and quite adept with his fists.

Aleron had not always lived in the village, only moving there about three years prior. They lived alone in the forest, far to the north, until one day Grandfather stated that they should move to a town, so Aleron could learn about other people. He didn't always like the things he learned about other people. Geldun and Barathol were the only boys his age in town, and he quickly joined their alliance against the cruel older boys of the village.

One day, somewhere near his ninth birthday, he wandered home with a bloody nose and a bruised cheekbone; they were unable to outrun the older boys that time. Jessamine set immediately to cleaning up the bloodied, teary-eyed youth, attempting to comfort his bruised ego, as well as his physical injuries. Grandfather looked at him and, with kind amusement in his eyes, said "It looks like it's time for you to learn how to fight." From that day forward, Grandfather spent one or two bells each day teaching Aleron fighting techniques. He claimed to have been a soldier once, long ago and to have lived many years among the elves, learning from them as well. The training started with simple punches, kicks, and grapples, progressing over the years to more advanced techniques for subduing an opponent, as well as various weapon forms.

Though Grandfather warned him not to reveal too much of what he learned to those outside the family, he felt the need to practice with boys more his own size and he showed what he learned to his two close friends. As it turned out, Barathol was a natural talent, taking to the techniques like a fish to water and quickly surpassing Aleron in skill, while Geldun proved to be of middling talent, though solid in his tenacity.

The boys often dreamed of leaving their small village of farmers and woodsmen, to become sailors or soldiers for the Kingdom of Sudea; still a kingdom though it had no king for over a thousand years. Their town was only a few miles from the coast, so all three of them had seen the navy ships moored at the bay and the sailors swaggering through the streets of the port city, dropping coin like it was their last day with the living.

Though Grandfather didn't appear to have any particular line of work to apprentice Aleron to, he encouraged Aleron to help the neighbors whenever possible. Aleron especially liked helping the woodsmen, because that had been his father's trade and it gave him a sense of connection to the man for whom he had but fleeting memories. When townsfolk became curious about Hadaras' apparently comfortable retirement, they were told he was a retired soldier, generously rewarded for his time in service, who decided to move to the countryside in order to better raise his orphaned grandchildren.

Aleron's companions were both the sons of farmers and days like today were becoming rare, as their responsibilities at home consumed more of their time. It was widely assumed that Aleron, not having a trade to follow his father into, would be the one most likely to take to the sea or join the army.

THE HALFBLOOD KING

Hadaras watched the boy leaving that morning, and thought of how much Aleron reminded him of his daughter, Audina, who had given birth to the boy. He was tall for his age, and had inherited the golden-brown hair, and silver eyes of his mother, as well as her stubborn streak. The lad had it in his mind that he would become a soldier or a sailor, and there was no detracting him from that line of thinking, though Hadaras was certain that he was destined for far greater things than that. He thought back on that day, over fifteen years ago, when his daughter announced that she was getting married:

"*Father, I have decided to be married,*" *she told him.*

"*That is certainly good news,*" *he replied. Audina had been born in the colonies, well after the Great War, so she was relatively young, but at five centuries of age, it was about time she chose a mate.* "*Do I know him?*"

"*I'm sure that you do Father; he is from a fine old family.*"

"*Good, what is his name and what family?*"

"*Valgier, of House Sudea,*" *she replied frankly.*

Hadaras' demeanor took on a dark cast, as he stated, "*That is a human, who does not even know the house to which he is heir to. House Sudea is extinct, as far as men are concerned. I have already determined that he is not the one.*"

"*I am aware of that, Father and I have been watching him since he was a babe, just as you have. I have seen that I can love him, for he is pure of heart and a vision has told me that he is to be the sire of the one.*"

"*And what makes you believe that you are to be the mother of the one? I have watched this family for nearly a thousand years, ever since I discovered the bastard nephew of Alagric's, the son of his dead brother, living on the streets of Arundell. I have waited since, for the right time and the right heir, to come together. I have worked all these years to assure the family remains far from power, to avoid any inopportune discovery of their birthright. What makes you think you know better?*"

"*Father, the prophecies have all stated that a millennium will pass before a new king rises to the throne. If the heir is to be born, it must be soon,*" *she spoke.*

"*The prophecies were not that specific; they were all written to say "millennia" not precisely how many. Plus, they say nothing of how you are to be involved,*" *he retorted.* "*I should know, I wrote some of them myself!*"

"*Though I realize why you hide who you are from our people, it does not change the fact that we are of the royal house of Elvenholm, and you abdicated in favor of your younger brother. A child of this union would reestablish the half-elven royal line, with greater legitimacy than ever before, having blood ties to both Royal House Sudea and Royal House Elvenholm,*" *she replied coolly.* "*In addition, the vision came to me, because it pertained to me. Perhaps you should seek revelation as it pertains to you, Father, as to whether what I tell you is true or not. Regardless, my decision is made, and I will be journeying to Sudea soon."*

Hadaras often thought of that fateful day and of those that followed, when he would pass through, posing as an itinerant craftsman, plying his wares to the remote villages. Valgier never knew it was his father-in-law who stopped by every few months, selling tools and trinkets, repairing tack and shoeing horses and mules as needed, though the old farrier always took an interest in how Aleron was doing.

Hadaras thought most of all about the day he had been too late to save them from the Kolixtlani assassin who murdered the young couple. The agents of the Adversary knew of Aleron's existence and though they may not know that he is anything but a halfblood, that fact would be enough for them to want him. Halfbloods often developed frightening powers, when the pure spirit of the elf blended with the impure heart of the man. A halfblood sorcerer could master both dark and light aspects of magic and they were highly sought after by the Nameless One during his time in power. This casting about for them by his agents indicated an increase in his power. The old wards of binding had weakened after all these years. He renewed them after the murders, travelling in secret through the jungle to Immin Bul, but he was certain the Adversary would find some way around them eventually.

✳✳✳

By mid-afternoon, Aleron was on his way home with two good-sized carp dangling from a stringer. They were having a good haul, but his friends needed to return home for their chores. Aleron needed to get back home as well and to get the fish cleaned quickly. Grandfather promised to start teaching him an elvish dual-scimitar form that looked viciously effective when he demonstrated it yesterday.

Chapter 2

Zorekday, Day 18, Squash Moon, 8759 Sudean Calendar

Sweat dripped into Aleron's eyes as he circled Hadaras around the makeshift ring in the stable. They were practicing greatsword this afternoon and the summer heat was oppressive. Somehow, the heat never seemed to bother the old man; he was barely perspiring. Aleron shook his head to dislodge some of the moisture. If he were to reach up to wipe his brow, the bout would be lost. Hadaras was incredibly fast and never let an opening pass. Aleron had the bruises to show for it too. Both were fighting in a right-handed stance and Hadaras stepped forward with his left foot, taking a low chop to Aleron's forward leg. Aleron dodged back to avoid the blow, then surged forward to take his grandfather's exposed left shoulder. The old man rolled left, bringing the sword up vertically to block the incoming strike, then counterstriking to Aleron's left collarbone, bringing him back to his original guard position. Aleron barely rolled his wooden practice sword left to protect his shoulder and then it was as if his reflexes saw the next move before his mind had even processed it. As Hadaras' sword was deflected, Aleron snapped the tip of his into a backhand strike to Hadaras' own shoulder. Then, as his grandfather released his right hand from the hilt, Aleron rolled his blade into the same offside leg strike his opponent had just attempted. Having no way to defend his forward leg, Hadaras took the blow and dropped to his knees. Aleron circled Hadaras, looking for an opening, as the old man pivoted to remain facing him. To yield was never an option during these bouts with his grandfather, so he would have to finish it. He teased out feints, which Hadaras either ignored, or deftly blocked. Finally, as

5

Aleron saw his opening and closed in for the kill, the opening suddenly disappeared and the tip of Hadaras' sword took Aleron in the midsection, knocking the wind out of him.

As Aleron stooped into a crouch, attempting to breathe again, Hadaras stood, saying, "Remember this Aleron: It is always possible to transform a position of disadvantage into one of strength, whether in combat, or elsewhere in your life. You simply need to think your way through the problem and wait for your opening." He patted the boy on the shoulder as he passed and said, "Put your gear up and clean yourself off at the trough my boy. Supper will be ready soon."

Aleron caught his breath quickly. The padded leather practice coat had rigid plates attached at key locations, to discourage serious injury. As well, the five years of daily martial training his grandfather enforced had whipped the now fourteen-year-old Aleron into excellent physical condition. Hadaras tired the youth out with pushups, pull-ups, and sprints around the yard, before any of the actual combat training took place. He often resented the warm-up training and suspected that his grandfather was only doing it so that Aleron would not win the bouts. Hadaras always told him that it was important to warm up first, to avoid injury. That did not explain why his grandfather never needed a warmup. What he failed to realize, was that his grandfather was building his strength and endurance. At the same time, he was showing him what it would be like to fight tired from the physical exertion often required to get within range of an enemy. He made his way to the cabinet where they stowed their practice gear. He removed his heavy leather gauntlets first, then the practice helm, with its skirt of heavy chain mail protecting his neck and finally the coat. He wiped down all the metal parts with an oily cloth and placed the equipment on the appropriate hanger for each. He wiped down the sword, carved from a straight-grained stave of ironwood, with the same oily cloth and placed it upon the weapon rack.

Aleron made his way to the water trough, pulling off his sodden tunic as he went. He dunked his head and shoulders into the cold water for two or three seconds. The breath exploded from his lungs when he came back up. He doused his tunic in the trough, then hung it over a fence rail to drip dry. Despite the cold water, Aleron's face, neck and torso were still flushed red with heat. *At least I'm not sweating so much anymore,* he said to himself. *Why does it seem like this never gets any easier? No matter how much better I get, each time is just as hard as the last.* It seemed as if his grandfather had an endless capacity for ever-higher levels of combative skill. No matter what Aleron brought to the fight, Hadaras had the counterattack to match it. *If the old man is still this good now, I wonder, what was he like in his prime? He must have been damn near unstoppable.* Aleron had seen other old soldiers in the city before. He had noticed that his grandfather did not bear the numerous scars that those old veterans had one-and-all.

Hadaras was impressed with Aleron's performance that afternoon. *That was the first time in a very long time, that anyone has managed to tag me like that,* he thought. *His speed and agility are becoming more elvish than human every day.* He recalled from before the war, the half-elf children of the Sudean nobles. They usually matured much earlier than their elvish cousins, reaching nearly the same level of physical prowess in sixteen years that an elf child would wait forty years to achieve. Hadaras had fought in the Great War, under a different name, over four thousand years before, and Aleron was beginning to remind him of the boy's namesake. *He looks like the man and fights like him. It's amazing that the traits could breed true after so many generations. It's as if I'm looking at the young prince again, after forty-one hundred years,* he thought as he watched Aleron approach the house.

The king was one-hundred and five, just in his prime, when the Nameless One cut him down on that barren plain, in the midst of the vast central jungle. Crown Prince Aelwynn, Hadaras' younger brother, fought beside the man who was his best friend and blood brother. The two grew up together in each other's households and were fast friends for decades. Members of House Sudea were the only humans ever allowed to visit Elvenholm. The way was barred to the ships of men and even the greatest mariners of Sudea could not so much as catch a glimpse of the island nation.

"Hey Jessie, what's for supper? Aleron hollered as he strode through the door. "I'm starving."

"I roasted a pork shoulder, since you didn't bring home any fish this morning, Aleron," she replied. "Did you wash?" she asked him pointedly.

"Of course I did Jesse."

"Don't you give me that "Of course I did" line," she scolded. "With you, it's definitely not a given. Now go get a clean tunic on and make sure the dirty one gets to the laundry."

"I cleaned it already." Aleron declared.

"Rinsed in the trough and hung on the fence does not make it clean!" Jessamine informed the boy. "Make sure it gets inside before dark, or the coyotes will be wearing it tomorrow."

"Yes Ma'am."

After a hearty meal of pork, potatoes, and greens, followed by the daily chores of cleaning up after supper, Aleron took a lantern and retreated to his room. He was tired and sore from the afternoon's exertions. Lying prone upon his bed, he resumed reading the latest book Hadaras had assigned, this one on the history of Sudea. He was just getting to the part where Azrael, the last high governor, declares the independence of Sudea from Elvenholm. The governor knew that he was nearing the end of his life and wished for his half-blooded son to follow him in leading the colony. Before then, the position was not hereditary and high governors were always elves, appointed by the king at Elvenholm. The king acquiesced, in part because he feared how a protracted war would damage his kingdom. Men were far more numerous than elves and halfblood sorcerers were extremely common in Sudea. A war between Sudea and Elvenholm would have resulted in massive losses to both sides. Aleron had read many different histories these last several years. Histories of elves, men, and dwarves, some by authors of the people discussed, others written by outsiders looking in. Hadaras taught him to read Elvish, Sudean and Dwarvish and was in the process of teaching him Coptic, the language of their neighbors to the northeast. Elvish and Sudean were nearly the same language, and he could find some common words between Sudean and Coptic, but Dwarvish was very different. Dwarves seemed to run words into each other, forming ever-larger words to communicate ideas, rather than building sentences. Hadaras told him that the language of the westmen was similar, as was that of the Kolixtlani. His grandfather even professed that the languages of the westmen and the dwarves bore so many similarities, that they must have been the same people at some time in the distant past. It seemed to be Hadaras' intent to teach Aleron every major language in the world, for the apparent purpose of forcing him to read every single history book in the world. Aleron often wondered why his grandfather thought so highly of scholarship. He did not believe soldiers were scholarly, as a rule. At these times, his grandfather reminded him of some aged university professor. At least, how Aleron imagined one would be since he had never been anywhere near a university. There was, however, no questioning the man's martial abilities.

Hadaras sensed Aleron drifting off to sleep. He sat across the table from Jessamine. They both let their guises down, knowing Aleron to be sleeping and no one near the house. To spy upon this pair would be next to impossible for any being in existence. Hadaras' elvish features gave him a much younger visage than he normally wore. The only clue to his advanced age was his snow-white hair. Jessamine was obviously not man or elf, but something else, her skin literally glowing golden, in the dim light of the kitchen. She was aelient, an immortal child of the aelir, the ancient teachers of elves and men. Her chosen form was that of a wood nymph, the golden skin of her face and hands merging seamlessly into her gown of deep green leaves and her dark hair seemingly intertwined with vines.

Hadaras spoke first: "That boy is almost grown now. Soon, he will want to get on with his life."

"What you say is true, my love," she replied. "The children of men are ever so eager to make their way in the world, their time in it being so short. They are like sparks from the fire, burning so brightly, but winking out so soon."

"Yes, they speak of the virtue of patience, because it is a concept so alien to them."

"I have often thought that they have just as much life in them as your people, but by their nature, they plow through it in a fraction of the time. Always in a hurry, they strive for progress and conquest, to the point that they are ever on the brink of mutual destruction," she surmised.

"They were always so inclined, were they not?" he asked.

"Yes, they were. Even so far back, as when they were all of one race, dwarves and westmen included, they quarreled among themselves, imagining differences between groups as an excuse for competition. Eventually, the imaginary divisions they created became real," she informed him.

"Do you realize, that for all the centuries we've known each other, this is the first time you have validated my suspicion that dwarves and westmen were once the same people? And on top of that, you claim they have a common origin with men as well?" Hadaras inquired, with surprise.

"Yes… I suppose I let that slip," she answered coyly. "We aren't supposed to tell you that, but I guess our long familiarity has eroded my guard to some extent."

"So, what were they like, these first men?"

"Well, I guess there's no point in concealment anymore. The first men came into being in the grassland, north of the southeastern desert, in what is now Coptia. They had faces much like the westmen, but their bodies were taller and slenderer. Their skin was very dark, like the Coptians."

"Coptia has no grasslands today. The land goes back to jungle as soon as it's no longer tilled.

"Aertu was much colder then. The sea ice reached all the way to the northern and southern coasts and thick sheets of ice covered the far northern and southern lands. With so much water locked in ice, that there was little rain to sustain the forests. Aertu was a world of ice and grass in those days."

"How long of a time was this…how long ago?" he asked.

"That particular episode lasted for over one hundred fifty millennia. It happens in cycles and that one ended around fifteen millennia ago," she answered. "Just so you know, it's moving in that direction again. The world was much warmer ten thousand years ago."

"And I thought it was just my old bones making me think the winters were getting colder," he observed. "Men, westmen and dwarves act very differently. How were the first men?"

"They were very much like the men of today. westmen and dwarves became less warlike when they adapted to the cold of the north," she replied.

"Interesting, that the harsher conditions would lead to a less competitive people," he observed. "You would think that the opposite would be the case."

"It seems with men, that hardship often breeds cooperation. When they have all that they need, that is when they quarrel the most," she said, then adding, "but remember, my love, there is nothing quite as fearsome in this world as a cornered dwarf, and no one would wish to face a westman on the warpath. They all have the capacity for incredible violence. Your people had to be taught how to fight. The peoples of this land have it ingrained in their very being. I believe it was the Allfather's means of ensuring their survival in the presence of the Adversary's creations."

"Too true," Hadaras replied, "but back to the subject, Aleron will soon be in a hurry to do something with his life. He has no way of knowing that he stands to live ten times the span of a normal man's life."

"You can only hope that we have raised him properly, so that his hastiness does not lead him down the wrong path. I do not think that anyone could have done better in preparing Aleron to rule than you, my love," she reassured him.

"Thank you, My Dear. I just know that he has much further to go before he is ready to assume his inheritance. After one thousand years kingless, Sudea does not need a boy-king on the throne. Better to let the Steward guide the kingdom, until Aleron is truly ready. The problem is what to do with him until that moment arrives."

"I'm sure that dilemma will work itself out, and your old friend will continue to guide the kingdom to greater prosperity. He still has a couple of years before he will be ready to leave the safety of our nest. Now come to bed you old fool."

"Who are you calling old?" He joked, as he rose to comply.

"I'm not old," she answered, as her features transformed to those of a beautiful, dark-haired elf. "I'm "Timeless.""

Chapter 3

Corballday, Day 21, Sowing Moon, 8760 Sudean Calendar

Aleron walked along the narrow lane that led to the village from Hobart's farm, Hobart being Geldun's father. It was late afternoon and Barathol and Geldun walked beside him. The boys had worked the last two days to get Hobart's planting done. Tomorrow they would do the same at the farm of Danel, Barathol's father. They had a few coins in their pockets and being thirsty after a hard day planting, were heading for the inn for a draught. The summer beer was light enough that the boys could afford one or two pints before evening chores. Aleron had a few days off from his training to help his friends, so he could afford it as well.

"So, you're leaving next week?" Geldun asked him as they walked along. He was still the smallest of the trio, but wiry and strong. He had just turned fifteen and was developing a chiseled handsomeness that, along with his golden hair and quick tongue, was quickly making him popular with the girls of the village.

"Yes," Aleron answered, "we leave on the new moon, in just four days." Aleron had yet to turn fifteen and though taller than the others, at nearly six feet, he still had his boyish looks. He wondered if he would ever grow a beard, the wispy moustache he cultivated being the only hair growing upon his face.

"Why are you going again, right before summer?" Barathol asked, somewhat upset that one of his two best friends was leaving, for the first time in six years. Barathol, the oldest of the group, as well as the most mature looking, had a full black beard as opposed to Geldun's blonde fringe and Aleron's wispy lip growth. He was nearly as tall as Aleron, and more solidly built than many of the grown men in the village, with unusually dark skin, like the desert dwellers to the east.

"My grandfather thinks it's important for me to travel and meet new people." Aleron answered. "I'm not really happy about it either. It means no fishing this summer."

"Where will you be going? Geldun asked.

"First, we will be visiting the dwarves. Hadaras says there are some of my father's old business associates there that would like to see me. I'm not sure if they think I might be going into the charcoal business or something. I'll be sorry to disappoint them if that's the case." He answered. "Then we're supposed to go see the elves and visit some of grandfather's old friends there."

"That should be fun." Geldun replied. "I've never heard of anyone getting to visit elves and dwarves. How did old Hadaras get in so good with the elves anyway? I've heard that they're not too friendly to outsiders. Even though the border is not closed, it might as well be."

"He says the army sometimes sends troops in to help on the border with the wild men. He lived up there for years, even after he retired. I think he liked all the books they have up there."

"Still making you read every night?" Barathol asked wryly.

"Without fail," Aleron replied.

"So, what are you planning to do for work?" Geldun inquired. "You can't go on forever helping out, not if you want to have a family or anything. Are you still thinking of the Army?"

"I still haven't decided between the Army and the Navy." He answered. "I like the woodsman thing enough, you know, like what my father did, but I want to see more of the world before I settle into something like that. Anyway, it seems like my grandfather has been training me for the military for the last six years. He says I'm free to do whatever I want, and he always said I should help the farmers and woodsmen, to get the feel of it. But I think he would be disappointed if I didn't choose to serve the kingdom first."

They were about to enter the inn when Barathol said, "I'm thinking of doing a stint in the Army before I take over the farm. Ol' Da won't be ready to retire for quite a few years yet and it would be good to salt away some money before I settle down and take a wife."

"No luck on finding a girl who will have you, eh?" Geldun teased.

"Watch your tongue pretty boy," he replied, cuffing Geldun as they entered the common room. "I'm just not in any rush."

"Nor are the ladies," Aleron quipped, dodging another swipe from Barathol.

The boys took a table in the back corner, still joking as they took their seats. Lutea, the serving girl approached with a smile. She was nineteen and had known the trio since they were children, in Barathol and Geldun's case, their entire lives. They were friendly, likeable boys, though they had gained a reputation as ones not to be trifled with.

"Three pints of ale please, Lulu," Geldun called out to her. They continued their conversation and when she made her way back with three full tankards, he followed with, "Just set those down on the table and set yourself right here on my lap."

"Save your smooth charms for the little girls Geldun." She admonished him after setting the drinks down. "Remember, I used to wipe your boogers when you were little."

Geldun looked crestfallen and Barathol added, "You did have quite a lot of them," as Aleron nearly spit his beer out stifling a laugh.

"Now look what you almost made me do." Aleron complained. "That would have been a waste of perfectly good ale. I think some got up my nose." He added, sniffing.

✳✳✳

As the boys were busy carousing at the inn, Hadaras and Jessamine were getting ready for the trip. Inventory and packing of supplies and equipment took up the afternoon. They had decided that Aleron could spend as much time with his friends as possible, since they would be gone for most of the year. Hadaras had re-shoed the horses that morning and was now inspecting their gear. Their travelling clothes consisted of light chain hauberks and boiled leather paneled spangenhelms. Each would wear a hand and a half sword and long dagger while travelling and pack a light sword and dagger for wear about town. He packed the two Chebek horsebows in their cases and set them with the four quivers of fifty arrows each. Hadaras preferred the longbow of the elves, but the Chebek bows were more practical on horseback. Additionally, the horn and sinew construction allowed them to remain strung for days on end. Were he travelling alone, Hadaras would need none of this weaponry, but he could not reveal his sorcerous abilities to Aleron. One day, the boy would learn of his true heritage, but the time was not yet right for that. In the meantime, they would need to be prepared for any eventuality. Jessamine was wrapping dried meat into bundles, placing them with the flour and oil to await further packing. "I hope those boys don't drink too much this evening," she stated. "The alcohol is not good for their young brains."

"I'm sure they will be fine. The other two still have the evening milking to contend with, so they cannot stay at the inn too long." Hadaras stated.

As the evening drew into night, Aleron entered the house. "Boots outside!" Jessamine called out as he walked through the door.

"Sometimes I think you can see through walls Jessie."

"No Aleron, I just know you too well. Now get those boots off in the mudroom and come get some supper."

After the meal, Aleron set to helping with the supplies and equipment. As they inventoried, Hadaras made notes of what he needed to pick up in town the following day. "So, how are your friends today?" He asked.

"They are doing well," Aleron replied. "We were talking about what we will do next year."

"And what exactly did you discuss?"

"Well, Barathol and Geldun are both thinking of joining up in the fall of next year, you know, after they turn sixteen and after the harvest is in."

Hadaras mulled on the information for a moment and then said, "That is a little surprising. What about their farms?"

"They're thinking that they will do a three-year stint to make some money before they settle down on the farm," Aleron explained. "Both of their fathers are still young, and they have younger brothers who will be big enough to help next year."

"That's a sensible enough plan," his grandfather agreed. "Have they decided on the army or the navy yet?"

"Hmmm…they're kind of waiting for me to decide that, Grandfather."

"Is that so? Will you be deciding for them, or with them?"

"With them, Grandfather."

"You know Aleron…" Hadaras began, "I never wanted you to feel pressured to join just because I was a soldier. You can be a woodsman, like your father, or a farmer, or a tradesman and I will be proud of you just the same."

"Then why have you been training me to fight all these years?" Aleron asked.

"Because I want you to be able to fend for yourself and you needed to have something to apply yourself to. I do not have enough work around here for you remain occupied and not become soft and lazy."

"So, it was only to keep me busy?"

"Yes," Hadaras replied, but Aleron did not believe him for a moment.

"I still think it might be the best thing for me Grandfather. I've been thinking about it a lot lately and I'm not really interested in anything else. I want to see some of the world, and I know that will not happen if I'm stuck on some farm."

"You will get to see plenty of it this year. We will see if you still feel that way next spring." Hadaras replied with a wry tone.

Aleron lay awake in his bed that night. The bit of drowsiness from the ale had long since worn off and though he was tired from the long day planting, he was too excited about the upcoming journey. A whole year away from the village he had called home for nearly six years. He imagined returning home next spring, nearly sixteen years old and seasoned world traveler. He wondered if he would have a beard by that time. *The girls would be impressed then*, he thought. His thoughts drifted to soldiering and sailing. He imagined leading a column of soldiers against evil Kolixtlanis, goblins and wild men, or sailing the high seas on the deck of a Sudean warship, fighting Thallasian corsairs and exploring strange shores. With these thoughts, he drifted off to sleep.

✳✳✳

Hadaras spoke to Jessamine after Aleron slipped into the land of dreams. "He is still adamant about the military when he turns sixteen."

"Were you expecting anything different from the boy you raised," she replied. "He is a more accomplished fighter than half the soldiers in the army already, under your tutelage."

"True enough, my dear, but I've also taught him to read and write four languages. Why not an interest in university instead?"

"That's simply not exciting for a fifteen-year-old boy, my love. He will have plenty of time for that later."

"I suppose so," he admitted. "Time for bed?"

"I suppose so," she replied, as she sauntered towards the bedroom, hips swaying seductively.

Chapter 4

Gurlachday, Day 25, Sowing Moon, 8760 Sudean Calendar

"Are the horses saddled yet, Aleron?"

"Yes Grandfather," Aleron replied.

"Did you remember to wait for them to exhale, before you tightened the girth straps?"

"Yes, I did, Grandfather."

"Good boy; now get the saddlebags while I finish this," Hadaras instructed as he finished loading the packhorse with the sundries they would need to sustain them on the road. It was just before dawn and there was enough chill in the air that the horses blew steam from their nostrils as they snorted at the indignities imposed on them by their handlers.

After finishing with the horses, they donned their mail hauberks and strapped on their sword belts. Hanging their helms on the saddles, they were ready to depart the farmyard. Jessamine came out to see them off. She would stay behind to keep an eye on the homestead. "Have a safe journey and keep your grandfather out of trouble," she said to Aleron. *Fare well my love and stay safe,* she spoke in Hadaras' mind. *I will miss you this season.*

And I you, he replied in kind. *It will be as a blink of an eye to one such as you, my dear.*

True, but my sense of time is skewed to that of the mortal realm as I reside with you. Time is more precious when one knows it may be limited.

I understand my love. We will return as swiftly as we are able, he spoke to her mind, as his voice said, "Take care of yourself Jessamine; we will be home before you know it."

They mounted their horses and rode out at a light canter, with Aleron to Hadaras' left and the packhorse trailing behind Hadaras' mount. Aleron asked, "Are you sure Jessie will be all right out here by herself Grandfather? I'm worried that we being so far from the village might be dangerous for her all alone."

"Jessamine is quite capable of taking care of herself, my boy. You need not worry about her."

"But I still do," Aleron replied, as they turned onto the main track heading east. "Will it be long before we reach the dwarves?"

"We should reach Arundell in three weeks and we will stay a few days to rest the horses. Then it will take us at least six weeks to reach the dwarf road in the Blue Mountains and another four weeks until we reach Dhargul.

"We're going to the capital too?" Aleron asked excitedly. He had never been to the largest city in Sudea and the prospect of it had him quivering in anticipation. Then it started to sink into Aleron's brain, that they would be travelling three months to reach the seat of the dwarf kingdom.

"I thought we should visit, so you can see firsthand the things you have been reading about. Plus, we would have been passing so close on our way, that it would have been a shame to pass it by."

"How long will we stay in Dhargul?" Aleron inquired. He was still in the dark in regard to many of the details of the trip. It seemed as if every time he asked, more destinations appeared on their itinerary.

"We will stay for a week and then make our way through the Blue Mountains, to Nhargul, in the Northern Kingdom."

"Did my father do business with them as well?" Aleron asked, already knowing the simple answer, but wondering what machinations his guardian was up to in dragging him around the world this summer.

"No, of course not, at least not directly, though some of his product could have been traded to the north from the south, since the north has few friendly borders with men," he answered. "No, I simply thought it would be good for you to see the two kingdoms for yourself. Though they are adjacent to one another, they have developed quite differently."

"So the circuitous route is entirely for my benefit?"

"Aleron, this entire trip is entirely for your benefit. I thought you realized that. I've been to these places, many times over, but I no longer have any business that takes me to them. It is for you to see them and in turn, gain experience of the outside world. That is why we are going. So that you have more knowledge when it comes to making decisions that will affect the rest of your life."

"Is this about me joining the military? I can't figure out if you want me to or not, Grandfather. Sometimes you seem to encourage it and then other times you do your best to discourage me. What do you want me to do?"

"I want you to do what is right for you, not what you think I want you to do. You could be a farmer, or the king of Sudea and I would be equally proud, as long as you were following your heart. If that means the military, then so be it. I just want you to realize that there are other ways to see the world, if that is the only draw it has for you," his grandfather emphatically declared.

"Ha, king of Sudea, like that could ever happen, but I do get your point, Grandfather" Aleron assured him. "Seeing the world is only one of the reasons I'm thinking of joining. All those histories you've had me read; they all speak of the sacrifices people have made to help make Sudea a great kingdom. I just feel like I need to do my part too, to honor their memory."

"That is the best sentiment I could have heard coming from you Aleron," Hadaras replied to his grandson, a warm feeling filling him. *The words of a prince, once again reminding me of the man so many years ago.* "If that is truly how you feel and you still feel that way next year, you have my blessing."

"That is how I feel Grandfather and I'm sure I will still feel that way when I turn sixteen."

"We will see, my boy. A year and a half is a long time out to make predictions," Hadaras stated, chuckling to himself over how short a year and a half really was, in the grand scheme of things. *I can vaguely remember how slowly the years seemed to pass in my youth, but that was nine thousand years ago. I have seen the glory of civilizations wax and wane in that time. One day soon, I will have had enough of this life and return to the Allfather, but not yet, not with the Nameless One's minions still moving in the world.* "Time to put your helm on now Aleron. We're far enough out in the countryside for bandits to be lurking about."

"Yes Grandfather," Aleron answered, as he grabbed the helm hanging from his saddle horn. The fields had given way to forest, as the land was too rocky to farm, the realm of the woodsman and the outlaw. At times, the two were one and the same and wealthy looking travelers must be always on their guard.

Later, as they rode on along the trail, Hadaras could feel eyes upon them from the dark forest. He sensed ill intent, but unease at the same time. *No, we don't look like easy marks, but if there are enough of them, they will muster up the courage to attack.* "Stay alert Aleron. I do not think we are alone. Fortunately, bandits are usually cowards, but we should put some distance between us and them." They continued uneventfully for several more hours, the bandits evidently deciding to wait for easier pickings. Soon, the forest gave way to open fields again and the road widened, as smaller paths joined the flow, like streams joining the greater river. It was midafternoon by this time.

The road they were following began to veer east and they could see a large village in the distance. Hadaras chose a smaller path that headed more northeast, in the direction of Arundell. They were far from needing a resupply and he had no desire to slow their progress with a visit to the town. They would camp outside tonight. The leagues flowed by beneath the horses' hooves and as dusk drew near, they found a place to camp by a small stream. They unloaded the horses and rubbed them down well to avoid stiff muscles. Then Aleron baited a couple hooks and set the lines in a calm pool he found just downstream. When he came back up to help Hadaras with the fire, he said, "Maybe we'll get some fresh fish for supper tonight."

"That would be nice," the old man answered. "The more we forage, the less we drain our supplies. Once we set up, you can go back to tending your lines and I will see to feeding the horses. They should be cooled down enough for some food and water now."

Later in the evening, as they enjoyed grilled trout and bannock, cooked over their modest fire, Aleron asked, "Should we gather more wood for the night, to stay warm?"

"We have enough," Hadaras replied. "There is a saying among the Chebek. They say, 'The plainsman keeps warm with a small fire and staying close to it. The villager keeps warm with a big fire and running for more wood.' Now go to sleep. I'll take the first watch and we will rotate every two hours."

Aleron settled into his bedroll, tired and stiff from riding all day and quickly drifted off to sleep. Hadaras sat with his back to the fire. He could have kept watch all night, from his bed, setting out mental feelers that would wake him to the slightest hint of danger. *Instead, we must do this the hard way. The boy needs to learn the basic ways first. Simply having the mental discipline to stay awake when you need to is a necessary step on the way to self-mastery.* Hadaras often wondered just when Aleron's sorcerous abilities would emerge, or if they would at all. All elves had at least some degree of ability and the majority of halfbloods did as well. Usually, with halfbloods, the ability manifested between sixteen and eighteen years of age. He hoped that it would happen before the lad went off to the military.

Dusk found Jessamine busy finishing the last few chores around the homestead. With only one horse left in the stable, there wasn't much to do. She left the lonely animal with warm thoughts of companionship to comfort it through the night and puttered around the yard, making sure everything was in its place. As she bent over the trough fishing out debris to keep the water fresh, she could sense the man moving out from the concealment of the hedgerow. What the miscreant could not sense, was the vines reaching out from the hedge behind him. She turned to him, after hearing his yelp of surprise and witnessed the vines rapidly entwine him into a green cocoon. She heard the muffled wheeze, as the vines constricted, crushing the life out of her would-be assailant. The vines recoiled to the base of the hedge and began dragging the twitching cocoon into the earth. *That section of hedgerow will be exceptionally green next year,* she thought. *Not a nice way to go, but it serves him right, having rape and murder on his mind. I gave him the benefit of the doubt, in case he only wanted to look but not act.* As darkness fell, she went back inside the cottage and settled in for the night.

✱✱✱

Hadaras sat in a trancelike state, as Aleron dozed beside him, keenly aware of everything within a half mile of the camp. Jessamine spoke to him in his mind as he sat there. They would communicate in this manner throughout their time apart. *You did the right thing my love,* he said to ease her conscience. *If not you, he would have gone on to victimize some other innocent.*

I know, but I hate to make any living thing suffer and I fear I let my anger get the best of me. I didn't end it as cleanly as I should have.

It sounds to me, like it was expedient and quick, even if a little creative, My Dear.

I suppose so. I just feel guilty when forced to take a life, she replied. *That's why I always make you kill the livestock.*

I know, My Darling. Now get some rest. Not that you need it, but I need to shut down this part of my mind, if I intend to be on top of my game tomorrow.

Very well, good night My Love.

Good night, Darling.

Chapter 5

Gurlachday, Day 25, Sowing Moon, 8760 Sudean Calendar

The tall figure lurked about the black walls of the fortress Immin Bul. He had been pacing around the ancient fortress for several hours. The once sharp angles of the obsidian stronghold now somewhat rounded after four thousand years of weathering from the daily rainstorms of the jungle. The individual had been slowly circling the edifice since mid-afternoon and night was quickly descending. A close look would reveal to anyone, that this was not a man. The pointed ears and set of the eyes said elf, but his skin was dark, like unto the jungle men and no respectable elf would be loitering at the prison of the Nameless One. Whatever he was, he had journeyed long to reach this place, thousands of leagues over sea and land. The men of the jungle who guarded this place sensed something about him and left him alone. The one leopard that was watching from its concealed perch sensed the same and let him be. He radiated malevolence to the point that it was a palpable thing. The deepening darkness meant nothing to this one. His night vision was excellent, though he did not truly need his eyes to see.

Dusk gave way to night and the faint sliver of the new moon hung over the western horizon. Soon it would follow the sun below the horizon and night would be complete. The stranger could see the faint glow from Kolixtla far to the East. The stars glittered thickly in the black sky of the Central Jungle. They reflected perfectly off the glassy surface of Lake Bul, calm for the moment, in the heavy tropical air. As the moon left the western sky, the stranger heard a voice in his mind.

Welcome, my son, did you journey well?

Yes Father, the stranger replied. *I set out as soon as I could after receiving your summons. It took some time to assemble a proper crew and to fit a ship for a journey of such distance. I am sorry that it took nearly two years to reach here.*

Do not feel sorry, my son. I have grown patient here in my prison. I realized it would take some time to reach me. Are my people prospering on our island? I had such high hopes for them. The voice inquired.

Yes, Father, your people number in the millions now. You would be proud of the progress we have made. As king over these thousands of years, I have sired scores of children. Every living Arkan carries some of your blood in their veins.

Are there none left of the first generations then, those that came before I sired you?

Once the breed was well established and numerous, Father, we disposed of the original progenitors. The elves proved to be untrustworthy, and their part-goblin offspring were unpredictable at best.

And what of your mother? When I chose her, she was the strongest and brightest of the quarter-goblin generation.

The stranger hesitated for a moment, then, *Father, I hope you are not upset. She contributed greatly to the advancement of our breed, dam to many of the eighth-goblin generation. But that generation was bred only to each other after that point and to myself. Eventually she outlived her usefulness and was disposed of with the rest of the old breeding stock.*

I am not upset with you. The voice replied, with a melancholy tone. *You did what was necessary for the race. I was only thinking that I would like to have seen her again.*

Father, when you free yourself, you will have your choice of any maiden in the kingdom and freed you will soon be, he added, emphatically.

That is a good thought, my child, but there is much for you to do to make that happen. You must spread the word among the men of this land. They are still loyal after all these centuries. Then you must send word to your people and muster them to this land. Finally, you must return to me my axe.

Father, can you speak to your servants here, as you do to me now?

I was once able to. For many years, I felt the bindings weaken, with the makers of the wards all dead for centuries. I spoke to the priests of my temples in Kolixtlan and the sacrifices to me resumed. My power swelled as they spilled blood in my name, and I cast my web further afield. It was then that I sensed something amiss. There was a halfblood child whom I sensed had claim to the long empty throne of my old enemy, Sudea. I sent out an assassin from the temple to capture the boy. Though we warded him well against all magic, an elvish sorcerer thwarted the mission.

How could this elf have defeated your wards, Father?

That is a good question. The priest who imbued the wards with my power perished immediately when this elf dispelled their magic. I sensed the priest saw the attacker through the eyes of the assassin, but the encounter destroyed his mind. Then, suddenly, the bindings on my prison renewed, as strong as the day they were laid. I could no longer speak to my temples here. There was ever only one that powerful among the elves and he should have been long dead, but this renewal had his flavor upon it.

How then, can you speak to me? The dark elf asked, somewhat perplexed. *It is a far greater distance to Arkus, where you summoned me.*

I discovered one small gap in the bindings that confine me. It is not enough for me to cast my web fully upon the land, but I am able to cast a single thread to one of my own blood. I can speak to my followers only when they are in close proximity to me. I am only able, when darkness is complete, and my power is strongest. I was able to contact you through the fortuitous combination of a moonless and overcast sky and a mass sacrifice by my priests in Kolixtlan. Only then was my power great enough to reach across the seas to you. I can speak to you now because you are close, and the darkness is full. Our power is always stronger in darkness, just as the elves' magic thrives in the light.

How shall we free you from this binding, Father? I feel that these wards are beyond my ability to dispel.

That is why I need my axe, Zadehmal, the faceless voice answered. *I invested much of my power in that weapon. Separation from it weakens me greatly.*

Where is your axe now, Father? I will bring it to you.

I sense that it is very far away and has not moved for many thousands of years. It is somewhere cold and remote. You must find it for me. It is a focal point of dark power and has my particular flavor about it. You will be able to recognize it when you are near. When you bring it here, I will be able to draw enough power from it to break the wards binding me here.

I will bring you Zadehmal, Father and you will be free. Then we will crush our enemies and extend your dominion over all of Aertu. All living beings will worship you Father, as their god and king.

Yes Zormat, my son and as lord over my chosen people, you will lead their armies in the battles to come. In turn, you will lead the goblins and trolls, my people on this continent, the men loyal to me, and the other beings I created. Your allies shall be the dark Aelient, loyal to me since the creation of this world. You bear my mark and all loyal to me shall bow to you, my chosen one. One day soon, that will be all of Aertu, but there will be many enemies to overcome.

But Father, do you not desire to rule over all of Aertu?

I desire worship by all of Aertu and those that do not, to be sacrificed in my name. It is through worship and the blood of sacrifice that I gain power. You shall be my representative and rule in my name, as the Son of the True God. Now go and do as I have directed you.

I will do as you have bid me to, Father.

Go to the edge of the lake, son. There you will find something that will speed your journey to your comrades. May the Darkness always be with you, my son.

And also with you, Father.

And so, Zormat, Son of the Nameless One, King of Arkus and the most powerful sorcerer of the Arkans, left the prison of his father. He strode to the dark lakeshore and, seeing nothing, waited. Soon he detected a rippling of the water, far from shore. The water parted for the massive bulk of a huge reptilian creature. The long sinuous neck bore a large crocodilian head, with elongated jaws full of dagger like teeth. Its thick trunk bore four long flippers, which it used like feet on land. The long tail had a flattened cross section, like a leaf shaped blade. Overall, the creature was easily over fifty feet long. It looked expectantly at Zormat, as it waddled onto shore. He walked to the animal and lightly sprang onto its back. The huge lizard lumbered back into the water and began swimming. The creature shot across Lake Bul on a northwesterly course that Zormat knew would take them to the outlet of the lake. They skimmed the surface of the water, the lizard's tail sweeping side to side, propelling them at an impressive pace. He estimated that they were travelling at a speed of at least forty knots. If the beast were capable of maintaining this pace nonstop and down the course of the rivers, they would complete in a day, what had taken him a month to accomplish on foot.

Dawn found them exiting the lake into the wide lazy river. The beast did not slack in its pace. Zormat believed they would reach the far shores of the next small lake by late morning. *Whether we can proceed past that point is the question,* he thought. The river draining that lake to the sea was much narrower and faster than the one they now travelled. He doubted this massive beast would fit the narrow channel.

By mid-morning, they entered the small lake. The magnificent beast he rode had never once slackened its pace and they cut across the glassy surface like a hot knife through butter. True to his suspicions, they made directly for the far shore, not the outlet. The beast obviously knew where it did or did not fit. The giant lizard lumbered ashore at the site of a small village of thatched huts. The village looked deserted, and the beast bellowed a horrific roar. Zormat dismounted and patting the beast's neck said, "Thank you friend. Now go find some food." The lizard grumbled and turned back to the water, looking back to the village once longingly, before sliding back into the lake. It was obviously disappointed at finding the shore deserted.

The Arkan drew his sword and, resting the blade on his shoulder, proceeded into the village. The sword glowed deep red, imbued with the magic of the Nameless One. Two figures stepped out from the cover of the huts. They were tall and dark skinned, with a greenish tint. They wore hide loincloths and capes of woven palm fiber and carried short spears with foot-long black iron blades. Straight black hair extended to the brow lines of the vaguely ape-like faces. *Some sort of goblin, it appears, though not one I am familiar with. They look a bit like the Arkan half-goblin breeders we once had, but darker. I think this is a cross with men,* Zormat surmised.

The elves of Arkus were a work in progress at the time of the Great War and became separated from their founder before learning of his breeding programs on the continent. Zormat knew nothing of the hobgoblin and half-troll races his father developed from breeding his creations to men and westmen. Here, the Adversary bred men to elves, to create fast maturing halfblood sorcerers to counter those of Sudea and bred goblins and trolls to men and westmen, to refine his creations and imbue them with more intelligence. The Arkans, with their one-eighth goblin heritage, he intended as a long-term project to create a master race of elves, attuned to the wielding of dark magic. Zormat was the first of the one-eighths. To conceive him, the Adversary assumed the form of an elf and bred himself to the best specimen of the quarter-goblin females. Thus, Zormat is the original Arkan and directed the breeding of the race, in his father's absence, himself mating with many generations of females, to assure that his father's legacy permeated the race.

"Greetings stranger," The first hobgoblin said in a guttural dialect of Zormat's own language. "You bear the mark of our Lord, the Nameless God," referring to the eight-pointed star tattooed on Zormat's forehead, "and you bear a weapon of his power. We have never seen one tame a korkor. They are the fiercest hunters in these waters. You must have great power. What sort of being are you."

"We call ourselves Arkans and live far across the sea from here. The beast you call a korkor is one of my father's creations and as such, it will obey me," he answered as he sheathed the sword. "And what sort of being are you? You look like some sort of goblin, but not any that I have seen before."

The other two's eyes widened in shock. "You are the son of our Lord?" the second one asked in disbelief. "Please grant us mercy Lord," he pleaded, as the two fell to their knees and kowtowed. "We meant no disrespect in how we addressed you."

"Please, stop groveling and answer my question. I took no insult, and I may have use for you. You need not fear me, for the moment."

The hobgoblins lifted their heads from the ground, though they remained kneeling. "We are called hobgoblins, Lord," the first one answered. "We were bred by the Nameless God, for the Great War against the men and elves who worship the false gods."

"Interesting, my father has been absent from our land, since his imprisonment. We are unfamiliar with what he was accomplishing elsewhere in the world. Were any other new races created by my father in these lands?"

"Living in the hills to the south and the northwest, my Lord, there are trolls. Our legends say that they were bred alongside us for the Great War, and they are very different from the mountain trolls they were bred from. They are fierce and crafty warriors, Lord."

"Do you know what races you were bred from?" Zormat asked.

"Our legends say that we have the blood of men in our veins, Lord," the second hobgoblin replied.

As I suspected, he thought, *now to see if they could help with my journey.* He still had fifty-five leagues left to reach where he moored his ship. "That is as I thought. Now, to business, do you have any means of transport faster than by foot? I have six days to travel yet, to reach the coast where my ship awaits."

"Lord," the first one again, "we have boats that could run the river, out to the sea, but that way is long and treacherous. Better for you, Lord, would be to ride a yag."

"Show me one of these 'yags' of which you speak."

Chapter 6

Shilwezday, Day 26, Sowing Moon, 8760 Sudean Calendar

Hadaras roused himself at dawn, leaving the trance state in which he spent each night. He could not afford the luxury of true sleep while on the road, but the trance allowed enough rest for his body and mind to maintain. He could keep it up for years, if needed and he had many times in his life. He was impressed to see Aleron already tidying up camp. "Good Aleron, I'm glad you've gotten started already. This will speed us on our way."

"Thank you, Grandfather. I was beginning to get sleepy, so I figured I would get to work to keep myself awake. I just fed the horses, so after we eat, we should be ready to go," Aleron explained.

After a quick breakfast of bannock, from the night before, cheese and dried sausages, they were back on their horses. Aleron could feel each hoof beat, as his sore behind bounced on the stiff leather saddle. He winced quite often and Hadaras chuckled to himself. *It's amazing that I can still find mindless humor in things after nine thousand years in this world. I have seen such things in my life as would purge the mirth from anyone.* He often wondered why he had lived so long. Three thousand years was an average lifespan for an elf. Twice that was not unheard of, but he had lived three times what was typical. His own father had lived nearly six thousand years, which may explain it to some extent. Hadaras' mother gave birth to him when his father, Balgare, was a mere nine hundred years old. Hadaras believed then that if he were to ascend to the throne of Elvenholm, it would be an exceptionally short reign. Hadaras' mother, Chaldee, disappeared when he was two hundred-fifty-four, leaving King Balgare heartbroken. For centuries,

Elvenholm had no queen, due to his mourning. Eventually, the king remarried and when his half-brother Aelwynn was born in 5861, by the elvish calendar, Hadaras gladly passed the title of crown prince to his younger sibling. The job of high sorcerer was more than enough for him at the time. Aelwynn, as well, lived over four thousand years, passing through the veil to rejoin the Allfather little more than a century ago, but still Hadaras lived on. *I've outlived my parents, siblings and even my children. Will I even outlive this precious grandchild riding beside me?*

✳✳✳

Jessamine sat upon a bench outside the cottage, enjoying the morning sun. At one point, she glanced over to the hedge that had snared her attacker the night before. She still felt some misgivings for that, but there was nothing that could change what had happened. She prayed that the man's spirit was not so maligned that it would reject the embrace of the Allfather when it crossed the veil. She could sense the thoughts going through the mind of her lover. Having been conceived when the Cosmos was young, she possessed knowledge that even one so old as Hadaras could not hope to comprehend. She suspected that his mother, who he knew as Queen Chaldee, was not an elf at all. None but the Allfather can know when or if Hadaras might die of natural causes. She could tell that he was not immune to death by injury, and he displayed some superficial signs of ageing, but there was something else, not altogether elvish about him. Jessamine also wondered what import this ancestry would have on her young charge Aleron. He was heir to the Sudean throne, by direct male lineage, forty generations removed. Additionally, he was great-grandson of the first high king of Elvenholm and whatever his consort was. Aleron's was likely the most unique lineage of any man that had ever lived, even among halfbloods.

✳✳✳

As the morning wore on, Aleron became more comfortable in the saddle. The muscles of his legs warmed up and his behind just went numb. His thoughts mostly revolved around how tired he was. Four hours of sleep, broken into two-hour intervals, was not what he was used to. He yawned deeply as he took in the scenery. The hedge rowed fields had given way to mixed wooded rangeland. He noted a shepherd tending his flock off to the left. Ahead and to the right, he could see a small herd of what looked like aurochs. They all appeared to be brown cows, with none of the larger black bulls among them. He wondered if they would see elk or wisent on this trip. He hoped so, but preferably at a distance for the wisent. The wild cattle had a reputation for unpredictable

28

aggressiveness. *Grandfather is deep in thought. He hasn't spoken in over an hour. I wonder what he is thinking right now.* But mostly, Aleron wondered how Hadaras could be so alert with only half a night's sleep. Aleron could hardly keep his eyes open, even with the horse jostling him constantly.

Zormat looked doubtfully at the odd creature before him. The yag was superficially like a horse, appearing to be, in some way, related. It stood about five feet tall at the shoulder, the stout body supported on thick sturdy legs. The feet were the strangest part, being three toed hooves, instead of single or cloven. The head was vaguely horse like, but short, wide and housing a full set of sharp canine teeth. Across the pen, he witnessed another yag dart forward and snap up a lizard that made the mistake of sunning itself on a fencepost. Others in the pen were grazing on forage as normal horses would. "You ride these things?" he asked the hobgoblins incredulously.

"Yes, my Lord," the one he knew now as "Shaggat" told him. "Horses do not do well here, but the yag is from this land."

"Is it faster than walking?"

"Not by much, my Lord, but it should get you to the coast a day earlier and better rested than on foot."

"I suppose that is better than walking," Zormat replied, not quite believing his own statement. "And how will you retrieve your animal? The coast is several days ride from here."

"I will accompany you, as your guide and protection my Lord, if that is acceptable to you," Shaggat answered, swatting the yag as it nipped at him.

"That is an acceptable solution," Zormat agreed. "I will welcome your company and protection, my friend." He had no need of guidance or protection from this creature, however, he felt it best to humor him. *I think it may be advantageous let these hobgoblins feel useful and important. Happy loyal minions perform better than those held merely by fear of retribution.* He planned to use these people in the war to come. They looked to be stronger and more robust than the original breeds of goblin, as well as more intelligent and articulate. He might even consider bringing some of these to Arkus, along with some men, to improve the breed of goblin there. These hobgoblins were still ugly but were more pleasant to look at than those goblins with which he was familiar.

This Shaggat was a passable fighter as well. After the communal midday meal Zormat attended, as guest of honor, a young male stood to challenge Shaggat for his position as chief over the band. Shaggat knifed the upstart between the ribs, mere minutes into the duel, exclaiming, "Here's the meat for tonight's supper," as the youth spasmed in the dust, forming red mud from the blood pouring freely from his chest. Up until that moment, Zormat wondered if this new sort of goblin was too civilized to be effective. He saw then that these hobgoblins possessed the ruthless streak common to all goblins.

Riding out from the hobgoblin village, Zormat struggled to control the unruly three-toed ass. This was not one of his father's creations and as such, he had no special command of this beast. Shaggat was faring only slightly better, continually slapping his mount and formulating ever more colorful strings of curses. And so, they bounced along on their days long journey to the coast where the ship and its crew awaited.

＊＊＊

The sun was low in the western sky when Hadaras remarked, "We should probably find a spot to camp for the night," startling Aleron awake. "That hilltop to the northeast looks like it has some cover," he continued, pointing ahead and to the left at a wooded hilltop. They were travelling through an area of rolling hills with mixed patches of forest and shrubby grassland. They had spooked several deer, but the two had resisted the temptation to take one, as they had not the time to process a large game animal. They did, however, take three rabbits with blunted arrows that afternoon, so they would dine well that night.

Aleron yawned and stretched, then stated, "I can't wait to slip into my bedroll tonight. I'm so tired I'll be asleep before my head hits the ground."

"If we get settled in early enough, Aleron, I'll take a longer first watch, so you can get more sleep."

"That wouldn't be fair, Grandfather. I'll take my full share of the watch."

"My boy, when you get to be my age, you don't need as much sleep as a lad still growing, like yourself," Hadaras explained. "I can see that you need a few hours of uninterrupted sleep. Otherwise, you are likely to get sick if you go night after night without sleep."

"All right," Aleron agreed. "I sure could use some sleep."

They came upon a narrow track leading off the main path to the left. It appeared to lead to the hilltop in question and they followed it. They halted at a stream crossing to allow the horses a brief drink and to refill the water skins. Though there was no shortage of water in this part of the world, a smart traveler never passed up the opportunity to top off. They continued to follow the path and were happy to note that, a bit further along, it rejoined and followed the stream towards the base of the hill. That was good news, as it meant that they would have less of a walk to water the horses after they cooled down. Nearing the base of the hill small trickle branched off from the main stream and the path followed that up the hill. The smaller stream led to a spring that was enlarged into two pools, the higher one for travelers and the lower for livestock. Both pools were smartly edged with stone, bringing the water level higher to form deep troughs. This was obviously a maintained rest stop but maintained by who was the question.

As the two continued up the path, the brush gave way to larger trees, mostly oak, with some ash. They could smell the smoke of a cook fire ahead and knew that they would not be alone that night. "Be on your guard Aleron. We cannot know what sort of people we might encounter on the road, or what their intentions might be."

"I understand, Grandfather," He answered.

A bit further, they were able to hear faint music, from some sort of stringed instrument. They proceeded with caution. What bothered Hadaras was not so much that there was someone ahead, but that he had no sense of the one ahead. *I can pick out the minds of most men from miles away, but of this, I sense nothing.* When they rounded the last bend of the trail and came within sight of the sheltered glade, just below the top of the hill, they saw the man. Seated on the ground, with his back against a log, he had his legs stretched toward a modest fire and was playing a zither, held in his lap. The intricate tune he plucked from the strings was hauntingly beautiful. He ignored the newcomers, until his song was complete. Hadaras and Aleron dismounted and simply stood immersed in the strange melody.

The stranger stopped playing, looked up at the pair and said, "Welcome friends. I hope you enjoyed my meager attempt at musician-hood. Please, make yourselves at home. I have little, but what I have is yours to share. My name is Cladus." He stood then, gently leaning the instrument against the log. He was tall and generally handsome, with long brown hair and moustache, but no beard. His eyes were a bright emerald green that seemed ill matched to the man's complexion. He wore sturdy boots, with trousers and tunic that, though worn and mended in a few spots, were of good quality and clean. He wore no sword, but he had a pair of long knives fixed horizontally to the back of his belt. His lone horse was picketed beneath a large sheltering oak.

"Well met Cladus, I am Hadaras and my young charge here is Aleron. We have food to share as well and would welcome a place at your fire."

"Excellent, let me help you with the horses then."

After they unpacked and rubbed down the horses, Aleron led them back down to the waterhole to drink their fill. When he led them back up the hill to picket then and tie on their feedbags, Hadaras and Cladus had the rabbits dressed and spitted over the fire. Hadaras had mixed up a pot of bannock. Now he was busy winding the dough around sticks for baking over the fire. Cladus used one of his long knives to reduce longer limbs to usable firewood lengths. The knife's blade was over a foot long and thick, with a spear point shape and a single cutting edge. It seemed more like a butcher's cleaver than a fighting weapon.

Hadaras commented, "That's a Sultean seaxe, isn't it? Not too common this side of the mountains."

"Yes, I spent a few years with the westmen. The people are nice and friendly up there, though the girls play a little rough," he added, in jest. He looked at Aleron as he said it, with a mischievous glint in his eye. Aleron was happy the light of the fire masked the redness of his face as he settled down by the men. Cladus continued, "Looks like you need to get this youngster to bed. He looks dead on his feet."

Before Aleron could reply, Hadaras agreed, "That's the plan. He didn't get much rest last night with the two of us swapping watch shifts."

"Don't worry, young man," Cladus said to Aleron, "you will eventually learn how to sleep with one eye open. All of us who travel the wilderness alone acquire the skill."

After they ate, Aleron settled into his bedroll and promptly fell asleep, as Cladus played a new tune on the zither. He'd identified himself to the others as a travelling bard, earning his keep with songs, stories and news, wherever he went. After the boy was sound asleep, the bard stated, "Let's not pretend anymore; shall we, my friend? The two of you have some secrets about you, as do I." He continued, "I could sense the horses and the boy from a mile away, but your presence was a complete surprise."

"I, as well, could smell the fire and hear the music, but no mind could I sense," Hadaras offered. "It seems you have some ability. May I ask, from where?"

"Let's just say, that I was born a couple hundred years ago on the northwest coast, right on the border with the colonies in fact."

"Was it your mother or father?"

"My father was the source of my elvish blood," Cladus answered. "He took good care of my mother and me, until I was grown, and she passed away. Then, he disappeared back to the elvish lands. I have not seen him in nearly one hundred fifty years. So yes, that boy you have there is not the only halfblood wandering these lands. I have encountered a few of us over the years. As for you, my new friend, I sense nothing of Man in you."

"Fair enough," Hadaras conceded, his human features smoothly morphing to elvish. "The boy is my grandson, my daughter's son. I've been raising him since he was two."

"Does he know what he is?"

"No"

"What happened to his parents?"

"They passed through the veil nearly thirteen years ago."

"Thirteen years eh," Cladus mused, "thirteen years ago, the Kolixtlanis were looking for a halfblood boy. Word of it travelled quickly among us magicians who knew of one another. Is this the boy? Is that what became of his parents?"

Chapter 7

Gurlachday, Day 1, Growing Moon, 8760 Sudean Calendar

After five bone-jarring days of riding, Zormat had only thoughts of murder for the yag. Unruly, cantankerous, and omnivorous, it was the perfect mount for a goblin, but not necessarily an elf, even an elf that was one-eighth goblin. They rounded a bend in the trail, and it opened to a clear grassy sward, with the beachhead just beyond. He scanned southward down the beach and could see his ship moored in the distance. There appeared to be a small group massed on the beach. They rode down the beach at a vigorous trot, the yag's odd feet floating on the loose sandy soil. As they neared the group, he could see that they were men, dressed in light armor and appearing to be soldiers of some sort. Closing to within thirty paces of the group, they halted the mounts and Zormat handed the reins to Shaggat. He dismounted and strode purposefully to the group. The apparent leader shouted something at him in a language he did not understand and the six lancers flanking him raised their weapons to a guard position. Two archers, armed with longbows, moved to the outer flanks to provide cover. Zormat drew his sword, glowing like red flame, even in the bright afternoon sun. The eight-pointed star on his forehead flared with the same fire. The leader gave a quick hand signal and the soldiers stood down. He said something else that Zormat did not understand, but its tone sounded reasonable.

We do not speak the same tongue, so I will communicate with you in this manner, Zormat spoke into the mind of the leader, sheathing his sword as he came to a halt. *Speak as you normally would, and I will understand you while we are so connected.*

"I can understand you, stranger," the leader offered, then asked, "Who are you and why do you travel with the goblin? Do you belong to this vessel?"

The ship is mine, yes and this goblin has been my guide from the jungle interior. I have journeyed to and from Immin Bul and I have much work remaining.

You bear the mark of the Nameless God, but I do not recognize you from any folk who worship him. What is your business in Kolixtlan?

I come at my Father's bidding, from a far-off land, to spread the word amongst his people that he will soon be freed from his prison.

With the wordless transmission of thought, the full import of the title "Father" hit the man like a battering ram. He immediately genuflected, saying, "Son of the Nameless God, please forgive me my insolence." At their leader's words and actions, the other soldiers dropped their weapons in the sand and dropped to one knee as well, averting their eyes to the ground.

To the group he said, *Rise, my friends. I took no insult from you performing your duties. I am still unknown in these lands. I am Zormat, King of Arkus.* To Shaggat he said, "Ride back to your people, my friend and spread the word that our day approaches. Prepare for war!"

The hobgoblin wheeled his mount, tugging the reigns of the second yag to follow, saying, "Yes Lord, I will spread the news to all of my people!" before riding off at a brisk trot.

To the leader of the men he said, *I must journey to your capital and speak to your king and his priests. What is your name and what rank do you hold among your people?*

"My Lord," the man replied, now standing again, "I am Matlal, captain of the army garrison at Ixtauhac, just north of here. We have been monitoring your vessel for over a week and we have sent riders south to alert the nearest naval ships in port. There will be warships making their way up the coast by now."

I imagined as much would be afoot and that could add unnecessary complication. Will they be likely to attack or hail first?

"Most likely, they will attack and then search the ship when all the crew are killed or captured, My Lord."

That would not happen, but I would prefer not to destroy the ships of my allies. Is there one among you that you can spare to accompany us? Moreover, a banner, perhaps, that we might display friendly intent?

Matlal replied, "I will be the one to accompany you, My Lord, if you will have me. We can fly my unit banner off the bow. It will confuse them at first, but they will recognize it as Kolixtlani. That will keep them from attacking before they ask to board."

Will you not be missed at your post, Captain?

"I will send word to my Lieutenant to assume command, Lord. He is a capable young man who will do fine running the garrison for a couple weeks," the captain answered. To one of the lancers he said, "Soldier, get me the banner and move smartly." As the soldier moved out, an Arkan, rowing a small boat from the ship, was almost within reach of the shore.

✳✳✳

As Aleron readied the horses that morning, Hadaras recalled the words Cladus had left him with several mornings past, *Keep a close watch on that boy, my friend. There is something about him that goes beyond him being a half-blood. The lad is a focal point of both light and dark and I sense unfathomable power within him. One of my gifts is a keen sense for potential and I sense in him, depths of potential I have never before sensed in an individual. Given the chance, that boy of yours might even surpass the power of Goromir of old.* The words troubled him, as he could not sense Aleron's potential in such concrete terms. Every sorcerer had his or her own special gifts and if that was Cladus', he dared not ignore the warning. Also troubling, was the casual resurgence of the name he had not used in four thousand years.

"I think we're ready, Grandfather," Aleron called, breaking Hadaras from his contemplation of the events of days past. He was leading the horses to the spot where Hadaras and the bags were waiting. They worked together to finish loading the animals, then donned their helms and mounted. Neither spoke much that morning, as if both were deeply involved in their own thoughts.

A bell or more had passed when Aleron spoke up, "Grandfather, I had a strange dream last night. I was wondering if you could tell me if it means anything."

"I can try to help you make sense of it, Aleron," Hadaras replied. "Just bear in mind that most dreams are meaningless, just your minds way of rearranging its memories while you sleep. Only rarely does a dream involve revelation of any sort."

"Well," Aleron ventured, "something is telling me that this one means something, Grandfather."

"Go on."

"I dreamed that I was in some strange garden somewhere. It was nighttime, but the moon was full overhead, and it was nearly bright as daylight. The garden had pools and fountains scattered through it and all the stonework looked very old. Not many of the figures carved into the fountains looked human at all."

"Interesting, so far, go on."

"Well, that wasn't the strangest thing about the fountains," Aleron continued, "The water in the fountains was all different colors and it glowed like it was lit from inside." Hadaras began listening intently now. Aleron went on, "You and Cladus were there, together. You were sitting at the edge of a fountain with bright blue water, dipping your mugs into the flow and drinking the glowing blue water. There were others drinking there as well, but I think they were elves, not men."

"And, what of the other pools?"

"There was another pool, in a dark corner of the garden that had this deep red water. It looked like glowing blood. There were strange men and elves drinking from that one, along with other strange creatures that I didn't recognize. Everything about that pool said disorder. The stonework was rough but strong and the carvings were a riot of different designs, all clashing with each other. It seemed like the opposite of the blue fountain, where everything was so ordered it was almost too perfect."

"Were those the only pools? I thought you said there were several."

"Oh, there were, Grandfather, one for every color of the rainbow."

"Really and who was at these pools?"

"No men or elves, that's for sure, but lots of other strange creatures. There was a bright green one with some creature that looked like a walking tree drinking from it. Then it poured a mug-full on the dirt and new plants just sprouted there. There was another that was bright gold, like the sun, which was able to heal things. Sick and broken animals were crawling to it, only to walk away strong and healthy."

"Were you able to drink from any of the pools," Hadaras inquired with great interest.

"That's the odd part, Grandfather. I was able to drink from all of them, even the red one. The people at the red one did not want me to drink there, but I just shoved them aside and drank. I drank from every pool in the garden. Then I found an empty basin, in the center of the garden. It looked like it was to have been the focal point but was never filled."

"What did you do at that pool?"

"Do you think that it means something?"

"It might, I'll have to think on it a bit more."

"I didn't like the pool being empty, so I brought water from all the pools and poured it in the empty basin."

"And what happened when you mixed the colored waters together?"

"Kind of what you would expect to happen, the colors mixed to make new colors. The only thing that was different was when I had mixed all the colors.

When I've mixed lots of colors of paint together, I always end up with some sort of brown. When I mixed all the water from the different pools together, the water turned white and glowed too brightly for me to look at it anymore," Aleron elaborated. "Why do you suppose that happened, Grandfather?"

"Well," Hadaras began, "some scholars have ideas about how light works. When sunlight passes through a glass prism, it is split into all the separate colors. So, they think that white light is an even mix of all the colors. But, when we paint something, green perhaps, the paint reflects back the green light and absorbs all the other colors. Because of that, when you mix all the colors of paint, it absorbs all the colors, little to no light is reflected and appears black or brown," he explained. "That is the best explanation that I have heard for it. It was originally from a physical philosopher from the university at Kaas and I believe most scholars have adopted that view as well."

"That would make sense," Aleron ventured, "since the waters were all glowing from within. They were giving off light, not reflecting it."

"Did anything else happen with the white water? Did you drink that as well?"

"Yes Grandfather, though I was not able to look directly at it, I dipped my cup in and drank."

"What happened then?"

"After I drank, I could look directly into the white water. Then, when I looked around, I could see into the minds of everyone in the garden. I didn't like what I saw in some of them, especially the ones at the red fountain."

"What did you see that you didn't like," Hadaras inquired.

"I saw a lot of dark thoughts, especially with the red fountain people," the boy continued, "but also at the other fountains too. There were a few at the blue fountain that seemed pure, but not all. I got the impression that the blue stood for order and the red stood for chaos."

"You said the red stood for chaos, but not evil?" Hadaras asked.

"No, not evil, but the people with evil in their hearts were mostly drawn to that one. It seemed like no one in the garden was completely evil and none were all good. Some just had more of it than others," Aleron replied and then went on, "There were only a few who had none at all. There was the tree thing and the keeper of the golden pool and a couple of the elves at the blue fountain. They were the only ones with no evil, but there were none with no good at all," he finished.

"That certainly was an interesting dream, my boy."

"Do you think it means something? I don't usually remember dreams this well."

"I think this one definitely falls into the vision, over the dream, category," Hadaras offered. "I will need to think on it for a while before I can make sense of it, though."

"Thank you for listening, Grandfather. I have wanted to talk about it. It seemed important, but I couldn't make any sense of it."

Hadaras rode on thinking, *Important, maybe, perhaps only as important as the unification of all the branches of magic. What importance could that have?*

Chapter 8

Corballday, Day 15, Growing Moon, 8760 Sudean Calendar

The pair rode through wooded, hilly country as they had all morning. The forest alternated between dark conifer stands, where little light made it to the ground and brighter stands of hardwoods. The overall prevalence of certain species indicated that this was no wild forest, but an intensely managed woodlot. "Look, Aleron," Hadaras said to get the boy's attention, "do you see the holes in the bark of these maples surrounding us?"

"Yes, I see them," Aleron replied. "They look like they were drilled. Why would people drill holes in trees?"

"They do it to drain the sap," he explained. "In the early spring, the local people here draw sap from the trees and drink it as a tonic. There is enough sugar in the sap that they can boil it down to make a sort of beer, or even boil it down to make hard sugar."

"Sugar from trees?" Aleron asked in disbelief. "Why don't they do that where we live?"

"It has to do with the altitude, I've been told," Hadaras related. "We don't have the right kind of maples because it is too warm where we live. Moreover, even where these grow, they need deep snow and a drawn-out thawing period to produce much sap. Up here, it takes a long time for winter to release its grasp."

"What happens if it thaws too quickly? Doesn't the sap run anyway?

"From what I understand, it happens too quickly, and they are not able to capture as much before it's over. But, in a completely unrelated point, our passing through this region means we are getting close to Arundell," he said as they crested a small ridge.

As if on cue, the forest path opened into a small clearing. From their vantage point, the entire Arun River Valley opened up below them. It was a nine-hundred-foot descent to the valley floor. They could barely make out Arundell through the haze, far to the north, between the west and north branches of the river. They had slowly gained elevation for the three weeks they had been travelling. Now, the massive canyon that formed the upper reaches of the Arun Valley, over thirty leagues wide in places, cut the plateau. The trail descended the steep slope in a series of switchbacks. This was definitely not a cart path. They would have to descend carefully, so as not to injure the horses. "It's beautiful Grandfather!" Aleron exclaimed and then continued, "How long do you suppose it will take us to get down there?"

"This will take a few bells to negotiate," Hadaras answered. "It would actually be quicker without the horses. We will have to take it slow, then camp somewhere on the valley floor tonight. We should be able to reach the ferry crossing by mid-afternoon tomorrow. Then, we will be in Arundell by nightfall."

"It will be nice to sleep in a bed again," Aleron said, followed by a sigh.

"Who said we would sleep in a bed?" His grandfather chided.

"Grandfather!"

"Just kidding," Hadaras said, chuckling. "I just wanted to see the look on your face when I said that."

Hadaras was still chuckling as they started their mounts down the trail. It was rapidly becoming steeper and soon they would need to dismount. The Arun glittered crystal blue in the far distance. The river formed a seaway, two leagues or more in width, allowing Arundell to become a major port city, as well as being the capital of Sudea.

✳✳✳

Zormat sat in his private cabin, pleased with his progress of the past week. Cutting across the open sea, they managed to avoid any warships sent to intercept them on the way in. The port authorities at Kolixtla stopped them, of course and Captain Matlal's presence proved useful in negotiating their passage. His few days of contact with the Kolixtlani officer allowed Zormat to absorb a passable knowledge of the local language prior to meeting with the king. It was a strange language, difficult to grasp due to many sub-words making longer words, whose meaning would take an entire sentence to convey in other tongues. The meetings with King Quauhtli and his High Priest Itzcoatl were very productive. Kolixtlan was the most powerful of the nations loyal to the Nameless One and their allegiance to the cause was assured. He instructed Itzcoatl to discontinue sacrifices for the near term, saving the captives for a mass sacrifice when the time was right. Zormat also blessed Itzcoatl and some of his higher echelon priests with the ability to discern true believers from unbelievers. The upcoming inquisition would weed unbelievers from the populace and swell the number of potential sacrifices. When he returned Zadehmal to the gates of Immin Bul, thousands would die, and the power of the blood sacrifice would flow into his father. Then, together, they would have the strength to burst the bonds holding the Nameless God captive. As well, he instructed the priests to begin referring to his father as the 'One True God'. He was nameless only because he needed no name. All other gods were false. *Next stop will be Zyx on the Adar coast, then Corin on the Thallasian coast. Both are more backward than the Kolixtlani and lack a strong priesthood, but the missionaries I instructed to be sent will help in that respect. Apparently, the Thallasians were never much more than pirates, looking for an advantage. A few years of missionary effort, followed by an inquisition will remedy that problem. Time to get some sleep.* They would set sail at dusk, with the king's second counselor and a prelate of the newly renamed Church of the One True God. Men were not comfortable sailing at night, but an Arkan's vision penetrated the darkness like that of a cat. Zormat was looking forward to this trip.

As Cladus made his way to Swaincott, the small village Aleron and his family called home, he came upon the well-maintained cottage of Hadaras and his family, with its meticulously manicured gardens and hedges. As he rode into the courtyard, he saw a content old mare wandering free, cropping the grass. He dismounted and led his mount to the hitching post. The horse looked indignantly at him as he prepared to tie the reins. "You want to visit, don't you, old friend?" The magician/bard said to the animal. "Go ahead and play; just stay out of trouble." He looped the reins around the saddle horn, to keep them from tangling and patted the horse's flank. *So, this is where the old elf was raising the lad, very nice spread. Something keeps telling me that boy's name was no accident at all. Could it be true? The prophecies did state that a new king would arise after a millennia's absence. With the raw power he could sense at the core of Aleron's being, it was quite a believable prospect.* He made his way to the cottage door; it opened in anticipation of his arrival. The dark-haired beauty in the doorway nearly took his breath away.

"Welcome Cladus, I've been expecting you," Jessamine greeted him. "Come in please and make yourself at home."

"That would be improper of me Milady, what with the men of the house away," he replied, stammering slightly. He rarely lost his composure, and it was a bit disconcerting. Looking into her eyes, he caught a sense of primordial forests, the likes of which no living man had ever seen and beyond that, the fathomless depths of the space between the stars. *This is no more a daughter of men than Hadaras is a son.*

"Nonsense," she retorted, "you will sleep in a proper bed tonight and eat a home cooked meal. Now, unsaddle that horse and come inside, take your boots off at the door and bring your instrument. You can sing for your supper, bard."

"Of course, Milady," he answered, composure regained. "Jessamine, I presume?" he continued, with a half-bow and flourish.

"You presume correctly. Now tend to your mount and come inside. I believe we may have a few things to talk about before you start singing. You may store your saddle in the stable if you like."

✳✳✳

As they slowly picked their way down the narrow, switch backed trail, Hadaras thought on the dreams his young charge was having of late. Always the dreams revolved around the common thread of colors. Sometimes liquid, sometimes light or vapors, sometimes even solids or his own flesh, the colors and their associated powers, were always the central focus of the dreams. It was a concept the old sorcerer was familiar with, from his long study of magic. The blue power of order was, traditionally, the only form available to elves. The Adversary and his halfblood sorcerers preferred the red power of chaos. The other colors he knew, but they were available exclusively to the Alient, not mortals. The boy impeccably described the properties of the various colors. In one such dream, he was healing the injured with glowing yellow hands. In another, he described pulling down a mountainside with the red light of chaos. He then raised a forest upon the destruction with a shower of glowing green rain. Hadaras knew that these were visions, not dreams. Somehow, the Allfather was communicating to the boy and instructing him in the ways of magic, while he slept. Most interesting, was the lad's description of white, the blend of all colors. Aleron described it as the power of transformation. With the white, he could change one substance to another, or change himself into something else. He described running free across the plains as a wolf and flying high above Aertu as a bird. In so doing, he accurately described places he had never been, to the point that his grandfather knew the exact location to which he was referring. What Hadaras found most troubling were Aleron's descriptions of elvish wielders of red magic. They were a supposed impossibility, but they were scattered throughout the boy's dreams. He could not let on to his grandson how much he knew about everything the boy was telling him. Posing as a man, he could not seem to possess any more than a scholarly knowledge of magic. Sorcerous ability cropped up only rarely among men in these days since the halfblood caste was diluted. Granted, there were the scattered halfbloods like Cladus roaming Aertu, but for the ability to manifest in an ordinary man, was highly improbable. Though not unheard of, it involved a concentration into a single individual, of elvish traits present only at low levels in the population.

One afternoon, when Aleron asked him whether he was dreaming about magic, Hadaras answered, "That appears to be the case Aleron," continuing, "but I know not why you would be dreaming of such things nearly every night. It must mean something though."

"But I only recall reading about the blue and red, when it comes to magic. The story of the final battle of the Great War said that blue and red magic shot like lightning across the sky and the weapons glowed in those colors too."

"Those two are the colors allowed for elves and men. Elves wielded the blue exclusively, while men were capable of wielding either, depending on their alignment," Hadaras answered.

"Where there ever men who wielded both?" Aleron inquired.

"Yes, there were some, who began on the side of good, who were swayed by the lies of the Nameless one. Once they wielded the red power of the Adversary, they never returned to the wielding of blue."

"That's odd," the boy mused. "In my dreams, I can switch from one to the other easily and sometimes I blend the two. When I do that, it makes this purple light, that's good for moving big things. It's like a mix of brute force and precision. I dreamed I was using it to lift huge boulders and hurl them to a spot leagues away, where they were needed to build something. Then I used the blue light to cut them into perfectly square blocks."

"What were you building?"

"It looked like some sort of fortress, a tower with walls four arm-spans thick, but what about the other colors Grandfather?"

"A tower, interesting…The other colors were known to exist, but from what I've read from scholars of magic, the others were not for mortals."

"Oh…" The boy stopped his questioning and rode along, seemingly deep in thought.

Hadaras thought on that and other conversations he and Aleron had on the subject of the boy's dreams. *Could the red be wielded without the wielder becoming evil? Red was associated with death and decay, but were those forces not necessary for new life to arise? The red force of disorder could be seen as complimentary to the green force of growth, as much as it opposes the blue force of order. The lad claims that none of the forces seemed inherently good or evil, just that good or evil individuals preferred one to the others, definitely food for thought.* He wondered what all these visions meant for Aleron. They were starting early, for one thing. Most halfbloods didn't start showing signs of ability until well into their seventeenth year and elves, much later than that. For Aleron to be experiencing visions, not even into his sixteenth year, was prodigious, to say the least. His thoughts returned to the trail. The narrowing, just ahead, meant they would dismount and lead the horses on foot.

Cladus took in the details of the kitchen, as Jessamine prepared tea for them. It was comfortably spacious, but just so, without being wasteful of space. The architecture of the cottage was simple, spare and unadorned, but still quite graceful, very elvish in its sensibilities. The hardwood planks of the floor were beautifully polished and waxed, a rarity in a country cottage. "You have a very beautiful house," he said, for lack of anything better to break the ice.

"Thank you Cladus. That's kind of you to say about our modest little abode," Jessamine replied. "Hadaras told me about you. He said you possess remarkable abilities of perception."

"I suppose so," the bard agreed. "It comes in handy in my profession, to anticipate what the customer would like to hear next."

"So, what do you perceive in me?" She asked, as she set the teacups on the table and took her seat across from him.

He hesitated a moment, before replying, "Like Hadaras, I sense you are not a child of men, though you may appear to be. But I also sense that you are not an elf, but something more ancient still."

"That will suffice, I believe you are as Hadaras said you were," she concluded. "At this time, it is probably best not to go into detail about who I am, though I'm sure you can come to your own conclusions."

"Understood Milady."

"Now, what did you perceive about my dear Hadaras?" she inquired.

"I have arrived at my own conclusions on that as well, Milady. I sensed that he is impossibly old, even for an elf and 'Hadaras' is only one of many names he has gone by. There is something beyond elvish in his makeup. He is possibly the most powerful sorcerer I have ever encountered. That was all I could gather from him; the rest was too closely guarded."

"That is certainly an impressive skill you have there, Cladus and it appears to be a passive one, that doesn't require you to probe the individual you read. I felt no intrusion, though your assessment of me was accurate," she admitted. "What did you sense of our young Aleron?"

"Well, with that lad, there it becomes complicated."

Chapter 9

Carpathday, Day 16, Growing Moon, 8760 Sudean Calendar

"One silver piece for you, a half for the boy and one and a half for each of the horses," The ferryman said. "That makes for four and a half silver."

"I don't have any half-pieces with me," Hadaras explained. "Will you take four even?"

"Don't you worry my good man," the ferryman replied. "I have plenty of half pieces. Give me five and I'll give you back a half."

"Very well," Hadaras agreed, opening his coin pouch. The man was obviously not interested in haggling.

"Thank you, kind sir," the old man said, after receiving his money. The boat won't depart for another half-bell or so. Have to wait and see if a few more customers show up." He had the look of an old sailor and probably saved his pennies for years to buy this boat and the rights to this route. The dozen oarsmen rested in place, obviously not interested in embarking any sooner than necessary. "That's a strappin' young lad you have there. He your grandson?"

"Yes, he is," Hadaras replied.

"Does he know how to use that sword on his side?" the ferryman asked, with doubt in his tone.

"More than passably," Hadaras answered, adding, "He's probably more than a match for most of the trained recruits in the ranks." A couple of the bored looking oarsmen perked up at the statement.

"I'm going to join the army or the navy next year, after I turn sixteen," Aleron interjected, beaming at his grandfather's compliment.

"Go for the navy youngster," the old sailor offered. "Sea pay is better'n land pay, plus you get to see more of the world, 'cause you get places faster. If you're really that good with a sword, the marines would likely take you in a heartbeat."

"Thank you, sir, I'll definitely take that into account."

The ferryman smiled and patted Aleron on the shoulder, as they guided the horses up the loading ramp and onto the boat. As they tied off the horses to the center railing, they saw dust in the distance. Soon two riders came into view, hurrying to catch the ferry. Apparently, they would have company after all on this trip.

The new arrivals dismounted and commenced negotiating the fare with the boat's owner. The horsemen were decked out in the Sudean royal livery of blue tabards emblazoned with a four-pointed star, in gold. "Royal couriers, by the look of them," Hadaras said of the men as they paid the fare. They led the lathered mounts onto the boat, as the ferryman scanned the distance for any more late arrivals. He untied from the dock and hopped onboard, pulled up the loading gate and proceeded to the tiller. On cue, the oarsmen lowered the oars into the water and pulled in unison. The ferry pulled away from the dock as the pilot lowered the tiller and pushed as if attempting a hard left. As the oarsmen pulled, the ferry canted into the current, appearing as if to aim far to the north of the city, when in fact they were travelling straight across to the dock on the opposite bank. Fully half their effort went toward fighting the current of the Arun as it flowed to the sea.

"Are you really Royal Couriers?" Aleron inquired of the men who had joined them.

"Aye," said one, a tall red-haired man of about thirty, with what looked to be perpetual sunburn.

He didn't seem interested in elaborating, but that did not deter Aleron from asking, "Do you like it? I mean, is it exciting?"

"It's a job, just like any other," said the second courier, a bit younger than the first and not as tall, with sandy hair. He was a bit friendlier to the boy, continuing, "It's better than soldiering at least. The hours are still long, but I get to sleep in my own bed more often than when I was in the ranks. Not nearly as exciting though. This is more of a settling down and raising a family job, than an exciting one."

"Aye, that it is," agreed the tall redhead, loosening up a bit. "Being a soldier's a young man's job. Once you got a wife and younguns, bein' out campaigning isn't so much fun anymore."

"I keep telling the lad he should think about university, but he wants a career at arms," Hadaras said.

"He can read?" asked the older courier.

"Four languages and working on the fifth," Hadaras informed him.

"Damn boy, you could be a court scribe. Why would you want a soldier's life when you could live at the palace and make twice the money?"

"What Grandfather isn't telling you, is that he's been teaching me to fight for almost as long as he's been teaching me to read," Aleron interjected.

"Your good with that sword then?" the younger one asked, looking from Aleron to Hadaras for confirmation.

Hadaras nodded, as Aleron answered, "I'm not too bad, I think. It's hard to say, since I only fight my grandfather and a couple of my friends."

"I wouldn't mind sparring with you for a bit, if you're willing and your grandfather doesn't mind," the young courier announced. "We have a little time, don't we Karl?"

"We can spare a few minutes Bruno," the elder answered.

"I have no problem with it," Hadaras agreed, "as long as we lay down a few ground rules first."

"Agreed then," Aleron stated.

The ferry was nearing the opposite bank and the ferryman lifted the tiller out of the water. The oarsmen on the left side reversed direction, pushing the oars, rather than pulling and the ferry spun around to bring the stern to the dock. The pilot deftly tossed a loop of rope over a post on the dock, as the rearmost oarsmen stowed their oars and joined him in pulling the boat tight to the dock. He tied off the up-current side of the stern, saying, "Good work boys."

"Thanks Dad," one of the hulking oarsmen replied.

"Looks like we're gonna have a show. We're ahead of schedule, so we might as well take break boys," The ferryman said to his men.

After offloading the ferry, the oarsmen followed the passengers off the boat. A few passengers were waiting on the return trip and the ferryman announced, "We're taking a short break, ladies and gentlemen and we will board in about half a bell." Some of the potential passengers grumbled among themselves, but none spoke up to complain.

Karl, Bruno, Aleron and Hadaras hitched their horses and found a clear area near the docks. The ferry crew dragged benches over so they could watch, while they took their mid-morning break. The new passengers and some dockworkers noticed the activity and wandered over as well. Hadaras spoke up, "Now, if the boy is to do this, there will be some rules. Until now, he has only sparred with practice swords, never live steel. Aleron, you will wear your helm. Bruno, it's your choice to wear yours or not."

"Aye," Bruno agreed, while Aleron nodded in affirmation and went to retrieve his helm. Bruno simply pulled his mail coif over his head and fastened the gorget across his throat. Aleron did the same and placed his helm on his head.

"You will strike with the flats only," Hadaras continued, "with no thrusting and no intentional strikes to the head and neck. Daggers are to be used for blocking only. Are we agreed?"

"Yes Grandfather," Aleron agreed.

"Of course," Bruno replied. "I've no intention of harming the lad. I just want to see how well you've trained him."

"Then let's get started," Hadaras announced.

The two faced off against each other, separated by four paces. They both drew their dagger and tossed them to their left hands, following with their swords. When Aleron drew his, Karl remarked, "That's an elvish blade if I've ever seen one." The blade was long and slender, with a leaf shape and a long central fuller that changed width along with the blade. The quillons arced gracefully forward, and a teardrop shaped pommel completed the hand and a half hilt. Bruno's sword was a typical Sudean issue arming sword, the blade four fingers wide at the hilt and tapering abruptly to the armor piercing point. "Where are you folks from?" inquired Karl.

"We come from Swaincott, near Ellesfort, on the bay, but I served up in the colonies years ago and acquired a few souvenirs," Hadaras replied.

"That's some rough duty up on the border," Karl commented. "I was always glad the dwarves never asked for our help up there," he continued.

"Are you ready lad?" Bruno asked.

"Ready!" Aleron answered.

They slowly circled one another to the right, as right-handed fighters often do. Suddenly, Bruno darted to the left, attempting an offhand strike to Aleron's right hip. Aleron deftly executed a low block and then whipped his own blade in a graceful arc, trying to connect with Bruno's shoulder. If not for the ground rules, he would have gone for a head shot. Bruno barely parried the shot, his eyes widening at the speed of the counterattack. The dance went on for several more minutes, with neither swordsman scoring on the other. Finally, as Aleron blocked with his dagger, he managed to catch the other's sword with the forward pointing quillons, locking the blade with a twist of his wrist. Bruno, surprised by the teenager's strength, was unable to free his blade, as Aleron took his sword arm in a blindingly fast attack. The strike to the arm was immediately followed by a strike to the opposite leg, so fast that the onlookers could barely see the flash of steel in the sunlight. Bruno let drop his weapons, raising his hands palm outward to signify his ceding the match. As the weapons clattered to the ground, a few of the oarsmen cheered, while the others groaned. Apparently, a few wagers had been made on the outcome.

"Corball's Balls!" Karl exclaimed, "The lad's as fast as an elf too! How old is the boy?"

"Not quite fifteen," Hadaras replied, chuckling at the ancient soldier's explicative.

Karl raised one eyebrow, "And he already fights like that and that big too? He just beat one of the best in Bruno there."

"Fine work lad!" Bruno exclaimed, closing in to embrace the boy. "Your grandpa wasn't joking about you. You're the best I've fought in a long while."

"Th-thank you sir," Aleron stammered. "You are very good yourself, though I've only fought my friends and my Grandfather here. You're almost as fast as Grandfather."

Karl raised the eyebrow again, this time at Hadaras, then said, "Come on Bruno, we need to get going, or there'll be hell to pay when we're late. You folks have a good day," he finished, as he moved off to their horses.

"Good day to you lad," Bruno said before collecting his weapons. "Keep working at it and you could be the best swordsman in the kingdom before long."

As the couriers rode off, Karl said to Bruno, "They're from Swaincott, a little cow town near Ellesfort. Last place I expected to find a nest of scorpions."

"You aren't joking Karl," Bruno replied, "That kid was the fastest I've ever run up against, excepting a couple elves and he said his grandpa is faster.

"The old man claims he served up in the elf lands, on the border. He doesn't look like he has a scratch on him though. He'd have to be damn good just to get sent there and better than good to make it back in one piece."

That explains the elf-blade the boy wields." The men continued discussing the bout as they rode towards the city at a brisk trot. Bruno was not used to losing and wanted to know everything he did wrong. Karl didn't have much to tell him other than that he just wasn't fast enough.

The oarsmen were laughing and slapping each other on the back as they exchanged coin. Win or lose, they all enjoyed the show. The ferryman began accepting fares and the passengers began filing onto the boat. Many of them laughed as they talked about the match they had just witnessed. Aleron stowed his helm and untied his and the packhorse, as Hadaras untied his own mount. They mounted up and Hadaras led the way toward Arundell.

"That went well," Aleron commented, "Bruno was really good and a pretty nice fellow too. I half expected him to be angry when I beat him."

"I think he was too perplexed to be angry," his grandfather replied. "According to Karl, Bruno is one of the best swordsmen in the city. They recruit the royal couriers from the best of the army ranks."

"Huh…" was all Aleron said in response, as they rode to the city gates.

Chapter 10

Carpathday, Day 16, Growing Moon, 8760 Sudean Calendar

By late morning, they passed through the city gates, leaving the dusty road behind them. Aleron had never seen anything like the walls of Arundell. Five arm-spans thick and ten high, with watchtowers every fifty paces and zigzagged with redoubts, providing a clear view of every inch of the perimeter, the city walls appeared impregnable. Dual portcullises formed the gate, to facilitate heavy traffic in both directions and travelers had to cross a drawbridge, spanning a deep moat, to enter or leave the city. Though the gate and drawbridge were easily five arm-spans wide, travelers still bottlenecked in both directions, and it took quite some time to gain access to the city. The two couriers were far ahead, as soldiers positioned at the drawbridge halted traffic to allow them to pass unhindered. After passing through the walls, the street opened to a vast marketplace. Wooden stands and carts dotted the cobblestone expanse, while shops of a more permanent nature, lined the outer edges. Beyond the market could be seen orderly blocks of low stone houses, divided by narrow streets and occasionally punctuated by tall mansions of polished granite and marble or the imposing spires of the occasional temple. Far in the distance, he could see the towering minarets of the Royal Palace. "Where will we be going first, Grandfather?" he asked, trying to take in all the sights.

"First thing my boy is to get to the inn, stow our gear and care for the horses. Then some food and a hot bath are in order," Hadaras answered.

"Will we get to look around the city?" Aleron inquired, looking a bit crestfallen.

"Don't worry Aleron, after a short rest, we'll be able to wander the markets. The one by the docks is even bigger than this one, with much more interesting merchandise, but we won't get to that one until at least tomorrow."

"All right," the boy conceded.

Hadaras knew exactly where he was going and they rode straight through the crowded marketplace, in an easterly direction. Exiting the market square, they travelled two city blocks before coming upon an inn, on the opposite corner of the street intersection. The sign above the door read, 'The Golden Dragon', over a realistic portrayal of just such a beast. A smaller sign on the corner of the building read 'Stables in Rear', with an arrow pointing left. They waited on a large, important looking carriage coming from the other direction before crossing to the entrance. Hadaras dismounted after passing the reins to Aleron, saying, "I'll go in and see if there are any rooms available. You wait here." Aleron waited until his grandfather came out again.

"As luck would have it, they've a double room available for the next five nights. I've stayed here in the past and it's a reputable establishment. Let's get the horses taken care of so we can rest."

After three and a half weeks on the road, Aleron would have gladly settled for less than reputable, as long as there was a bed involved. "Great," he replied as he dismounted, "I can't wait to get settled into something with four walls and a bed." They led the horses to the stable and got them settled in, taking turns bringing saddles and baggage to the rooms. When all their belongings were stowed, they unbuckled their swords and, keeping their daggers, went back to the stables to brush down, feed and water the horses. By the time they finished and returned to the room, they were several bells past midday and had not eaten since dawn. "Are we going to get some food soon Grandfather?" Aleron inquired. "I'm famished."

"Let's head to the common room then," his grandfather answered. "This establishment always has something cooking." They proceeded to the common room and Hadaras requested of the proprietor for a couple of hot baths for the room. The innkeeper obliged, informing him that it would cost two silvers extra for the service. They saw that braised venison haunch was on the menu, so he ordered two platters with sides of bread and boiled cabbage.

As it turned out, the inn, like many residences in Arundell, had running water inside the building. The city was supplied by springs, high above in the hills and transported via underground aqueducts. Metal pipes tapped into the pressurized aqueducts to carry water into the buildings without the need for pumping. The inn had the added feature of routing the water through black copper tanks on the rooftop, preheating the bath and cooking water to save fuel. Often, in the summer months, the bathwater would be so hot as to require tempering with cold water before use. After their meal and a hot bath, to wash away the weeks of road grime, the pair donned fresh clothes and buckled on the small swords and daggers they had packed for wear about town. Hadaras locked the door behind them with the large padlock provided and they headed out to the market.

***

The market square was still bustling with activity when Aleron and Hadaras arrived. They perused the stalls and shops together. Aleron had never seen such a selection of goods in one place. There was merchandise not only from across Sudea, but all over the Aertu as well. Aleron hefted a Sunjibi broadsword in one shop, wondering aloud who in the world could wield a five-pound, single-handed sword. His grandfather informed him that westman arms and armor were often much heavier than the norm, due to the great strength of that people. The two separated as Hadaras stopped to speak to one of the vendors, while Aleron continued browsing. Aleron looked up and saw a young, auburn-haired girl of around fourteen, dressed in a fine gown of sky blue and surrounded by four armed retainers. Their eyes met and Aleron thought hers might be the greenest eyes he had ever seen. She smiled at him and one of the retainers, noticing the exchange, scowled at him in turn. Since he wasn't watching where he was going, Aleron bumped into another young man, who was perusing the wares. "I'm sorry," Aleron said to the other, who appeared only slightly older than he did.

"And so you should be," the other youth stated in a loud voice, shoving Aleron backwards. The other youth was about Aleron's size, with black hair and a fringe of a beard.

"I said I was sorry!" Aleron stated, as the other reached to shove him again. Aleron grabbed his aggressor's right hand and twisted inward, until the palm faced the sky, bending the thumb back towards the ground. As his attacker fell to his knees, groaning in pain, Aleron noticed another youth, darting for the dagger on his right side. Aleron shifted slightly and mule-kicked the second attacker in the midsection. He thought he felt a rib crack beneath his heel and the second youth was curled on the ground, coughing. He twisted all the harder, as he repositioned himself to see both attackers. He said to the first, "I'm going to refrain from breaking your arm and you should tend to your friend. I think he may have a broken rib or two. If I notice either of you follow me, I will assume the worst and I will kill you. Are we understood?" The other nodded in affirmation. Aleron released him and stepped back, hand on his dagger hilt in an ice pick grip. The black-haired youth scrambled to the aid of his companion and Aleron looked around for the first time since the altercation began. The market goers had given them a wide berth and the girl, who Aleron had quite forgotten about, was watching him wide-eyed, with her retainers keeping a wary eye on him as well. Hadaras was watching from the other side and with a slight grin, motioned him over.

"You must try to stay out of trouble, my boy," Hadaras admonished the youth, jokingly.

"I didn't do anything to him, other than bump into him," Aleron defended. "I don't know what his problem was."

"I believe the problem had more to do with the pretty girl you were both eying before you bumped into each other," his grandfather offered. "I'm fairly certain that those two lads know her, or at least know who she is, which would explain the posturing."

"I never understood that Grandfather."

"You never understood what?"

"The fellows who think that pushing the others around will impress the girls," he answered. "Most girls are not impressed by that, from what I've seen."

"Just enough of them are, to keep it going and it's been going on since men first came into being. You can bet your last copper on that to be true. Come on and let's see what else they have here."

They spent the remainder of the afternoon and well into the evening, perusing the various offerings of the vendors. Aleron had some silver with him, but Hadaras reminded him several times, that they would be travelling for the better part of a year, and they would not want a lot of extra weight. Therefore, the swords, knives and armor that caught his eye, did not make it off the vendors shelves into his possession. He bought a few cakes and something to drink. As well, he purchased a new pair of gauntlets that appeared to be made from the hide of some sort of large snake or lizard, the dark green scales glittering in the sunlight.

With the day behind them, they returned to the inn for a hearty supper and retreated to the room, for a long-awaited sleep.

Chapter 11

Zorekday, Day 18, Growing Moon, 8760 Sudean Calendar

Mid-morning on their third day in Arundell brought Aleron and Hadaras to the palace gates. Zorekday, devoted to the God of the Sea and the last day of the week, was traditionally a rest day in the city, especially for the government, so Hadaras deemed it the best day to tour the palace grounds. The usual frantic activity would commence tomorrow, on Gurlachday and casual visiting was discouraged. As they entered into the expansive front courtyard, a minor official announced, "Gentlemen, if you are interested, a tour will start on the next bell."

"Thank you, Sir, but that's quite alright," Hadaras replied. "I know my way around well enough."

"Very well Sir, enjoy your visit."

The courtyard and gardens were open to the public every day, but Zorekday was the only day the old throne room was open. They crossed the wide flagstone courtyard, easily large enough to review an entire regiment, on their way to the public gardens. The gardens were equally as expansive as the courtyard. Wide paths meandered through impeccably maintained beds of flowers and incredibly detailed topiary. Statuary abounded, depicting characters and scenes from Sudean history. At the center of the garden, Hadaras led them to a larger-than-life statue in marble, of a tall man in armor, mustached but beardless, his right hand resting high on the hilt of a greatsword. "Meet your namesake lad," Hadaras announced, "Aleron, king of Sudea." Hadaras was impressed that the facial features still seemed accurate, this likely being the tenth such statue erected to honor the great king. Marble only lasted so long, after all. *They must have a proof hidden in a vault somewhere,* he thought.

"So that's what he looked like," Aleron stated, unconsciously stroking the wispy moustache on his lip and thinking no beard may not be the worst thing that could happen. The statue had a familiarity that he could not put his finger on. "He looks like somebody I know, but I can't think of whom."

Hadaras knew that if he had a mirror, he might have made the connection more easily. The statue looked like an older version of the boy standing before him. "Come on, my boy; let's get a look at the throne room before it gets too crowded."

Aleron turned to face Hadaras and then suddenly his eyes got wide. "That fountain, it's the one from my dreams!" He pointed to the fountain the statue of Aleron was facing. He had not noticed it when they approached. The ornate fountain was situated at the very center of the garden.

"Are you sure it's the same one?" Hadaras asked as Aleron rushed to touch the construct.

"Yes, Grandfather, it's unmistakable. All the markings are the same as in my dreams. I'm sure of it," he answered as he ran his fingers along the smooth marble rim. "This is the fountain of the white water." Water poured from the jugs held by the statues four maidens, facing the cardinal directions, with their backs to a sacred oak. Numerous magical glyphs were carved into the pedestal on which the maidens stood, most of them involving blessings of peace and prosperity for the kingdom. Aleron felt a tingling in his fingertips as he touched the stone and, unable to help himself, he dipped his hand into the fountain and scooped up a mouthful of the water. It was refreshingly cold, but otherwise, he felt nothing.

"Now don't be doing that," Hadaras admonished him. "People might find drinking from the fountains a bit uncouth." Sure enough, a few passersby did look crossly at them.

"How could I have dreamed about something I've never seen before?"

"I don't know Aleron, but I am sure that those are not mere dreams you have been having. I just don't know what to make of them yet. Now come on, let's go to the palace before the crowds arrive."

To enter the inner courtyard, leading to palace doors, they had to give up their weapons to the guards. In return, they received a colored and numbered ticket. Several sword belts and miscellaneous other personal weapons were already hanging on the numbered hooks beside the guardhouse. "Now don't lose that ticket, or we will have to come back tomorrow and pay to get your weapons from impound," Hadaras implored. "That is, if no one else takes a liking to them first and pays the fine, claiming them as their own. This is a good place to find inexpensive weapons if one lacks honesty."

"I won't lose it Grandfather," Aleron assured him. "Here, I'll put it in my coin purse and then back in my belt pouch it goes."

Hadaras nodded, satisfied with the boy's solution. "Let us proceed then, my boy." He led the way to the expansive main doorway, four yards wide and tall. The gilded steel doors swung inward on massive hinges, to reveal a huge antechamber. They stepped into the marble chamber that could have held two hundred comfortably, though they shared the space with only a half dozen others. Hadaras watched as Aleron took in the sight of the pristine white room, with its high vaulted ceilings and ornate carvings. Golden sunlight filtered in through narrow windows set high on the walls. Another set of doors, matching the first and hinged to open into the antechamber as well, remained closed and barred from within. Beside the huge doorway were two smaller ones, one on either side and also constructed of thick steel and gilded. These were open, with pikemen, still as statues in full military regalia, standing guard. "Don't let the fancy uniforms fool you lad," Hadaras said when he noticed Aleron looking them over. "The palace guards are like the couriers. They glean them from the best of the best."

"I don't doubt it, Grandfather," Aleron replied. He noticed the long scar, running temple to chin, on the one and the crisscrossed scars on the forearms of two others. These men were all veterans and definitely not dandies. They proceeded through the door to the right as the guards stared unflinchingly ahead, as if Aleron and his grandfather did not exist. If the antechamber was impressive, then the throne room itself was spectacular. Fifty paces long and twenty-five wide, the vaulted ceilings reached at least fifty feet to where the arches intersected. The pillars supporting the arches were carved to look like tree trunks and the arches like limbs. The room gave the impression that one was in a forest of gleaming white marble. Leaf like tracery in silver and gold covered the ceilings. Countless banners and pennants, commemorating thousands of years' worth of military campaigns, were festooned between the pillars lining the central aisle and tapestries depicting significant events in Sudean history lined the outer walls. Contrasting all this was the massive black granite throne at the far end, empty for over one thousand years. The clean simple lines of the weathered granite seemed at odds with the ornate and polished nature of the room. Aleron knew from his reading, that the seat was far older than the hall it sat in and nearly as old as the kingdom itself. King Aleron had the new hall completed just a few years before the great war against the Adversary, and moved the ancient throne of his kingdom, rather than have a new one built to match the space.

As they moved closer to the seat, Aleron saw something glittering blue in the sunlight. Hadaras noticed it too and hoped no one else could see it seemed to be glowing with an inner light, too bright to be the fault of the sun alone. He secretly cast a shade about the dais, to conceal the glow that was getting ever brighter as Aleron approached. *No doubts now,* he thought, *the sword recognizes its master.* The blue glow came from the sapphire studded pommel of Andhanimwhid, the sword known in the vernacular as the 'Sign of the King'. It glowed with blue radiance in the presence of the rightful king and only that one could draw it from the stone of the throne's back that encased the blade.

There were others touring the place as well. The old hall was no longer used for any official government business. That was done in the steward's offices deep within the palace. Aleron panned the room and to his surprise, there was the auburn-haired girl from the market, along with two of her bodyguards, and speaking to a well-dressed and handsome older gentleman. She was pointing at Aleron and whispering into his ear when Aleron spotted her. She quickly dropped her hand and turned to avoid his eyes. He nudged his grandfather, saying, "Grandfather, it's the girl from the market the other day." As Hadaras turned to face them, the older gentleman's eyes widened in recognition.

"Hadaras, you old badger," he shouted, "I thought I'd never see you in the capital again."

Hadaras laughed and replied, "Gealton, good to see you. I thought as much myself. Come on Aleron," he said, clapping him on the shoulder, "let's go meet the Steward of Sudea." Aleron followed in shocked disbelief as they crossed the floor to the highest-ranking official in the kingdom. Hadaras dropped to one knee and bowed his head when he came to one pace from the Steward and Aleron followed suit, to his immediate left.

"Get up old friend," Gealton cried, moving to grasp Hadaras' shoulders, "and you too lad," he directed Aleron. "How have you been, old friend," he asked, embracing Hadaras as he got to his feet.

"I've been well, old friend, living in the country for the last twenty years or so," Hadaras answered, "And you?"

"I'm doing well enough, I suppose, though I never had the option of melting into the landscape, much as I'd like to some days. I would like for you to meet my youngest daughter, Eilowyn and her esteemed bodyguards, Hans and Simeon." The two large men bowed, and the girl curtsied.

"Pleased to meet you Milady and Gentlemen," Hadaras replied, returning a deep bow, with Aleron awkwardly following suit. "This is my grandson, Aleron, son of my daughter Audina and Valgier." Aleron bowed again, more gracefully this time and was answered with still more bows and a curtsy. "You have a lovely young lady there, my friend," he continued, as the girl blushed.

"Thank you; she is an exceptional girl. That's a fine strapping young lad you have there, with a fine name as well. Eilowyn and her guardians told me a story of a young lad dispatching a pair of ruffians at the market. They said it was over in the blink of an eye. It's not so surprising, now that I see he's the grandson of the fastest sword in the kingdom." At that, Aleron looked to his grandfather in surprise.

"You flatter me Gealton."

"That I do not, Hadaras," the Steward retorted. He addressed the others, saying, "I've seen this man win against six spearmen at once, came through without a scratch. We served together on the elvish borderlands. He saved my arse more than once when we battled the jungle men. He one time plucked one of their poison darts right out of the air, just as it was to take me in the eye. I literally owe my life to this man. How long have you been training the lad here?"

"Nearly six years now."

"He started when I was nine, Milord," Aleron added, feeling a bit more comfortable now.

"Nine, which makes you about fifteen then son?" the Steward asked.

"Almost, Milord," Aleron answered, "I turn fifteen in the summer.

"Big for his age," Gealton said to Hadaras. "Those lads he took on in the market are both seventeen, sons of minor vassals, both of them. They should be in the military by now, but they're too busy lording it over the commoners to be bothered. It's a growing problem with the younger generation of nobles. They think the people exist to serve them, not the other way around. It does not bode well for the kingdom if you ask me. I'm considering mandatory service for all able-bodied noble sons. It should not have to be a law though. So, what are your plans for the future, my boy?" he inquired of Aleron.

"I'm having trouble deciding between the army and navy, Milord, so I'm thinking the marines might be the best of both worlds," answered the boy.

"Excellent, is the lad's father a soldier?" he asked Hadaras.

"No, my daughter chose a fine honest woodsman for her mate. We lost them both twelve years back and I've been raising the lad since." A sad expression crossed Aleron's face, as it reminded him of his lost parents, accompanied by a soft gasp of sympathy from Eilowyn. Aleron glanced over to see her brilliant green eyes regarding him and quickly looked down again, blushing himself, this time. She smiled slightly at that, but he did not see it.

"So sorry to hear that lad," Gealton said to Aleron, "but I can't think of a better man to have raised you than old Hadaras here. Come, my friend, let's talk," he said, grasping Hadaras' arm, "I want to know what you have been up to for the last twenty years." They walked off together, leaving the young people with Hans and Simeon.

"Aleron, is it? I like that name," the girl offered, to start conversation.

"Yes, Milady," Aleron affirmed, "that is my name," lifting his eyes to meet her gaze again.

"You can call me 'Ellie', all my friends do and none of this 'Milady', unless there are folks about of course. Would you like me to show you around a bit?"

"Yes, I would like that…Ellie," Aleron answered, "if it's all right with your father, of course."

"I think we will be fine," she replied. "Simeon and Hans won't let us out of their sight, I'm sure," she said, directing it as much to her bodyguards as to Aleron.

"Of course not, Milady," Simeon replied, "your safety is our utmost concern, over our own lives." Aleron recognized him as the one who scowled at him in the market two days past.

"Could my privacy be at least a minor concern as well?" she asked, sweetly. "Please give us a little space."

"As you wish, Milady," Hans conceded. The bodyguards allowed the teenagers to advance a few paces before following. "They make a handsome couple, don't they Sim?" he whispered.

"Aye," Simeon agreed, "but they don't stand a chance, with the boy being a commoner and all."

"Aye, too bad that and it looks like she really fancies him," Hans added before the two fanned out to cover more area. "But, if that's Lord Marshal Hadaras…"

"Not sure if his title extends to his descendants. I'm no scholar, but maybe…"

"Would you like to see the throne of your namesake, Aleron?" Eilowyn asked.

"Sure," he replied. "That would be great," his eyes of silver meeting hers of emerald with more confidence than before.

Chapter 12

Zorekday, Day 18, Growing Moon, 8760 Sudean Calendar

Eilowyn reached over and grabbed Aleron's hand. "Come then, let's go see it. I'm so glad you are here. I haven't had anyone new to talk to in such a long time, especially none as handsome as you," she teased. Aleron blushed again but said nothing for the moment. "You would not believe what it's like to live here, with people about you all the time. I have no privacy from the moment I open my eyes in the morning, to the moment I close them at night, all for my 'protection', they say."

"That would be hard to deal with," Aleron agreed. "I don't know if I could bear living in a palace, nice as it seems."

"What was it like living in the country?"

"I don't know, really, how to describe it. I did a lot of fishing with my friends, helping them with their farm work and helping the woodsmen and townsfolk with their work. Grandfather always wanted me to stay busy. He said it was so I could find my trade."

"Did you discover your calling then?"

"I think I did as soon as Grandfather began teaching me to fight. He told me all the stories of his time in the army, and I knew I wanted something like that, to be a soldier or a sailor."

"Father has always spoken of your grandfather, as long as I can remember. He said that your grandfather was, hands down, the finest fighter in the kingdom, and that he owed him his life, many times over."

"I'm beginning to think Grandfather glossed over some of his accomplishments, when he told me the stories," Aleron commented, "but that would explain why I can never beat him. The funny thing is, he put even more effort into teaching me to read."

"You can read and write Sudean too?" she said. "That's unusual for a farm boy, isn't it?"

"I guess so, but I had more time on my hands than the real farm boys and Grandfather made sure I was occupied. Actually, I can read Elvish, Dwarvish and Coptic too."

She looked at him in utter disbelief. "Did he want you to be a scribe or a soldier?"

"I've never been sure what he wanted. He told me he wanted me to have choices in life and that I should be able to take care of myself, no matter what the situation."

"I think you're trying to play with me Aleron. If you can read Elvish, what does that inscription there read?" She pointed to an ancient bronze plaque bolted to the dais upon which sat the throne.

Aleron looked at the plaque and replied, "By the hand of the Allfather, may the kingdom be blessed with peace and prosperity for all the ages yet to come."

"Well, I'll be a…never mind," she said, with some consternation. "Can you read that one?" she asked pointing to another bronze plaque that, like the first, had been mounted to commemorate the opening of the hall, over a thousand years ago.

Aleron looked at the Dwarvish runes and having to ponder a little longer, had Eilowyn thinking he was stumped. Then he recited, "By the Allfather and Gurlach, may the steel of your swords be always sharp and limber and your armor hard like stone. Strength in battle to all your generations, until the end of time." As she stared at him, slack jawed, he continued, "Kind of funny how the two blessings sort of contradict each other. Together, they both call for success, but of very different kinds."

"You're not a normal country boy, are you?"

"I suppose not, though I'm pretty normal with my friends. We fish and joke around, fight with the other boys and mostly have a good time."

"Well it's good to hear you have other interests than fighting and reading. Do you want to come look at the sword?"

"Is it allowed?" Aleron asked nervously.

"Of course it is. People touch it all the time. It's the most sacred relic of the kingdom and it's indestructible, as far as anyone can see." She assured him. "It's four thousand years old and it's been stuck in the back of the throne for a thousand of them, but the hilt still looks bright as new." She took his hand again and led him up onto the dais and then to another raised platform, behind the throne. "They built this here so people wouldn't have to stand on the throne to touch the sword," she explained. "No one sits or stands on it, ever, but every New Year's Day they let people line up to try to pull the sword out. We've been doing it since King Alagric died without an heir, a thousand years ago. Go ahead, try it." As Aleron got closer to the hilt, the jeweled pommel seemed to glow with an inner light. "That's odd," Eilowyn noted. "The light in here must be different. Those jewels seem brighter than I've ever seen them."

Aleron reached out and took hold of the hilt and the sapphires suddenly shone incandescent. Hadaras shouted, "Aleron, no!" from across the hall, but it was too late. The blue glowing blade of the ancient elvish weapon was already partway out of its granite scabbard, before Aleron slammed it back in, a look of shock and fear on his face. "Boy, what have you done?" Hadaras asked in dismay, as he and the Steward rushed over.

"I don't know, Grandfather!" Aleron cried. "I didn't mean any harm. I just meant to touch it and then it jumped out at me!"

"Guards, clear the hall now!" Gealton bellowed at the top of his lungs. "You two," he shouted at the bodyguards, "get Ellie to the royal chambers."

"Daddy, what's going on? I don't want to leave!" she protested.

"Don't argue right now, girl and do as you're told!"

"Yes Father," she acquiesced, turning, and walking with her flanking guards to a doorway behind the dais.

Once the girl and her guards were gone and the hall was clear, the Steward directed the remaining guards to exit and close the doors behind them. Then he said. "Hadaras, old friend, it looks to me like you have some explaining to do." Hadaras nodded gravely. "Now lad, why don't you grasp that old sword again and pull it out all the way." Wordlessly complying, Aleron grasped the hilt again and once again, the sapphires shone with piercing blue light. He stretched to his full height to draw the four-foot-long blade from the stone and then stood there in shocked disbelief, holding the sword before him. The blade shone with an inner radiance, that nearly matched that of the jeweled hilt, but softer. The older men could see the visible manifestation of the swords magic infusing Aleron's body as well. His skin glowed faintly, and the whites of his eyes were radiant blue. "Now go ahead and put it back." Aleron did as he was told, sliding the blade back into the stone of the granite throne. "Now you try it, Hadaras, if you would." Hadaras stepped up, as Aleron moved aside. He grabbed the hilt with both hands and pulled, but nothing happened. "Now it's my turn," Gealton asserted. The others stepped aside, as the Steward attempted the same as

Hadaras, with the same results. "I do believe we need to retire somewhere private and discuss matters."

"Agreed," Hadaras replied.

"Can anyone tell me what is going on here?" Aleron pleaded.

"In good time, lad, all in good time," his grandfather answered. First, the Steward and I have some things to talk over.

"Follow me, please," the Steward directed, and they walked to the same door Eilowyn and the guards had used. They emerged into a large reception room, richly furnished, but otherwise unused looking. Ellie was seated on a small, ornate chair in one corner, looking worried, while the guards stood at the ready, to either side of the room. "Aleron, please stay here with my daughter, while I speak to your grandfather privately. Come, old friend, here's a place we can speak in private." Gealton led Hadaras to a side door, leading into a private chamber.

As soon as they were gone, Eilowyn asked, "What happened out there, Aleron? What were you three doing after he sent me out?"

"I don't know what's going on," Aleron answered, looking vexed. "Your father had me pull the sword out again, then he had Grandfather try and then he tried himself."

"Were you able to pull it out again?"

"Yes, but I don't know what that's supposed to mean."

"Were they able to pull it out of the stone?"

"No."

"You and I both know what that means, Aleron," and then she asked, "What did the sword look like when you held it?"

"It glowed blue…but that's impossible. My father was a woodsman, not a prince or anything."

"Let's think about this, Aleron. You don't know your father's ancestry that far back, do you?" To his hesitant headshake, she replied, "Right and you know it's not through your grandfather, or he would have been able to draw the sword too, but what about your mother, through your grandmother? The reason they have that line up every New Year is in the hopes that the royal line survived somewhere. You appear to be it."

"But I just want to be a soldier, not a king!" he cried, falling into the chair next to her. Hans wore a sympathetic look as he glanced over to Simeon, who nodded in agreement.

***

Gealton closed the door behind them, and they found themselves in what appeared to be a private office. "The old office of the steward, from back when the throne room was used for official business. We replace the furnishings every hundred years or so, as needed, just in case we need to start using it again. It looks like that time may be upon us. Have a seat, Hadaras," he gestured to a chair, taking the one opposite. "It occurs to me, considering your warning shout, that this is not entirely surprising to you."

"No, it is not, Gealton. He is the rightful heir and I have long known it."

"How is that so? It is not through you; we saw that much in the hall."

"It is through his father. He is a direct, male-line, descendent. Do you remember Alagric had a younger brother?"

"Yes, Adelard, the drunkard, he died in a ditch, choked on his own puke, a year or so before the king."

"He died, yes, but not before siring a bastard son, with a local prostitute."

"How do you know this, Hadaras?"

"I found the boy myself, living on the streets after his mother died."

"You found him!" the Steward exclaimed, flabbergasted. "How could that be? It was a thousand years ago."

"Friend, I have trusted my life to you in the past and I still trust you today, but I have not been altogether truthful with you over the years." As he said this, he let fall the glamour he normally maintained over his appearance. His face smoothly morphed into one with the high cheekbones, arched brows and pointed ears of an elf. "I have walked Aertu for over nine thousand years and have gone by many names."

Gealton froze in his chair, rendered speechless. When he finally spoke again, he stuttered, "B-but even elves don't live that long. Who and what, are you?"

"I will tell you this and you must bear in mind, that you are one of only a couple mortals to know my true name. I am Goromir, the one of old and no other. I forged Andhanimwhid and I was there when Aleron fell. It was I who bound the Nameless One in the depths of Immin Bul. I do not know why I have lived so long in this world, but I suspect that my purpose here is not fulfilled as long as the Adversary lives."

"Why do you hide among us as a man and is the boy truly your grandson? I do not understand what is going on here. Why did you not bring forth the heir a thousand years ago?"

"I was guided by prophesy and revelation, that the bastard child was not to be the king and that millennia would pass before the king returned to the throne. I have watched over his line and yours, ever since Alagric's death. In answer to your first question, he is my daughter's son."

"So he's a halfblood and heir to the throne, amazing that this would happen in my time," Gealton said, a look of joy coming across his face.

"You do not worry for your base of power, my friend?" Hadaras inquired.

"Hadaras, or should I call you Goromir...? The Steward has always run the kingdom, while the king commands the armies. The generals and admirals need to worry more than I," the Steward replied, "but what's this about watching over my line as well?"

"My revelation told me that the line of Stewards must be preserved, for if either line failed, the kingdom would be doomed. That is why I was with you in the jungle, to make certain you made it home alive. It seems that you and yours have parts to play in this story."

"Ellie...?"

"That could very well be," Hadaras replied. "I have seen, over these nine millennia that very little happens by chance. I'm sure that Eilowyn was meant to meet Aleron today and she was meant to bring him to Andhanimwhid. Whether her part is over, or she has a greater part in the overall story, I cannot say."

"Wait a bit; it occurs to me, that if you are who you say, then that boy is descended of the kings of Elvenholm as well."

"Yes, Aleron is a joining of both lines. That was from my daughter, Audina. She received a revelation to which I was not privy. It told her that she would wed Valgier and together they would beget the one of whom the prophecies speak. I was against it, for I saw only doom at the time."

"How were his parents lost?"

"A Kolixtlani assassin killed them and kidnapped the boy. I killed the assassin and took back my grandson. Once I made him safe, I travelled to Immin Bul and renewed the bindings of the Adversary."

"I am sorry for your loss. Does the lad have any clue as to who he is?" Gealton asked.

"I'm certain he does now, as well as your daughter and the guards, but before now, no. We were not yet ready for this turn of events. I did not plan to seat a boy-king to rule Sudea."

"I see your point, old friend. As joyful as this news is for Sudea, he is young and untested. Furthermore, not having grown up at court, he likely knows nothing of politics, does he?"

"Not a bit, he would be vulnerable in his naiveté to those who would try to influence him. That is not the only concern I have, Gealton. There is another prophecy, separate from that of the king's return and the boy may have a role in that as well."

"What prophecy would that be?"

"There is an old prophecy among the elves, that upon the return to power of the Nameless One, a sorcerer of such power that the world has yet to see would stand between him and the free peoples of Aertu. Recent events have indicated that Aleron may be that sorcerer."

"How is that so, what events?"

"The boy has yet to manifest any ability, but he dreams of it almost nightly. He dreams of places he has never seen, but I recognize them. In his first such dream, he saw the central fountain in your public garden, then recognized it this morning. In these dreams, he wields all types of magic equally, even blending them into new forms. A fellow sorcerer, with far greater perceptive abilities than my own, saw in him a well of power unlike anything he has seen before. All indications are that, when Aleron's abilities manifest, they will be unlike anything the world has known."

"Is it possible to wield and blend multiple forms of magic? I have never heard of such a thing, even from the days when sorcerers were common in Sudea."

"Elves can wield the blue. Men with the ability can wield the blue or the red, though I've never known any to use both at the same time. The Aelient are able to use other colors, not available to us. I remember from when I was young and the Aelir still walked among us, that they could wield all the colors, but I never witnessed them blend them into new forms. They used each in its individual capacity. Aleron dreams that he can blend all the colors, even the red, into a new form that is white in aspect. He claims the white has the power to transform one thing to another. As far as I know, only the Allfather has such power."

"What do you plan to do with the boy now? I sense there is danger in having him exposed this early," Gealton asked. "If the Kolixtlanis were after him once, they likely still want him."

"That is my primary concern," Hadaras agreed. "The Adversary found him once and my daughter and her husband paid for that mistake. He wanted him alive and unharmed as well. My guess is that he intended to turn him over to darkness, but to which prophecy was he reacting? If he meant to raise the heir to the throne to be loyal to him, the Adversary could have Sudea in his pocket. Likewise, if he manages to turn the loyalty of the one meant to oppose him, no one on Aertu could stand before them."

"So we need to keep this under wraps for now, I would say."

"Exactly my point," Hadaras agreed, "we need to keep him out of the public eye, squash any rumors about what happened today and let him grow up first.

When he comes into his power and matures, then he will be ready to take over the kingdom."

"And so, the damage control begins, starting with those four in there."

Chapter 13

Carpathday, Day 22, Growing Moon, 8760 Sudean Calendar

I hope the rest of your journey goes well for you Aleron," Eilowyn told him, as he performed one last check of his mount's tack. "It was nice having you here."

"Thank you, Ellie. It has been…nice," he agreed, looking up to meet her eyes. After the events four days past, he and his grandfather stayed at the palace. The steward sent for their belongings at the Golden Dragon, and they did not leave the palace grounds for two days. The guards on duty that morning were questioned, but none aside from Simeon and Hans had witnessed the event. Thankfully, the throne room was nearly empty of the public and apparently, there had been no other witnesses. Palace spies were sent about to ascertain if any new rumors abounded, about strange occurrences at the palace. They came back empty handed and after two days and three nights, they were permitted to explore the city again. Aleron couldn't complain though. The days spent at the palace had been mostly spent with Ellie, and Hans and Simeon, of course. The bodyguards were sworn to absolute secrecy on the matter of the sword and Aleron's identity.

"You will be on the road many months yet and it is very dangerous out there. I want you to pay attention and be careful. I want to see you again," she said sternly. "I'm going to miss you, you big dopy farm boy!"

"I'll miss you too Ellie," he answered, "and I'm not a farm boy. We still have most of a year to go, before we get home again. I'll try to get out here to see you again after that. I can be your third cousin from Ellesfort again, if that's all right," he added, with a grin.

"Whatever gets you into the palace," she agreed. 'Just make sure you do it before you run off and join the marines. That will take you out for another year, before I get to see you again."

"I'll make sure Ellie. You can count on it." Aleron spent many hours in counsel with his grandfather and the Steward. Together, they decided that he would go on with his plan to join the marines after his sixteenth birthday. Once he got over the shock of discovering he was a halfblood, heir to the kingship and his grandfather was really a nine-thousand-year-old elvish sorcerer, the rest of the discussion had been easy. He was going to do what he already wanted to do, and they would wait for the right time to claim the throne of the most powerful kingdom on Aertu, simple.

"You had better make sure of it farm boy and remember, it's a lot faster to get here by boat." His dumbfounded expression made it clear, that he hadn't considered the fact that the trip would have only taken a week by ship, rather than the three weeks it took on horseback. "See: 'Big dopy farm boy'," she joked, before reaching up and taking hold of both sides of his face. She stood on her toes and planted a kiss right on his lips.

"Eilowyn!" Gealton scolded. "Let the poor lad ready his mount, for the gods' sake."

"Yes Daddy," she acquiesced, "but he doesn't look like he minds all that much." Aleron was blushing and couldn't wipe the silly grin from his face. "Come back and see me soon," she directed at Aleron. "I can't believe you have to go, and I miss you already," she said, turning to go.

"I will, Ellie, soon," he assured her, unable to see the tear running down her cheek as she moved to join her father. She wiped it discretely before turning to face him again. Hadaras was already mounted, his goodbyes complete. Aleron mounted his horse and the pair set out, Hadaras in the lead and the packhorse trailing Aleron. They waved goodbye to Gealton, Eilowyn, Hans and Simeon. No one else was present to witness their early morning departure.

"Safe travel, friends," Gealton called out, "and make sure you keep that old man out of trouble, lad!"

"I'll do my best, Milord," Aleron returned, "but I can't make any promises."

Hadaras laughed and answered, "I think I can manage to stay out of trouble. Thank you for your hospitality, Milord."

"Farewell," said Eilowyn, raising her hand to wave and trying to maintain a cheerful expression, with little success.

"Goodbye, Milady," Hadaras replied.

"Goodbye, Ellie. I will return soon," Aleron answered in turn.

As the pair of riders moved off towards the back gate of the palace compound, the Steward said to his daughter, "Do not worry Ellie; he will be back for you. I am certain of it."

"How can you be sure of that Father?" she asked. "He's going to travel for a year, see new places and meet new girls. He's a halfblood and he's going to the elvish lands. Who's to say he won't find an elf maid to be his queen. That's what he should do, to reestablish the Halfblood Line, not marry a simple mortal girl."

"Dearest girl, I saw how he looks at you since the moment he met you. He will be back for you," her father reassured her. "The Halfblood Caste has been diminished for three thousand years and will not be renewed with a single marriage. All the children of all the high houses would need to choose elven mates to reestablish the caste viably and that simply will not happen. That was the product of a bygone age. If the king's line were to choose only elven mates, the royal line would become elvish, not human and the people will not stand for that."

"I suppose that makes sense, but it still doesn't guarantee he won't find someone he likes more."

"Ellie, dear, even if I were to confine him to the palace grounds, there is no guarantee against that. You can't keep him prisoner and expect love to be true," her father instructed. "Who knows, maybe you will be the one to change your mind."

"That won't happen, Father. I will wait for him," she replied, adamantly.

The heavy iron portcullis lifted to allow their passage, the guards staring steely eyed into the city as they passed. The back gate of the palace compound opened onto the wide flagstone streets of the Noble Quarter. Ancient stone mansions lined the streets, most dating back to the period in which the noble houses were of the Halfblood Caste. After the devastation of the Great War, many of the noble houses dwindled and died out and then the remaining ones were forced to intermarry with the common folk to avoid inbreeding. Thus, the Halfblood Caste ceased to exist just two generations after the war. The elvish traits of longevity and sorcery do not consistently carry to those only one-quarter elven, so the nobles became no different from the common man. Hadaras guided them left, on a route that would take them from the Noble Quarter and loop them through the Merchant's Quarter back to the gate. "I think she likes me, Grandfather," Aleron stated, the foolish grin coming back to his face.

"What tipped you off, lad, the kiss or the tearful goodbye?" Hadaras asked, sarcastically. "How much do you like her in return?"

"I like her a lot, Grandfather. She's different from any of the girls I know back home. She's smart and funny. She can read, Sudean and some Elvish too. And I got the idea that even without Simeon and Hans around, she wouldn't be quick for a roll in the hay, if you know what I mean."

"Have you done much hay-rolling, my boy?" Hadaras questioned, one eyebrow raised.

"No Grandfather," he replied, "that was supposed to be this summer."

Hadaras laughed heartily and for what seemed to Aleron too long, before saying, "It's good to know that I'm keeping you out of trouble, lad, good to know." He continued chuckling as they rode along. A bell or so later, they made their way back to the market square they had entered through a week prior. The early morning throngs, mostly farmers and merchants with goods for the market, were already pressing into the city. The outbound gate being mostly clear, they carefully picked their way around the crowd spreading over the square. Soon they made it to the open road, headed west.

***

Far away, in the port city of Zyx, capital of Adar, Zormat knew in his heart that something was amiss. Four days past, while still at sea, his fair mood went suddenly dark, and he could not ascertain why it would be so. Favorable winds brought them to the port days ahead of schedule and his initial meeting with the Khan and his Chief Necromancer this morning went very well. The faith was stronger here than he expected to find, it just took a different form than that of Kolixtlan. Here, rather than the mass sacrifices of the Kolixtlani priests, the necromancers drew the maximum power from each death, by prolonging the process of dying, through torture and starvation. It was a much more efficient strategy, well suited to lower available population of Adar. All was going better than he had hoped, but he could not shake the sudden sense of dread he was feeling. *I need to get over it. I am the most powerful being walking free on the face of this world. I am the son of a god and I have much work to do. In five days, we set sail for Thallasia.*

Chapter 14

Corballday, Day 9, Haymaking Moon, 8760 Sudean Calendar

One day shy of three weeks from the day they left Arundell, found them in the wild foothills of the Blue Mountains. For the first week, it became steadily warmer as they travelled north, until they began the steady climb to the mountains and the temperature stabilized, though they still travelled further north each day. A week past, on Aleron's fifteenth birthday, they descended into the hot steamy valley of the Fall River, crossing the ancient stone bridge over the yawning chasm, with the water rushing two hundred feet below. Grandfather told him then, that the dwarves built the bridge, over six thousand years ago, to facilitate trade with Arundell and it stood today as a testament to their skill. Climbing out of that valley brought them back to cooler air and the trip had been reasonably comfortable since. "How high up are we now?" Aleron asked, curious as he gazed at the Blue Mountains looming before them. "And how long before we find another village?" They had travelled all morning without seeing any others on the road and passing no settlements. The road was well travelled, following the Arun Valley all the way to Dhargul, the dwarf capital at the headwaters of the Arun River.

"I believe we are over nine hundred feet above the level of the sea. As to your second question, we are about a day from Freemarket, the last settlement of men before we reach the Southern Kingdom." Just then, an arrow flew from the dark forest, straight at Aleron. He barely raised his buckler in time to block and the bodkin neatly pierced the shield, vambrace and forearm together. He froze, momentarily, at the sight of the bloody arrowhead sticking two inches through his inner forearm. "Goblins!" Hadaras shouted. His sword was already out, and he chopped the black-fletched shaft from the boy's buckler. "Draw your blade, lad and be at the ready!" He gestured and raised a dome of shimmering blue around them. More arrows rained down upon them but were incinerated upon contact with the dome of magical energy, as was the first goblin warrior to charge the pair. The momentum of his charge carried him headlong into the blue light and they witnessed his body dissolve into gray ash, from front to back. This stopped the others from charging, and they surrounded the pair instead, shooting the occasional arrow and hurling the odd spear, only to watch them flare against the dome. "Leave the arrow in for now, boy; it plugs the hole. Are you well enough to shoot your bow?"

"I think so, Grandfather," Aleron answered. "It really doesn't hurt." At the moment, his wound was numb more than painful. He moved to retrieve his bow from his saddle, the quiver already on his hip. The goblins had them completely encircled now. There were nineteen in all, along with a half dozen of their half-tame wolf dogs.

"They know I can only maintain this for a little while and they will wait until I tire and falter. Take out as many as you can before then."

"I'll do my best," Aleron replied, as he dismounted with bow in hand. He winced as the bow forced his forearm to twist against the shaft piercing it, bringing pain at last. *I'll have to remember not to do that again.* Luckily, he was wearing a Chebek forearm buckler, with an arrow pass cutout, so he did not need to remove it to shoot.

The goblins jeered at him, one yelling, "What you gonna do, Man-child, kill us all with your little bow." That one died with an arrow up one apelike nostril and a second one went down with a shaft through the eye.

"As a matter of fact, yes," he replied, as a third took an arrow through the heart. With three of their comrades down in just a few seconds, the goblins began shouting in their own tongue and scurrying for cover. The dogs still circled the perimeter and Aleron picked them off, one by one, as he circled just within the blue light. A goblin tried to climb into a tree and Aleron shot him through the armpit. It fell squealing to the ground. It was then, that Aleron noticed something, tendrils of blue light connecting every living thing in the vicinity to Hadaras. The energy the old sorcerer wielded was life force, concentrated and directed. He was even drawing it from the goblins. He saw too, that the dead and dying goblins and dogs had a different energy about them. Along with their actual blood, there was a crimson glow about them and as he looked about, the faint crimson was present all about him. It was the color of death, just as natural as that of life, the two existing side-by-side. He stretched out his hand toward the pool of red about a recently deceased goblin and found he could move it to his will. He set down the bow, closed his eyes, felt for the red energy all around him and began drawing it to himself.

"Aleron, no!" Hadaras shouted, finally noticing what the boy was doing. "You cannot wield that magic, it's too dangerous!"

"Trust me, Grandfather; it's as natural as rain, just seems a little unruly." He drew the red energy to himself and formed a vision in his mind. He directed the red magic and it obeyed, forming a deep pool along the bottom edge of the blue dome and then sheeting up the dome, combining with the blue to form a deep maroon color. "Do you remember what I used this color for in my dream, Grandfather?"

After a moment, he replied, "Yes."

"Good, on the count of three, let go of your magic and let me take over, all right?"

"All right, Aleron, on the count of three," Hadaras agreed, raising his sword to guard, ready for the worst.

"One...two...three!" Aleron counted, shouting the last number. He took control of the power, as Hadaras released his grip. The maroon dome reformed into a torus and flashed outward. Trees uprooted as a wall of earth and timber moved outward in a wave. They heard the muffled screams, as the remaining goblins were buried and crushed. The unmounted horses spooked, but quickly discovered that there was nowhere for them to run. They stood upon a small flat island, at the center of a massive crater, plowed into the bedrock. Aleron dropped to one knee, a sudden wave of dizziness overcoming him. As was common, his first time wielding magic left the boy physically spent. Eventually, he would need to learn to meter the flow of energy through his body, to be able to maintain sorcerous effort over time.

Hadaras leapt off the horse, then quickly cast about to sense for any remaining goblins. Those he could sense were rapidly expiring beneath the heaped mass of soil, rock and timber. "Buried alive," he muttered aloud, "damn sad way to go, even for a goblin." Sensing no imminent danger, he hurried over to Aleron. "Let's have a look at that arm now. How do you feel, lad?"

"I'm a little woozy, Grandfather, but I think I'll be all right." After the effort of speaking, he lurched forward and emptied the contents of his stomach onto what was left of the road. "Or not," he added, between spitting.

"If you can talk, you will be fine," The old elf assured him. "Wielding magic is tough on the body, until you learn to control it. That was a massive amount of energy you just directed. With that much coursing through your body at once, it's difficult to conserve your core life-force and use only what is around you."

He knelt down and took up Aleron's shield arm. With a flicker of blue radiance, he sliced the splintered shaft off smooth. Carefully, he unbuckled and removed the shield and laid it aside. "It's a barbed point, so I need to pull it through; all right?"

"I'll be all right, Grandfather," he answered, but looked away as Hadaras prepared to remove the object. He felt a sharp pinch as he yanked shaft free, followed by a dull throbbing ache in his forearm. "That wasn't so bad," he said looking back to see the blood welling through the hole in his leather vambrace. He looked away again, narrowly avoiding losing the remainder of his breakfast.

"You're lucky it wasn't poisoned, and the bleeding is good; it cleans out the wound. Also lucky it wasn't a broadhead, or you would be bleeding a lot more than you are." Hadaras removed the vambrace and said, "Let me get something to wrap the wound." As his grandfather moved to the horses, to retrieve a dressing from the baggage, Aleron took a deep breath and looked back to his injured forearm. An idea occurred to him, and he formed a mental image around it. Hadaras sensed a fresh unleashing of magic and turned to see Aleron, his face set in concentration, with a golden yellow glow emanating from the wound on his arm. The glow then infused his entire body for a moment, before winking out. Hadaras grabbed a water skin and, foregoing the bandage, strode back to his grandson.

"I think I'm good now, Grandfather," the youth told him as Hadaras returned. "I feel pretty good now, actually." Hadaras noticed the paleness he had seen earlier on the boy's face replaced by its normal healthy glow. The forearm was still bloody, but the wound appeared to be gone.

"Let me wash off that arm and take a look." He poured water on Aleron's arm and scrubbed the blood away, rinsing his hand and the forearm clean. He saw barely a trace of the puncture left on the boy's arm. "Can you move it and roll your wrist like before?"

Aleron rotated his wrist several times and stated, "Yes, it seems fine and doesn't even hurt at all now. I think I feel better than I did before I got shot."

"That was healing magic you just used, and you likely healed everything that was amiss, including fatigue," Hadaras informed him. "I've seen it used in the past, but only by the Aelient and Aelir, never by a mortal. You are full of surprises this morning. Now we need to get the path back in order, so we can move along. When that raiding party fails to return, the goblins will send out another, to find out why.

With the coaching of his grandfather, Aleron once again harnessed the maroon-colored energy and dragged the soil, rock and debris back into the crater, more carefully this time. Unfortunately, this action unearthed most of the goblin and dog carcasses, along with much splintered timber. Hadaras used his blue fire to dispose of the corpses and debris. Aleron helped with the burning, though he was not as efficient as the elder sorcerer was. He also used the maroon energy to reduce some of the larger rubble, in order to clear a path. When the work was complete, a large ring of rubble and ash surrounded their little island and Aleron was once again exhausted. "Saddle up lad," Hadaras called to him, "We need to put some miles between us and those goblins. They will know something is amiss when they find that patch of burnt ground and there is no hiding from their wolves."

Xarch ran as if his life depended on it, for he was quite sure it did. *Elves, damn bloody elves, they had to be,* he thought as he ran, on all fours when he came to hills and obstacles. Goblins can move like wildfire when the need arises. He had narrowly escaped the exploding wall of earth that had engulfed his party, lucky to be far enough back and behind a massive hickory when the debris hit. He lost his bow, but still had his knife, his wits and his feet. *They might whip me for surviving to bring bad news, but the Chief needs to know about elves travelling in disguise through the lands of men.* Xarch was sure the Chief would welcome the information and he would be rewarded in the end, even if he was in for a beating first.

***

Eilowyn sat in her chamber, escaping the heat of mid-day. A terrible feeling of unease came over her and she worried for Aleron's safety. The feeling passed as suddenly as it came, and she was left to wonder about her feelings for the young man. Doubt crept into her mind as she thought; *Do I only like him because I know he will be king someday? No, I liked him when I thought he was a commoner. I was trying to find a way to sneak around the guards and kiss him when the thing with the sword happened. No, it's not that he will be king, but it does make it better.* Knowing her father would not forbid a union put it into the realm of possibility, rather than fantasy. She could actually marry him someday, which would never be allowed were he common. *I just hope he is safe. That feeling was too real a moment ago.*

***

Hadaras and Aleron rode along at a brisk trot. They would ride through the night, for if they stopped, they would certainly deal with more goblins. They would reach Freemarket by early morning, possibly with a horde of goblins on their heels. Hadaras knew it to be a well-fortified frontier town, with a large garrison to defend it. The goblins would not likely attempt a frontal assault, unless they massed at far greater numbers than the usual scattered raiding parties. They should be safe at Freemarket.

Zormat sat alone in his cabin, deep in thought, as he often spent his days and nights at sea. Thirteen days into this leg of the journey, they had still a month to go before they would reach the port city of Corin, capital of Thallasia. His sleep was interrupted by another premonition. It was very much the same feeling he felt two weeks before that, only this time, it came in the form of a dream. The dream was of vague flashes of power, the flavor of which, he was not familiar. *Someone is unleashing powerful magic in the world, someone dangerous.* He was certain that was the case. The question at hand was, is this someone a potential ally or a foe? He felt that the time was near, that he would find out.

Chapter 15

Carpathday, Day 10, Haymaking Moon, 8760 Sudean Calendar

Dawn brought them to the walls of Freemarket, after a hard night of riding. About two bells prior, the horses were near collapse, with the riders not much better. Hadaras said, "We need to stop and rest before we kill the horses." They had come to a stream crossing and the pair dismounted to allow the horses to drink.

As the thirsty animals drank, Aleron reached out and placed his hand upon the neck of his own mount. The same golden radiance he had used to heal his arm infused the exhausted animal. The horse jerked its head up in surprise, snorting and pawing the ground with newfound energy. The boy grabbed its bridle and rubbed its neck to calm it down, saying, "Easy there, old girl, keep drinking, we have a way to go yet." He continued on the other horses, with similar effect.

Hadaras watched as his grandson healed their tired mounts and packhorse. When Aleron came to place his hand upon him, Hadaras said, "Not me lad, I'll be all right. Save that for the horses. You don't want to wear yourself out."

Grandfather, this one makes me feel better as I use it. Let me help you. I feel as if I've slept the whole night through, right now."

"Very well, but nothing comes without a cost. That magic must come from somewhere."

Aleron placed a hand on Hadaras' shoulder and concentrated. Hadaras felt the warm glow infuse his entire being. Suddenly he was no longer tired, thirsty, or hungry. It seemed like he felt better than he had in years, though that was likely due to the extreme fatigue he had recently been experiencing. Aleron broke his concentration, replying, "This one seems to come right out of the ground. It's especially strong in the water here. I can feel it going back upstream to the springs that feed this stream."

Now they found themselves at the gates of the last village of men, with relatively fresh mounts. As for themselves, they felt as if they had slept the night through and simply had an early start that morning. Hadaras thought: *Were this magic in common use, armies could march night and day across the continent and the wounded would be healed and sent straight back to battle. Forget spreading comfort among the masses, this would make mass warfare seem that much more affordable to an ambitious tyrant. The Allfather must have had a reason to limit our access to the two forms allowed us, but why should it be different for this boy?* "Try to look tired," he instructed Aleron, as they approached the gatekeepers. "Good morning to you," he hailed the guards.

"And to you Sir," answered one of them, through the heavy bars of the gate, "State your business…What brings you to Freemarket?" The pair was, judging by the livery they sported, Sudean general infantry, likely here on a six-month rotation to guard the outpost.

"We simply seek lodging for a few days' rest, my good man," Hadaras replied.

"On your way to the South Kingdom then, you come from Arundell?" The one speaking wore a silver chain, denoting sergeant's rank; the other wore none, signifying he was a private.

"We came through there, yes, but originally from down Ellesfort way. Just to let you know," he continued, "We had a run in with a band of goblins mid-day yesterday. We've been riding ever since, to put some distance between us and we've no idea whether or not they have been following us."

"Well, if they are following you, it won't be anything new here. They test us nearly every night. Odd for them to have attacked you during the day; they usually wait for dark."

"I agree; they must have thought us an easy target, being only two. We managed to drive them back and break contact."

"How did you manage that, with only two o' ya?" the private inquired.

"It was a small party and we're both good with a bow," Hadaras answered, "so after we killed a few, the others backed off." Aleron remained silent throughout the exchange.

"Neither here nor there," the sergeant commented. "If they are on your trail, we'll kill em just like we kill all the others that try to get in here. Goblins are pretty easy to kill. It's the trolls that give us trouble. It takes a heavy bow to pierce one of their hides and they'll shed an axe blow like heavy plate. You go on in and tend to your animals. They don't look too bad for running since noon yesterday, but I'm sure they could use some rest, oats and water. Your boy looks ready to fall out of the saddle, though."

"Let's go Aleron. Thank you, gentlemen and enjoy the rest of your day."

"Oh, I'm sure we will," the sergeant replied sarcastically, as the other guard opened the gate for them to pass.

They passed the massive iron gates and through the thick stone wall, twenty feet high. More guards patrolled the ramparts. It was obvious that Freemarket existed only through force of arms, in this goblin infested territory. Hadaras commented, "Goblins and trolls tend to congregate near roads and settlements in the wildlands, hoping to prey upon travelers and unwary townsfolk, just like bandits in the more settled lands. Good job acting exhausted, by the way," he added when they passed out of earshot of the guards.

"Why, thank you, Grandfather. Don't they have bandits out here as well?"

"Some, but not as many, due to the goblins and trolls. They make an easier living closer to civilization. When you do find them, however, they are big trouble. Usually, they form large bands for mutual protection and live in fortified villages, for the same reason. Freemarket was once such a town. After a few generations, the thieves became legitimate businessmen." The stables hadn't moved since last Hadaras had visited. They made directly there to put the horses up. Luckily, they had locked storage available, for an additional fee, so they did not need to lug all their gear to the inn.

Later that morning, after securing rooms and a large breakfast, Aleron asked, "So what are we doing next, Grandfather?"

"I think it would be best to lie low today and get some real sleep. We should try to fit the story that we rode sunrise to sunrise. It wouldn't due for us to be seen wandering around, if our story becomes known. In addition, we do not know what the long-term effects of your intervention may be. I wouldn't want the effect to suddenly wear off somewhere inconvenient." And so, they settled into their room. The furnishings seemed somewhat coarse and rustic, but clean, nonetheless. The following day, they would explore the outpost and lay in supplies for the long trip to Dhargul.

"Grandfather, who is Jessamine, really?" Aleron asked, after they had settled in. He had been pondering many questions since discovering the truth of the legacy he was heir to and asked periodically, as new ones came to him. He now knew the details of his parent's death, at the hands of an assassin. He knew that Hadaras was really Goromir, High Sorcerer of Elvenholm, from the histories, likely the oldest elf on Aertu. He learned that his grandfather had fathered many children and had outlived them all. It occurred to him, that Hadaras had no other children, recently, aside from Aleron's mother, so Jessamine was unlikely to be an actual relation of his. He was somewhat hurt and resentful at the years of deception, but it was not in his nature to hold grudges. Young as he was, he understood the necessity of what his grandfather did, after the Kolixtlani killed his parents. "She's not really my cousin, is she?"

"No, she is not, my boy," Hadaras answered. "She is a friend, who cares very much about you and me. We have been friends for many years, and she agreed to help me take care of you."

"Is she an elf too, or a human, or is she something else?"

"Something else, lad, let's just leave it at that for now."

Aleron knew when he wasn't going to get any more information out of his grandfather, so he cut his line of inquiry short. It did not require much imagination to figure out what "something else" could mean. She obviously was not a dwarf, goblin, or troll, so the only thing left was aelient.

✳✳✳

Later that evening, when Hadaras spoke to Jessamine on the events of the past day, all she had to say on the subject was: *Well, it looks as if our little boy is growing up. I cannot say why the Allfather is allowing him access to magic usually reserved for my kind.*

He was able to wield the red alongside the blue, to no ill effect. I have never seen a man who chose the red, able to return to using the blue. He claims that there is nothing inherently evil in the magic, just that it is chaotic in nature, the ancient sorcerer related.

It could be that chaotic power is the inevitable choice of those who choose evil, not that it turns them to evil. It may be that both blue and red were always open to men, and we simply misunderstood the nature of the red and avoided its use for the purpose of good, she hypothesized. *The blending of powers is what strikes me as the most unusual aspect. That ability may place him on par with the Aelir. Even we Aelient cannot accomplish that.*

I see the outcome I fear becoming the more likely each day that Aleron is as much the fulfillment of the old prophecy, as he is the new.

That does appear to be the case, my love. For what it's worth, I am sorry for that.

Chapter 16

Zorekday, Day 30, Haymaking Moon, 8760 Sudean Calendar

Three more weeks of travel brought Aleron and Hadaras nearly to the headwaters of the Arun River. They were moving less than twenty miles per day through the steep, rugged terrain. Fifteen days earlier, they reached the ten-thousand-foot elevation marker and the border crossing with the dwarves. Hadaras' name alone was enough to gain them passage and Aleron reflected upon how well known his grandfather was, even under his assumed name. Grandfather told him some of the other names he had lived under, in the four millennia since Goromir disappeared from the knowledge of Aertu. Many of the other names were also prominent in the historical accounts Aleron read since early childhood. The old elf was continually moving the world as he moved within it. They worked their way slowly along the narrow path, barely wide enough for two small carts to pass, hewn directly into the side of a sheer cliff. To their left and arching overhead, was a smooth finished rock wall. To the right, was a low stone railing that appeared as it would do little to keep one from toppling over the side and falling to the foaming water hundreds of feet below, where small fields were visible along the far side of the river. The dwarves used every inch of arable farmland within their harsh environment, specially adapting crops to the high altitude and short growing season. "Isn't today supposed to be a day of rest, Grandfather?" Aleron asked, between yawning.

"Would you prefer that we rest right here?" Hadaras asked in turn. "It may be a bit inconvenient to have to break camp every time someone needs to pass us by. I think, perhaps, that we should wait until we reach a turn out, constructed for such purposes."

"Sorry Grandfather, I didn't mean that I wanted to stop right now. It just seems like we've been riding forever." Aside from the occasional way station, spaced several days apart on the trail, there had been little to break the monotony of the trip. Once or twice a day they would pass trader's carts heading back to the lands of men, loaded with manufactured goods and occasionally they would pass up a cart loaded with foodstuffs or fabric, heading to Dhargul.

"It certainly is a long journey," Hadaras agreed, "but well worth it. Dhargul is a sight worth seeing and very few non-dwarves are permitted entry into the city proper."

"How is it that you are so well known here, Grandfather?"

"I did a favor for King Faergas Goldhammer, long ago. He is still quite grateful for it."

"What did you do for him and why do they call him 'Goldhammer'?"

"As for your first question, my boy, I helped rid him of a minor case of demonic possession," Hadaras explained. "He is one of the few individuals alive who know my full identity. As for your second question, he has a gold hammer. He says he prefers the heft of it for fighting mountain trolls, which he still enjoys doing, on occasion."

"He still goes out and fights trolls himself?" Aleron asked. "Isn't he too important for that sort of thing? I mean, what if he gets killed?"

"Aleron, my dear boy, what I am about to tell you, I hope you take to heart and never forget. A king who styles himself too important to himself defend his territory and people, is no longer a king in truth. The king exists for the people, not the other way around. The kingdom belongs to the people and the king belongs to the kingdom and thus the people. When a ruler believes that the kingdom and people exist for his own benefit, he becomes a tyrant, and the people eventually overthrow tyrants. No one person is indispensable, not even the king." That left Aleron to ponder the words of his grandfather, quite possibly the oldest and wisest mortal being on the face of Aertu. He recalled the histories of some other nations, such as Ebareiza, whose kings and emperors faced regular usurpation over the ages. "Look, here's a place to rest now." The dwarves quarried away a spur of the mountain, leaving an area over thirty paces across. Fast growing grasses and shrubs, bred by the dwarves for this purpose, provided much needed forage for horses. Hadaras led them of the path, and they dismounted, picketing the horses alongside the most recovered looking sward. "This would be a good place to camp, but it is too early in the day for that. There will be other opportunities further along the path." The builders also carved several alcoves into the face of the mountain, as well as a larger, covered stable area.

The tremendous amount of effort expended by the dwarves to build this road and the way stations along it was mind boggling to anyone who took the time to think about it. This fact was not lost on Aleron, who asked, "Grandfather, how long did it take the dwarves to build this road? It seems like an awful lot of work."

"This being the major artery between Dhargul and Arundell, the dwarves have developed this route more than others," Hadaras answered, "and if I recall correctly, it took them well over a thousand years to establish it to the point you see today."

"A thousand years…?"

"Yes, but bear in mind, the route was established much earlier and what you see now is the result of improvements. This section of the trail used to follow the river and then climb steeply out of the valley at the falls. This gradual climb took centuries to carve into the cliff face. Dwarves build nothing shoddily, so once they build a road, they spend very little on its upkeep and it endures for thousands of years."

"That's not the way men build, is it Grandfather?"

"No, unfortunately lad, men, being the short-lived creatures they are, look for quick results and don't often build things to last. There were exceptions of course, like the monuments of Cop and the royal hall at Arundell, but nothing built on Aertu can match a dwarvish structure for longevity."

"How about elves, how do they build?"

"Elves build for beauty. We care not that it will not last forever, for we value the aesthetic above all else. Our structures are quite durable, nonetheless, but no match for those built by dwarves."

"Thank you, Grandfather." Aleron seemed satisfied with the answer. "I'd like to look around a little, if that's all right." Hadaras nodded in affirmation and Aleron wandered off to explore the shelters and stables. He found the manure heap, next to the stables. It was obvious that someone came through regularly to clean the area and the manure likely used to fertilize the grass and shrubs. A raven flapped in, taking roost on an outcropping overhead. Aleron looked up at it and it in turn, eyed him quizzically. Thinking little of the bird, Aleron decided to practice magic while they waited. He did as Hadaras had shown him and projected a thin beam of blue radiance from his hand, using it to reduce a stray stone into precisely spaced slices, like a loaf of bread. He found that he could feel the measurements through the power he wielded. He tried to do the same to another stone with the red power, but found the precision was not there. The stone split violently and haphazardly, and he soon had a small pile of rubble where the stone once was. He then picked up one of the wafers he made and held it in his right palm. Around the stone, he generated a blue glow, while in his left palm he produced red. Closing both palms around the disk, he focused on a cliff wall facing him from across the valley and visualized the disk striking a point on the rock face. In a flash of maroon light, the stone shot across the valley, to the point Aleron focused upon. He saw a puff of dust and several seconds later, heard the crack from the impact.

Hadaras looked up from his repose on the finely crafted stone bench he chose to lie on. "Easy boy, you don't know who might be here in these hills to witness. Be careful."

"Yes, Grandfather, I'm sorry. I won't do it again."

A voice cackled behind him, "Indeed, good advice my grandson gives you." Aleron whipped around to see the raven had hopped down to wall of the refuse bin. "I haven't seen the likes of that in many an age." As Aleron's jaw dropped in disbelief, the black bird continued, "Why don't you try mixing all the colors, like I showed you." The bird underwent a transformation before his eyes, going from black to luminous white. Without another word, it took wing and shot impossibly fast up the cliff face and into the sky, dwindling to a point of light before winking out.

Aleron rushed to his grandfather and in a shaky voice asked, "Did you see that?"

"See what? You were just flinging stones and I closed my eyes for a quick nap," he replied.

"That raven just spoke to me."

"It spoke?" he asked, sitting suddenly upright. "What did it say to you?" He knew that aelient could take many guises and not all were benevolent.

"It said it hadn't seen anything like that for many an age." Hadaras looked even more worried and Aleron continued. "Then it said that I should try mixing all the colors, like 'IT' showed me to."

"As if it were the source of the dreams you were having?"

"I think so, Grandfather, then it changed its color to white and flew off."

'You're saying it became a white raven before it left you?" Hadaras asked, sounding more excited.

"Yes, it was definitely still a raven, just white and glowing, sort of. Is that something important?"

"The White Raven is a symbol for the Allfather, the world over, so yes, it's a little important. And it's good news, considering what the alternative might be."

"What would the alternative be?" the boy asked.

"The alternative would be a spirit, good or otherwise, there's no way of knowing, but by all accounts, the White Raven is forbidden to all but the one, under pain of utter destruction for any imposters. You may have just been visited by the Creator, my boy. Now, the only question is why?"

"Um, Grandfather, he said one more thing, which might seem a bit odd."

"What was that?

"He said that his 'grandson' gave me good advice, meaning you Grandfather."

"That must be some sort of riddle." Hadaras asserted. "We are all his children, and he is a notorious riddler and trickster when he takes on the raven form. Grandson is an odd way to put it, but I wouldn't worry overmuch," he assured Aleron, though he was in fact troubled by the odd affirmation. *Why would he say 'grandson', when we are all equally his children?* He would pose this to Jessamine, when next they spoke.

"Maybe I should try mixing them now, like he said to do?" Aleron offered.

"Maybe you should," Hadaras agreed, having trouble believing he was having this conversation with a lad barely fifteen. Touching the sword triggered something and the raw power that Cladus foresaw was rapidly coming to the fore. *I need to make a strong effort to keep this boy on the straight and narrow, lest he become a bane, rather than a boon to the people of Aertu.*

Chapter 17

Zorekday, Day 30, Haymaking Moon, 8760 Sudean Calendar

By the way, I'm curious if you have tried mixing the red and green?" Hadaras inquired, as they prepared for their experiment.

"No, Grandfather, I haven't. Why do you ask?"

"With light, a mix of red and green is perceived by the eye as yellow, but yellow light exists by itself in a pure form as well. I know that the healing energy is a pure form of magic, so I wonder what the mix of red and green power would be and how it would appear."

"I haven't really used the green for anything yet," Aleron mused. "I remember from the dreams that it was for making things grow and the red is from things that are dying."

"And the blue comes from things that are living," Hadaras finished. "I believe that the green feeds life and the blue is fed by life, so they are somewhat related. The yellow relates to green as well, in that it mends life. I think this is why we perceive them as colors, in the positions of the spectrum that they are. If you look at a rainbow, blue and red appear at opposite sides, with green and yellow between. It would be interesting to see what red and yellow produce as well. Let's go try some things out, shall we?"

"I'm up for it," Aleron agreed, "but what should we try it on?"

"It should be something alive, since most of what we're working with affects the living. Let's play with the shrubbery." Hadaras led the way to a group of bushes, well away from the horses. "Try these, to start."

Aleron concentrated and like before, pooled the red and green energies in each palm and then brought his hands together. When he opened his palms, he held a pool of golden energy, which felt fundamentally different from healing magic. He let the color wash over the first bush. It glowed golden, then faded. Nothing about the bush seemed to change though. "Maybe they just cancel each other out," Aleron guessed. "It didn't seem to do anything."

"Let me check," Hadaras said, as he coiled his senses about the plant. "In a way, you are right Aleron. They did cancel each other out. This plant is neither growing nor dying. Though it appears to be alive, it gives off no life force. You placed it in some sort of stasis."

"What should I do, use healing to bring it back?

"I don't think so, since it is not injured. Try growth instead." At Hadaras' instruction, Aleron generated a green radiance that enveloped the bush. "That was it; it's alive and growing again. Now let us try something else. They attempted several other combinations. Green and yellow proved unsurprising, leading to healing and growth, the same as they would if used separately. Red and yellow yielded an orange energy that caused sudden death, without the destructive aspect of the red alone. Blue and green together caused rapid but orderly growth, the bush acquiring the appearance of a groomed garden specimen. None of the colors or combinations could help the one they killed with orange, until they tried blue and yellow. It produced a green hue, which led to no growth in the live bushes, nor to any other reaction from the plants. After examining the plants and finding nothing out of the ordinary, Hadaras suggested, "Try it on the dead one Aleron." Aleron complied and bathed the wilting bush in the green radiance. They waited a moment and Hadaras exclaimed, "It's alive! You did it boy! You brought a living thing back from death."

"Is that even possible?" Aleron asked, shaken by the revelation.

"Never before," his grandfather stated, more gravely than before. "This brings up a lot of questions."

"What sort of questions?"

"Questions like what the Allfather's intent is, for allowing these powers to be placed in the hands of a mortal," he explained. "I think we should get on with the final mix now and see what it does. We could play forever with combinations of three, but I think it will be easy to predict the results. Let's see what white magic can do."

"All right, Grandfather," Aleron agreed, and he began to concentrate again. He drew blue from within and red from the soil all around, yellow from the bedrock and green from the sky. The four hues blended in his cupped palms, forming a blinding white light. He let it flow onto the bush he resurrected, and it glowed with white radiance, but no other reaction took place.

"Wasn't this one a transformative magic?" Hadaras asked. "Maybe it needs a visualization to do anything." He could sense no changes to the shrub, despite its saturation with the strange power. Aleron thought for a moment and formed a picture in his mind of the rose bush Jessamine maintained outside the door to their cottage. In a shimmer of white light, the bush veered into the form of a rose bush, the light then fading. "Well, isn't that something?" Hadaras stated at the sight of the rose bush and its bright orange blooms. "What I sense from the bush, is that it still thinks itself a locust, even though it looks like a rose. It even has the proper number of leaflets; the thorns look right, and the flowers appear correct as well."

"I think it's because I looked at that rose bush of Jessie's every time I walked into the house, Grandfather," Aleron offered. "I had a pretty detailed image of it in my mind."

"That makes sense, but it's still locust, even though it looks like a rose on the outside. It's likely because you never felt through a rose, only seeing it from the outside. Try the growth magic on it and see what happens." Aleron did as he was told and when the green energy flowed into the rose bush, a new growth of locust twigs erupted from tips of its branches. "That's certainly an odd-looking bush. In good time, I'm sure it will return to normal on its own, but perhaps you should turn it back to locust now."

"I think you're right, Grandfather. Anyone else seeing this is bound to realize something is afoot." Aleron, once again, conjured the white energy and returned the bush to its normal conformation, then had a thought. He reached into the pocket of the vest he wore over his chain and his hand closed over the silver coin there. He turned his awareness to the coin, attempting to feel the essence of the silver itself. Then he picked up a pebble and in a flash of white, held a lump of silver in his palm. "Here Grandfather, it seems to work on things not living, as well." He handed the nugget to Hadaras and said, with a grin, "It looks like we'll never have to worry about money."

Hadaras took the nugget and replied, "Very impressive…the transmutation of minerals has never before been achieved, but then again, neither has the restoration of life, so this is a great day for firsts. However, we must be careful of what we do with these newfound powers of yours. Imagine what would happen, if you were to make gold as cheap and commonplace as stone."

"What would be wrong with that, Grandfather? Then everyone could have all the gold they wanted."

"And all that gold would be worthless," Hadaras continued, "and all who had wealth in gold would suddenly find themselves destitute, while those who held inventory in goods would become the only wealthy ones. Kingdoms would no longer have the funds to pay their workers and soldiers. Governments and economies would collapse. No, let's keep what is precious, that way."

"I hadn't thought of it that way," the boy conceded. "That wouldn't be good at all."

"No, it would not," Hadaras agreed, "and when you are blessed with power, you must think through all the possible repercussions of what you do with that power. What may seem like a helpful kindness could unleash unforeseen chaos in the future. And another thing, I think you should avoid the green energy for the time being."

"Why do you say that?" Aleron asked, in a slightly deeper voice than he possessed that morning. Hadaras noticed as well, that the boy's moustache seemed a bit fuller and his features a bit harder edged than before.

"I think it may prematurely mature you, just as the yellow inadvertently heals you as you wield it. Though you may think you want to be a grown man, I don't believe you would enjoy being a fifteen-year-old grown man."

"Why would that be so bad?" Aleron inquired, thinking it wouldn't be bad at all to be grown.

"Making eyes at a fourteen-year-old girl doesn't go over as well if you look twenty-five, lad."

"Oh," Aleron replied, Eilowyn suddenly coming to his mind. He missed her and was often saddened by the thought of not seeing her for over a year. He was sure she would find another suitor before that time. How could she not, the daughter of the Steward, beautiful and with all those young noblemen in the city. "Grandfather, how long am I likely to live?"

"Halfbloods like yourself typically live over three hundred years, some much longer. Why do you ask?"

"Just wondering, Grandfather, how I'm going to find a wife when I am grown," he revealed. "There are not a lot of halfbloods around anymore and I will outlive a normal girl by hundreds of years."

"There is no easy answer for that question, my boy," his grandfather conceded. "I have outlived three wives and ten children. It is no easy thing to see those you love fade and die, but you move on with your life. I take comfort in the knowledge that they have all returned to the halls of the Allfather, where they will dwell forever in comfort. Believing one serves a higher power and purpose helps one to move on." Hadaras watched his grandson, as he digested the words just spoken. The late morning sun shone on the boy's handsome face, as his concerned expression was replaced by one of stoic resolve. *Being forced to grow up fast, this boy is. It's difficult for him, but necessary. We will need a strong man on that throne, sooner rather than later.*

"I like Eilowyn and if she'll have me, I think I will deal with the outcome," Aleron resolved. "Thank you, Grandfather. Do you think we should go now?"

"Yes, that would be wise. Those look like storm clouds building to the east and it behooves us to find shelter again before they find us."

Gealton sat at the ornate desk, in his private office, deep inside the palace. Here the gray limestone walls were sheathed in rich mahogany, unlike most rooms in the structure. Two large oil lamps illuminated the room with warm yellow light with an additional lamp positioned on the desk. He was reading the latest report to indicate strange happenings afoot in the land. On the road to Dhargul, about a day's ride from Freemarket, travelers reported a patch of land scorched and devoid of trees, the land looking as if it had been tilled for planting and boulders reduced to rubble. Soldiers investigating discovered some goblin carcasses buried, along with shattered trees and debris. One of the soldiers recalled a couple well-armed strangers wandering into Freemarket with the story of having repulsed a goblin attack. *Oh, here it says, one of the goblins had a Chebek arrow through its side. Hadaras and Aleron, it's good to see you're all right, but try to be a little less obtrusive please.* He recalled the interview with the courier, Bruno, two weeks prior. After the spies reported the story circulating about the sparring match at the docks, he called the courier in. Bruno verified that he had been bested in a friendly match by a fifteen-year-old lad named Aleron. *Said he was the fastest swordsman he'd fought in years, if ever. This coming from one of the most feared duelists in the city, though he had mellowed much since his hotheaded youth.* This, along with the account from the market by Simeon, Hans and his daughter, painted an interesting picture of his future king. According to his grandfather, a kind and compassionate lad and polite enough by Gealton's own observation, he could in turn, be a most deadly adversary. No rumors surfaced yet on the sword or a new king, so all was well on that front. *It will definitely be an interesting day, when we unveil our discovery to the people of Sudea,* he thought, *interesting indeed.*

Chapter 18

Gurlachday, Day 7, Squash Moon, 8760 Sudean Calendar

Fortuitously, they entered Dhargul midmorning on Gurlachday. The structures of the dwarvish and Sudean calendars are identical, with the same six-day week and five-week month, the only difference being the names designating the months. The consensus among scholars is that the calendar originated with the dwarves, but it is likely the dwarves borrowed the names for the weekdays from Sudea, as they do not venerate any gods aside from the Allfather and Gurlach, the smith god. Gurlach being the patron god of the dwarves, his day is one of rest for dwarves, just as Zorekday is for Sudeans. The gate guards, however, did not have the day off. One of the guards was a youngster, with only a short red, but still heavy, beard. The other was older, with a black beard reaching his knees. Both wore heavy mail and plate armor, but still moved easily under the weight. Armed with tall double bitted axes in hand and short swords belted to their sides, they made for a formidable pair. "Good morning gentlefolk," the senior guard greeted them. Most dwarves are bilingual to some degree in Sudean, and gate guards are required to be fluent. "What business brings you to Dhargul?"

"No business really, other than resupply, of course," Hadaras replied, they had dismounted and were walking the horses. "I'm Hadaras the Wanderer and I come simply to introduce my grandson to some old friends." The eyes of both guards widened slightly at the announcement.

"We are honored by your presence Lord," the guard said as he bowed low, his beard brushing the paving stones, a gesture of great honor for a dwarf. The younger guard quickly did the same. "I thought you looked familiar," he continued after returning upright. "I was just a lad, like this one here, the last time you passed through the city. He barked instructions to the younger guard in Dwarvish then said, "We are sending word to the city gate of your arrival Sir. Faergas Goldhammer will be pleased with the news." Rather than running off with the news, the younger dwarf began tapping on the key to an odd apparatus, in a halting but somewhat rhythmic pattern. Soon afterward, the apparatus made clicking sounds in reply, similar to the pattern the guard had just tapped.

"I am honored by the fact you remember me," Hadaras answered, bowing low in return. Aleron followed suit.

"They acknowledge Sir." The young guard said in Dwarvish, to his superior.

"Gentlefolk, please enjoy your stay in our beautiful city," said the senior guard, as he and the other stood aside, holding their axes in the position of salute.

"Thank you, I'm certain we will kind Sir. Come along Aleron," Hadaras instructed the boy.

"Thank you, Gentlefolk," Aleron said to the guards as he passed. He and his Grandfather towered head and shoulders above the stout pair, though the guards likely massed more than the elf and halfblood. They stepped through the gate and into the high vaulted tunnel through the massive stone wall, formed of impossibly large blocks. "How did they move stones this size?" he asked his grandfather. The stones lining the tunnel were fifteen feet tall, twenty wide and judging from what he had seen on the outside wall, forty feet long.

"That detail is known only to the dwarves, my boy. No one was here to witness them build these cities," The old elf answered. "Just remember, the dwarves were working stone when elves and men were still roaming the wilds naked and hunting for their keep. They passed through the wall and into the merchant's square that served as a buffer between the outer wall and the city proper. This area is as far as most travelers get when they visit Dhargul and is much like the merchant's quarter of any city among men. Many shops and a couple of inns lined the outer edges of the space, but most of the business was taking place out in the open, as traders transferred goods from one wagon to another. Wagons loaded with tools, weapons, armor, jewelry and precious stones and metals made their way to the outer gate, back to the lands of men. Meanwhile, carts loaded with foodstuffs, wood, charcoal, and fabric moved toward the city gates. Heavily armed caravan guards accompanied the outgoing wagons, especially those loaded with gold and silver. They made their way through the throng towards the gates of the city. The overcast sky was beginning to drizzle, and they meant to get under cover before they would need to dry off all their equipment. As they approached the inner gate, the guards there snapped to attention and one asked, "Lord Hadaras?"

"Yes, my good dwarf," he replied.

The guards executed deep bows, like those at the outer gate and Hadaras and Aleron returned the gesture. "Ahead and to the left, you will find the stables, Lord and someone will be there to greet you shortly and guide you to your lodging. Enjoy your stay in Dhargul, Lord."

"Thank you, gentlefolk, for your assistance. I am certain that we will enjoy our stay in your beautiful city," Hadaras answered in Dwarvish, giving the response required of dwarvish etiquette. He and Aleron entered, passing the thick, outward opening, steel doors, decorated with gold and silver. A massive portcullis loomed over the far end of the corridor, before it opened into the underground city. Upon moving into the city, Aleron experienced a sight seen by few outside the dwarven world. Massive stone columns, hewn from the living rock, supported vaulted ceilings, well over one hundred feet above their heads. Some columns bore helical staircases, indicating levels above the one on which they stood. Terraced galleries lined the sides of the expansive underground plaza, switchbacks providing cart access from one level to the next. Ornate carvings seemed to decorate every surface. Hadaras spotted the stable area and they made towards it.

"Did they hollow out the entire mountain?" Aleron asked, awed by the sheer expanse and grandeur of the dwarvish city.

"Essentially, yes," Hadaras replied, "this mountain is riddled from top to bottom. There are countless levels above and below this main one." He continued, "It is even rumored, that one can travel from here to Nhargul, completely underground."

"But that's hundreds of leagues away."

"And they have had thousands of years in which to accomplish it," his grandfather reminded him. When he considered the scale of the excavation before his eyes, it was not difficult to believe that the dwarves could have tunneled the three hundred leagues between the cities.

"Grandfather, what are those lamps burning overhead?" the boy asked. "It's not the right color for any oil lamp I've ever seen." The lamps to which Aleron referred hung high in the ceiling and shone with a flickering, blue-white light.

"Those lamps operate on the same principle as a bolt of lightning. Essentially, they are a continuous spark of lightning, contained in a glass vessel. As I recall, they employ rods of an extremely pure form of coal, so pure, that it does not readily burn, like other types. A spark of lightning is maintained between two coal rods," Hadaras explained.

"What kind of magic do they use to harness lightning?"

"This is not magic. They have devised a way to generate the same energy as lightning, through mechanical means, but on a smaller scale and can store it for later use. The machine the guards used to communicate works on the same energy. It readily travels on wires made of metal and seems to be in some way related to loadstones."

"How do they make lightning?"

"The machines I saw years ago, used loadstones mounted on a disk, spinning past coils of wire. Somehow, the loadstones create lightning energy in the wire coils, and they use it to power other things, like lamps or that distance talker. They employ water mills at their dammed reservoir to spin the loadstone disks and generate the energy. Dwarves are very ingenious when it comes to mechanical things. Faergas told me once that they learned to make artificial loadstones, many times stronger than the natural ones and use them in their energy mills."

"Why don't men use this kind of energy, instead of burning oil in lamps?" Aleron wondered.

"The dwarves are not quick to share their secrets with outsiders. Men will likely discover this soon enough. Another thing Faergas told me was that after they began using these lamps, rickets became all but unknown among dwarf children. It seems even, that one can receive sunburn from working too close to these lamps and rickets occurs in children who do not receive enough sunlight."

"The light seems whiter than the sun; it kind of hurts to look at it."

"No, I don't believe it is a good idea to look directly at them, any more than it is to stare directly at the sun."

They arrived at the stables and a groom came out to meet them. His bushy black beard covered nearly his whole face. "G'mornin Lairds," he greeted in thickly accented Sudean. "Dunt git many o ye tall folk an yer tall harses, but we'll find ye sum reume." Aleron could barely understand the dwarf through the accent.

Hadaras replied in fluent Dwarvish, "*Thank you kind sir. Where may we offload our baggage and equipment?*"

The groom seemed delighted that a foreigner took the time to become fluent in his tongue and replied, "*You can offload your bags right here Sir. No one will bother them.*" Dwarves, as a rule, abhor the concept of theft and will not take anything that is not their own. Often, they will go to great lengths to find the rightful owner of a lost or discarded item and if that is not possible, will donate the item to a charitable cause, rather than keep it for themselves. Because dwarves are also hard working, as a rule, they have little need for charity and their charitable donation warehouses overflow with items, some quite ancient. Only during times of war or natural disaster, do they draw down their stockpiles. The groom continued, *"You can store your saddles here and we can get a cart to carry your bags to lodging, if need be. But seeing as you're not dwarves and you made it past the gate, I assume you're important folk and someone will be along to collect you."*

"Yes, the guards said a representative from the palace will be along shortly to bring us to where we will be lodged."

"Guests of King Faergas, important folk indeed," The groom stated, looking impressed. Aleron found he could understand most of the conversation, but it was moving too fast for him to actually join in. He discovered that being able to read another language does not necessarily mean that you are conversational in it. *"Well, let us get these oversized ponies settled in before they get here. I've a few larger pens for when the foreign dignitaries visit. I even have a long-handled brush to rub them down with. I'll take good care of them for you. They look like fine animals."* He started in on unloading the packhorse. Hadaras and Aleron started on their own mounts as well.

"How much will we owe you for your services, Sir, for each day of lodging," Hadaras asked, as they unpacked and set the baggage and gear to the side.

"Not a thing my Lord," the groom answered him. *"I'm an employee of the kingdom and this is a free service to guests of the city, as is the lodging, if you were to need it. Outside, in the merchant's square, it's another story. You would pay for everything out there.* After they brought the horses in and stowed the saddles, with the groom chatting the whole time, he finally got around to asking, *"So, may I inquire as to your names, Gentlefolk?"*

"Certainly, Sir, I am Hadaras, and this is my grandson, Aleron."

The dwarf's face went white, and his eyes got wide. *"Lord Hadaras, the Wanderer?"* he asked then he bowed deeply, like all the guards before, saying, *"Please pardon my insolence, Lord. I had no idea you were a Protector of the Realm, ten thousand pardons Sir."*

"Please rise my friend. There is no need. I was glad for your conversation," Hadaras assured the dwarf, extending his hand in friendship. The groom straightened and took the elf's hand in a vise-like grip.

"Sir, it is a great honor to meet you," he stated, emphatically, pumping Hadaras' arm vigorously. *"Laddie, dids yer gramper tell yu he's da only outsider in da histry o' da fur kindoms evar neemed a Prutectur o' da Realm? Dat's ar heist oner."*

"No Sir, he did not," Aleron replied. "I've come to find out that my Grandfather is not one to boast on his achievements."

"Aye, yoo b' prood; e's eh greet mon," the dwarf told him, as he slapped Aleron on the back with enough force to knock the wind out of the boy. He apologized as Aleron wheezed to regain his breath, "Surry laddie, Iy furgut ye min urnt so stoot is oos."

"No problem, Sir," Aleron assured him, as he regained his composure.

Hadaras just laughed heartily at the exchange. *"And may I ask of your name, Good Sir?"*

"Daegle, at your service, my Lord," the dwarf said, bowing low, once again.

"An honor to meet you, as well, Sir," Hadaras announced, bowing in return as Daegle straightened from his bow. Just then, an ornate carriage appeared, drawn by, albeit somewhat smaller than average, horses, rather than ponies. The driver was clad in gilded chain mail, with a surcoat of black and red, bearing the image of a golden hammer on the chest. His golden hair and beard were braided elaborately. The door to the carriage opened and another individual stepped out. This one, with red hair, dressed in the same livery as the driver, with the addition of a silver torque and vambraces, indicative of high office.

"Lord Protector Hadaras, the king cordially requests the presence of you and your charge, as soon as you are able," the important looking dwarf announced, importantly.

"Certainly, Lord Chamberlain," Hadaras answered. *"It was a pleasure to meet you Daegle,"* then to Aleron, he said, "Let's grab our things, my boy and go meet the king." The driver set the brake and hopped lightly down. He and the Chamberlain moved to help with the baggage, as did Daegle and they loaded them onto the carriage roof in a few short minutes. Aleron and Hadaras entered the carriage, followed by the Chamberlain. Soon, the cart set out toward the royal palace.

Chapter 19

Gurlachday, Day 7, Squash Moon, 8760 Sudean Calendar

Good winds from this storm and it looks like it will swing north, missing landfall, Zormat surmised. They would reach Corin today but given the choice, he would weather a storm like this one at sea. The Adari envoy informed him of the Thallasian coast's regular battering by cyclones each summer. The sun's rays, only just revealing themselves, accentuated the bank of black clouds on the eastern horizon. Today looked be a sleepless day for the Arkans, as they would reach the capital's harbor by mid-morning and the work would start. A meeting needed arrangement between him and the pirate king, then with whatever remnant of the priesthood still existed there.

"Three ships ahead to starboard!" the watchman shouted from the crow's nest. They had been keeping the coast within sight since nearing Thallasia and an intercepting patrol was inevitable.

"Cut sails and change course to intercept. We will meet them head on, not outrun them," Zormat directed the crew. "Drop the sea anchor when they get near."

"Yes, my Liege," the helmsman replied, and others of the crew scrambled through the rigging to adjust their sail.

The banner of Arkus flew from the forward mast, black eight-pointed star on a red background, looking like a fat spider. Below it, flew the flags of Kolixtlan and Adar. *The Black Sun is the symbol of my father, the One True God. If these fools fail to recognize, they will pay dearly.* He moved to the foredeck. He could sense the reassuring presence, many fathoms below. It followed the ship since he summoned it weeks ago. Zormat could sense it was not comfortable in these warm waters, far from its home in the north, but it was bound to obey him, as all his father's creations were.

"Captain, they fly the colors of Kolixtlan and Adar, below a flag I do not recognize," the lookout shouted down to Captain Baruk, lowering his spyglass.

"What does it look like?" the captain yelled back. He, like his crew, was black of skin, like a Coptian, but straight of hair, like a Castian or Chuan. The Thallasians, as a people, had roots with many different peoples. Outcasts from throughout Aertu found refuge in the piracy of the eastern shores, since time immemorial.

"Three masts, square rigged, narrow low hull, looks fast sir."

"Not the boat you idiot, the flag. I can see the blasted boat without a spyglass."

"Right sir, it's a black star on a red field."

"How many points does that black star have?" The captain asked, an uneasy feeling coming over him.

"Looks like eight, Sir."

An eight-pointed black star, on a red field, Baruk thought. *The Black Sun has not flown in four thousand years.* "Ready the fire and signal the other ships to do the same!" he shouted to the crew. *It will not fly to the ruin of my people again, if I have any say in the matter.* The signal went out and the crews fed more wood to the fires maintained beneath great kettles of naphtha and sulfur. They set torches within the iron maw of each dragon-headed prow. The other two ships would move to flank the alien vessel to catch it at the intersection of three gouts of liquid flame. They drilled this maneuver often, though today's wind might prove problematic. There would be no plunder today. This was a maneuver to destroy the enemy, not merely disable. The crew did not question Baruk's orders. Ships of all nations are fair game to Thallasians in their home waters and even if they wondered at his decision to destroy the ship, they knew better than to second-guess their commander.

The Thallasian corsairs closed fast on the lone Arkan clipper. Zormat waited for them to get closer, to gauge their intent. They were flanking him, but that was no reason to assume hostile intent. *I could destroy them out of hand, but I am here for allies, not enemies.* He cast his thoughts about, probing for the thoughts of the Thallasian crewmen. For the most part, he found thoughts of anticipation mixed with obedience. *More professional and disciplined than I imagined they would be.* His first and second officers were beside him now, their minds linked in wordless synchronization. It was an interesting sensation to see the world through six eyes. Suddenly, his senses locked on the one with murder on his mind, who appeared to be the leader. Gouts of yellow fire suddenly erupted from the dragon-headed prow of each corsair. Flames engulfed the Arkan ship and oily black smoke billowed, only to be swept away by the wind. The spouting flame persisted for over fifty heartbeats, before dying to a trickle, dripping from the chin of each iron head. The Thallasians witnessed the flames slide off the sides of the foreign vessel, enveloped by a glowing red nimbus, to be swallowed and extinguished by the choppy sea. *Now why did you have to go and do that?* He projected to the mind of the captain to his immediate front, as hundreds of pallid white tentacles rose from the sea, surrounding the Thallasian ships. The tentacles closed upon the three corsairs and with a sickening groan, followed by several loud cracks, the Thallasian ships were crushed and pulled under the waves. Men screamed as they were crushed, along with their vessels, or snatched by still more tentacles, if they tried to jump clear. *My beast eats well today,* Zormat thought, as he watched the hapless Thallasians pulled to their doom. He made the beast save the captain for last, to allow the import of the situation to settle in before he died. *Remarkably efficient creature,* he marveled at his father's creation. *Father always had an eye for the efficient. When I rule Aertu, efficiency will be the guiding force of my realm. All will embrace efficiency or embrace death. After all, what's more efficient than only one god to worship.* Upon witnessing the captain go under, he signaled the crew to proceed. The sea anchor was drawn up and the sails once more unfurled to the wind.

Baruk kept his wits about him and took a deep breath as soon as he felt the tentacle wrap around his leg. He feared that none of his men were as lucky. The foreign sorcerer was obviously toying with him sadistically, but that gave him enough time to kick off his boots and unbuckle his sword belt. The sword was drawn and, in his hand, when he went under, his flame bladed dagger in the off hand. He knew of this beast and knew it was out of place in these warm waters. As he was drawn below the waves, the pressure crushed the air in his lungs, just like when he dove for pearl oysters, as a boy. Little light made it to these depths, but he was able to see by the monster's sickly yellow-green glow. The light allowed him to see the last of his crewmen being fed into the beast's tripart beak, clouds of dark blood filled the water around the creature. *Looks as if I am indeed meant to be the last morsel. Not today, my friend.* As he came to the wide-open jaws, he shifted forward and jammed the tip of the sword into the flesh of its lower jaw and wedged the hilt into one of the upper sections, using the dagger for traction against the beast's rubbery hide. Beside the beak, one large eye opened wide, and he stabbed at it with the dagger. Blinded and in pain, the beast flailed him at the end of the tentacle. Baruk nearly lost his grip on the dagger as he was torn away from the beast's face. Once the flailing slowed, he used the blade to rip through the tentacle holding his left leg and kicked for the surface. Almost out of air, he knew he would black out soon, if he did not make it. Breaking the surface, he managed two deep breaths before the beast grappled him again. This time he was grabbed by multiple tentacles and knew he would likely be torn limb from limb. Just then, a piercing beam of light projected from the distant shore. Baruk felt the warmth from it as it passed over him and the creature loosened its grip. The light panned back to him and was joined by another beam. Apparently, the heat and light were too much for the monster and it released Baruk. He swam for a timber floating in the choppy water and lifted his upper body onto the sodden wood and began kicking for shore. One spotlight remained trained on him as he swam, while the other focused on the incoming ship.

Zormat turned away from the blinding light and shouted, "Get the men on deck…NOW!" *They focus sunlight and it saps our power. I feel weak as a kitten.* The Kolixtlani priest and the Adari necromancer hurried above deck.

"Your Grace," the Kolixtlani was the first to speak. "What is it that you need of us?

"What is this weapon they use against us?

"I know not, Your Grace. I have heard of nothing like this before."

"I have," Nergui, the necromancer, interjected. He was taller than the average Adari and gaunt to the point of disbelief. Beardless and bald, with a long white moustache, his cruel eyes revealed the blackness of his heart. Undoubtedly one of the most skilled torturers on Aertu, there was no trace of fear in those eyes as he addressed the elf. "Those are the lighthouses. They use mirrors to focus the sunlight. At night, they use them with fire, to guide the ships in. In the day, they can use them to roast men in their own skins, like potatoes."

"Why did you not warn me of these?" Zormat screamed at the Adari.

"Didn't think you were going to sink three of their ships just outside their own harbor, Your Grace," he replied, saying the last part in a most sarcastic tone. "You should probably consider turning around, as I don't think they'll be too keen on a truce now," he continued. "This is not the hornet's nest you want to poke."

"I will poke where I want," Zormat railed, "and I will lay their city to waste, if they do not cooperate."

"Not if they burn your ship down to the waterline, with us on it," the Adari retorted, "but if you insist on proceeding, so be it. I have lived long enough." Tenoch, the Kolixtlani priest, remained silent through the whole exchange, looking positively terrified.

"Have you anything to add, priest," Zormat asked the Kolixtlani, "any suggestions for our next course of action?"

"N-no, Your Grace," he stammered, "whatever you decide will be best."

"Spineless twit, I am asking for useful ideas."

"Sorry, Your Grace."

A second and then a third spotlight found them. The temperature rose noticeably and Zormat knew he and the other sorcerers were next to powerless. Red magic can accomplish many things, but it has no power over sunlight. On the contrary, it is strongest in darkness and bright sunlight saps its power tremendously. Zormat came to a decision. "Turn about!" he shouted. "We will return after darkness falls."

"It's working Marshal! They're turning about!" the excited guard announced. The lighthouse mirrors were an engineering marvel. They could be focused for any range out to a mile, and would hold that focus, four hundred silver plated mirrors moving in unison, as the operator tracked them to the sun, enabling the engagement of moving targets. Within a hundred yards of the tower, they were deadly, setting ships afire and roasting men where they stood.

"Of course it did," Marshal Tangir agreed. "Those are red wizards aboard that ship, and they don't like the bright light. Don't you worry, they'll be back after dark. We'll notify the High Admiral," he continued, "and he will engage the Wizard's Guild. It will cost him some gold, but we have red and blue wizards of our own. Gartuk! Send out a boat for that poor slob who managed to escape the thrule. Gods only know what it was doing this far south." *If there's one on board that ship that can command a thrule, the Wizard's Guild will have a good fight on their hands.*

Baruk continued kicking. The waves carried him steadily toward shore. The spotlight left him, and he hoped the thrule was gone for good. The light was a mixed blessing anyway. It drove off the thrule, but at the same time accented his silhouette for any sharks in the vicinity. He looked over his shoulder to see the clipper turning about, with three lights trained upon it. *Must not like the heat either. Damn red wizards. I don't even trust ours.* Soon, he saw a small skiff depart the docks. "Ah, my rescue approaches," he said aloud.

Chapter 20

Gurlachday, Day 7, Squash Moon, 8760 Sudean Calendar

They entered the throne room, Aleron still marveling at the "levitator", his grandfather had called it, which brought the carriage, horses and all, eight hundred feet to the palace level, on massive steel cables. They stopped in the entrance, while the Lord Chamberlain announced, "Lord Hadaras, Protector of the Realm and his charge, Aleron."

"Bid them enter," a booming voice directed. The Lord Chamberlain stepped aside, gestured for them to proceed and then fell in behind them. The voice belonged to the black bearded dwarf seated upon the iron throne atop the dais to their front. They approached and as he was coached on the way up, Aleron dropped to his right knee, alongside Hadaras. "Twenty years it's been. What makes you think you can just saunter in here after twenty years and expect a warm welcome from me?"

"My charm and winning nature, perhaps, Your Grace?" Hadaras offered.

"Ha, just as cheeky as you ever were," the king stated, laughing. Faergas Goldhammer rose from his iron seat and stepped down to greet his old friend. "Get up Hadaras. I told you twenty years ago; you kneel for no one in my kingdom and that includes me. You as well, boy, get on up. Ulrick, hold the throne down for a while. We're retiring to my chambers, and I wouldn't want it floating away on me."

"Of course, Your Grace, you need not concern yourself; it will not move an inch in your absence," the red-bearded dwarf letting slip only the slightest of grins, before returning to his usual solemn expression.

"Good," the king replied, "now let's go have some ale and talk. I want to know what this old stoat has been up to for the past two decades. Come, my friend and your boy too, my chambers and my ale barrel await." He gestured them to follow and headed for an ornate iron door, set directly into the stone of the mountain. Aleron noticed very little actual masonry. Nearly everything seemed to be carved directly from the stone of the mountain. He could see no sign of a doorknob, or any other means to open the door. Faergas pressed a series of raised studs on the door panel, and with a hissing sound, it recessed into the wall and then slid to one side. After they entered, he pushed a single stud on the inside wall and the door slid closed with a hiss and a dull clunk. Aleron could barely make out the seam in the stone that belied the mechanism hidden within the wall. "You don't have doors like that where you're from, do you lad?" the king asked Aleron.

"No, Your Grace, nor lamps like yours either," Aleron replied.

"Aye, lad, our engineers have come up with some amazing inventions in the last hundred years. The door runs on compressed air and that's pumped using the same power as runs the lamps."

"What is compressed air, Your Grace, if you don't mind me asking?" the boy inquired.

"Air is substance, boy and it takes up space," Faergas explained, obviously proud of his people's innovation. "Birds fly on it, and you can see how it takes up space if you turn a clear glass cup over and try to push it under the surface of a tub of water. Unlike liquids or solids, you can push more air into a container than naturally fits there, store it for later and make it do work for you. Do you understand now, lad?"

"I think so, Your Grace, thank you for the explanation."

"Think nothing of it, lad. Now I want to know what this one has been up to all these years and why he took so long to pay me a visit. But first, let me get us some refreshment." He moved to the large keg, snatched three large earthenware tankards off their hooks and filled them from the spigot. He grabbed all three in one hand and walked to a heavy round wooden table in the middle of the room. "Come, have a seat my friends." He set the tankards down in front of three short sturdy stools.

"Thank you Faergas, it has indeed been too long, but I have been fairly busy these last fifteen years or so," Hadaras explained.

"I see that. I take it the lad here is fifteen, your son?"

"No, Aleron is my grandson, son of my daughter, Audina," Hadaras explained as they took their seats. The king sat at the head, Hadaras took the seat to his left and Aleron the next one down.

"Audina, beautiful lass, how is she? I haven't seen her in a troll's age."

"Gone I'm afraid," Hadaras declared, "nigh on thirteen years now."

"I'm sorry old friend," the king offered, "and the boy's father?"

"Passed on as well. I've raised Aleron since he was two."

"That's sad news indeed," Faergas said and then to Aleron, "At least you had your grandfather here to take care of you. He's a fine fellow, as far as elves go. You can let down your disguise, lad, no secrets here." Hadaras had let the glamour drop as soon as he entered the chamber. Most dwarves, at least those that gave it any thought at all, believed he was a halfblood, to explain his longevity, but still a man.

"Your Grace, there is no disguise; this is how I look."

Faergas looked to Hadaras and asked, "A halfblood, this one is? I thought he seemed big for an elf at that age."

"Yes, he's a halfblood and there are a few other things that he is, that bear discussion."

"You have my interest, please, go on."

"I did not plan for this to come to light for a few more years. I did not think my grandson was ready yet, but we had an incident in Arundell, that altered the track of my plans." Faergas, resting his chin on one palm, arched his bushy eyebrows questioningly, as Hadaras continued, "We were in the throne room and Aleron laid his hand upon Andhanimwhid. The sword practically jumped into his hand." At that revelation, the king sat up straight in his stool and slammed both palms on the tabletop.

Looking at Aleron, he said, "You mean to tell me that I have the king of Sudea here before me?"

"Yes," Hadaras replied, "that is exactly what I mean to tell you. This was meant to be a friendly tour, so Aleron could see some of the world, but it is turning out far different than I had anticipated."

Aleron just sat, sipping his ale, as the adults conversed about him. "Who else knows about it?" Faergas inquired.

"Only the Steward, his daughter and her bodyguards, so far." Hadaras proceeded to recount the events of that day and the ones to follow, as well as the history that led to the event. It took a while, as Faergas interjected questions periodically and Aleron refilled the tankards once during the exchange.

"Got something for young Lady Eilowyn I see," he said at one point to Aleron. "Can't say I blame you; she's a pretty little lass. Copper and emeralds go well together, don't they lad?"

"Uh, I guess so, Your Grace," he agreed, not knowing what else to say and flushing as he said it.

"Enough with the 'Your Grace' thing, boy, you're the blasted king of Sudea, whether anyone else knows it yet, or not. Call me Faergas."

"Yes, Your Gr…Sir, I mean Faergas."

"You'll get it straight eventually," the king said, chuckling. "Go on old friend and fill me in on what happened after Arundell." As Hadaras recounted the events on the road to Dhargul, Faergas took a keen interest in the encounter with the goblins. He looked at Aleron and said, "New forms of magic, now that's quite an invention, my boy." He asked if they had come up with any other combinations and Hadaras went into more detail on the experiments they undertook on the road through the mountains. "Do you still have that nugget, lad?" Aleron nodded in affirmation, drew the silver piece from his pocket and handed it to Faergas. He examined it and said, "Looks like a casting of a piece of gravel, can you turn it back to stone?" He was understandably skeptical and wanted to see for himself, though he was being polite about it.

"I'll see if I can," Aleron replied. "Some magic is scarce this far underground." He took back the nugget and concentrated. Blue and yellow were plentiful enough, but he had to search to find a few scraps of green and red. In a flash of white, he once again held a granite pebble in his palm and handed it back to Faergas.

"Well, I'll be a billygoat's daddy! It's true!" he exclaimed, not quite believing in the thing he had just witnessed. "I have to agree with your grandpa, lad. You can't go making gold and silver as cheap as gravel." He handed the pebble back to Aleron and in another flash, it became silver once again. "What's interesting to me is that the lad can go from blue to red and back to blue," he elaborated to Hadaras. "Why is it that no other wizard has ever done the same?"

"Not knowing the minds of any of the red sorcerers, it's hard to say," Hadaras began, "but we think that those men became evil first, then were drawn to the chaotic nature of the red. The Adversary was capable of using any form he wished, but he invariably chose the red for the destructive power of it."

"And this new maroon power you describe, it's not destructive as well? It seems like you destroyed a troop of goblins pretty effectively."

"It's not so much destructive as powerful," Hadaras explained. "I could use the blue power that is available to my kind, to move a boulder the size of a house, but it would require great effort and I would be exhausted after a short time. I could, however, slice the same boulder in two, with great precision. A wielder of red could do the same with little effort but would require intense concentration and control to avoid pulverizing the boulder in the process. Aleron's maroon power combines the precision of the blue, with the power of the red. He could take the same boulder and hurl it over the mountain, if he wished."

Faergas looked across the table to Aleron, his eyes like liquid onyx, below bushy black brows. "Now that's some power, lad. With power like that, a man needs self-control and strong character. Otherwise, it takes control of you, instead of the other way around, and you crave more and more power. That's how a ruler becomes a tyrant and that's not a path you want to tread. Do you believe you have the character to handle what you have been blessed with, lad?"

"I hope so," Aleron answered, not nearly as confident as he was a few moments before.

"The boy has a kind and generous heart, Faergas," Hadaras interjected. "If anyone can handle this power, it's young Aleron here," he reassured the dwarvish king.

"I hope you are right, my friend. He does seem like a good-hearted lad," he replied to Hadaras and then to Aleron said, "Don't worry lad, you'll do fine," in answer to the worried look in Aleron's eyes.

"He'll do fine, as long as he's not rushed onto that throne," Hadaras replied.

"Agreed, there will be no mention of it from this quarter, I can assure you. All in due time."

"Now, my friend, enough about us and our business," Hadaras stated, to shift the conversation, "how have you been? You don't seem a day older that when I last saw you."

"I don't feel a day older either and it's beginning to worry me," the dwarf answered. "I'm sixty-six and I don't feel a day over forty. I should be old and gray by now, with a beard to my ankles. Instead, I'm still running about, smashing troll skulls like a youngster."

"Do you mind if I check?" Hadaras asked the king.

"Certainly, check all you want. I'm surprised you haven't already."

Hadaras laid his hand upon the king's shoulder and concentrated a moment. Upon opening his eyes again, he exclaimed, "You are, not a day over forty. I think that Aelient I expulsed thirty years ago made some changes in you. She must have had some long-range plans for you because you have nearly ceased to age."

"You mean I'm going to live forever, like you? Gods no."

"It does appear to be the case, my friend. Not so much forever, but you are ageing more like an elf than a dwarf."

"How could an aelient have done something like that, Grandfather?" Aleron inquired, momentarily interrupting the flow of the conversation. "I thought that only the Allfather and maybe the Aelir had access to the white magic."

"Good question, my boy," the old elf conceded, "but all forms of magic have multiple applications," he explained. "I can still destroy with the blue, for instance, but it destroys with great precision. It's not so much that she transformed the king into something else. It's more like she made some subtle adjustments, making him more elf-like, than he was before." Speaking to Faergas, he said, "Since dwarves are already a long-lived race, she was likely to have better long-term results than if she had attempted the same on a man."

"Well, I better figure out what I'm going to do for the next couple thousand years then. I don't think I can get away with being spry in my old age for much longer." The king continued, on a different tack, "I think I've held you up for long enough. Time to get you to your quarters and a hot bath. The smell of the road lies heavy upon you, no offense."

"None taken, my friend," Hadaras replied, "we would welcome a hot bath."

"Good then, I'll have you shown to your rooms. You will find some light victuals there, as well as a steaming hot tub. I'll see you for dinner." With that, they arose and left the chamber. Upon exiting, Faergas said, "Ulrick, please show these gentlefolk to their chambers."

"Yes, Your Grace," the High Chamberlain replied and then gestured for them to follow and saying, "My Lords, please follow me and I will get you settled in."

Chapter 21

Gurlachday, Day 7, Squash Moon, 8760 Sudean Calendar

Captain Baruk stood in the antechamber to the High Admiral's office, in dry clothes, with his spare sword and new boots he had not intended to put into service yet. *Now I need to buy a new backup sword and boots.* It was mid-afternoon. After his rescue, Velin, the marshal of the city guard debriefed him on the morning's incident in which his ships were lost. Upon hearing the details, the marshal left to consult with the Grand Marshal Haldor. A bell or so later, the marshal returned with the news that Baruk would make himself presentable, as they would be meeting with High Admiral Kor in two bells. The marshals had been in the office for over a bell, along with the grand admiral, he found out from the orderly stationed at the door. As a closed society, Thallasia is little known to the outside world. Trader ships ply the Kolixtlani Sea to Kolixtlan and Adar, as well as the coast of Elmenia. Foreign ships, however, are not tolerated in their territorial waters. Most believe that piracy still reigns when in fact, Thallasia has become a meritocracy, ruled by a military government. Never having had an aristocracy, they were loath to invent the concept when they progressed from anarchy to governance. The High Admiral Kor, the son of a goatherd, is the supreme commander of the Thallasian people, with the grand admiral and grand marshal his second in command of naval and ground forces, respectively.

Marshal Velin stepped into the waiting area and stated, "Please come in captain; they are ready for you now." As a captain, Baruk's rank was approximately equal to that of the marshal.

"Thank you, marshal," he replied and strode smartly into the office, saluting with his right hand to his temple, palm open and facing the officers seated at the conference table. "Captain Baruk, reporting as ordered, high admiral."

"Come in captain and have a seat. You've had an eventful morning," High Admiral Kor answered, as he returned the salute. "I assume you are familiar with Grand Admiral Lim and Grand Marshal Haldor?"

"Yes, Sir and thank you," he replied, dropping the salute and moving to take his seat, next to Marshal Velin.

"So, Captain Baruk, it's not every day that I hear of someone fighting off a thrule," Kor continued. "In fact, none of us has ever heard of it, but Marshal Velin saw you go under, then resurface. Please relate to us, in your own words, what happened." Baruk recounted the event to his superiors, emphasizing the impression that he was purposely left for last, which allowed him time to prepare, unlike his hapless crew. Midway through the account, Kor asked, "Why did you choose to flame the ship, rather that attempt boarding, captain?"

"Sir, when I saw them flying the Black Sun, I assumed there were wizards aboard and wished to take them by surprise. I hoped to destroy them before they had opportunity to react, Sir."

"Good, that was a solid assessment captain, but unfortunately they did react in time," the high admiral commented. "I believe the wizard on board likely read your intentions in your thoughts and was thus ready for you. Considering how he left you for last, as punishment it seems, he must have singled you out as the leader. Go on, captain, continue." Baruk continued his account, relating how the spotlights seemed to drive the thrule away. "Your story corroborates with what you briefed Marshal Velin and with what he witnessed from the lighthouse. Thank you, captain, for your faithful service and please leave us for a few moments, while we discuss things. Do not leave but stay in the waiting area. We will have need for you again."

"Yes, Sir," Baruk replied, as he stood and rendered a salute. The high admiral returned the salute and Baruk pushed his chair in, turned on his heel and left the office, without another word.

"Gentlemen, it appears we have an unprecedented situation on our hands," Kor related to the assembled officers. "I have no intention of allowing the Nameless God dominion over our lands again, but it seems as we are likely to have a boatload of angry red wizards on our shores as soon as night falls." The others nodded in agreement and the High Admiral went on, "We will need the wizard's guild for this, and we need to mobilize them quickly. Haldor, you are charged with this task. Contact the guild and negotiate a price. Brief them on the entire situation and try to impress upon them the necessity for quick action.

Velin, you will coordinate the city defenses, of course. You will also coordinate with the wizards and emplace them in your formation. Go quickly; we will meet at the harbor a bell before dusk." After the two men took their leave, he said to the grand admiral, "Lim, you and I have been friends for a long time, right?"

"Yes, Sir," Lim replied, "we came up through the ranks together."

"What I have for you, Lim, is a bit more difficult than what Haldor is tasked with, because it has never been done." He waited for the acknowledgement in his friend's eyes before continuing. "I need for you to establish the first Thallasian diplomatic corps."

"The first what?" Lim asked, in astonishment. "We're Thallasia; we have no diplomats."

"Exactly my point, and we need to get some quickly. I've been considering this for some time now, and the events of today move what was a long-term goal to an immediate imperative. Your first recruit is in the next room."

"Captain Baruk, you mean? He has a stellar record up to this point, but he just lost three ships and ninety men this morning."

"Yes, men were lost," Kor replied, "but his decision was sound, and his quick thinking saved his own life, at least. Choking a thrule with his sword, ha! That was some quick thinking. He will be a liability if we leave him knocking about the city without a command, once the loss of his crew sinks in. I don't want him anywhere near the harbor tonight, Lim. He's likely to try something stupid if he sees that ship again."

"I agree with you there, Kor. So, where are we sending our new diplomat?"

"We will send ships to Chu, Coptia and Castia, under the flag of truce, once we know more about this new threat. Those will be a relatively fast run, so you will have ample time to pick representatives and crew for those three missions. Your first priority will be to bring the good Captain up to speed and outfit him for his voyage to Sudea.

"Sudea," Lim murmured, "do you think they will greet us as friends? We've been sinking each other's ships on sight for four thousand years."

"We have to hope that they will, my friend," the High Admiral replied. "There's a war coming, and I want us to be on the right side this time. We need to put our old enmities aside and hope that our old adversaries are willing to do the same. For Sudea, I need a man who can think on his feet and make fast decisions under pressure. I need this for all our ambassadors, but especially Sudea. I believe the man in the next room fills those requirements.

I had this made several weeks back, as an identifying insignia for the diplomatic corps, since I do not wish for them to display a military uniform of any type. That is not the presentation I wish for our ambassadors to foreign realms," he continued, as he rose, turned, opened the door to a tall compartment behind his desk. From it, he withdrew an ornate sword, and handed it to Lim. "Just a moment, while I find something to wrap that in."

The admirals stepped into the antechamber where Baruk and the orderly waited. Both snapped to attention when the superior officers entered. "Captain Baruk," Kor began, "Grand Admiral Lim has a proposition for you, which I hope you will fully consider and accept."

"Certainly, Sir, I will give it my utmost consideration," Baruk promised.

"Good," the high admiral replied, clapping Baruk on the shoulder as he passed. "There is much for me to do this afternoon, so I will leave you in the capable hands of the grand admiral. Good day all."

"Good day, Sir," all three replied, saluting as their leader exited the room.

"Come with me to my office, Captain," Lim directed, as he strode to the door. Baruk followed him out and fell into step to Lim's left, as they continued down the hallway. He noticed the grand admiral carried a wrapped bundle but thought better than to inquire about it. "In here," Lim directed him to a door on the left. They entered an antechamber, identical to the one they had just left, complete with a nearly identical orderly, who snapped to attention as the grand admiral entered. "Relax Chilo," Lim directed to sailor. "The Captain and I have some important matters to discuss. Let no one disturb us, unless they be the grand marshal or the high admiral; am I understood?"

"Understood, Sir," Chilo replied, then opened the door to the inner office. Lim's office was only slightly smaller than Kor's and was similarly spartan in its furnishings. The admirals were lifelong seamen and tended not to over clutter their workspaces with unnecessary accoutrements.

After the door closed behind them, Lim turned to Baruk and asked, "So, how good is your Sudean?"

"Passable, Sir," Baruk replied. "It's not far off from Thallasian and I've had a bit of experience interrogating captured Sudeans."

"Good, because you will need that if you accept our offer for a new position, just opening up."

"A new position, Sir...of what sort?"

"Sort of a lateral, as well as upward promotion," Lim began to explain. "Do you recognize this, Captain Baruk?" He unwrapped the bundle to reveal a cutlass of unfamiliar design, with an S-shaped cross-hilt of gold, rather than a full knuckle bow and a silver wire-wrapped dogleg grip. The heavy gold pommel was formed as a stylized osprey head, symbolizing Thallasia. The scabbard was of red dyed ray skin with silver fittings and bound in crisscrossing gold cord. Baruk thought it looked a bit gaudy, to say the least.

"No, Sir, I do not recognize that sword, should I?"

"No captain, you shouldn't, as it's never been seen before, aside from the smith who made it and the high admiral. He had these made as part of a plan he has had in the works for a time now." Lim drew the sword partway from the scabbard, revealing a highly polished blade of watered steel. "This is an ambassador's sword, a symbol of office for the diplomatic corps."

"Diplomatic corps?" Baruk questioned. "I didn't know we had one, Sir."

"We don't, as of yet, Captain Baruk. How would you like to be the first member?" Lim asked and then went into explaining the high admiral's intentions, to the best of his knowledge. He finished by saying, "As an ambassador, you will be equivalent in rank to admiral or field marshal and will report directly to the high admiral. Eventually, as the corps grows, it will likely be necessary to appoint a grand ambassador, or some such equivalent and we will most likely promote to that position from within the corps. As envoy to Sudea, we expect yours to be the most challenging position of the original lot and as the first appointee, you will be senior to the others as well. Your star appears to be rising, despite the setback this morning captain, or should I say ambassador?" Lim held out the sword to Baruk, as he completed his spiel.

Baruk hesitated only a moment, before reaching out to grab the cutlass. He knew he would be stupid to balk at this opportunity, despite the unexpected nature of it. "Sir, I would be honored to accept this charge." This appointment effectively catapulted him two ranks, despite the fact that he would not have even been up for commodore for two more years, accelerating his career by at least eight years.

"No time to think on it ambassador?" Lim remarked wryly as he relinquished the sword to Baruk. "I guess Kor was correct in his estimation of you; you certainly do make quick decisions."

"I would have to be an idiot to pass it up, Sir and I hope it wouldn't require additional thought for me to be an idiot," Baruk replied, with just a hint of a smile.

Well put, Ambassador Baruk," Lim said, with a laugh. "Now I need you to return to your quarters and get some rest. Report to me tomorrow, one bell past dawn and we will begin planning your journey. One more thing, ambassador, stay away from the waterfront this evening. That is a direct order from the high admiral.

Walking across the courtyard to his apartment in the single officer's quarters, he thought on the fortunes of the day, *I started this morning commanding a trident and now this evening, all my men are dead, and I'm promoted. Somehow, it doesn't feel right. I would give anything to go back to this morning. If I ever get my hands on that bastard of a red wizard, I'll cut him to bits, slowly, starting with his fingertips.* He thought then of the condolence letters, he would be needing to write, starting in the morning. Many of his men had families and he would need to assure they received compensation. ambassador or not, he still needed to discharge his final duties as captain. He knew exactly why he was forbidden to be at the harbor this evening. The red bastard would come back after sundown, with the spotlights then powerless to drive him off. *I hope the wizard's guild has something good planned for him,* he thought, as he headed off to his landside quarters.

Chapter 22

Gurlachday, Day 7, Squash Moon, 8760 Sudean Calendar

"Are you sure you wish to poke this nest, Your Grace," Nergui asked, as the elvish sailors lowered the gangplank to the dock. They sailed into the harbor of Corin unchallenged, which was suspicious enough and now the docks seemed deserted as well. The necromancer put out his feelers but could sense not so much as a wharf rat in the vicinity. Torches guttered against the darkness, lighting well the docks, but nothing further in. "I don't care for the fact that I can't sense anything, living or dead here."

"They may have tricks, necromancer and tricks are all they will amount to," Zormat replied. "They will not withstand my power as I act in the name of the One True God." Tenoch looked terrified, as was usual and Zormat was quickly becoming weary of the timid Kolixtlani priest. He was wearier of the sarcastic Adari, with his barbed comments, who just rolled his eyes, put on the stoic expression of one who expected to die soon and was at peace with the revelation. The son of the Nameless One drew his flaming sword and the black star tattooed on his forehead flared red at the edges, matching the crimson glow of the blade. He signaled his elves and the two men to follow him down the gangplank. "Be alert for signs of ambush," he exhorted them. "They are likely to attempt something of the sort and I can sense nothing of their intentions. They are well masked, wherever they may be." He was the first down the gangplank, his second behind him, followed by the men and a squad of twelve more sailors, armed with sword and shield. His first, along with a skeleton crew, remained on board to secure the ship. They hit the dock and rapidly fanned into a protective wedge, weapons, and armor glittering with barely visible red energy from the latent power imbued unto them. Rigging snapped in the wind, still blowing strong, though the storm had passed to the north, and masking any sounds that may have emanated from the apparently abandoned docks. Five paces up the dock and the red luminance of their weapons and armor winked out, Zormat's included. The tattoo on his forehead went dark and he felt as though he had been punched in the midsection. His internal store of power disappeared in the space of a heartbeat. The others felt it as well and the formation halted suddenly. A bright blue tracery of energy suddenly rose about them.

"Missing something wizard?" a voice asked out of the darkness, in the trader's tongue the Adari necromancer taught him on the voyage. High Admiral Kor stepped into the torchlight, along with Grand Marshal Haldor and a tall, hooded figure in blue robes. The sailor to Zormat's right flank swung his sword at the blue web and the blade clattered across the dock in five neat slices, leaving him with a hand width stub forward of the hilt. He dropped it and drew his long dagger instead. "As you can see, it would not be advisable to rush our perimeter, unless you would like to be cubed into shark bait," Kor continued. "Now this is a first; elvish red wizards, in cahoots with an Adari and a Kolixtlani. Oh, how the world is changing. I assure you, wizard, that I have more than your number of blue wizards and as many red, prepared to obliterate you and your pretty little boat. Now tell me, what brings you here and why did you return, after sinking three of my ships and killing ninety of my men? Did you think you would receive a warm reception, or did you, in your arrogance, believe your little crew could roll right over us after nightfall?"

"I come in the name of my father, the One True God, to whom you are vassal," Zormat answered, continuing with, "Your ships intended to destroy us outright, without so much as hailing us first. I merely acted to defend my ship and crew."

"One True God, eh, I don't have much time for gods, but I always thought that was the Allfather. He doesn't fly the Black Sun, as far as I know. That belongs to his deviant son, the Nameless God and you say you're his son? That's really new; the Nameless One has a son and it's an elf!" He chuckled audibly at the revelation. "Your friends should have told you that we tolerate no trespass in our territorial waters. If you had flown the Thallasian flag, you would have been hailed, rather than flamed."

"The one you refer to is an impostor, who stole my father's dominion from him at the time of creation. Your nation fought for him in the last war. Why do you reject him now?" Zormat was enraged by this worthless man's insolence, but he was powerless to do anything about it.

"Let's see…," Kor mused, "that 'Great War', as the westerners call it, wasn't so great for us on the losing side. It took us centuries to recover from that and we have no intention of finding ourselves on the wrong side of that fight again. I would as soon we stayed out of it completely, but we likely won't have that option. Now, aren't you just a little curious as to where all your power went? This is no fun if you don't care."

"I don't care," Zormat replied drily. A spear of red energy shot from the bridge of the elvish ship, toward the High Admiral, only to dissipate suddenly, as it passed over the dock. Twin shafts of red and blue shot out of the darkness, plastering the remains of Zormat's First Mate across the bridge. Pink gore dripped from the railings and the faces and tunics of the two crewmembers on the bridge. They coughed and retched, slipping in the slime that was once their leader, as a hail of pebbles catapulted onto their deck.

"Not the best idea," Kor remarked, "that will take some serious cleaning." Zormat's rage grew at the man's callous demeanor. Kor went on to say, "Care or not, I just have to tell you about the most amazing substance we discovered. We call it bloodstone and it's quarried in the desert to the north." He held out a stone in one hand. It glowed with an inner light that Zormat immediately recognized, with a hunger, as the energy missing from his core. "It has the interesting property of soaking up every available drop of red magic anywhere near it." He tossed the stone to Zormat. It bounced off one of the blue strands with a twang, like a plucked harp string, but the elf managed to catch it in his off hand. The stone felt unnaturally cold to him, as it absorbed any residual energy he still had. He dropped it quickly and it bounced back through the web. He looked over to the robed figure and saw he sported five rings of the same substance on his right hand, the one gripping a finely carved wooden staff with a glowing blue crystal mounted on top. The man's face was obscured by the shadow of his hood, but Zormat was certain he could see a blue glow where the eyes should be. "Now, wizard, you have two choices. Number one is to get on your ship, turn around and tell your daddy we aren't interested in his offer, this time around. Number two, is to rot in a cell, paved and walled in bloodstone, for the rest of your life, or until we get sick of feeding you and hang you from the gallows. So, what's your choice?"

"We will choose the first," Zormat answered, "but bear in mind, when my father comes back into his dominion, he will have no mercy for those who betrayed him."

"We'll just have to take our chances then," the High Admiral replied. "Oh, by the way, there's a few thousand bloodstone pebbles scattered across your decks. That may take you a while to clear out of all the nooks and crannies of your boat," he finished with a chuckle. The web of blue opened behind them, serving to corral the group back to the gangplank.

"Clean up this mess!" Zormat shouted, as they boarded the ship. The remnants of his first mate had already begun to dry onto the surfaces of the bridge. If they didn't clean it soon, they would live with it for a long time. The two who were caught in the blast had stripped off their soiled tunics, throwing them overboard in disgust after using the cleaner backsides to wipe their faces. One of them had added vomit to the gore on the bridge, so the stench there was horrid.

Kor, Haldor, and the figure in blue stood and watched the elvish crew prepare to disembark. With thirty wizards of the guild at their backs, along with a hundred bowmen and men at arms of the city watch, they had little to fear from retaliation. The leader of the elves paced furiously up and down the deck, shouting orders at his crew in an unfamiliar language. "Do either of you recognize the tongue they speak?" Kor asked the other two.

"Sounds like a dialect of goblin to me," the blue robed figure replied. "I recognize most of the words and the structure seems to match as well."

"What do you make of that, Blue, elves speaking goblin and using red magic? I've never heard of such a thing. Have you, Haldor?"

"No Sir," the grand marshal replied, "and what about him claiming to be the son of the Nameless One?"

"Demigods are not unheard of," replied the Grand Wizard of the Blue. Members of the wizard's guild never reveal their true names to anyone, so the grand wizards are known to those outside, simply as 'Red', and 'Blue'. "The gods meddled in the affairs of mortals during their stay with us. There is some indication that a certain elvish wizard of great renown was a demigod. He disappeared after the Great War, but certain events in the last four millennia have had his taint upon them."

"You speak of Goromir?" Kor asked, in surprise. "Do you think he is still alive? That would make him ten thousand years old."

"Only a little over nine thousand your Excellency and yes, we think he may still be about. If his mother was truly a goddess, as we suspect, he may not have a maximum lifespan and may linger on Aertu until the end of time. We believe they can be killed though, unlike the gods themselves. There was a Sunjibi king, many ages ago, who was the only known wizard among the westmen and arose before the arrival of elves to our continent. He was killed in battle against the Wabani. It was said that his body refused to rot, and the carrion birds would not touch it upon the funerary rack. They finally entombed him, for lack of a better course of action."

"So, this elf may be who he says he is? How many of these demigods roam Aertu, anyway?" Kor asked.

"That is difficult to say, Excellency, but they will mostly have had to survive over eight millennia since the gods departed our world. Aside from Goromir, there is no evidence that any others have lived that long. Now this one, claiming paternity of the Nameless One, will only have needed to survive the four millennia since the war. There is a chance that he fathered more, but we have never heard of any others. I believe the Nameless One must have captured some elves, ages ago and twisted them to his purposes. Normally, elves are incapable of using the red. These appear to be incapable of using the blue, a purposeful counterpoint to the elves with which we are familiar."

"Most interesting, Blue," the high admiral commented, as they watched the elvish crew drawing up buckets of water and breaking out scrub brushes in an attempt to bring the bridge back to useable condition. A less squeamish crewmember took hold of the helm as the anchor was drawn up and sails trimmed to the brisk crosswind. The ship slowly angled away from the dock and then steadily picked up speed as it moved into the open water of the harbor. "Now I have to wonder where in Aertu they came from and how blasted many there might be. How is it that we never heard of them before now?"

"They may be hidden, like the homeland of the elves," Haldor offered.

"Yes, but we still know about where Elvenholm is. We just can't sail there, but we know how big it is by the amount of area it excludes us from."

"It could be that they are far to the north or south, Sir. That ship looked to be outfitted for cold weather, though I'm no sailor."

"I think you may be right, Hal. The widest stretch of open sea is between here and Elvenholm and we've never found anything but uninhabited islands out there. There may just be a large island or two along the ice somewhere in the eastern sea. I'll have to study the charts to see if there are any inaccessible areas along the ice sheets, maybe someplace the ice seems to extend too far north or south. What do you think, Blue?"

"That's as good a guess as any, Excellency," the blue wizard replied. "They may use an illusion of ice to deter investigation. An alteration of the wind and ocean currents is too obvious if you're trying to conceal your very existence. It may not be an illusion either. If their magic is powerful enough, they could maintain actual ice and open channels when needed. Shall we keep the docks seeded with bloodstone a while yet, in case they return? At worst, it will keep my red brethren off the docks for the duration, not that they frequent them anyhow."

"I think that would be best," Kor decided. "I don't think they will be back soon, but it pays to be careful. It will take them some time to ferret out all the bloodstone gravel we pelted their ship with, and they will be weak until they rid themselves of it. What is it you normally use that stuff for?"

"We blue wizards like to have it around. We build it into our houses and studies. It keeps the air clean and uncluttered for our own magic. The red wizards use it as a repository for their power, as well. They cannot handle it directly, so they build it into special warded mechanisms that allow them to draw energy from the stone. When the time comes, my people will come to collect the stones we secreted, but only after the threat has passed."

"Don't you blue wizards have something similar? What is that crystal at the top of your staff?"

"Yes, Excellency, the blue quartz is similar in the way it stores energy, excepting that it does not forcibly draw the energy to itself. It is more passive, allowing us to add or withdraw power as needed, without the need for special devices. Red wizards use it in devices to rid their areas of blue energy, just as we use bloodstone to purge ours of red."

"Well, that's all very interesting, boys, but we still have work to do. Hal, I need you to continue reinforcement along our coastal defenses and if we could get a red and a blue wizard to each of the outposts and warships, that would be wonderful, Blue."

"Certainly, Excellency, the council is unanimous in our agreement to protect our lands from this new threat by the Nameless One. As long as we can work out a plan to cover our incidental expenses, we will require no additional recompense."

"Yes, your people will be integrated into the garrison forces of each outpost and the crews of each ship. They will receive pay at the grade of lieutenant, if that is acceptable."

"I will consult with Red, Excellency, but I am certain those terms will be acceptable."

"They will be!" a voice shouted from the darkness. More torches winked into life, as the trio turned to see the Grand Wizard of the Red, revealed in extravagant robes of red and gold and a wide-brimmed conical hat of the same colors. A large pendant of bloodstone, within a cage of gold filigree, hung from his neck. "Your offer is quite acceptable, Excellency. If those Black Sun bastards take over, we'll all be slaves again, just like we were four thousand years ago. This is as far as I can go, with all this unshielded bloodstone scattered about, so if you would be so kind as to join me…"

"Are you good, Hal?' Kor asked the grand marshal.

"Of course, Sir and if I have your leave, I will go put things in order now." The grand marshal saluted his leader and Kor returned the salute smartly. Haldor turned on his heel and strode down the dock toward the city.

"Don't you think the hat is a bit over the top, brother?" Blue called out as he and Kor walked to join the red wizard. It was common knowledge that the grand wizards of the red and the blue were identical twin brothers, though their personalities were polar opposites.

"I happen to like it," Red replied. "It looks wizardly, unlike that bland hood of mystery you favor. Honestly, I think you enjoy everyone thinking you're ancient. We're only forty-two, but everyone thinks you're a hundred. Nice touch with the glowing blue eyes, by the way, made you look like some sort of specter, very unnerving.

"Why thank you, Red. That may be the nicest thing you've ever said to me."

"You're welcome, brother. Now, if we're finished here, I believe there's a pint with my name on it somewhere. Anyone care to join me, Excellency, brother?"

"I would love to, Red, but there is still much for me to do," Kor replied. "Have a good night gentlemen. Will you get the word out to your people tonight?"

"Already done," both wizards said, in unison.

Kor walked off to his office with the realization that the pair of wizards had contacted their subordinates and engaged in negotiations, without uttering a single word outside of their inane conversation about hats.

Chapter 23

Gurlachday, Day 13, Squash Moon, 8760 Sudean Calendar

The past week at Dhargul proved most enjoyable for Aleron. As being the Lord Protector's grandson, afforded him a large degree of freedom and respect, allowing him to see things not normally permitted for outsiders. Several days prior, guided by Faergas' sixteen-year-old youngest son Ierick, he saw the dynamo plant producing the energy used to light the city. Massive water wheels, moved at ponderously slow speeds. Connected through a series of belts and pulleys, the wheels spun disks bearing coils of copper wire at blinding velocities against other loadstone bearing disks. A low hum permeated the cavern housing the dynamos, overlaid by the sizzle of sparks, coming from copper brushes pressing against copper plates mounted to the spinning shafts. "What are those sparking things?" He asked Ierick. The youth was tall, for his people, and had the same dark looks as his father. Already broad of chest, he would grow to be a formidable dwarf in adulthood.

"We call those switches," Ierick replied. "When the power comes off the dynamo, it moves back and forth through the wires. The switches work to change it to moving in only one direction through the wires."

"Why do you need to do that?"

"We can use it that way, to light the lamps and such, but when we change it, we can store it for later." The young dwarf then showed him to a room filled with huge stoneware crocks, coated in tar, with tar coated copper wires leading out either side of the lids and connecting to heavy copper bars, suspended from the ceiling. He told Aleron that the crocks held lead plates and acid so powerful that it burns through clothing and skin. "These are the piles. We like to call them pickle crocks. We pump the power into these, and we can use it later, when we need more than we are making."

"What are those for?" Aleron asked pointing out the rapidly spinning blades, positioned in front of holes cut into the ceiling. They appeared to be moving under their own power.

"Ventilation fans," Ierick answered. "They run off the piles. If we don't have those, fumes build up in here and before you know what happened, the roof blows off the pile room." Ierick showed him many other things that day and those that followed, and they soon became fast friends. From huge blast furnaces, processing tons of molten metal, to jewel-smithing shops, producing the most intricate forms in bright metals and stones, Aleron observed things he never dreamed were possible. Dwarves do not use magic of their own, but they more than make up for it in sheer ingenuity. They even had a way to plate precious metals onto less valuable ones, for instance, making a bronze ornament look like gold or silver. *Someday men will have this knowledge and it will change the world,* Aleron thought, as he witnessed wonder after wonder in the underground city. So far, the dwarves had been tight-lipped about their precious "technology" with outsiders, but Aleron knew that it was only a matter of time before the scholars of men would discover the same things the dwarves had. His grandfather told him that, since the decline of sorcery among men, scholars had been devoting more time to the study of the mundane physical world and had made many new discoveries over the years. Aleron envisioned machines running under the power of the dynamo and pile, transforming agriculture and transportation in the years to come, as well as giant foundries established in the cities of men. It would be many years coming, but he was certain that it would be so, some day.

Now it was time for them to leave, if they were to make it over the high passes before the snow began to fly. Winter comes early to the mountains and smart travelers do not wait for it to set in before attempting to cross. Aleron and Hadaras were at the stables, loading the horses for their journey to Nhargul, the capital of the Northern Kingdom. "The next leg will take us at least six weeks," Hadaras said in answer to Aleron's inquiry. Daegle was helping them, as before, along with a younger dwarf named Fingal, whom he was training as a new stable hand. It's a rare dwarf who actually enjoys working with animals over mining and smithing. Fingal was a valuable find for the crusty old groom, and he was going to train him up right.

"Now make sure you get the blanket positioned properly lad, so the load doesn't chafe the poor animal's back," he informed the youngster. "We hass a toof time wit yur tall

harses, Gintulfulk," he told Hadaras and Aleron, "boot da laddy needs da sperience."

"*Quite all right,*" Hadaras assured the groom, in Dwarvish. "*We are in no major hurry and it's still early.*"

"*He's doing a great job too,*" Aleron added, his Dwarvish improving greatly over the week they spent at Dhargul.

Fingal grinned at that, saying, "*Thank you, Lords. I'm trying my best.*"

"*Couldn't have done it better myself,*" Daegle assured him. "*This lad will do just fine. He actually likes horses, which is uncommon as hen's teeth.*" Fingal grinned even broader at that and moved on to the next animal. "*Now I know you gentlefolk can take care of yourselves but take extra care in the high passes. Aside from the snow, there's still mountain trolls out there and they're thicker along the road, hoping to catch travelers at unawares. There's worse stuff out there than trolls too, so be on your guard.*"

"*We will be, my friend,*" Hadaras assured him. "*I've travelled these mountains before and seen what dark things they harbor. We will be on our guard.*"

It was then that the royal coach came clattering into view. As it pulled up to stop before them, the coach door opened and out hopped the Lord Chamberlain, who proceeded to announce, "*All bow and pay homage to His Majesty, high king of the Southern Kingdom of the Blue Mountain Dwarves, Faergas Goldhammer!*"

"*Oh, shovel off this steaming pile of dung, Ulrick! They know bloody well who I am, and they don't need to bow either.*" The king hopped lightly out of the coach, followed by Ierick. Fingal snickered at the exchange, which drew him a sharp glare from Daegle, whereupon his expression quickly sobered. Daegle bowed low anyway and his apprentice quickly followed suit. "*Rise, loyal subjects, rise. I said no bowing right now. Save it for when there's folks about Daegle.*"

"*Apologies for both of us, Majesty,*" Daegle replied, as he recovered.

"*Daegle here is one of the best horse grooms in the kingdom,*" Faergas exclaimed, "*I'll have him in the royal stables as soon as old Golan retires. How's the new lad coming along?*"

"*Fingal is doing just fine, Your Majesty,*" Daegle answered the king. "*He's the best I've had come through here in a long time, actually enjoys working with the animals.*"

Fingal beamed visibly at the praise from his master, before the king. "*Good to hear, that's a rare quality among us, I well know,*" Faergas stated. "*Carry on Daegle. I don't wish to hold you up from your duties. Get our friends' mounts saddled up right, so we can send them off on a good note.*"

"*Right away, Your Majesty.*" With that, Daegle and his helper resumed saddling and loading the horses.

"I hope the provisions will prove adequate for the next leg of your journey," The king directed at Hadaras.

"You have been most generous, Your Majesty," Hadaras replied. "I had every intention of purchasing what we needed for the road to Nhargul, but you have provisioned us beyond my intentions, thank you so very much."

"You know your money is no good here, old friend. You've done more to aid this kingdom than we could ever repay you. If not for you, that evil bitch would still rule through my body and the people would suffer." He went on in a lower voice, moving closer to Hadaras, "Now take good care of that lad. If that other thing we spoke of is true, then all of Aertu will depend on him in the end. Rest assured, if it comes down to that, he will have our pikes and axes at his disposal, as well as my hammer. He's a good lad. I can see the pure light shining in his eyes, but all that can change if he falls under the wrong influence."

"I will, my friend," Hadaras answered, barely above a whisper. "Thank you for the pledge; we may have to take you up on it, if what I suspect is true. Pray that it is still years in the future."

"Aye, that's for certain. I'll pray to the Allfather and all the gods for that."

Meanwhile, the youths were holding their own conversation. "I wonder what the old ones are scheming over there?" Ierick mused. "Looks like it's something serious. Usually, my father is loud as a cave bear."

"I think the king has some business for my grandfather to attend to in Nhargul," Aleron seemed to theorize, knowing full well they were likely talking about him. Ierick could not yet know who he was. "They did a lot of secret meeting, just the two of them, this week."

"Your Grandfather is some sort of halfblood wizard, right?"

"Yeah, something like that, I suppose. Why do you ask?"

"So, you would be something like one eighth elf; what does that make you?"

"Beardless for life, apparently and not much else," Aleron joked, knowing there was no truth in it. He was a terrible liar, and the current line of this conversation was making him a bit uncomfortable. He didn't enjoy having to be less than honest with his new friend. He began to worry again, about what he would tell his friends back home, when he returned. A few months ago, he was nobody special. Now he was a halfblood sorcerer and heir to a throne, vacant for a thousand years.

"Ha, that's a good one. I guess I was just hoping I could have a wizard friend, like my father," Ierick admitted, "but you'll do, I suppose," he continued, with a mischievous grin.

"Sorry to disappoint you, but who knows, maybe it will crop up some day."

"One can only hope," Ierick surmised and then he said, "It looks like you're ready to go. The old ones are finished talking and the horses are loaded. Fare thee well my friend. I hope to see you again someday."

"I'm sure we'll be back someday. Thank you for showing me around. This is an amazing city."

"Come along, my boy, we need to get moving now," Hadaras called out to him. "The sun is well above the horizon outside these caverns, and we need to put some miles behind us this day." Aleron hurried to join his guardian and mounted his horse, newly shod, as it turned out. Repeating goodbyes all around, they rode out of Dhargul with no additional fanfare, into the bright morning sunshine. The sun was a handbreadth above the mountains to the east, making it mid-morning, as they left the magnificent city of the dwarves, third oldest city in the world, behind. Snowcapped peaks, like a row of glittering white teeth, rose before them, to the north. Somewhere ahead lay the pass that would take them through the otherwise impassable range. The day still young, they rode on in high spirits.

✳✳✳

Baruk stood at the bow, if you could call it that, of the fastest long-range catamaran in the Thallasian fleet. Even traveling over sixty leagues a day, it would take them two months to reach the capital of Sudea. Dressed in more finery than he was used to, with the gaudy sword at his side, he felt out of place on this ship. *I'm a sailor, not a damned diplomat. What am I doing here, anyway?* Nevertheless, the wind did feel good in his face. He knew this mission was of utmost importance to his country. Thallasia could not be allowed to fall under the dominion of the Nameless God again. The elf who claimed to be his son had already swayed Kolixtlan and Adar, leaving Thallasia with no allies in the world. Elmenia was friendly, in general, but had no central government and couldn't be counted on as a true ally. Baruk's great-grandfather was Elmenian, in fact, banished from his clan for some wrongdoing and hopping on the first Thallasian trader that was hiring. Thallasia needed strong allies among the free peoples and Sudea was still the strongest of them all, despite its decline from the glory of ages past. The ship flew the white flag of truce, a universal symbol among the civilized peoples of Aertu and even some not so civilized. Baruk hoped that it would be enough to keep the Sudean navy from killing them outright, then scuttling the ship. This was a long-range scout, designed to outrun pursuit, not a warship. This mission, however, would not allow for them to turn and run at the first sign of trouble. *Please, Allfather, I pray to you now. Let me find success, for the sake of my people. I give you thanks and promise always and everywhere to serve you.* Never a very religious man, recent events caused Baruk to reassess his life and remember some of the covenants he had made with his god as a child.

His parents were simple tradespeople and strict adherents to the sole veneration of the Allfather. No graven images of other gods and goddesses were allowed in the home in which he was raised. It was not that they did not believe in the existence of the gods; they just knew who the creator of all things was, including the gods. He pulled the white raven pendant out from the neck of his tunic. It was a gift from his mother, when he entered the navy, so many years ago. He always wore it close and now he wondered if it had anything to do with his being spared in the attack that took his men. *Was it my resourcefulness, or was it you looking out for me, Allfather?* He would never know for sure, of course, but such is the nature of faith.

Chapter 24

Zorekday, Day 18, Harvest Moon, 8760 Sudean Calendar

The road crossing the spine of the Blue Mountains, is among the most heavily fortified routes on Aertu, due to the prevalence of trolls in the highlands. For that reason, the travelers spent their nights in the way stations closely spaced along the highway during the long excursion between the dwarvish capitals. After more than a month traveling, they found themselves at the gates to Nhargul, capital of the Northern Kingdom and the oldest city of dwarves on Aertu. Entry to the city was handled in much the same manner as at Dhargul, though with far less fanfare. Hadaras' name was known here but carried not the weight it did in the Southern Kingdom. They proceeded through the gate, passing stone blocks equal in size to those Aleron saw in the south and made their way to the stables to board their mounts.

After seeing to the horses, the pair headed to the boarding house Hadaras remembered as the best the city had to offer. The dwarvish inscription above the entrance translated to *"The Brown Bear's Repose"* and skillfully carved figures of bears curled in sleep graced the platforms to either side.

"This is where we will be staying for the next week," Hadaras stated, "unless the establishment has declined in the thirteen years since I last visited."

With saddlebags slung over their shoulders, they stepped into a grand foyer, the walls and ceilings decorated with intricate carvings and colorful stone inlays. To Aleron's untrained eye, the décor seemed equal to any he had seen in the royal palace at Dhargul. "Grandfather, are you sure this is a boarding house? It seems more like a palace."

131

"This has been the best Nhargul has to offer for centuries and as such, commands the highest prices and attracts the most foreign clientele," Hadaras explained. "They can afford to decorate like a king and their clients expect it. *Ho, Grimbel!*" he called to the white-maned dwarf manning the counter. *"It's good to see that you're still running this place."*

"Is that you, Hadaras?" the ancient dwarf inquired. *"My beard had a lot less gray in it the last time you paid a visit, but you look like you hardly aged a day in what must be a dozen years. Who is this young companion, son, grandson?"*

"Yes, my friend, it has indeed been a long time," Hadaras agreed. The last time he stayed was on his return journey from Immin Bul. *"This is my grandson, Aleron. Aleron, I would like you to meet Grimbel, the finest innkeeper in the Northern Kingdom. He has run this establishment nigh on one hundred and fifty years."*

"I'm pleased to meet you Sir," Aleron said. *"You certainly have a beautiful place."*

"Pleased to meet you as well, lad. I see old Hadaras taught you good manners and your Dwarvish is quite good."

"Thank you, Sir."

"We would like a room with two beds please," Hadaras requested, *"and please have two tubs brought in for bathing. It would be good to wash off the stink of the road."*

"No issues with the room," Grimbel answered, *"but the tubs are another thing. We've done a bit of a renovation since you were here last. The old copper tubs are gone. You can get a room with a tub built in and take turns, or you can get the room without a tub cheaper and use the common baths."*

"What might be your prices for such rooms?

"In Sudean coin, four silver a night for the tub, two and a half for the one without."

After a moment of internal deliberation, Hadaras replied, *"We will take the room with the tub. We'll be staying at least five nights, so here is one gold piece."* He opened his money pouch and laid the small gold coin on the counter, conserving the bulkier silver pieces for other purposes. They would visit the bank to change more gold over to silver before they left the city. *"Is dinner still included with the price of the room?"*

"Most certainly and in the morning, if you're early enough, there's likely to be some pastries left from the night prior, but you're on your own for the midday meal."

"Perfect, my friend, now, if someone could please show us our room, we'll make ourselves presentable before dinner."

As if on cue, a sharply dressed young porter appeared from a back room, gold buttons gleaming against his black waistcoat. *"Dalbek, please see these fine gentlemen to room fifteen,"* Grimbel instructed, handing the key to the porter.

"Of course, Sir," Dalbek replied. *"Gentlemen, may I take your bags?"*

"Thank you, but no need for that," Hadaras replied. *"Our load is light."*

132

"Very well, Sir, if it would please you to follow me…" The porter turned on his heel and led them down a corridor into the east wing of the building. As in the Southern Kingdom, all interior areas of the entirely subterranean city were lit with the glass orbs that somehow channeled the power of lightning to produce light and heat. Arriving at their room, he unlocked the heavy door of carved wood, opened it and held the key out to Hadaras. *"Your room, Gentlemen. I will wait here to assure it meets with your approval."*

Hadaras accepted the key and stepped in to inspect the room, setting down his saddlebags just inside. Aleron did the same as he followed his grandfather in. The room was well decorated, though not as lavishly as the foyer. Finely woven tapestries hung from the walls at intervals to mimic windows. Aleron checked the bath as Hadaras inspected the two large beds. The door was tightly fitted, and he realized why when the wave of humidity hit him headlong. The one-piece marble tub, luxuriously large for one, ran with steaming water, a tinge of sulfur in the air indicative of a hot spring source to the ever-replenishing flow. Yet another tightly fitted door revealed the privy.

Hadaras stole a quick glance into the bath area before returning to Dalbek. *"This room will do quite nicely, thank you."*

"Grandfather, do you mind if I check out the common baths?" Aleron inquired, before the porter had a chance to leave. "I think it might save us some time and I'm really hungry."

"That would be fine, Aleron, but please try to speak the local tongue where you are able. It's the polite thing to do," Hadaras admonished.

"Oh, that is quite all right," Dalbek reassured them. "I understand Sudean quite well."

"No, my grandfather is right, Dalbek. It was impolite of me to exclude you from the conversation, not knowing you could speak our language. For that, I apologize."

"No apology necessary, good Sir. It is our pleasure to serve you. I will stay to guide you to the bath house, if you so desire," the dwarf offered.

"Thank you, that would be wonderful," Aleron agreed. *"Please give me a moment to get my clothes."*

"Thank you for all your help, Dalbek," Hadaras said, pressing a full silver piece into the young dwarf's hand, while Aleron returned with a rolled bundle of clothing.

"Thank you, Sir!" he replied, followed by, *"Please follow me, Sir."*

Aleron found himself in an expansive chamber with vaulted ceilings. A large pool, big enough to swim in, filled the center of the room. He tested the water and found it not hot, but comfortably neutral, likely mountain stream water, tempered with hot spring water. Several smaller pools of steaming water lined the sides, each large enough for several occupants. Aleron took a towel from a stack near the door, set it and his clothing on a bench by the nearest hot pool and disrobed. Nearby, a shower flowed from a brass fixture projecting from the wall, next to a shelf full of fresh bar soap, allowing him to wash away the grime before settling into the clean hot bath.

Soon he lounged, submerged up to his neck in luxuriously hot water. He dunked his head for a few seconds, slicked his hair out of his face and then leaned back into the stone headrest, eyes closed. Shortly afterward, he opened his eyes at the sound of soft footsteps. A young woman of fifteen or sixteen stood before him, eying him quizzically. At the sight of her, he covered himself with his hands under the water, causing her to giggle.

"You Sudeans are ever so proper," she remarked, with only a trace of a Castian accent. She looked to be eastern Castian, her skin lighter and her hair dark brown and wavy, rather than black and straight like the western folk. That hair cascaded over her back, past her knees and her dark almond-shaped eyes sparkled with mirth. "I am Didia Aurelia," she introduced herself, "and who might you be?"

"I might be Aleron," he replied. Nearly forgetting himself, he began to stand to render a bow, but recovered in time, repositioning his hands to maintain decency. "Wait…you're one of the Castian royal family, aren't you? Please forgive me for my insolence, Your Grace."

"Ever so proper and always so formal," she continued, as she pulled her simple but delicately embroidered dress over her head, revealing that she was completely naked underneath. She gave it a quick fold before placing it on the same bench as Aleron's clothing, kicked off her slippers and proceeded to the shower. Aleron tried to look away, out of courtesy, but glimpses from the edge of his vision kept pulling his eye to her. She caught him peeking and laughed again. "It's fine if you want to watch, Aleron. I don't mind," she half taunted, before coming straight back to his pool and lowering herself into the steaming water. "Besides, it's rude to not look at someone when you're talking with them."

"Of course, Your Grace," he replied, turning to look straight into her eyes, though he couldn't help but see everything below her eyes.

"Please forego the formality," she implored him. "My friends call me Didi. Do you always go by Aleron?"

"No, most people call me Al, except for my grandfather. He always uses my full name."

Noticing he was still covering himself below the water, she commented, "You Sudeans don't really do public baths, do you?"

"Not really," Aleron replied. He readjusted by crossing his legs to free his hands.

"To what house do you belong?"

"I belong to no house," he answered, true enough, considering House Sudea was not yet reestablished.

"Oh, are you a merchant then?"

"No, we are just traveling. My grandfather thought it important for me to see some of the world."

"Interesting. Who is your grandfather, who is not a noble, nor a merchant, but can afford to travel in such manner? This is a very expensive inn."

"Well, I grew up thinking he was a retired soldier, but I just recently found out that he was Lord Marshal for a time. He left with a fairly hefty pension from that post."

"That might explain it," she replied, settling further down into the pool, "but I sense that there is more to you than all that. I have a very good sense of things like that, but I won't pry into your private affairs."

He noticed her toes lightly stroking his ankle after she sank deeper into the water. "I assure you that we have nothing to hide," he answered, as he began planning his escape. *I need to get back to the room soon,* he thought, but Didia seemed to have something else in mind, as her toes crept up Aleron's shin.

"I think you are lying to me Aleron," she replied with a mischievous grin, "but I'm sure I can get the truth out of you...eventually."

Abandoning any plans for a modest exit, Aleron levered himself out of the pool and onto the deck in one fluid motion. "I'm sorry, Your Grace, but I really must get back to my room. Grandfather is waiting on me for supper," he explained, heading directly for his towel for which he was forced to walk around to her side. "I really did enjoy meeting you."

"You as well. It's a shame you couldn't stay longer," Didia stated as she rose to exit the pool as well. She studied him with unveiled amusement while he attempted to dry off without exposing himself. "You say that you are common folk, Aleron, but you have the build of a fighter. Most commoners don't develop that sort of a build until sometime after they enter the military. You look like you've trained your entire life, just like a high-born son."

"Grandfather was the Lord Marshal, after all," he said, pulling on his breeches. "He always believed in training." He was buttoning his shirt, with the girl in front of languidly patting herself dry and doing nothing to conceal her body from him. *I've heard Castians are loose with modesty, but this is too much,* he thought before saying, "It was very nice meeting you Didi, but I do have to go."

She was only then reaching for her shift and replied, "It was nice meeting you as well, Aleron. I do so prefer your full name over just Al. Perhaps I will see you at supper?"

"Perhaps," he replied as he turned to leave, "but if not, I hope you have a wonderful evening."

Aleron returned to the room to find Hadaras dressed and buckling on his sword and dagger. "Are we going armed in the city Grandfather? We didn't do that in Dhargul."

"Yes Aleron, it is customary to be always armed in the north," his grandfather replied.

As it turns out, the Northern Kingdom of the Blue Mountain Dwarves is quite different in atmosphere from the Southern Kingdom. Due to the border shared with the Central Jungle and Kolixtlan, the northerners deal with near constant incursions of wild-men, half-trolls and hobgoblins from the jungle. They are the most militarized of the four dwarvish kingdoms, maintaining the largest standing army. All male dwarves train as warriors and any of the kingdoms are able to muster armies if needed, but professional soldiers are generally volunteers and rare. The Northern Kingdom, in contrast, requires a mandatory period of four years' military service from all able-bodied dwarves, beginning a week after their twentieth birthday. A large number of them choose to stay on longer, receiving a generous pension after forty or more years of service and often still young enough to go into business for themselves, dwarves often living over two hundred years.

"What took you so long getting back?" Hadaras inquired of his charge.

"I met someone, and it was hard to get away."

"Really," Hadaras replied, with a knowing glint in his eye, "and who was she?"

Aleron, knowing full well that his grandfather was on to him, replied, "Didia Aurelia, the Castian Princess."

"Ah, yes, second in line for the throne, after her older sister. I had heard that her father was taking her abroad to learn the business side of her family's dealings. How was she?"

"She was very nice," Aleron answered, blushing as he said it, "very casual, for a princess."

"Yes, the Castians do have a gift for the casual. Welcome that, as you will not find it so when we reach the elvish lands."

Eventually, they arrived at the dinner meal. Being served buffet style, the diners grabbed plates and served themselves. Soon after seating, they heard, "Hadaras! Please join me for a drink!" They looked over to the source of the invitation to see King Aurelius, ruler of Castia, waving to Hadaras to join him. Didia, her mother, and several courtiers were also in the group. Hadaras set down his plate and joined the Castians. Aurelius poured an amphora into several glasses and offering one to Hadaras said, "What brings you to Nhargul, you old rascal? I thought you long since retired."

"I have, but I needed for my grandson to see some of the world," he replied.

"Ah, yes, Didia mentioned meeting him in the baths, and that is a good thing for a grandfather to do. Mine did much the same for me, when I was a boy, after he handed the throne to my father. What of the parents, too busy to travel?"

"Passed away, I'm afraid. I've raised Aleron since the age of two."

"I am so sorry to hear that old friend," Aurelius replied with sincere empathy. "I lost two brothers and my parents, and I was inconsolable both times. I can only imagine what it must be like to lose a child. How old is the boy now?"

"He is fifteen years, by a couple months now. I know that he is tall and well spoken, but as yet, he is quite young."

"Yes, I would have taken him for at least sixteen. My daughter said that he claims to be common but has the build of a fighter. Knowing that you raised him explains that well enough." Then he leaned in and whispered to Hadaras, "But I must come to my point, Hadaras. I respect you and would gladly welcome your line into my family. My girl likes your grandson. What are his prospects for marriage?"

"As much as I would welcome such a match, Your Grace," Hadaras replied, "I believe the lad has already promised himself to the Steward of Sudea's daughter. I'm not certain of this and I am sure they have done nothing to consummate the agreement, but I have a strong suspicion that such is the case."

"That would explain his cold reception to my daughter's advances," the king surmised, chuckling softly. "Unfortunate as it may be, and as angry as she may be, I will explain the situation to her."

"Thank you, old friend. Life is becoming complicated these days."

"You know it's true," the king replied. "Had I only a single boy, amongst my wife and all my concubines, I would not be going through the trials I am today." The whispered exchange complete, they continued to trade pleasantries for a few moments until the king declared, "How rude of me to keep you here, while your supper grows cold. Go and eat, my friend. We can catch up over a glass of wine after the meal."

"Thank you, Your Grace. I will return with Aleron straightaway after we eat."

After Hadaras' departure Aurelius explained to Didia, "Dearest, the boy is promised to another. I am not saying you should not pursue, but the task may not be so easy." Lowering his voice, he continued, "This must not go further than this table, but I know for a fact that Hadaras is an elf, disguising himself as a man. That boy is at least a quarter-elf, if not a full halfblood and so his lineage is a moot point, but he is promised to the Sudean Steward's last daughter. He will be a difficult catch, but if you catch him, you will have a man worth the effort."

"Understood, Father," Didia replied.

✳✳✳

Once again, the sun rose on Zorekday and Aleron's week in Nhargul was over. He did not enjoy his stay in the north quite as much as when they visited Dhargul. Because of the dearth of friendly neighbors, northerners tend to be reserved with strangers. Aleron saw that although the architecture and the level of technical advancement seemed to be about the same between the north and south, the southerners appeared able to enjoy the fruits of their labor more fully than their northern cousins were. He liked a few things about the Northern Kingdom though. As they prepared to leave, he remarked to his grandfather, "Grandfather, I think I like the idea of compulsory service that they use here. I think I might use it when I'm king."

"Really and how would you propose going about with this plan?" Hadaras asked, continuing, "I think you may find the population of Sudea to be a bit large for any universal conscription to be feasible."

"Oh, I wasn't thinking about that for the common people, Grandfather. You're right; there are far too many people for that. I was thinking along the lines of what the Steward said that one time. He said that all noble sons should serve, and I believe he is right. Otherwise, what purpose do the nobility serve, if they do not serve the kingdom?"

"That, my boy, makes more sense," Hadaras agreed, "and I believe that would be a good thing for Sudea, that the nobles do not forget for what they exist."

The inimical nature of the locals aside, another stressor for Aleron was Didia's steady stream of advances. No matter where he went in the city, he managed to bump into her at least once over the course of the day, besides seeing her every night at supper. She would not be deterred, even after he explained to her that he was interested in another. He admitted to himself that he did like her and in other circumstances, he would not be so reticent, though his Sudean sensibilities were a bit affronted by such an aggressive pursuit by a woman. Had he really thought about it, he would have realized that Eilowyn was every bit as aggressive, but in a much more refined manner.

Finished with saddling and loading the horses, the pair led the animals out of the stables and to the city gate, just in time to see the portcullis rise, allowing the score of waiting travelers to exit into the wilderness beyond. It was a bell past the dawn, allowing the patrols time to sweep the immediate area prior to opening the gate.

Chapter 25

Sildaenday, Day 5, Falling Leaves Moon, 8760 Sudean Calendar

The journey to Wynn took the Aleron and Hadaras more than two months, traveling from high mountains, through dense interior jungles and finally idyllic coastal palm forests. They took the west road, running alongside the border with Sudea, over the more direct east road, which lay dangerously close to the Central Jungle border. There is little chance of running into hobgoblins, half trolls, or wild men in the western parts of the Elvish Colony, though goblins are as common there as anywhere else.

Rounding a corner, the riders came upon the wide covered wooden bridge spanning the Wytheryn River and spied the golden city beyond. Ornately carved timbers, seeming too thin to support any great weight, interlocked to form scissor trusses supporting a wide thatched roof three fathoms above the planked deck. The bridge formed four lanes, separated by railings, to accommodate inbound and outbound trade wagons as well as individual riders and foot traffic. A pair of guards, burnished armor gleaming in the late morning sun, stood either side of the two inner lanes, scanning the forest to the east. Each held a bow, with arrow nocked and wore a pair of short swords at their hips. Aleron noticed several small glyphs, glowing faintly blue, imbedded in the center post at the entrance. Looking to his left, he saw several large crocodiles sunning themselves on the riverbank, only twenty paces away.

The guards gave them a brief once-over as the pair dismounted and led their horses across the bridge, choosing the left of the two narrow inner lanes. They guarded the bridge to raise the alarm, in the event of attack from the forest, rather than to restrict access. The colony had border crossings, city and village gate guards to control entry. The thudding of shod hooves against thick oak planks accompanied the clink of their spurs as they crossed. A caravan of six massive trade wagons passed on the right, each pulled by a team of ten draft mules, causing the bridge to flex and creak underfoot. The elvish merchants, wagons likely loaded down with honey, the colonies' biggest export, made their way to Sudean or dwarvish trading posts at the border. They met several such caravans on the road from Nhargul.

Aleron welcomed the shade of the wide thatched roof. The late morning sun was already oppressively hot, this near to the equator and it was not yet time for the regular early afternoon deluge that made the rest of the day bearable. It's hard to believe that we're approaching Winter back home, with the Harvest Festival over a month past, he thought to himself. It's not even Autumn here; we're above the Equator, so it's Spring, not that that makes a difference here. He decided that he didn't much care for the tropics, with their consistently hot humid weather. Hadaras told him earlier that the northern tropics were just now moving into their rainy season, while places in the southern tropics, like Coptia, were moving into their dry season. Aleron thought the timing only too perfect, as he was weary of the daily oiling their tack and gear required in this climate. At least here on the coast, sea breezes moved the air about more than in the interior. The week they spent between descending from the mountains and reaching the coast road was the hottest Aleron ever felt in his life.

They remounted on the north side of the river, with about a thousand paces to go before reaching the city gates. The difference in the architecture immediately impressed Aleron. He had become used to the solid massiveness of dwarvish building. Otherwise, he knew only the somewhat boxy utilitarianism of Sudean building. Aside from the royal palace of Arundell, most Sudean buildings are low structures, seldom exceeding two stories. In Wynn, Aleron noted that soaring arches and tall spires were the norm. Elves build upward, rather than outward, leaving ample room between structures to allow for open space at ground level. Hadaras told him once, that the earliest elves lived in tree houses, and many still did, in the countryside. Whether constructed of stone, or wood, the structures of the capital city often rose to dizzying heights. Though not as solid as the underground cities of the dwarves, the elvish structures were breathtaking in their delicate aesthetics, often seeming to float on thin air, with elevated walkways connecting buildings at many levels. The elves constructed entire city from blond wood, hence the golden appearance, with little evidence of any paint at all to preserve it.

"How do they keep all the wood looking so new?" Aleron wondered.

"First, they coat everything in a mixture of wood spirits and either beeswax or pine gum," Hadaras answered. "Did you see the wards as we entered the bridge?"

"Yes Grandfather, I could see the power in them, but didn't have time to read them."

"Those are wards of preservation and protection. Some prevent the wood from decaying, while others deter dangerous animals, like those crocodiles, from venturing too close. Every elvish building receives similar warding; it greatly reduces the cost of upkeep."

The elves kept the area surrounding the city cleared of trees for about six furlongs from the city walls, primarily for agriculture, but also for visibility in the event of an attack. Orchards, vineyards, and gardens clustered against the city walls, while herds of cattle and sheep grazed the surrounding pastures. Aleron noted larger versions of the same wards he saw at the bridge lining the walls surrounding the city. As they drew nearer, it seemed to him that the whole city glowed with a faint blue aura, and he began to feel the power in the air. "I can feel it, Grandfather. The air is thick with power. It's as if the city itself were alive."

"Yes, Aleron, it would feel that way. Since the blue is the power of life, the concentration of it in the warding makes it feel as though there is much more life here than there is. That and the accumulators many elves build to store the power for later use contribute to the effect. Those are primarily employed by ones who manufacture wards in large volume. The sword you touched in Arundell has such an accumulator built into its hilt, albeit a small one."

"Is that to store power for use in battle?"

"Yes, it confers other advantages as well, but the primary application is to provide a storehouse of power in the event of a fight. It also works to power the warding on the weapon itself, making it practically indestructible, though the dwarvish forging methods I employed made Andhanimwhid nearly that way before I warded it."

"Dwarvish steel is that strong?" Aleron asked.

"The dwarves learned to smelt iron long before the Aelir came to teach it to men and elves," the old elf replied. "We were still chipping spear points from flint and obsidian when they forged the first steel. They shared with me secrets ancient to them but still unknown outside of the mountain kingdoms." He continued, "The blades we forged for the Great War were formulated to never rust, hold an edge through ridiculous levels of abuse, be unbreakable through any natural amount of force and all before we applied any warding."

"And now they have had another four thousand years since then," Aleron mused. "I wonder what they've come up with since then?"

"Considering that even then, they didn't share their recent developments, I would have to say quite a lot. You saw their armor and mail, but did you ever get the chance to hold or wear any of it?"

"No," the youngster replied, "why?"

"The metals look like silvered steel or bronze, but they weigh almost nothing and are impossibly strong. The fabric of their gambesons can't be cut with a knife and repel bodkins as if they were blunted arrows. I've never heard of a dwarvish sword or axe breaking; they rarely dull and when they do, you must bring them to the maker for sharpening." Hadaras concluded with, "I'm certain they have many developments they have yet to share with outsiders, just as when I studied under them."

As Hadaras finished his explanation of dwarvish technology, the pair found themselves at the gates to Wynn, capital city of the Elvish Colonies. Aleron noted the guards here wore much heavier armor than the archers at the bridge, wielding long bladed glaives, with armor piercing punch-bucklers adorning their off hands. Archers, equipped like those at the bridge, lined the upper battlements. One elf, appearing to outrank the others, positioned himself at the entrance to check the credentials of those entering.

"Good morn to you, gentlefolk," he greeted them in fluent Sudean, as they stopped and dismounted, "What might be your business in Wynn today?" He scrutinized them carefully as they appeared to be neither merchants nor scribes, the most common visitors to the city.

"We come simply to visit, for the sake of nostalgia, on my part," Hadaras answered. "My name is Hadaras, and this is my grandson Aleron," he said, gesturing to his companion. "I served here with the Sudean Army many moons ago."

"Hadaras, I do remember you," the officer stated. "You were the Lord Marshal protecting the Steward's son, Gealton. I am Patrilir. I was a young lieutenant when we served on the border."

"*Ah, yes, Patrilir, how is your father, Engletan?*" Hadaras inquired, in Elvish.

"*He is as well as can be expected, for one so old. He just passed his three thousand and fifty eighth year.*"

"*Perhaps we could visit him,*" Hadaras offered. "*I do miss his anecdotes.*"

It was not lost on Aleron that his grandfather was referring to an elf one third his own age, with the respect one reserved for the old and doddering. He realized something was amiss with his grandfather living to three times the normal lifespan of an elf, while still being spry to the point of outright youthfulness.

"I think he would enjoy that," Patrilir answered. *"His mind is still as sharp as his body is failing. You still look to be doing well. You must be quite old for a man if you don't mind me asking?"*

"Old enough to know better, I suppose. *Where does he reside?"* Hadaras replied, sidestepping the question.

"On 40 North and 57 West. He has a young maid looking after him, as Mother passed several years back, so you might have to brave a few pointed questions to see him."

"I suppose we could brave the gauntlet on that. I see traffic piling up behind us, so I guess we should be moving on. It is good to see you again."

"You as well," the officer replied.

Aleron and his grandfather led their mounts through the portcullis and into the city beyond.

"You are nearly three times the age of that elf's father," Aleron stated, when they were out of Patrilir's hearing. "How is that possible, Grandfather, if Engletan is doddering in his old age."

"I do not know, my grandson," Hadaras replied, with a wistful look. "I have outlived spouses, children and most of my children died natural deaths, unlike your mother. I suspect that the scheme of time has as yet unknown purposes for me, as long as the Adversary lives. I only try to do my best, in anticipation of what those purposes might be."

"And the prophesies about me?"

"I'm still unravelling those, to the point that I'm not yet fully convinced they involve you, but that may be my ultimate purpose, to see those prophecies fulfilled."

Aleron knew a strange misgiving at his pursuit of the current line of questioning. Somehow, he felt it was not proper to inquire about his grandfather's ancient origins. "Forgive me, Grandfather. I didn't mean to pry into your personal affairs."

"No apologies necessary, Aleron. My history is your history, and you deserve to know. If I myself knew, I would tell you."

✳✳✳

Meanwhile, thousands of leagues away, Jessamine thought along the same lines, My love has lived over nine-thousand rotations around this star, all the while showing only the slightest silvering of age. Silvering is only a sign of dominance among these people, associated with infirmity only at the twilight of their lives, but normally preceding it by decades. If he is indeed the offspring of Iselle, is he any less than one of the Aelient, progeny of paired Aelir, though his father was a mortal elf? She pondered this conundrum as she passed into what her people would call sleep. Unlike the sleep of mortals, hers was a reconnection to the primordial realm, where all are connected to the Allfather, save those who rebelled. She realized, as she drifted off, that Hadaras, though entitled, was somehow denied this privilege. She wondered why his lot was cast with the mortals, as it was.

✳✳✳

Aleron wondered aloud about the several men and women he saw among the elvish population. In fact, Hadaras chose to maintain his guise, in order to avoid questions regarding his non-elf grandson. He told Aleron that they were likely sorcerers. "So, most of the men and women I see here are sorcerers?" Aleron asked.

"Yes, Aleron, though many are simply scholars, interested in the accumulated knowledge of the elves. It is quite common for scholars and sorcerers alike, to study among the elves, at their numerous colleges and libraries."

"But I thought sorcery had pretty much died out, since the decline of the noble houses."

"It has, among the high houses, become no more frequent than it is among the common folk. However, there is some elvish ancestry in all men of the south, even into Coptia and Castia, so occasionally the traits line up in an individual and a sorcerer is born. Many of them end up here, due to the distrust of the general population towards them. Also, there are a few true halfbloods, like you and Cladus, roaming around." He added that, "There is a sorcerer's guild in Arundell, but it is small and highly secretive."

Shortly, they arrived at the inn. The Rough-Cut Emerald seemed of average accommodations and considering his grandfather's tendency towards the best of what a particular locale had to offer, Aleron had to wonder at the choice. "Grandfather, if you don't mind me asking, this seems a trifle more modest than what you normally settle for," after the porter led them to the small room, with two small beds.

"True, Grandson, but here, I try to keep as low a profile as possible. Some might make the connection with the Sudean Lord Marshal, but here, it's less than likely, considering how self-centered most elves are. What I am more concerned with are those who might connect the Lord Marshal to my true identity."

"So, you're less concerned with reports of a hero of men reaching the masses than reports of an ancient elf?"

"Exactly," the ancient elf replied.

Their accommodations were far from spartan, though not as luxurious as they were with the dwarves. No individual baths here, they were forced to use the public facilities, but other than that, they were well treated. After the baths, fortunately not very crowded at that hour, they returned to the room to finish dressing. "Where will we go first, Grandfather?", Aleron asked.

"First, we will visit my old friend Engletan,' he replied. "Then we will see another old friend of mine, Morguilis, with a rather odd specialty. Hopefully, you can learn a few things from him."

"Does he know anything that you don't?"

"He employs very different methods than I," Hadaras replied, "though we often arrive at the same ends. He calls himself a shaman, after the priests of the jungle. I think it important for you to see different techniques."

"Aren't the jungle folk evil?"

"Not entirely, just as the Kolixtlanis are not. No man is entirely evil, no matter how far he may seem to have descended, just as no man is entirely good. The jungle men have traditions rooted long before their coming under the sway of the Adversary."

✳✳✳

Engletan's nurse, Aelfwicca, was very young, for an elf, barely into her age of majority at forty-one, but she was extremely protective of her charge. *"And by what do you know him by?"* she inquired of Hadaras.

"I and his son, Patrilir, served together on the border, many years past. I met Patrilir at the crossing and he told me where to find his father."

"And who is this other one?" she asked, eying Aleron with bit of suspicion, and possibly a little interest.

"This is my grandson, Aleron," he replied. *"I am bringing him to meet my friends and acquaintances, so that he might carry on my business dealings in this area."*

"Is he part elf?" She inquired, sensing more to Aleron's nature than most.

So, this one is another empath, Hadaras thought. I shall have to teach the boy to shield without raising suspicion. *"I think not, though, I know not for certain,"* he replied. It is possible to shield one's mind entirely, expending little effort, as Hadaras normally did among men, to hide his presence from the odd sorcerer. Among elves, however, where every person you meet has some level of ability, the practice would only identify you as a sorcerer. In order to completely mask

146

his identity here, Hadaras projected the thought patterns of a normal man, while masking his true identity.

"It is nice to meet you Mistress Aelfwicca," Aleron extended to the vigilant woman. *"I do look forward to meeting Colonel Engletan. My grandfather says he is full of interesting stories."*

"He is certainly full of something, and it is nice meeting you as well, Aleron," she stated, finally cracking a smile. *"You both seem legitimate, so I do not see any reason you should not visit Engletan."* To Hadaras, she said, *"Your grandson speaks very good Elvish; you have taught him well. You may have a sorcerer on your hands with him. I have a sense about such things, and I am usually right about them."*

"It may be so," he replied. *"I certainly wouldn't know, but if that is the case, I may have to bring him back here to live, so that he might receive the proper training. Besides, sorcerers are not terribly popular in the lands of men these days."*

"It is a sad thing when a natural talent is eschewed by those who fail to possess it. Let us join the Colonel in his study now. This is the best time of day, as soon he will be down for a nap." She beckoned them to follow her as she left the foyer, moving toward the back of the house.

Aleron noticed that, unlike the bright wood exterior, the interior of the home was finished in fine white plaster, for the walls and polished white stone floors. *"Grandfather, I've never seen stone like what we are walking on. What is it?"*

"It's a type of limestone, Aleron," Hadaras answered. *"They quarry it near Aestryll, north, in the Iron Hills. The stone forms below the hot springs there."*

Aelfwicca smiled at Aleron and added, *"My father worked many years in those quarries. He told me that it was the only sensible source of stone in the colonies, being constantly replenished by the flow of spring water."*

"Yes," Hadaras agreed, *"There is little stone otherwise available here. Fortunately for the colonies, there also exist several significant deposits of metal ore in the Iron Hills as well. Otherwise, they would be forced to rely entirely on imports."*

They arrived at the study, finding Engletan thoroughly engaged in a book. He looked up to see the visitors accompanying his caretaker. "Hadaras?"

"Yes, old friend, it is me. How are you faring?"

"As well as can be expected, for one as old as I," the old elf replied, echoing the words spoken earlier by his son, as he carefully placed a bookmark and set down the text he was reading. He laboriously rose with the help of a walker framed from bamboo. He slowly walked to the group and held out his hand. *"It is so good to see you again. What has it been, twenty years?"*

"Twenty-two, I believe," Hadaras replied, grasping the proffered hand in greeting. He could have walked to where Engletan was sitting to save him the

effort, but Hadaras was wise enough to allow the old elf the opportunity to be a proper host, despite his advanced age and frailty.

Up to this point, Aleron had not the opportunity to meet many elves. With only his grandfather for reference, he was surprised to see one this old and frail. Hadaras had warned him that elves decline quite rapidly at the end. Though they commonly live up to fifty times the lifespan of men, their period of old age and decline is much the same length, if not shorter than that of men. He knew from this that Engletan was likely spry and active up until about ten years past.

"Ah, yes, twenty-two it was. I only retired from service twelve years ago. I got to enjoy a few years of that before this old body started to fail me."

"You look good," Hadaras reassured him. *"I would like for you to meet my grandson, Aleron. I'm attempting to show him a bit of the world before he goes off on his own."*

"Grandson, eh? I wasn't aware you were a family man, but I guess you must have been hiding a wife back in Sudea."

"Yes, he's the son of Audina, my only daughter and her husband Valgier. They both perished in a fire, so I've been raising the boy since the age of two." The fact was that Hadaras had a completely different elvish identity that he used when residing in the colonies and Audina had lived with him there, along with her mother Quiana, though both of them lived in Sudea for a time, under human guise as well.

"He looks to have some elf in him, if you were to ask me," Engletan surmised, much the same as Aelfwicca had.

"Well, I suppose that's possible; your Aelfwicca thought the same. He takes after his father's side, and they are from the border region. He's fifteen years now, so we should see in the next year whether anything manifests. If he turns out to be a sorcerer, we will likely move back here to keep him away from trouble back in Sudea."

"It's a shame," Engletan mused, *"to see how far old Sudea has fallen, from being ruled by halfblood sorcerers, to being suspicious of anyone with ability."*

"I fully agree, old friend. The current state of affairs is unfortunate. I, for one, always welcomed the assistance of a sorcerer wielding blue, though many did not."

Aleron wondered, after hearing so many negative statements about magic wielders in the lands of men. *What am I to do then, if the people I'm to rule over will not trust me for my very nature?*

Chapter 26

Sildaenday, Day 5, Falling Leaves Moon, 8760 Sudean Calendar

After several pounds of the massive bronze knocker, Morguilis answered the door. "Goromir? What brings you back to these parts?"

Aleron was surprised to see that Morguilis was a very swarthy complexed man, not a fair skinned elf. He was even darker than Aleron's friend Barathol. He looked to be southern Coptian, or maybe one of the desert men. His name sounded like it may be elvicised Castian. Even more surprising was his correct identification of his grandfather.

"Please don't utter that name here," Hadaras implored. "Don't you realize where we are?"

"Sorry… Hadaras. I'm on mezcalo right now, so I forget where I am in the physical plane. Please come in. I was just walking the dream plane before the knock brought me back." Mezcalo is a hallucinogenic cactus that grows in the Great Southeastern Desert and southern Coptia, far from the Elvish Colonies. Morguilis used it regularly, along with ayuska, a blend of local herbals used by the jungle shamans.

"If that's what works for you, far be it from me…" Hadaras left it hanging, as they stepped into the foyer, hinting at his opinion of those who rely on drugs to perform magic.

"Hey, I can't help not being an elf, or a halfblood. I do what works for me. So, what brings you here, you old bugger?"

"You either have ability, or not, Morguilis. The drugs are a crutch."

"Be that as it may, it's what works. I am convinced that the dream plane has nothing to do with magic. I do not wield any particular color to enter it, nor do I when I'm there. I just enter the trance state and I'm there. Also, I have uncovered evidence that the jungle men were using ayuska for the purpose long before your people arrived at these shores."

"Really, what evidence?"

"Someone found some sculptures in the jungle, obviously showing their shamans brewing ayuska. A local sorcerer dated them to over ten-thousand years. I believe this is humanity's unique ability, as magic is for your people."

"Interesting indeed," Hadaras admitted, "but to the point of our visit here. I wanted my grandson to meet you. Aleron, this is my old friend Morguilis. Morguilis, this is my grandson, Aleron, Audina's son."

"Pleased to meet you, Aleron," the sorcerer extended. "Being Audina's son would make him at least a halfblood, I presume," he directed at Hadaras.

"Yes, his father was a man, and he already shows some ability."

To Aleron, the peculiar man said, "Don't worry about me, young man. I'm more than loyal to your old grandpa here. It's just that some things about oneself can't be hidden on the dream plane."

"That is true, Aleron. Morguilis knows what he knows, because of his mastery of the dream plane. And he is a good friend."

"Yes, your grandfather helped me out of a terrible bind, a couple decades back. In the process, he revealed his true identity to our common enemy. The realization that he was facing the greatest sorcerer that ever lived was enough of a shock for him that we gained the upper hand and defeated him."

Aleron looked to his grandfather inquiringly.

"Morguilis and I were involved in a business dealing with someone who turned out to be a dark aelient. My disclosure stunned him to the point that we were able to subdue him. Aelient are not always particularly intelligent. Morguilis worked the dream plane, while I worked the physical plane, the dark aelient bouncing between the two."

"But isn't Jessie aelient?"

"Jessamine is extremely intelligent and intuitive as well, as are most light aelient. It always seemed to me that the dark aelient were stunted in some way. They often act as children would. I feel that even the Adversary is much the same. It seems as if, once these beings were cut from the Allfather's fold, they ceased to grow."

"I concur," Morguilis added. "Dark aelient seem particularly dim, but they are still quite powerful."

"On a completely different note," Hadaras said, "Aleron can work multiple colors, even white magic."

"What did you just say?" Morguilis inquired.

"I said that Aleron can work multiple colors…"

"No one but Aelient can work multiple colors!" the sorcerer retorted. "And white magic? I've heard only legends of that, from when the Aelir walked among us."

"Nonetheless," Hadaras continued, "the lad can work all the colors, with seemingly equal efficacy, which is not common even among the Aelient and I have seen him combine them all into white."

"Well then," Morguilis replied, his previous fog seeming to dissipate in an instant, as his nearly black eyes drilled Aleron, making the boy decidedly uncomfortable, "It appears that you are something never before seen. Except, perhaps that Sunjibi king from eons ago, the one that refused to rot after he was killed. There were rumors of his having unprecedented abilities and being fathered by one of the Aelir."

"That has come to my mind as well, but I know not where that thread may lead," Hadaras agreed.

"I can think of something. Perhaps regarding suspicions about the parentage of a certain elvish sorcerer who has lived far longer than he ever should."

Aleron looked questioningly to his grandfather.

"I still do not give that old rumor much credence," the old elf replied. "I do not believe that my mother was of the Aelir. I think I have lived this long due to unfinished business with the Adversary."

"What of her mysterious disappearance at about the same time that the Aelir left this world?"

"Be that as it may, neither I, nor any of my children ever displayed an ability to wield anything but the blue. Why would it skip two generations and crop up in my grandson? I believe there is something else at work, but I cannot see the Allfather's plan."

"Come to my sitting room and make yourselves comfortable," the odd sorcerer invited.

Aleron was still trying to reconcile the man's name with his appearance, as he led to the back of the dwelling. He spoke perfectly unaccented Sudean, so that was no help. Perhaps he was of mixed Coptian and Castian parentage, raised in Sudea?

"If you don't mind, I would like to reenter the dream plane to seek some answers," Morguilis offered. "It will be a trifle boring for you, I'm afraid," he directed to Aleron.

"I was hoping you would offer, old friend," Hadaras agreed. "You have access to places I do not, and the Aelient I'm acquainted with are particularly close-lipped on the subject."

"Sharin, I would appreciate your assistance again," Morguilis shouted.

Shortly thereafter, a pretty young elf maid of about fifty years old entered the sitting room from the kitchen. "Master, would you like me to beat the drum again, or get you more mezcalo?" she inquired. She turned to see Aleron and Hadaras and added, "Would your friends like some mezcalo as well?" She looked Aleron over with a critical eye and seemed to dismiss him in the next instant. Aleron was a bit taken aback by her obvious body language, as he was unused to such a reaction. However, she displayed a much more appreciative expression when she saw Hadaras.

"I will have to go with the ayuska this time, since my friends here have woken me from my mezcalo trance," Morguilis replied. "Would you be a dear and make me some?"

"As you wish," she replied. "You know I can't resist those brown puppy eyes of yours."

As she exited, Hadaras inquired, "Romantic, or strictly business?"

"Started out business, but as it turned out, she likes the more mature type."

From that admission, Aleron felt less affronted by her lack of interest. Fifty is the approximate equivalent for an elf of eighteen for a man, in the sense of physical maturity, though the life experience is that of a full adult, so she looked to be about his age, but she only had eyes for the elder two. *At least I didn't suddenly turn ugly,* he thought.

"You realize, of course, that she is just now entering her childbearing years," Hadaras implied.

"She's already expecting with my child," the odd mystic replied. "She will bear a true halfblood son. I have seen it in the dream plane. I know that this is not readily acceptable here, but I love her, and she loves me. We will be alright."

"As long as it's good with the Allfather, be damned with opinion," Hadaras replied. "I've had about as much as I can handle with elvish intolerance and I'm the oldest elf on the face of Aertu, as far as I know."

"We might need these halfbloods in the future," Aleron added, "If we are to bring Sudea into the present."

Hadaras looked sharply at his grandson, not yet even sixteen, while Morguilis also looked to the boy with a bit of astonishment.

"What? Did I say something wrong?"

"No," Hadaras replied, "but I think Andhanimwhid may have influenced your thinking."

"Did this boy draw the sword?" an astonished Morguilis exclaimed. "Is this the king of Sudea before me? What in the frozen pit of hell are you bringing to me, Hadaras?"

"Aleron is the rightful king of Sudea," Hadaras replied. "Audina purposely married the heir, who I tracked for many years, in order to bring about the prophesied outcome. He drew the sword, but we have not yet publicized the event."

"Who else know?"

"The Steward knows, and I believe that Aleron is essentially betrothed to his youngest daughter, if I am not mistaken in such matters."

"Yes," Aleron replied, as he reflected upon the kiss she gave him before he left. As forward and persuasive as the Castian princess was, her charms could not eclipse the love he felt for Gealton's daughter, the firebrand that she was. "Eilowyn will be my wife, if I have anything to say about the matter."

"You are a young man, but I sense in you a level of determination that I will not pretend to underestimate." Morguilis offered, "but please make sure that your betrothed is as enthusiastic as you."

"I am pretty sure that she expects no less from me," Aleron replied. "We want to be together, but the required courtship period needs to be maintained."

"Notwithstanding the fact that you are only fourteen and fifteen years old," Hadaras added.

"Yes, no need to rush," Morguilis agreed. "You have many years ahead of you, possibly centuries."

The last comment again reminded Aleron of the prospect of outliving Eilowyn by hundreds of years.

Hadaras noticed the boy's expression darken and sensing what was on his mind added, "No need to worry about any of that now, lad. You are both barely into your youths."

"Yes, have a seat and put aside your cares awhile. I wish to see you from the dream plane, and it will help if your mind is relatively clear. You as well, Hadaras," Morguilis added. "When Sharin beats the drum, the two of you just relax and follow the rhythm. That will allow me to find you more easily."

Sharin returned bearing a mug of liquid that exuded a somewhat fetid scent. "Here you are Love," she said, handing Morguilis the mug where he sat cross-legged on a woven mat.

"Thank you Dearest," he replied, taking the mug, draining it in one pull and handing it back to the young elf.

She placed the mug on a side table, picked up a small drum, settled onto a small stool and began a slow rhythm, drumming at around the speed of a heartbeat. Morguilis closed his eyes and slowed his breathing, while the two visitors lounged on cushions in the dimly lit sitting room. Hadaras settled into the well-practiced trance that passed as sleep for him, while Aleron quickly relaxed to a dozing state with the cloying beat of the drum.

The hypnotic drumming helped Aleron to put his cares aside. *They are right. Why am I worried about something thirty or forty years in the future? Is Morguilis glowing?* He thought he could see a soft white glow coming from the shaman's form but lost the impression as he drifted off to sleep.

After a half bell had passed, Sharin rapped the drum seven times in rapid succession, to call Morguilis back, much as the door knock had earlier done. The shaman and Hadaras both opened their eyes slowly, but Aleron remained asleep on the cushion.

"Please come with me," Morguilis said softly to Hadaras, as he stood. "Sharin, please leave the shades, let the boy sleep and keep an eye on him. If he wakes, do not let him follow us." He motioned Hadaras to follow and made his way to the study at the other end of the dwelling.

"Why the secrecy, old friend?" the elf asked, as the man closed the study door behind them.

"That boy is something new, beyond being just a halfblood."

"How so? I realize he has some unprecedented abilities, but he is still only my daughter's son."

"I sense something more in him than just man and elf, the same as I sensed in you, but even more pronounced in him and different at the same time. His seems a conflict of light and dark, unlike in you. Maybe it's due to his half human ancestry, but I do not believe that. He has Aelir or Aelient ancestry, just as you do, whether or not you choose to admit it, but his is not entirely of the same source. I sense a bit of the Adversary in him, though overall, his heart is pure. Just something to consider."

"I cannot see how that could be," Hadaras stated, not willing to consider the substance underlying either of Morguilis' claims. "I have followed his father's line for a thousand years. They were just men, normal men, of no special ability."

"Yes, but what of all the matrilineal input over those thousand years? Did you follow all of those lines?"

"No, but it only makes sense that one of them would have shown ability of some sort, had any of them been half Aelient, as you propose."

"And Audina's mother?"

"Quiana's ancestry is well documented, as are most elves'. I don't see where the input could have occurred."

"Well, there is something in there," the shaman maintained, "a couple of somethings, if I am any judge."

✳✳✳

That evening, upon their return to the inn, they settled at a table in the common room for supper, assisted by a smartly dressed young elf. His attire appeared more typical of Sudea, than of elvish lands, but Aleron could see that most of the clientele were foreigners, men, and dwarves, so that made sense.

"We have spit-roasted boar with baked yam and mixed greens tonight," he declared in heavily accented Sudean, as they sat, "and of course, bread and honey."

"That sounds wonderful," Hadaras replied, choosing to not display his fluency in Elvish. "Please bring us two full orders and a pitcher of weak mead."

Aleron's stomach growled upon him smelling the aforementioned offering. Morguilis fed them a small mid-day meal of bread and honeycomb, but that was many hours past and the teenager was famished.

Shortly, the waiter returned with their order, another waiter in tow with the mead.

As Aleron dug into his meal with relish, Hadaras stated, "We shall stay for months, perhaps taking a trip to Aestryll, in the north, celebrate the Yule and New Year here, before returning home."

"That sounds good," the boy replied, after forcing down a mouthful.

The old elf regarded the boy thoughtfully, pondering on Morguilis' earlier revelation, before attacking his own meal.

Chapter 27

Corballday, Day 15, Sowing Moon, 8761 Sudean Calendar

After nearly a year on the road, Aleron and Hadaras once again found themselves in the familiar countryside of home, the cottage and farmyard visible in the distance. It was a warm spring and many farmers had already finished their planting, the rich black soil just beginning to show the green tinge of new growth. Several were out with hoes, dealing with the pernicious weeds sprouting among the crops. Those close by, waved when they recognized the pair. Bright green fields of hay and winter wheat were interspersed among the black patches of newly planted crops, creating a checkerboard effect, while sheep, goats and cattle grazed on the fresh new growth of the pastures. For Aleron, the familiar sights and smells placed his mind at ease, to a degree he had not experienced in ages. "It feels good to be home, Grandfather."

"Yes, it does, my boy; yes, it does," Hadaras agreed. "I just spoke to Jessamine, so she will be expecting us. I hope you're in the mood for brisket."

"I'm in the mood for anything other than dried beef and bannock, Grandfather," the young man replied. "I do miss Jessie's cooking." In the year they were away, Aleron had grown to over six feet tall and filled out as well. His moustache was thicker, but still no trace of a beard. Hadaras told him that it was unlikely that he would ever grow a full beard. Halfbloods, especially first-generation offspring, nearly always lacked facial hair to some extent, some even totally lacking, like elves. Hadaras sometimes wondered why halfblood children seemed to mature slightly faster than those of purely human stock, but never arrived at an answer.

Several casks of the strongly honey-scented liquor elves distill from mead burdened their long-suffering pack horse. The scent from the casks reminded Aleron of their time in Wynn. As a people, the elves seemed strange, yet familiar. He had, after all, been raised by an elf who was expert at impersonating men. Not surprisingly, Aleron found them to be serious and studious, compared to most men. All elves are literate, regardless of their social standing and abject poverty is unknown among them.

At one point, during their stay in the colonies Aleron asked, "Could the Halfblood Caste be reestablished from these human sorcerers?" He was beginning to formulate a plan for the future.

"Unfortunately, no," his grandfather answered. "Now that the elvish blood is so diluted, it does not consistently breed true. I have seen before, two sorcerers wed, but none of their children have the slightest inkling of ability. On the other hand, I've also seen powerful sorcerers born to completely mundane parents. Ability crops up very unpredictably. Even the Halfblood Caste of old occasionally produced some with no ability and they were actually more than half elvish. Now, I suppose you could breed for the trait, always pairing those with ability and discarding those without. Eventually you would reinforce the desired traits, just as we do in cattle and dogs."

"That doesn't sound right at all," Aleron observed.

"No Aleron, breeding men like cattle would be an atrocious assault to freedom, making us no better than the Adversary. He did as much before the Great War, enslaving elf maids and breeding them to his sorcerers to build his own halfblood caste. He did worse to the females of other races, breeding them to his trolls and goblins. One thing that many don't realize is that the Nameless One had no intention to destroy the free peoples, just enslave them. He would take away our free will for our own well-being, relieving us of the heavy burden of choice."

"It was just a thought."

"Just not a good one," Hadaras concluded. "The Halfblood Caste is a thing of the past, and only happened because there were enough of them to form a viable ruling class and exclude all others. There were quite a few moral quandaries surrounding that choice to begin with, but the Sudeans arrived at the system on their own. Both the mundane population and the halfbloods agreed to the arrangement and any were free to marry outside the caste, as long as they were willing to give up their titles." He went on to say, "When we elves returned to Sudea, we saw no reason to try to change the system, since the people arrived at it through the exercise of their own free will, even though we did not agree with the caste system ourselves."

"Didn't my mother intend to reestablish the Halfblood Caste through me, Grandfather?"

"Yes, my boy, that was her intent," he conceded, "but it was a misguided sentiment on her part. It takes more than one person to found a population, so where are all the other halfbloods to come from? Then, would you divest the noble families of their legacy and supplant them with these new halfbloods? Or would you force them all to marry elves? Where then would all these willing elves come from? It was never very feasible to begin with, plus she did not live in those times, to see the impingement on free will that the system entailed."

"I understand, Grandfather. I want to be able to marry who I want, and I wish the same for any children I may have too."

"Good," Hadaras replied, with a gentle smile. "I'm glad you are able to see the view from the mountain, rather than the bottom of the valley," puzzling Aleron with the metaphor. The boy would have to think about that one.

Aleron found the elves to be most charming and courteous, if a little stiff and aloof. He got the feeling that many of them believed themselves to be above him. He surprised more than a few with his intelligence and quick wit. Overall, they had an enjoyable stay, but when it was time to leave, Aleron was more than ready to move on. He could tell that his grandfather was tiring of the snobbery of his own people. Hadaras lived in the colonies for most of the last fifty-five hundred years, sometimes in the guise of a man, but mostly as an elf, under different names at different times. In every instance that he returned after living among men or dwarves, there was a period of adjustment to the strict social mores of his people. He liked it less each time he experienced it.

One intriguing piece of news came to them while at Wynn: Due to their ability to communicate over long distances, the elves receive news from their envoys around the world, far quicker than could ever be achieved through overland travel. Reports from around Aertu told of Thallasian envoys arriving at all the capitals of the east and south. So far, the elves and westmen seemed to have been left out, but it was likely that they would receive ambassadors as well, soon enough. The Thallasian diplomats, the one at Arundell especially, told of fresh entreaties by representatives of the Nameless God. It seemed that the Thallasians were not receptive to their advances and chose to seek allies elsewhere. It was dark and foreboding news, but good all the same to find that not all of the Adversary's former allies were pleased at the prospect of his return. Other reports, however, indicated that Kolixtlan and Adar were thoroughly in the Nameless One's pocket, with sacrifices and veneration to him on an upward trend. The most distressing part of the news was that these emissaries for the Nameless God were elves, wielding red magic. This news created quite a stir among the people of the colonies. Hadaras wondered how the Adversary managed to communicate with his followers, though he always believed that the god would someday find a way through the bindings that held him.

As they rode into the familiar yard, the old mare came trotting up to greet her long-lost companions and much snorting and nickering ensued. Jessamine stood at the doorway to the cottage, next to the rose bush Aleron remembered so well. It was definitely good to be home. "Hello strangers," she greeted as they approached. "Are you hungry? I have dinner nearly finished, if you are ready for it."

"We certainly are," Hadaras replied, dismounting lightly and bounding to her for an embrace, which she readily accepted, along with the long kiss that followed.

For Aleron, though he was now aware that their relationship was more than platonic, the sight of it made him slightly uncomfortable. "I'll take care of the horses," he volunteered, eager to be away from the couple.

After dinner and with the afternoon ahead, the mid-day meal being the largest for most Sudeans, Aleron asked, "Do you mind if I go out to find Geldun and Barathol?"

"That would be fine," Hadaras replied. "I know you have missed your friends, so go ahead."

Aleron set off down the path toward Geldun's farm, about five furlongs away. Nearing the farm, he spied his friend walking along the far edge of a field, a hoe upon his shoulder. "Geldun!" he shouted, waving, "I'm back!"

Geldun started, looked to the source of the noise, and returned a wave. "Welcome back! See you at the barn!" He then took off running and Aleron followed suit. They arrived at the barn together and, after catching his breath, Geldun said, "About time you showed up. We could have used your help planting this year."

"Looks to me like I am right on time."

"Whatever. Did you get swivin taller?" That's not even fair." To be fair, Geldun had also grown about a palm in height while his friend was away, about the same as Aleron, but that still put the halfblood nearly a span taller. "Your birthday is in a couple moons, isn't it?"

"Sure is…Are you lads ready to sign up then?"

"Well," Geldun hemmed, "Barry and I were talking about that, and we wouldn't feel right about leaving before the harvest."

"Umm…I wasn't planning to wait that long…"

"But what is it to you, really? Barry and I have responsibilities that you don't."

"I don't know...I guess that I can wait until you guys are ready. I've just been looking forward to it for so long. But you're right, it wouldn't be fair to your families to leave before harvest."

"Enough about that, how was your trip?"

"It was good. I met a girl in Arundell."

"A girl, you?" How did that go?"

"Well, I think we're engaged now..."

"Corball's Balls!" Geldun exclaimed, "Engaged!"

"Geldun!" the boy's mother screamed out the kitchen window.

"Sorry, Ma! Aleron just surprised me with some news!"

"You know how I feel about that sailor's language!"

"Won't happen again, Ma!" he yelled back, followed by a whispered, "Engaged? How in the frozen pit of Hell did you become engaged?"

"I don't know," Aleron replied. "We met at the palace, and we just hit it off. She kissed me before I left."

"At the palace? Just who did you meet at the palace?"

"Eilowyn, the Steward's daughter..."

"Cor...ugh...I mean, the Steward's daughter? How did you manage that?"

"It turns out that, years ago, Grandfather used to be the Lord Marshal. He and the Steward are old friends. They served together in the Army." Aleron purposely left out a few of the finer details.

"Well, that explains a few things that we could never put together. Your Grandpa always seemed a little too well to do for a simple veteran, but swivin hell, you're already engaged. You never had so much as a girlfriend."

"How about you? What have you been up to the past year?"

"Well, had a few girlfriends, but nothing that stuck. I think they were all scared off by the thought of me joining the military. Most girls around here can't imagine anything past Swaincott."

"Yeah, I guess that would be a problem," Aleron agreed. "Not an issue with Eilowyn. She expects as much. Every man in that family serves in the military. How about Barry?"

"You know the deal with him. All the girls are scared he might break them, if you get my meaning. He's just too big. Menlo's widow Gretchen is the only one who's shown interest, and she scares Barry."

"She is a burly gal and Menlo was a bruiser. Isn't he the only guy in town to ever best Barry in a fistfight?"

"I think so, but it really wasn't a fight. They were both laughing the whole time."

"They were both falling drunk, as I remember. Menlo got a broken nose before he knocked Barry out."

"Yeah, it's a shame what happened to him. Now Gretchen has their little boy and has to hire out a blacksmith to run their shop. Never heard of a forge bellows exploding like that."

"Grandfather said that it must have been a stuck valve and it sucked up the coal fumes. He was a good man. I miss him."

"The biggest guy in town and he never bullied us, like the others," Geldun agreed.

"More often than not, he fought off the others to save us. It's kind of too bad. Barry and Gretchen would be a good match."

"But she's older than him, by a few years. That scares him more than the fact that she might be able to take him. Plus, he doesn't want to settle down here just yet."

"I can see him coming back in a few years to settle down, maybe with a foreign wife. Same thing for you."

"And you?" Geldun inquired. You'll end up in Arundell, won't you?"

"Yeah… I don't think that I'll be able to move Eilowyn to Swaincott," he replied, with a chuckle. "Let's go find Barry!"

"All right, I have an idea of where he might be; they should be planting the front field today. Just let me put this away," the young man said, as he hung the hoe on a pair of hooks, just inside an attached lean-to. "Ma! Me and Al are going to find Barry!"

"Check with your little brothers to see if they're finished with the milking first!" she answered.

"All right Ma!" he answered. "Let me check in the barn first, and then we'll go."

Just as Geldun predicted, Barathol was finishing with smoothing the last rows of corn with his younger brother, Canwel, who was shaping up to be as large as his elder sibling, though not quite as dark of complexion.

"Barry!" Aleron yelled. "I'm back! Want to go to the pub?"

"Welcome home!" he yelled back in answer. "Let me check with my da first! He and our brothers are milking! Meet me at the barn!"

"See you there!" Aleron replied.

Of his brother he asked, "Do you mind finishing these last rows? I haven't seen Al in almost a year."

Canwel affected a pondering expression and, after a few heartbeats, replied, "I suppose I could do that for you, just this one time. Hi Al!" he called out to Aleron. "It's good to see you're back!"

"Hi Can, good to see you as well!"

"We can't cut across the field," Geldun commented, as Barathol headed home, "so we'll have to run to catch up with him."

"All right Gel," Aleron answered. "See you later Can!" He set off on a lope alongside his friend toward the distant farmyard.

"So...the Steward's daughter...engaged..." Barathol tried to digest what Aleron just told him, at the pub, over a pint if bitter. "Gurlach's hammer!" he exclaimed, causing a few patrons to glance over.

"Simmer down Barry," Lulu admonished him from across the room. "The other customers don't need to hear you cussing."

"Sorry Lulu," he answered and then turned back to his friends. "How on Aertu did you manage to land the Steward's daughter? Is she allowed to marry a commoner at all?"

"Well, apparently Grandfather's status as Lord Marshal elevated he and his family to the status of minor nobility, so it is legal for us to marry," Aleron answered. He was not lying to his friends, just not telling the whole truth, that he was more than minor nobility. Hadaras had coached him on what he could and should reveal to the people back home upon his return.

"Are we all still set to join up after the harvest?" Aleron asked, changing the subject.

"Yeah," Barathol answered, "My da is good with it, since my brothers are big enough to help out now."

"Same for me," Geldun added. "My da can do without me after the harvest."

"Good, then it's settled," Aleron replied. "Lulu, another round please."

Chapter 28

Corballday, Day 3, Storm Moon, 8761 Sudean Calendar

"Are you ready for this?" Geldun asked the other two.

They stood on the street before the Sudean military recruiting office in Ball Harbor, adjacent to the city of Ellesfort, and just over three leagues from Swaincott. The office was a plain, single-story building of the common local architecture, with tan plastered rammed earth walls and a steeply pitched slate roof, with wide overhangs, to protect the walls from the seasonal ocean squalls.

"I'm ready," Barathol replied.

Aleron hesitated.

"Are you good with this, Al?" Geldun inquired.

"Yes, I'm good with this," he replied. "I was just thinking." He was thinking about his life up to that point. He knew that after this point it would never be the same. He had visited Eilowyn that summer past and had seen the life of the court, firsthand.

"About what?" Barathol asked. "Are you sure you're good with this?"

"Yeah, just thinking about how everything is changing. Our summers of fishing in between chores is over. We'll be in the military, and I'll be marrying Ellie in a few years…"

"You know," Geldun interjected, "from what I've heard, if we go in the Marines, we're more likely to stay together. They tend to keep training groups together, where the Army and Navy split them up."

"Is that true?" Barathol asked. "If it is, that would be the clincher." They were leaning toward the Marines already but were willing to hear the other services out, before they made their decision.

"Grandfather, I have a question for you," Aleron asked in in mind. He and Hadaras were purposely maintaining contact through this event, so that he could covertly lend advice to the boys. He relayed the question at hand. *"Grandfather*

told me as much." Aleron offered, after he received an affirmation. "He said that, because of their smaller size, they usually keep basic training classes together as companies, with the instructors as leadership. They usually only separate the folks who can't get along with the others."

"Well, that settles it, doesn't it?" Barathol asked.

"It does for me," Geldun replied.

They walked into the building and straight to the Marine recruiter's office, not even glancing at the other two doors open to the lobby. It was situated between the Army and Navy offices, seemingly for those who had trouble making up their minds between the other two. In truth, the larger services commanded the spacious corner offices, due to their increased traffic, relegating the Marines to the narrow middle office.

Aleron led the way across the red tiled floor and into the office. "We would like to enlist, Sir," he announced.

"Good enough," the grizzled Master Sergeant replied. "Why the Marines? You know, we don't take just anyone. If the other two rejected you, we don't want you either."

'You are our first choice, Sir," Aleron replied, a bit taken aback by the response. "We thought it would be the best of both worlds and we've heard you're the best fighters."

"That's the answer I was looking for, or at least one of the answers." He peered at them a little closer. Their light summer tunics did nothing to hide their muscular physiques. "You boys look like you can already fight, by your builds, especially you, young man," he said to Aleron. "Not your average farm boys, by the looks. What are your names?" he inquired, picking up one of the new dwarvish fountain pens and a paper ledger.

"I am Aleron, son of Valgier," Aleron replied.

"Geldun, son of Hobart."

"Barathol, son of Danel."

"Well, two of you sound like local names," the recruiter remarked, "But you…must be old Hadaras' grandson…" he directed to Aleron. "We've been expecting you. You're a highborn, so you'll be going to the Officer's Corps."

The trio were visibly shaken by the revelation, glancing nervously to each other.

"I'd rather not, Sir," Aleron interjected, trepidation apparent in his voice. "See, we three are in this together. We'd rather not be separated. Is there any way you could leave that bit out?"

"It's your choice," he replied. "It's rare for a noble to choose the enlisted ranks, but not unheard of. It will be a note in your file," he continued, as he scribbled on the ledger. He set down the tablet and continued, "I fought alongside your grandpa once, before he was Lord Marshal and there're damn few of us left, after all these years. He was the best I've ever seen, both as a fighter and as a man. If he trained you boys, Corball help your benighted instructors."

"Thank you, Sir," Aleron said, relieved that he wouldn't have to part with his friends so soon.

"You will need to get out of the habit of calling everyone 'Sir'. That's for officers and civilians. You'll call me Master Sergeant from now on. The next transport leaves here in four days. Can you boys make it here with your stuff by then? Mind you, don't bring much, just a couple changes of clothes and something nice, in case you get a pass to go into the city. If you don't own anything nice, you'll have a chance to visit the seamstress, after you get your first pay. Don't bring a lot of money with you though. That just causes trouble early on."

"Thank you, Master Sergeant. We will be here first thing Gurlachday," Aleron replied.

"Good, but don't come here. Go straight to the docks and find me there. Now, I have some papers for you all to sign. Can you all read, or do I need to read them to you?"

It is a good decision, Hadaras thought, considering Aleron's choice after the brief discussion that took place in their minds. Though he himself served in the Army, that was because the Steward's son Gealton, now the Steward, served there. Gealton was an only child and Hadaras saw need at that time to protect that lineage, for the greater good of Sudea. A war of succession would likely have occurred, had the old Steward died heirless.

The Sudean Marines would provide the most well-rounded military training for Aleron, exposing him to both ground and naval tactics and going the enlisted route would give him an understanding of the lower echelons of the military services. The boy may be destined to rule, but a good ruler must understand the lowest levels of his domain. His upbringing gave him an understanding of the common folk, given he grew up as one of them. Hadaras could only hope that Aleron, with his lack of social experience, would adapt to the higher levels of society. Worried for his lack of experience in courtly life and intrigue, he hoped that the Steward's daughter would help him in that lane. She grew up in the court and would be a valuable resource for a young king, inexperienced in politics.

***

Eilowyn looked out an upper window of the Steward's section of the palace, across the Arun River, toward Swaincott. Today was the day Aleron would be signing up, according to his last letter. *Father said it would not do for me to meet him at the docks when his ship arrives in nine days, much as I would like to. It would just serve to embarrass him, Father said. But he ought to have someone there to greet him….* She would be there when the ship came in, even if Aleron had no idea she was watching. She did what she wanted to do, often to her father's chagrin, but he always forgave her in the end. *I won't do anything to embarrass him, but I will see him. He is the king, whether or not he wants to admit it, and I am his consort.* His visit this past summer, after his trip with his grandfather, allayed her fears of his finding someone more to his liking. From his words then, even the elf maids he encountered were no comparison to her. This thought warmed her heart as she contemplated her next move.

I hope that she is there when I arrive, Aleron thought, upon leaving the recruiting office. Though his thoughts then reflected on the potential for embarrassment, should she call him out from his peers. *I don't care,* he decided. *Let her call me out. I'll put anyone who chooses to make fun in their place,* he decided.

It was a good thing that Hadaras and Jessamine had raised Aleron to be the person that he was, countering his hot-headed nature. Though he might be naturally inclined to confrontation, they had taught him to measure his responses to adverse situations, bringing the likelihood of him coming to blows as low as possible. However, the young man was quite capable of coming to a decision with the barest of input and responding with extreme prejudice, as his actions against the goblins attributed.

I will greet her cordially, should she choose to meet me, he thought, *and if anyone has a problem with that…*

Chapter 29

Gurlachday, Day 7, Storm Moon, 8761 Sudean Calendar

"You boys take care of yourselves," Hadaras told the three young men, as they exited his carriage at the Ball Harbor docks, there to catch their ship to the marine training camp. Geldun and Barathol said their goodbyes earlier that day at their farms before he and Aleron picked them up. Hadaras had the nicest riding cart of the three families, and he did not need to return home as early as the farmers would have. "Here is a little something to help you in the first weeks," he said, handing them each a silver piece. "I know Master Sergeant Dulore probably told you not to bring much, and he was correct, but this much shouldn't get you into too much trouble."

"Thank you, Sir!" Geldun and Barathol said in unison, while Aleron said, "Thank you Grandfather."

"I think I see Dulore down on the dock," Hadaras continued. "Best to not keep him waiting." He stood by and waited for them to shoulder their bags and accompanied them to the dock, where the Marine recruiter stood waiting.

The Master Sergeant stood next to the gangplank of a smallish but fast looking caravel, moored there overnight. Sailors on deck and in the rigging busily prepared the ship to disembark. Aleron could see all the topside woodwork meticulously maintained and oiled. It sported the banner of the Sudean kingdom, a four-pointed gold star on a field of deep blue, as well as that of the Sudean Navy, a silver nautilus on a field of aquamarine.

"Ho, Lord Marshal Hadaras!" Dulore hailed. "I see you brought the lads right promptly. You only had one arrive before you," he continued, marking them off from his checklist. "Just waiting on two more, and the crew can move on to the next port."

"They were more than eager to arrive," Hadaras replied. "Aleron was badgering me hours before sunup to get on way."

"I figured as much," The Master Sergeant noted. "Never seen a more decisive group of recruits in all my time as a recruiter. Most of 'em hem and haw at what they want, 'cause they've got no idea. These boys walked in and told me exactly what they wanted."

"They have been looking forward to this for years," Hadaras explained. "Since they were young boys, they have wanted to serve."

Aleron and his friends beamed at the praise from the two older men.

"You boys head up the gangplank and see Corporal Langton. He will get you to your billets."

"Yes, Master Sergeant," Geldun replied, beating the other two, their mouths just opening, and snapping shut again. "Let's get our things stowed," he continued.

The trio hoisted their bags and headed up the gangplank of the waiting ship.

"So, just how good are these lads, if you don't mind me asking, old friend," Dulore inquired.

"I've been training Aleron since he was eight," Hadaras answered. "Soon enough, I realized that he was showing his little friends what I taught him at home, and I let it go on."

"Figured it couldn't hurt, eh?" the Master Sergeant asked with a chuckle.

"Yes, I had an inkling, even back then, that the boys would end up serving the realm in some capacity, so it wouldn't hurt for Aleron to show them a few tricks. For the past five moons, I've been training them as a group, and they work quite well together."

"That's good. If they work well together from the get-go, they'll be more likely to stay together," the old marine commented. "We see it more often with the officers, nobles trained together from childhood and all, but not unheard of with the enlisted, especially from military families. You know, I told your boy he should go to the officer corps, but he refused."

"I could have told you as much," Hadaras replied. "Those boys have been inseparable for half their young lives. He would never leave them behind."

"Maybe, for now...I caught wind of a rumor...He and the Steward's daughter?"

"That is true."

"I know you were elevated to the nobility when you were chosen for Lord Marshal, but isn't House Arundell a little high?"

"Maybe so, but there is no rule barring the lowest house from marrying into the highest. It's just not how the political levering usually works. Gealton and I have been friends for a very long time now, but neither of us were actively seeking this union. Aleron and Eilowyn just hit it off as soon as they met."

"Still, that political levering you mentioned, how did you manage it?"

"Oh, I believe that more than a few houses will be disappointed with the news and Gealton may lose some supporters, but those would be the fair-weather friends anyhow and he would lose most of those when she singled out a suitor. I think he was relieved to give her hand to someone whose house wanted nothing from him. He has already forged the alliances most important to him with the older girls." Hadaras was not being entirely truthful, as it was quite unlikely that the Steward would have approved of the union if Aleron's lineage had not come to light.

"Still surprising though."

"Yes, surprising, but I think his youngest daughter quite often gets what she wants."

"I've heard that rumor too," Dulore replied with a laugh. "Well, that looks like my last couple of recruits heading down now. It was nice catching up with you. Been a lot of years since we served on the border. Please don't be a stranger the next time you come to town."

"I will certainly stop by, but as you know, I don't come down very often. Maybe you could stop up for dinner on your next free day?" he offered. "Jessamine would love to have some company."

"Oh, that pretty niece of yours? How have you not managed to marry that one off? I bet half the lads in the county be lining up at your door."

"That could happen, now that the boy is off on his own. She came to help me take care of him, after his parents died. She's not blood to me, but to my wife and will likely go back to the north now, to be with her family."

"So sad for the boys round here. I have the first Gurlachday of next month off, if that works for you?"

"We'll be expecting you. Midday or evening?"

"Midday would be best," the recruiter answered. "I'm generally up early and early to bed, even on my off days."

"Midday it is. We'll see you then," Hadaras agreed.

Aleron, Geldun and Barathol made their way below decks as the corporal directed.

"This looks like as good a spot as any," Aleron proclaimed, tossing his bags on one of the open racks. There were several open in the same area.

"That one is taken," came a voice from the against the central bulkhead.

Another recruit lounged in a rack on that wall. He looked to be older than the three, perhaps nineteen or twenty.

"I don't see anybody's things there," Geldun stated.

"Don't care, still taken. Move down."

Apparently, the other had not noticed Barathol, who surged forward to grab the recruit by the collar and pull him from his rack, slamming him to the deck before twisting his grip to choke the other. "We will put our gear where we want you swivin fool." The other's eyes bulged at the pressure to his throat. "I think you need to change your attitude."

"Barry don't kill him," Geldun urged. "We don't need that right now."

"I have no intention of killing this fool," Barathol replied. "I know how to choke someone out. He'll be fine," he continued, as he grabbed the unconscious man by his collar and belt and threw him back onto his rack. "Let's settle our things before any other fools show up."

The boys did as he suggested and began stowing their belongings in the berths provided next to their racks, securing the doors to prevent anything falling out when the boat moved. As they did, two more young men came below with their bags.

"Where's Ban? ", one of them inquired as they entered. "He said he would save us a berth."

Chapter 30

Gurlachday, Day 13, Storm Moon, 8761 Sudean Calendar

Two sailors leapt to the dock, and swiftly turned to catch the mooring lines tossed to them from their comrades on the deck of the ship. It was early afternoon, as they tied off the recruit transport to the navy station docks at Arundell's harbor.

Two other sailors lowered the gangplank and the new recruits, twelve in all, filed off the boat and onto the docks. The boat and its crew had picked up six more recruits after the stop in Ball Harbor. They lined up in a single rank, baggage in-hand, as the corporal had instructed them, and looked around with curiosity at the bustle of activity surrounding them.

Ban and his companions, Halbet and Schill, avoided meeting the eyes the trio from Swaincott, particularly Barathol. A couple of additional altercations on their short voyage had taught them better than to court any more trouble. They wondered how Aleron could possibly be such a light sleeper as to preclude them from ever getting the drop on he and his friends. They had no idea that the halfblood needed no actual sleep, having learned the resting vigilance trance from Hadaras.

Aleron saw Eilowyn in the distance, with her bodyguards Hans and Simeon, as well as two others Aleron did not recognize. He met her eyes and smiled briefly, but otherwise made no moves to greet her. She, likewise, smiled but said nothing.

Corporal Langton stepped up and addressed the recruits: "Listen up! We are about to move to the training barracks. There, you will drop your bags and move on to the clinic, where the medical officer will examine you. After that, you will return to the barracks, empty your bags for inspection, and stow what we allow you to keep in the lockers we assign you. From there, we will proceed to the issue warehouse, where you will receive your training uniforms and kit. We will march on my order. Please attempt to stay in step."

The corporal squarely faced the makeshift squad, centered himself and called, "Right, face!" Several recruits sloppily obliged, shuffling their feet to turn roughly ninety degrees to the right of where they had been facing. Several others looked confused for a moment, before following suit. One faced left, finding himself nose-to-nose with another, before turning about, red-faced. "That was pretty ugly, but you will get better," Langton assured them, before calling, "Forward, march!" as he stepped off to the left and began calling out as he marched, "Left! Left! Left, right! On your left! Your left! Left, right!" The raw recruits stumbled along for a few paces, stepping on each other's heels, before achieving a rudimentary semblance of marching in-time, as he called out the commands.

Once they were moving relatively smoothly, the corporal announced: "We will be turning right on up ahead. I will call out all commands on my left foot. When I call out 'column right, march,' the front man will immediately step off to the right, with his right foot; the second man will take one more step, to arrive at the first man's position, before doing the same; the third will take two steps, and so on." He called out the command, and the squad, more or less, did as he instructed, though it was not pretty. Aleron and his friends had received some rudimentary marching instruction from Hadaras, but it was never a priority, so they fared only slightly better than their new companions.

Eilowyn beamed with pride as she watched her betrothed march off. She looked about to see her bodyguards, along with several sailors, grinning at the sight of the recruits and their sloppy marching. "What?" she asked.

Simeon answered, "Just funny to watch, Milady, and brings back lots of old memories. We were all that clumsy once."

"Not to worry," Hans added, "Your beau can already fight. The marching is just to teach order and discipline. He'll figure it out." Hans, Simeon, and others of her retinue had sparred with Aleron on his past visit to the capital city were all impressed with his ability.

"Well, no use loitering here any longer," she observed. "Let us return home now." She turned to leave, and her retainers formed a square formation, with her at the center. *Should I have said something to him?* She wondered as she left, but *No,* she thought. *His smile was enough, for now.*

THE HALFBLOOD KING

Later that morning, the recruits lined up, in pairs, in front of their "berths", upper and lower bunks built into the wall of the barracks to mimic those of an actual ship, with twin lockers below the bottom bunk for their belongings, those being somewhat lighter than what they arrived with. Their instructors confiscated weapons, alcohol, money over a couple silver pieces, and anything not considered proper or necessary. Essentially, the cadre allowed them a change of civilian clothing and some small mementos. Anything confiscated was inventoried and stored for return upon graduation, with a voucher issued to the recruit in question. Aleron could keep the braided ring of fiery red hair Eilowyn gifted him on his last visit, though the sergeant smirked as he handed it back.

They stood at attention in their new (to them) uniforms consisting of low slip-on boots, with wide legged canvas trousers tucked into the boots, and loose tunics, belted at the waist, all designed for easy escape, if the marine found themselves overboard at sea. The quartermaster informed them that they would learn how to tie off the legs and inflate the trousers for flotation in such an event.

"Now, you boys need to keep track of those vouchers you just packed away until graduation, or you wash out of training, whichever comes first," Sergeant Illian, their instructor advised. "If not, you'll have a chance to bid on it in the post-session auction, held the day after your graduation.

You will be here for three months, in which time, we will teach you all the basic skills you will need to function as a Sudean marine. That is, if you make it through the training." He paused for effect. "Only six of ten marines make it through the training, unlike the army and navy, which pass nine of ten." He paused again. "If you fail, you will be given the option of attempting army or navy basic training, provided we did not break you too badly, but you will not have the opportunity to repeat marine basic training. We will pick up a few more recruits over the next week, to round the group out to twenty for training. If by some chance we have more than a dozen of you left at the end, I will pick the top twelve as my squad, and we will be together for the next two years. By that time, some of you will have picked up some rank and will move on to other duties.

By the time you finish here, you should be somewhat proficient in your assigned weapon form, and at least familiar enough with the others to avoid maiming yourselves and those around you. Does anyone here have any prior weapons training? Raise your hand if you do."

Aleron, Geldun and Barathol raised their hands, along with Ban and Sethel, one of the recruits they picked up after Ball Harbor.

"What training?" he asked, pointing to Sethel.

"Quarterstaff, Sergeant," Sethel answered. "My da was in the army and he taught me."

Ban answered the same, when the sergeant pointed to him.

At Aleron's turn, he answered, "Most all of them I think, Sergeant: staff, spear, single sword, sword and shield, spear, spear and shield, glaive, greatsword, and axe…Oh, axe and shield, two-sword and knife."

Sergeant Illian just blinked for a few heartbeats and then asked, "What's your name, recruit?"

"Aleron, Sergeant."

Illian looked to his list for a moment and then said, "Oh, you're the high marshal's kid. Why did you go enlisted?"

"I wanted to stay with my friends, Sergeant. We went into this together."

"And I assume, these two jokers with their hands up are your friends?"

"Yes, Sergeant." Aleron knew, from several sources, that brevity was his friend in this situation.

"How many years have you trained?"

"Eight, Sergeant."

"Zorek's Spear! What have I gotten myself into? Never mind. How about you?" he asked, pointing to Geldun.

"I've tried them all, Sergeant, but just in the past year or so," he replied. "We've been doing the hand-to-hand stuff since we were wee lads, but Hadaras only started us on the weapons last season. I prefer the sword and shield."

"Alright," Illian acknowledged. "How about you?" he asked Barathol.

"Same as Geldun, Sergeant, but I like glaive. I seem to stay alive longer with that one."

The sergeant looked at Barathol and Geldun, assessing their builds, and replied, "Looks like a good fit for both of you, but we'll see over the next couple of months." He turned back to Aleron. "What form do you prefer?"

"Sergeant, I like two-sword the best, especially with them on sword and shield and glaive."

"Why"

"Well, Sergeant…That was the only setup we used that could beat my grandfather more often than not."

Sergeant Illian looked taken aback, but Aleron would not have dreamed to comment.

"You fought as a unit against him…alone?"

"Yes, Sergeant. Three-on-one is about fair with my grandfather. I never once beat him one-on-one, and he still beat us more often than not, with any other setup than sword and shield, glaive, and two-sword. I think that the extra blade factored in."

"Oh, Corball's Balls," Illian muttered. "Alright then, we'll sort out what you all know this coming Sildaenday, after the rest of the squad settles in. Until then, keep out of trouble. I'll be by to check up on you several time a day, and there will be work details. Once training begins, I will be on you like stink on shit. I have no family to distract me, so consider me your full-time companion. I will have to rely on you in combat, after this is over, so if I don't think you'll cut it in combat, I'll cut you, beforehand. See you this evening for supper chow formation. Until then…Dismissed!" Sergeant Illian turned and walked out of the barracks.

"What now?" Barathol asked.

"Hang out and polish our brass?" suggested Sethel.

"Sounds good," Ban concurred, and several others murmured agreement.

Chapter 31

Sildaenday, Day 17, Storm Moon, 8761 Sudean Calendar

Twenty one marine recruits made up the initial number of their squad. They all knew that, with luck, only twelve would remain at the end of three months. Most of them didn't really think about the alternatives.

At best, more than twelve would make it through training, and those not chosen to remain with the squad would move on to another squad that needed them. They might survive training with less than twelve and take on cast offs from other groups. In the worst-case scenario, they could lose twelve or more of their number and be dissolved, those remaining split up to fill vacancies in other squads. That would likely mean the separation of Aleron from his companions.

Aleron vowed to do whatever he could to help his group to succeed, even Ban and his group, if it meant that he could stay with his friends.

"You may have noticed the armor and weapons hung along the wall," Sergeant Illian stated, as they stood in two ranks in the practice yard. "You will pick a gambeson, breastplate and helmet that fits you. Corporals Halbert and Bors will assist you."

The corporals were as alike as they were different. Both men were short and stocky, muscular and not at all fat. However, Halbert was clean shaven, with black hair, blue eyes and skin even darker than Barathol's, while Bors blond, pale skinned, with brown eyes and a full beard. Both were a stark contrast to Illian, who was taller than Aleron, with brown hair and green eyes. The two men helped the recruits into their gear with few words spoken. They did not appear to be talkative types.

"Everyone grab a shield and practice sword," Illian instructed. "Find a partner and face off against one another. The leftover will face off against me."

Aleron hung back intentionally, waiting for the others to partner up. Barathol gave him a knowing look as he faced off against Geldun.

"Looks like it's you and me, lordling," Illian said, as he came over to face Aleron. He was a hand taller than Aleron and a good share heavier. He feinted a blow to Aleron's sword arm and immediately reversed to a strike to his shield side leg.

Aleron easily blocked and the shot and returned a series of blows that came in so fast that only an elf could have possibly followed them. The sergeant barely blocked the combination, more from his extreme level of training than from any conscious ability to see the shots coming in. As Aleron pinned the sergeant's sword against his shield, he leaned in and said, "I will carry these men to success, if it is the last thing I do."

"Understood," Illian hissed back. "We are after the same thing, so let's work together."

From there, Aleron dialed back his attacks, so as to not overwhelm Illian. It would not gain him any advantage to embarrass the man and gain his enmity.

As the morning progressed, they trained with spear, spear and shield, and spear in conjunction with sword and shield. Geldun, Barathol and Aleron consistently outperformed the other recruits throughout the various sessions. After the final break before the midday meal, Illian announced, "You three from Swaincott, let's see what old Hadaras taught you. Pick out your preferred weapons. The rest of you, alternate spear with sword and shield."

Aleron wielded two of the practice swords, while Barathol took a short spear, in leu of his preferred glaive. Geldun held his usual left-handed sword and shield form. They formed up with Barathol to Geldun's left rear and Aleron to his right rear. They faced the rest of the squad, nine each spear paired with sword and shield, with the squad's other two left-handers on the right flank.

"We need to take this carefully," Aleron told his companions. "We don't have any experience fighting large groups. The lefties on that right flank need to go. If we try to take them in the center, they will wrap around us, and if we try for the left, each shield we take out will be replaced, and they will have time to flank us. But, if we take out that shield on the right flank, and his spearman, they will be open on the sword arms, and we can work down the line."

The plan worked as expected. Though a veteran unit would likely have quickly dispatched the trio, with their lack of experience fighting groups, the friends from Swaincott had far more experience than this line of raw recruits. It took a few seconds to take out the first shield on the right flank. They spun left, as the line attempted to curve around to flank them, but once they took out the left-handed combatants, they tore through the line like a hound devouring links of sausage.

Subsequent rounds of fighting brought the rest of the squad around, and eventually, they were able to thwart the trio, but with great losses to their own.

"You Swaincott boys fight pretty good," Ban said to Barathol and the others, as they doffed their armor.

"Thanks, you lads didn't do too badly yourselves," he replied.

"Why did the sergeant call you 'lordling'," Ban asked Aleron.

"Well...My grandfather was the last lord marshal," he hesitantly answered. "They offered to put me in the officer's corps."

"But you wanted to stay with these clowns," Ban finished for him. "I can respect that."

Geldun and Barathol nodded, grinning slightly.

"I think we got off on the wrong foot back there on the boat," Ban suggested, "and I think we could have been friends if I wasn't acting a swivin ass that day." Schill and Halbet nodded alongside.

"I'm willing to let bygones be what they are," Aleron said. "How about you lads?"

"I never scrapped with anyone that I d'nt laugh over a pint about it with him later," Barathol replied.

"Sometimes beforehand," Geldun added, laughing.

"Settled then!" Aleron stated. "Allies from here on out?"

"Allies it is!" Ban agreed, with a grin.

After they finished wiping down and stowing their practice gear, Sergeant Illian proclaimed, "When we get back to the billets, you'll all wash off your goat smellin' arses in the practice pool. If you can't swim yet, you better learn quick!" The practice pool was five fathoms deep, with seawater pumped through at a stiff current, so excellent swimming was a must. He continued, "Three laps, and I'll consider you clean. You all worked hard today, so...There's a two-pint limit for you all at the chow hall. Don't make me regret it. Now form up!" he commanded.

They marched back with a quick step, all looking forward to their promised reward.

A few had difficulties with the current in the practice pool, though, thankfully, none of them were non-swimmers. The stronger swimmers helped them through their trials. Fortunately, Ban and Halbet were rescue swimmers, who normally helped with shipwrecks, and could help tow the weakest swimmers.

Aleron was impressed by the pair. He was a strong swimmer, but three times fore and back, towing a weaker swimmer, was far more than he thought he might be able to bring to the table.

As they quaffed their allotted pints with their dinner, Schill asked the Swaincott group, "Can you lads teach us the stuff the lord marshal taught you?" He and his friends looked to Aleron, expectantly, along with Sethel, who overheard the question.

"I think we could come up with something," he replied. "I think the sergeant and I have come to an understanding. I don't think he'll let me lead much during regular practice, so we'll need to ask about extra practice in our off time."

"Think you could teach us to swim like you lads," Geldun directed to Ban and Halbet.

"We could, if we can get the same deal from Illian."

They enjoyed their brief repast before Illian and the corporals arrived to move them out to the barracks. "Lordling!" Illian called. "Bring your skinny arse over here!"

"Yes Sergeant," Aleron replied as he hurried over.

"You and your buddies got some good stuff there, but you wouldn't last a minute against a battle experienced squad."

"I understand that Sergeant. We never had the opportunity back home to fight groups."

"I realize that, but I think you got somethin' to contribute." His rural accent came out more strongly in private conversation. "It's very rare we get anyone enlisted who has a noble's trainin', and your trainin' came from the Lord Marshal. I spoke to the Colonel while you lads was eatin' and drinkin'. He's seen your grandpa in action, said he was the best he's ever seen, before or since. If he trained ya, you could likely take out anyone in the army or marines, one-on-one, but ya don't know nothin' about melee fightin'."

"True," Aleron replied.

"I want you to take over training during our sessions, but I will direct you on group tactics." His country accent disappeared.

"That sounds good. I do need pointers on group fighting."

Chapter 32

Zorekday, Day 18, Allfather's Moon, 8762 Sudean Calendar

Graduation day had arrived. Out of twenty-one recruits, eighteen made it through training, an unheard-of success rate. Unfortunately, Sethel was not among their number, having dislocated his shoulder in the rigging two weeks earlier. Illian fought to keep all those who passed, but his superiors forced him to let go of four. These four kept to themselves a bit, as they had to be ready to join their new units before the ceremony, but there was still an element of joviality in their demeanors; they made it through the toughest training in the Sudean military, even if they were not staying with the squad.

Eilowyn sat in the VIP section of the stands, flanked by the school commandant, Colonel Viller, and the Marine and Navy commanders, General Corbak and Admiral Halger. Her bodyguards stood off to one side at attention, hands on sword hilts. They waited while the training battalions formed up. The 580 graduates made up three battalions of four companies, with four platoons, having four squads each.

As the commandant stood to address the graduates, Corbak leaned in and murmured, "Ellie, your beau is Hadaras' grandson, I believe?"

"Yes General," she answered formally, in case anyone was paying attention, though she had known the general most of her life. "Did you know Hadaras?"

"Oh, I knew him well enough, all right. He's an interesting one, for sure. After an extended pause, he leaned back in and asked, "do you know who he really is?"

"The Lord Marshal?" she asked innocently. "My father told me that when I first met Aleron."

"Yes, the Lord Marshal," he said knowingly.

Eilowyn was pensive for a moment. *How many people know who Hadaras really is?* She knew he was Goromir, from the old stories, and had reconciled that Aleron was not only heir to the throne of Sudea, but also directly connected to the rulers of Elvenholm. Despite his familiarity to her she wondered, *is this man a friend, or a possible threat?*

"Your father, Hadaras, and I all served on the jungle border, they in the Army, me as a marine envoy," he continued. The 'Lord Marshal' is one of my dearest friends, though he's been distant these last sixteen years or so. I may know a few things about him…"

Can I trust this man? She wondered again. This man was one of her father's closest friends, since before she was born. She made a decision. "My father had no idea until two summers ago. How do you know?"

"I guessed years ago, after I witnessed some things that were not possible. He swore me to secrecy, even to your father. Goromir," he whispered the name, barely audible, "knows that I know. If he raised your boyfriend, I would bet that he's worthy to be your husband. I will keep an eye on him for you if you would like."

"I hesitate to say yes," she replied, "but I would like that. Please be discrete."

"Of course, Milady. I will not get him any special privileges, just keep an eye on him, let you know how he is doing. I'm sure he is capable of staying out of trouble."

"Thank you," she replied, reassured that she may have an ally.

"If you don't mind me asking," still whispering, "is he a full halfblood, or only a quarter elf?"

"Yes," she whispered back. "His mother was Hadaras' full-elf daughter. His father was a woodsman up in the North Borderlands."

"Not unheard of," the general replied. "I'm privy to rumors that his martial ability is quite extraordinary. Elvish blood would explain some of that, Hadaras' training, the rest."

Halger eventually noticed their conspiratorial whispering, looked over at them, and Corbak broke off the conversation, with a quick grin to the admiral, his immediate superior. Halger was relatively new to his post, while Corbak had long been in Gealton's inner circle, so his familiarity with the steward's family was understandable. The admiral smiled back, and they all turned their attention back to the commandant's speech.

"…and as you embark on this most glorious journey, keep close your roots. You are the best Sudea has to offer," the commandant concluded.

"You're proud of him," Jessamine commented. "I can see it in your face."

"Yes, indeed I am," Hadaras replied, beaming.

They had seats in the VIP section as well, but much farther back than Eilowyn.

"I don't pretend to understand humans' preoccupation with ceremony, but this is an impressive display."

"Well, pride is an alien concept for you and yours, and that is not a bad thing."

✳✳✳

That evening, Aleron spent with Eilowyn at the palace, guest of the steward. Geldun and Barathol were out with Ban, Halbet, Schill and a few others from the squad. Aleron felt a bit of regret for not being with his friends this night, but he'd not spent time with Eilowyn in months, and priorities being what they were…

Eilowyn clung tightly to him, his right arm draped over her shoulder, and noticed that, unbelievably, he was even more muscular than before. His back was so broad that her arms barely reached around his chest, as they stood, listening to her father.

"This is quite the achievement, my lad!" Gealton exclaimed, "but I had no doubt you would succeed."

"Thank you, Milord," Aleron replied. He did not need to refer to the steward thusly, but that fact was not common knowledge.

Eilowyn's mother, Vetina commented. "You've gotten bigger, lad, since we last saw you. I take it there is no danger that we are starving the recruits?"

"No, Milady. They fed us quite well. We all got stronger with all the training, and we climb rigging like monkeys now."

"The Lord Marshal!" the lead servant announced, as Hadaras and Jessamine entered. Hadaras wore his usual visage, while Jessamine wore that of a young woman in her mid-twenties, the one with which Aleron was most familiar.

"Grandfather! Jesse!" Aleron exclaimed, seeing them.

"Aleron, my boy!" Hadaras exclaimed, striding over to embrace his grandson.

Jessamine followed with a hug as well. "Good to see you, cousin."

'Good to see you too Jesse." He well knew who and what she really was, but he did grow up with her as his elder cousin, so it felt natural.

"Some refreshments please," Gealton directed to the waitstaff. They had only a few staff in attendance, this being an intimate gathering.

Eilowyn's older sister Majori and her husband, Anderly, lord of House Bertome, as well as Hameln, her younger brother were the only others in attendance. Majori did not care for her sister's choice of a near-commoner for her mate, and Anderly was mostly indifferent to Aleron, likely believing his sister-in-law would get over this girlish crush in due time.

Gealton, and Hadaras had concocted a fiction, to explain away why the Steward's youngest daughter was to be engaged to a lowly marine private. The outward story was that Aleron, being of a minor noble house, had yet to accrue the necessary capital to purchase a commission. It was frequent practice for the sons of petty nobles to enlist in the ranks and save up to buy a commission. Many said that, indeed, they made better officers than their more well-to-do counterparts who directly purchased their commissions.

Hameln, on the other hand was enamored with Aleron, the thirteen-year-old trailing the young marine like a puppy.

Aleron wore his new marine dress uniform with red jacket, his private's rank pinned to the jacket collar, black trousers, a white belt and baldric supporting his cutlass and dagger in black scabbards with silver fittings. The other men and boy wore casual noble's clothing of dark jackets and trousers, with light dueling swords belted to their hips. The women wore light formal gowns, not as extravagant as full ball gowns, but dressier than everyday wear. Eilowyn wore green, as was her wont, and Aleron was pleased. Once again, he thought her the most beautiful woman he had ever seen.

Later that evening, Gealton had Aleron and Hadaras alone in his study for a brief aside. "Gentlemen, I believe we need to discuss this young man spending more time at court."

"Yes," Hadaras agreed. "How might we arrange that?"

Aleron looked from one to the other with curiosity. He had no idea how the steward might accomplish that.

"He will need to spend his first year abroad. Sorry lad, but there's no getting around that requirement."

"Understood," Hadaras replied, Aleron nodding in agreement. Regulations required all new marine companies serve at a remote outpost, either on the borders, or guarding embassies and ships at foreign ports of call.

"After the first year," Gealton continued, "I could recall the company to Arundell. Here, they will distribute your platoons among ship's contingents, spending as much time in port, as at sea. Of course, you would have the usual training requirements in garrison, but I can pull some strings to get you duties at the palace several times a week. That service typically lasts for three years, by which point, most leave the service. Those who stay, move on to train new companies, or take on other administrative duties."

"Sounds reasonable," Hadaras concluded.

"But, what about seeing the world?" Aleron questioned, with an apprehensive look on his face. "I joined the Marines to travel."

"Not to worry, my boy. You will have plenty of time on ships, sailing the globe. The duty is the same, regardless of the port of call. You will just be quartered here, rather than at some backwater port."

Aleron looked relieved at the revelation.

Chapter 33

Feast of Korelle

Zorekday, Day 6, Growing Moon, 8765 Sudean Calendar

Today is a good day to be a marine, Aleron thought. It was Zorekday, dedicated to the god of the sea and a traditional rest day for Sudeans. It was also the feast day of Korelle, the goddess of wind and sailing, meaning extra rations for all. He lounged on the foredeck with Barathol, Geldun and other fellow marines, passing around a jug of smoky tasting Elmenian usquebaugh. He was rubbing olive oil along the blades of his freshly sharpened cutlasses. Barathol reached over and grabbed the bottle of oil, pouring out a palm full and rubbing it into the new tattoo he acquired in Corin. An incredibly detailed viper, rendered in deep blue ink, now coiled around his heavily muscled upper right arm. Barathol took quite a fancy to the Thallasian custom, as had many Sudean sailors and marines since the two nations began collaborating nearly four years earlier. The young warrior now sported several pieces of body art. "You'll be quite the sight behind a plow in Swaincott, with all that artwork, Barry," Aleron commented.

"I'm not thinking that will ever happen, Al," he replied. "I think I like this line of work too much to go back to plows and cows."

"What, hacking up Kolixtlani and Adari sailors? I will admit, you are pretty good at it."

"We are, you mean," Barathol corrected him. The trio remained together after training because they proved to be such an effective assault team. Aleron, gifted with preternatural speed and agility, gravitated to the dual-sword form, while Barathol's solidity and strength made him an unmatched pikeman. Geldun favored a medium punch-buckler and cutlass, functioning as a tenacious obstacle, around which the other two worked. After serving a year on the four-kingdom border between Coptia, Castia and the two Blue Mountain dwarvish kingdoms, fighting goblin and troll incursions, and then two and a half years of patrols along the south, east and north coasts of the continent, experiencing ship-to-ship combat, as well as beach landings, the team could carve a path through an enemy formation like a hot knife through butter. Geldun had nothing to add to the conversation. When they looked to him for comment, they saw that he was asleep against the bulkhead, along with Ban. Apparently, the extra rations and liquor had taken their toll. The others had a chuckle at their expense and went back to what they were doing.

Their ship was six days south of Corin, heading back to Arundell for a three-month furlough at their homeport. They had spent the past six months in the northern sea off Chebek and Thallasia, patrolling for Kolixtlani and Adari warships. The idea that they would spend as much time in port as afloat had long been out of fashion, the low-level conflict with the enemy kingdoms slowly escalating over the years. Now, with winter in full swing for the northern half of the world, the northern waters proved too treacherous for the ships of the enemy. Though the coast remained heavily fortified, they could afford to minimize seagoing patrols. They spotted other unfamiliar ships over the years, but these always avoided the blockades and took flight when pursued. The Thallasians confirmed that the alien ships were similar to the ship sailed by the peculiar elvish emissaries for the Nameless God. A fleet remained to overwinter in the north, maintaining the blockade of the Wabani Inlet to the Kolixtlani Sea and to be ready, in case these strange elves arrived in force. Rather than attempt to run the blockade, the elvish vessels remained in the treacherous waters close to the northern ice. It seemed as if they were searching for something. As Thallasian patrols spotted them approaching from both east and west, High Admiral Kor believed they originated from the other side of the world, in an area where the sea ice seemed to run further south than was normal. He thought there to be an uncharted landmass in that area and the sea ice maintained through the magical efforts of these elves.

Aleron was curious about these strange elves as well. His grandfather suspected they were descended from the abductees of four millennia past and having somehow been twisted to the use of the chaotic red energy. The Thallasians said they were darker complexioned than was normal for elves, indicating an admixture of another race. Hadaras thought it was likely man or goblin.

At this moment, however, Aleron did not care about any of that. He was looking forward to seeing Eilowyn again, though there were still months to go before they would reach Arundell. He would once again feel the ire of the Arundell court, but he could deal with that. Many believed that Gealton was simply doting on his daughter and conceding to the whim of a spoiled child, especially those nobles who had hoped to arrange a match for their own sons with the Steward's daughter. It helped that Aleron rapidly gained a reputation as one of Arundell's most skilled fighters, at such a young age. His future career looked bright, and some believed he could ascend to the rank of General one day. Hadaras and Gealton, of course, knew that he would never be a General, but it was good reinforcement to their story.

Today, Aleron was a sergeant, and his two friends were corporals. Even now, Barathol and Geldun should have teams of their own and Aleron should be leading a squad, but the three were simply too effective as a team, for the command to break them up. There was much talk of sending them back to the marine training camp as combat instructors, but that would have to wait until this "war that wasn't a war" cooled down. In the meantime, Kolixtlan and Adar were being increasingly troublesome, while wild men and other denizens of the Central Jungle increased attacks on their neighbors. There were even reports of hobgoblins and half-trolls crossing Kolixtlan and making trouble in Castia. After three years of intermittent skirmishing, it did not look like things would cool down anytime soon.

Soon, Aleron and Barathol were dozing, along with Geldun and half the other marines on board. Sailors passing by either shook their heads and chuckled or scowled in disgust. Though some might be jealous of the marine's lack of responsibility when under sail, none would trade for their responsibilities upon boarding enemy ships or landfall on unfriendly shores.

Late that night, Aleron found himself in the storeroom adjacent to the galley. Sleep was eluding him, due in part to the redolent afternoon he enjoyed. He often took advantage of times like this, seeking a private place to practice magic. He cast out his senses and soon found one of the ubiquitous rats, prowling behind some barrels. It was not one that he had encountered before, so it came willingly when he called out to it. Most shipboard creatures he encountered previously scurried away quickly as soon as they sensed his presence. It was not that he was ever cruel to them; it was just that the things he did to them were a bit disconcerting for the poor animals. The ship's cat bolted whenever she caught sight of Aleron and oddly, became overly sympathetic to the rats and mice these past few weeks. He heard the cook complain that he would have thrown her overboard for uselessness, if he didn't think she was pregnant and there was hope for a good kitten. Aleron conceded to himself that he probably shouldn't have turned her into a mouse last month.

The little gray rat hopped into his palm and looked up at him with beady black eyes, twitching his whiskers, as rats do. Aleron concentrated and in a flash of white, a small parakeet stood on his palm, looking bewildered. He quickly gained control of the bird and calmed it, then he sensed through the creature. It was indistinguishable from the one he examined near Corin a week earlier, except that its mind was still that of a rat. The rat's mind, however, was rapidly realigning itself to the thought processes of the bird's brain it found itself inhabiting. Aleron sensed the dim intelligence of the rodent expanding to fill the exponentially greater capacity of the parakeet. The bird stretched its wings and hopped about his palm. Before it progressed much further, he bent his will and the little grey rat once again sat on his palm. He expected the creature to bolt, as soon as it gained its bearings again, but this one was different. It just sat and looked at him expectantly. He felt again for the rodent's thoughts and received a deep sense of longing from the animal. It wanted him to change it back. He tried to project an impression to the little creature that being a parakeet would not do in the cool dry lands where they were heading . Aleron did not think that a rat could mope, but that's just what this one did, as it flopped onto his palm and curled into a ball. He felt bad for the little rodent, having had a short glimmer of intelligence, only to return to its meager capacity again.

As he stroked the animal's fur with one finger, a solution came to him. He once again focused his will on the rat and another flash of white, along with a whoosh of inrushing air preceded the appearance of a young raven in the place of the little grey rat on his palm. *There, little friend,* he spoke into the bird's mind, *now you will be able to live where we are going.* He set his hand down on a barrel and the raven that was once a rat hopped off. It stretched out one, then the other wing, looking at each in turn and then it lifted one foot to examine it as well. Aleron reached into his pocket for a piece of hardtack he was saving and broke off a corner. He offered it to the bird, which took the bread and swallowed it in one gulp. He broke up the rest of the bread and set it atop the barrel for the bird.

Moving his own awareness into the head of the raven, he looked through its eyes as it plucked up the pieces of hardtack and swallowed them down. The rat's mind was in here as well, straining to fill the vast space now available. Aleron was surprised to discover that there seemed to be enough room for his mind in here as well. He had long avoided changing himself into anything other than a man, fearing that he would not have the intelligence to bring himself back. Here, however, was a mind with nearly the same capacity as his. When new and unformed, a raven's brain would be more than accommodating to his mind. The ravens he previously studied possessed minds already formed to their natural purpose and so he did not realize the potential mental capacity of these birds. He decided that this was a form he could use to move quickly, over large distances and still have hope of changing himself back to normal at the end of the trip.

Come along, my friend, he spoke to the raven, holding out his arm. *Let's get you out into the fresh air, where you can learn about the wind.* The young bird hopped atop Aleron's forearm, and he reentered the galley, extinguishing the glowing white orb he conjured to see in the dark storeroom. He grabbed another half loaf of bread someone had left on the table and made his way to the stairs. A portly night shift sailor trundled down to the galley, in search of a snack. He nodded to Aleron in recognition, as they passed at the foot of the stairs. Aleron cast a minor illusion so that the sailor saw only a marine, hands swinging at his sides, as he exited the galley.

On the main deck once again, he made his way to the forecastle, the upper deck of which, was currently empty. This far out to sea and under minimum sail, only one guard was required up in the crow's nest. Closer to shore, they would have shielded lanterns hanging from the bowsprit and at least two watchers on the foredeck, on the lookout for reefs and shoals. He bounded up the ladder, one-handed, the bread tucked under the arm holding the bird. He then set the raven on the deck, along with the half-loaf, saying, *now stay clear of the edge until you get your wings straight. If you fall over the edge before you learn to fly, you will be lost.* He picked up the stout rope meant to block the exit from the foredeck, where it dropped to the main deck and hooked it to the railing on either side. *Come on over here and grab hold of this rope. You can practice flying, while you hold on tight.* The bird understood, because Aleron was projecting the thoughts into its mind, rather than using any actual words. It hopped over to the rope, flapped its wings a few times and then looked up expectantly at Aleron. He reached down, it hopped onto his hand, and he helped it up to the rope. Once there, it spread its wings into the breeze , which, fortunately, blew from directly behind. *Good night, little friend; I will be back to check on you at dawn,* he reassured the raven, before swinging over the railing and dropping to the deck below. With only a few bells before dawn, he proceeded below decks to find his berth and get some real sleep.

Chapter 34

Sildaenday, Day 5, Haymaking Moon, 8765 Sudean Calendar

Nearly five weeks had passed since Aleron transformed the rat into a raven and Bob, as the raven was now known, had become something of a mascot for the ship. He lived atop the forecastle and one of the sailors fashioned a nest box for him. When he was first discovered, a few wanted to throw him over the side, but the others would not have it. Some sailors and marines pointed out that ravens are a fortuitous omen and sacred to Corball, as well. Now, nearly everyone on board checked on him and made sure he had food and water. He learned to fly and was oft seen perched in the rigging or flapping about the air above the ship. Everyone believed that Bob must have stowed away somehow, maybe falling from a nest at the harbor of Corin. Until now, they were too far out to sea for the young bird to find his way to land, so he just stayed with the ship. Today, however, they were approaching land. The Strait of Cordak, which separated the Sudean Mainland from Cordak Island and the slew of other South Sea islands, was dead ahead. Cordak is among the northernmost islands of a large archipelago, stretching from southern Sudea, to the southern sea ice and beyond. The vessel would hug the north shore of the island, keeping to deeper waters for the passage.

Aleron projected his thoughts to the bird perched atop the highest spar of the main mast. *You see the land, don't you?*

See something, no know what. I born ship, know ship. The raven's thoughts were much more like language now than the vague impressions Aleron first perceived from the rat's mind. *People nice, I stay ship.*

Aleron projected images of trees, rivers and mountains to the young bird. *That is where a raven is supposed to live, not on a boat. You'll find all of that on the island up ahead.*

What eat there? Food good here.

He projected more thoughts as to what ravens eat and where he would find it, then added, *there are female ravens over there and you'll never find one of those on the ship.*

I think it, the raven conceded.

Two bells later, the large black bird took to the air and winged off toward the now attainable shore off their port side. Someone yelled and everyone above decks stopped to watch Bob leave. "Goodbye Bob! Take care of yourself!" one of the marines shouted.

"He's off to find the lady-ravens, I would bet," Aleron announced, with a grin, relieved that his friend chose the most sensible, if not the easiest option. Several nodded and agreed, saying it must be, since Bob wanted for nothing else aboard the ship. Aleron was impressed by the near human level of intelligence Bob displayed. He resolved to attempt talking to some wild ones, when the opportunity presented itself. He thought it would be interesting to see if they were all as smart as Bob, or if he was somehow unique.

Later, they would adjust their course to a more westerly one and negotiate the channel taking them around South Cape. In nine or ten days, they were due to round the cape and dock at Cape Town. Aleron and the others looked forward to a day or two on solid ground for a change.

***

Zormat lounged upon a sumptuously cushioned divan, in his private quarters at the royal palace of Kolixtlan. *I could get used to this,* he thought. Luxury like this did not exist in Arkus, where everything was designed for utility over comfort and beauty, not even for the king. His languid reverie was interrupted by the approach of his first. Karsh entered without knocking, no formalities required between beings that could sense each other's presence across leagues. "Has my package arrived yet?" Zormat asked his aide.

"Not as yet, Sire," Karsh replied, "it is delayed by the need to spirit it across enemy territory, I'm afraid."

"Understood, I expected as much. So what business brings you here Karsh?"

"Sire, it's the other, what we have been searching for, all these years. We believe we are close."

"Zadehmal?" the Arkan king started, "Where?"

Far to the north Sire, across the ice to the desert beyond. The men who live on the ice worship a power there and we think it may be what we are looking for."

"That is news indeed, Karsh, my friend," Zormat stated, on his feet now, pacing about the room. "My father's weapon of power will soon be in my hands. With it, we will be able to free him and bring forth his new dominion over Aertu."

"Yes Sire," Karsh replied, "and yours as well, My Liege. Do you have any further instructions, Your Grace?"

"Yes, of course," he replied, pacing faster, "we must mount an expedition to retrieve it at once. The blockade will be a problem, but not an insurmountable one. We will simply mask our ship for the passage, then rejoin our people in the north."

"Your Grace, do you think it is wise to mount an expedition now? We are at the height of winter and the cold will be intense, not to mention the perpetual darkness when we pass into the far north."

"Do not question my authority Karsh, or I'll have you thrown into the sea, with your feet tied to a bloodstone boulder. We will mount the expedition, regardless of the conditions. My father would expect no less from his loyal son and his people."

"Yes, Your Grace, I never meant to question your wisdom and I apologize if I made such an impression."

"Good, I would not like to think that perhaps your faith is faltering."

"Sire, no, of course not," the first emphatically assured his leader.

"We will provision ourselves accordingly and there will be no men among our expedition. That will increase our chance of survival."

"Sire, do you intend to lead the expedition yourself?"

"Yes, this time I must. Only I will touch Zadehmal. I do not believe it safe for anyone else to handle the object. My father's power is too strong and if one is not up to the task, the axe may destroy them. Also, anyone who is up to the task is not likely to willingly relinquish the power once they hold it."

"Understood, Your Grace, when do you wish to depart?" Karsh was still uneasy about mounting a winter expedition into the frozen north, but had fewer reservations, the more Zormat explained his intentions.

"We will leave as soon as we are physically able," Zormat replied, stopping his pacing, "and it is up to you, Karsh, as my first, to assure that it is soon."

"Yes, Sire, and what of the package you are expecting? It will likely not arrive before we are ready to set out."

"The package will need to wait until we return. Identify a safe place to store it, where it will keep unspoiled, and I will deal with it upon my return. Now go see to provisioning my ship for the voyage ahead."

"Right away, Your Grace," Karsh answered, turning on his heel and exiting the chamber.

✳✳✳

"Where are we going today?" Eilowyn asked her captors, as she had every morning since her abduction.

"North," the shorter one answered, as he had every day for over eight weeks. "We'll be hitting another border crossing this morning and you know the drill. Open your pretty little mouth and you'll only get the border guards killed. If we must go through that again, you might not make it where you're going as clean and unspoiled as originally planned."

Eilowyn did not need reminding of the pair's killing efficiency. *She was on her way to the family's summer estate to join her mother, sister and her sister's children, when two horsemen appeared on the road ahead. As her entourage approached, the riders moved to either side of the road, as if to let them pass. Suddenly, crossbows appeared in their hands and before anyone could react, Hans and Simeon slumped dead in their saddles, each with a bolt lodged in their faces. She screamed and ten archers, with longbows, appeared from the wood line on either side, as the riders fell upon the rest of her train, cutting down the guardsmen and courtiers indiscriminately. The bowmen took out the archers in the retinue first, before moving to the other guardsmen, and within seconds, all but her were dead. She bolted, but her calm little mare was no warhorse. The shorter rider soon came alongside and cut to one side, driving her mount into a wide circle. He gained control of her bridle and brought both beasts to a halt.*

Holding his bloodied sword to her throat, he said, "Let's not try that again, little lady, unless you would like to join your friends in the afterlife. We'll get more for you alive, but your head is still worth something, if you prove troublesome."

"Mm-hm," was all she managed to respond, her throat too tight with fear to speak.

They returned to the scene of the carnage, where the tall one was quickly looting the bodies and wagons, searching for anything of value and assuring there were no survivors. The smell, like that of a slaughterhouse, wafted over her and she doubled over in the saddle, retching. "Hurry up with that. We need to go, now," her captor shouted to his companion, as he led her to a spot upwind. She regained her composure enough to see the other remount, with only a few items gleaned from the wreckage. Obviously, this was no simple act of banditry. They had come for her.

Leaving the roadway, they made their way down a narrow path through the woods, to a small clearing. There, another pair of horses awaited, one saddled like unto those of her captors and one pack animal. There, they forced her to change into the travelling clothes that a middle-class merchant might wear. The shorter one watched as she changed, so she turned away out of modesty and the hope that he would not notice the pendant she wore on a short silver chain. When she was finished, she turned back to them and he said, "Come, let's have a look at you." She stepped up to him, cautiously and he grabbed her arm and stuck his other hand in the top of her bodice, snatching the silver chain and dragging out the pendant. "So, what's this little trinket you're attempting to hide from us, My Lady?"

"Just a gift, from my betrothed," she answered meekly, somewhat surprised at his formal address.

"Aha, the great Aleron, of the Royal Marines. Some say he's the best swordsman in the kingdom. It would be fun to find out if he really is. Keep it; we're not here to rob you," he said, letting the pendant drop. "Take this and bind up your hair." He handed her a piece of cord, as she tucked the jewelry back in her bodice. After she bound her wavy auburn hair into a loose ponytail, he said, "Now mount up on that horse there. We have to move, or more of your people will die."

So it had been, for the past two months after parting ways with the hired bandit archers, they escorted her north, along paths little travelled, threatening violence if she spoke out of turn to others along the way, and skillfully avoiding any large parties. They spent most of the journey crossing Ebareiza and for the last week, the northwest corner of Coptia. Now, they had no choice but to use the main border crossing into Castia. The two kingdoms constructed a massive wall along their border, not so much for protection, but to regulate trade between the north and south. She knew where she was going. To the northwest of Castia, was Kolixtlan. She was a hostage, a prisoner of war.

Chapter 35

Corballday, Day 15, Haymaking Moon, 8765 Sudean Calendar

The morning broke bright and clear and the temperature was already rising. Cape Town is situated on the southern coast of the Great Southeastern Desert, and it was a week and a half before the Summer Solstice, nearly the height of summer. Aleron stood on the foredeck, the ship pulling up anchor and readying for its approach of the docks. He could tell that it was going to be a hot day. Last night, they entered the bay, too late to approach the docks, so they moored out in the middle of the harbor, with marker lights blazing. The crew was disappointed, as that meant one less night on shore, but the bars and brothels of Cape Town are open whenever there are paying customers.

"All hands on deck!" The order rang out and was rapidly echoed below decks. No one outside the infirmary was permitted to be asleep during the dawn and dusk shift changes, so sailors and marines soon were boiling out onto the decks, forming up by section. Captain Jorum began speaking, even before the entire crew was formed. "Inside the hour, men, we will be docked in Cape Town for two days and two nights shore leave. You already know that you won't have the whole two days off. There will be shifts and everyone will land one. The roster should have circulated among the leadership last night, so if you don't know when your shift is, ask your leader. If anyone asks me directly, you and your whole chain of command will be on shift for the next twelve bells. Have I made myself clear?" A chorus of "ayes" filled the air and he continued, "Anyone who decides not to show up for their shift, will be confined to the brig for the remainder of our stay and will be confined to the ship for the next shore leave.

If any of you fools gets thrown in jail while we're here, you will stay there until they let you go, or we come to get you when we are ready to sail. If you manage to miss your shift, because you're in jail, guess what; you stay on the boat for our next stop. Do you all understand?" Another chorus of "ayes" as he paused, then, "I know where most of you will be going from here and I have just one thing to say, the same thing I say every time. What is it?" He was answered with a resounding "Wrap your stick!" before he concluded, "That's right, men. You don't want to be bringing any presents home to your girl from here or leaving any to the girls here. Now, go out and have some fun!"

The formation broke up as leaders released their sections. Inevitably, several of the men had yet to see the shift roster and proceeded to badger their leaders for information. Those that landed early, or late shifts were happy with their lots, while those that landed shifts in the middle of the leave block, were not so pleased. Many tried to wheedle their way into a more favorable slot, with the most successful being those offering cash for a swap. Negotiations were still ongoing throughout the ship, a bell later, when the on-duty crew tossed the tow rope to the tugboat crew that would row them into position at the docks.

***

Later that afternoon, Aleron sat in The Thirsty Lizard, nursing a pint of ale. Barathol and Geldun had already found women and their empty tankards graced the table before him. Suddenly, Gram, one of the marines on shift, burst into the tavern. Red faced and out of breath, he exclaimed, "Al, thank Corball I found you in the first place I looked! Come quick; the captain needs to see you right away!"

"What's going on? I don't have shift until tomorrow."

"It's nothing to do with your shift, more like trouble at home. A royal courier came looking for you in particular. Aren't you betrothed to the Stewards daughter, or something? "

"Ellie? No, it can't be her! Maybe her da? I better go!" He jumped up from the table and grabbed a silver piece from his pocket and slapped it on the bar. "That should cover me," he said to the publicans, before chasing after Gram, out the door and back to the ship.

Arriving at the ship, he ran up the gangplank and straight to the captain's quarters. Gram ran up right behind him and back to his post, for a drink and to catch his breath. Aleron knocked on the captain's door, waited for the response and answered, "It's Aleron, Sir, reporting as ordered."

"Enter," he heard from Captain Jorum, so he opened the door and stepped in. His eyes widened in recognition when he saw Bruno, the courier he met five years earlier, standing beside the captain's desk. "Sit down, lad," Jorum ordered. "Courier Bruno has some news for you and it's not the best. Bruno?"

"Aleron, it's good to see you again, after all these years. I see you went ahead with your plan to become a marine. I bear a message from Steward Gealton. His daughter, Eilowyn, has disappeared. He thinks she was kidnapped."

Aleron was stunned to silence for a moment, then he recovered and asked, "When, how?"

"About ten weeks ago now," Bruno continued, "She was on her way to the summer house. Her escort was found butchered in the roadway and her horse was wandering loose, but no trace of her. The Steward believes she is being spirited to Kolixtlan, as a hostage to be used as political leverage."

"Her bodyguards, Simeon and Hans, how did they get through them?"

"It appeared that they were the first to die, crossbow bolts to the face and then the men at arms were put to the sword, followed by the women."

"Arien, her lady in waiting too?" The girl was only fifteen.

"Dead, along with the others," Bruno replied, shaking his head.

The blood drained from Aleron's face, but then his color returned, along with a determined clench to his jaw. "What does the Steward request of me?" he asked rising from the chair. At that moment, the other two could have sworn that a red glow flickered behind the young man's silver eyes, but they both figured that it must be from the oil lamp on the captain's desk.

Jorum spoke up this time, "This order, signed by the Steward, states that you are to be temporarily released from my command and you are to make your way to Arundell by the fastest means possible. He must be familiar with your team, because the next part states that any companions you choose shall also be released to accompany you. It's all signed, sealed and thoroughly official."

"I see, Sir," Aleron responded.

"Now, since the fastest way to the Capital is by sea, you will simply stay on until we reach Arundell and then you will be released. I assume you will want your pike man and shield man?"

"Yes Sir, I will want to take Barry and Gel, if that's possible."

"This order right here says it's possible. Now, were going to have to rush our loading and cut this shore leave short, so you might not be the most popular guy on board, if why we're leaving gets out."

"Sir, if I may, I would prefer to be released from here. I believe I can make my way overland quicker."

"That's not possible," Bruno interjected. "I came by boat because it only takes seven weeks. To go overland takes over seventeen and that's if you swap horses every day along the way. Even if you cut straight across the desert, it would take longer. It's over thirteen hundred leagues, there's no water and there's no place to swap out horses. Seven weeks by sea is the absolute fastest you can go from here."

"He's right, lad," the captain agreed. "There is no faster way."

"Would you say that it's thirteen hundred leagues, as the crow flies?"

"According to the map, yes," Bruno answered, "two thousand by road."

Aleron did a quick calculation and said, "I believe there is a way that I can do it in about four weeks if I have your leave Sir. If I am wrong, I will return straight away and rejoin the crew."

"I don't understand what you are planning," Jorum said, "but it can't hurt to let you check it out. Just make sure you make it back before we shove off if it doesn't work out. I don't want to be held responsible for you not making it back as early as possible."

"You may rest assured, Sir, that if we do not make it back in time to leave with the ship, we will be on our way, by other means."

"Go then, but first, take this, then go round up your crew." He tossed a small sack to Aleron, who upon catching it, realized it was a sack of coin. "It seems that Steward Gealton assumed you had something up your sleeve and sent cash for the journey."

"Thank you, Sir, Bruno; I have to go find the lads now." He saluted, turned on his heel and bolted out the door.

"He's a bit of an odd lad, that one," Jorum commented, "spectacular fighter, but odd. Where do you know him from?"

Met him and his grandfather on a ferry, a bit over five years back," Bruno replied. "Then, he bested me in a friendly pickup bout of sword and dagger."

"He just turned twenty the other day, I believe. Wouldn't that have put him at fifteen?"

"Not quite fifteen, Sir," the courier corrected him. "He and his grandpa said he'd been training since he was nine."

"Did you know his 'grandpa' is Lord Marshal Hadaras, of the Sudean Royal Guard, retired some twenty-five years ago?"

"At the time, Sir, I had no idea. It wasn't until afterwards, that the name clicked. I should be flattered though. He said I was almost as fast as his grandpa."

"That's a compliment indeed," the captain agreed.

✳✳✳

Aleron ran back to the Tavern to retrieve his friends. Bursting through the front door, he made for the stairs before the proprietor could say anything to slow him down. "Barry, Gel, we need to go, now!" he shouted down the long hallway upstairs. He continued to shout for them, causing other patrons to shout obscenities back at him, until he heard a response from Geldun.

"All right, already, what in Zorek's name do you need?"

Aleron stopped at the door the voice emanated from and opened it without considering the consequences. The young woman in the room was totally nude and made no effort to cover herself. "Oh, excuse me Mistress," he apologized, his eyes lingering a bit too long as she rolled off the bed and sauntered towards her robe, where it hung on the wall, smiling seductively the entire time.

"Damn it Al. Can't you knock first?" his friend demanded. "I was just getting started." Geldun had the bedcover pulled across his hips.

"Such a polite man," the woman exclaimed, "and cute too. Of course, you are excused."

"We need to go. I need to get to Arundell as soon as possible and I'll need your help."

"What for, what's going on in Arundell?

"They have Ellie and I need to track her down."

"What do you mean? Who're 'they'?"

"The Kolixtlanis, at least that's what the Steward thinks. Ellie was kidnapped two months ago, and they haven't been able to find her."

"Corball's Balls! All right, say no more, I'll help. Just give me a chance to get dressed. Gotta find my coin purse."

"Just get dressed Gel. We need to find Barry. Mistress, how much does my friend owe you?" Aleron began digging into his belt pouch.

"We weren't long at all Sir, so one silver piece will do." He handed her the coin as Geldun finished tying on his pants.

Soon, his shirt and boots were on, and he was ready to go. "Goodbye Carine, see you when I come back through.

"Sure, if I'm still here, love. Take care and don't let your well-mannered friend get you into too much trouble."

After a bit more yelling, searching and banging on a few wrong doors, they located Barathol, and much the same sort of thing ensued as with Geldun. The main difference being that Aleron had to pay off two women and apparently, Barathol got more work done as well, because it cost him three silver. As they made their way back to the ship, Geldun said, "It occurs to me, that the fastest way back to Arundell is to take the boat that we were going to board tomorrow anyway."

"Hey…yeah, that's right," Barathol sluggishly agreed. He drank enough for the other two as well that afternoon in the tavern. "Why we in such a mad rush, anyway? I wasn't done back there…mebbe if I go back now, we can pick up wh…"

"No, trust me, lads," Aleron said, cutting him off. "I have a way that should get us there in four weeks."

"What? You've gone stark raving mad!" Geldun exclaimed. "What are you planning to do, fly there?"

"Exactly," Aleron replied.

Chapter 36

Carpathday, Day 16, Haymaking Moon, 8765 Sudean Calendar

Morning broke with Aleron, Geldun and Barathol heading into the open desert, north of Cape Town. They left on foot, with their gear, a week's supply of food and not nearly enough water. The rest of the crew, plus quite a few townsfolk thought the trio had lost their minds for heading into the open desert with no horses. Even with horses, survival was unlikely. On foot, death was all but assured. "This had better be good Al," Barathol commented. "I think you've finally gone off the deep end. Must be all those books our grandpa shoved down your throat addled your brain."

"Trust me lads," Aleron assured them, "I won't let you down."

"If you turn out to be nuts, we're knocking you out and dragging you back to the boat," Geldun added. "This is not how I wanted to spend my shore leave."

"Grandfather is not really a man, just so you know," Aleron announced, as neared a group of granite outcrops.

"You're saying he's been a woman, posing as a man all this time?" Barathol enquired, barking a laugh afterward.

"No, not that, you twit, he's an elf, as was my mother."

"You mean to tell us you're a halfblood?" Geldun asked this time. "Does that make you some sort of a wizard or something?"

"Something like that," Aleron replied.

"Yeah right, prove it," Barathol demanded.

As they passed into the outcroppings sufficiently to obscure them from sight of those in the village, Aleron released a sliver of blue energy, neatly splitting a boulder in two. He followed on with a flash of red, instantly reducing the split stone to fine gravel. "Believe me now?" he asked his now slack-jawed friends.

"Ahhh…" was all Geldun managed to spit out. Barathol was still speechless.

"Good, now that I've made my point, there's something else I need to do. *I will have to talk to you like this from here on out, because I won't have a voice. Do you both understand me?"*

Both of his companions nodded, and he heard their unvoiced *"yes."*

In a shimmer of white, Aleron veered into the form of a raven and then began clumsily walking and hopping about on the sand. *"This is the first time I've tried anything like this. Now the trick is to see if I can change myself back."*

"You mean you don't know if you can change back?" Barathol asked. "What kind of trick is that anyway?"

"Nobody has ever done this before," he replied. *"According to my grandfather, I'm the only one who can do this. I've changed other things, but never myself."*

"Change yourself back then," Geldun insisted. "This is crazy."

In another shimmer, Aleron veered back to his normal form. "I just needed to see if I could change myself back again. I never dared try before."

"What if you couldn't change back," Geldun asked, "what then?"

"I'm not sure. I guess I'd stay a raven and you would go back to the ship and explain things to the captain."

"Oh, that would be really great," Barathol responded, "Our stupid crazy friend here is really a wizard and changed himself into this here raven. That would have gone over really well."

"I had to risk it lads. It's the only way I'm going to get on Ellie's trail quickly. A raven can fly six times the distance a horse can run in a day."

"And just how do you presume to take us with you and all our stuff too?" Geldun inquired.

"Well, my stuff just seemed to go away, when I turned into a raven and I didn't come back naked, when I turned back, so that's not an issue. As for you lads, I'll just turn you into ravens too."

"I was afraid you were going to say something like that."

After some extensive bickering negotiating and persuading, the other two conceded to Aleron turning them into ravens. He transformed the pair, followed by himself. *"There, now that that's done, all we need to do is learn how to fly."*

"You mean we don't know how to fly yet?" Barathol asked, surprised.

"I've no idea how much comes naturally and how much is learned. I remember it took Bob a day or two to figure it out."

"Bob wasn't really a raven?"

"No, he was a rat first," Aleron replied.

Geldun was the next to ask, *"Why didn't you turn him back?"*

"Once he was a bird, he didn't want to go back to being a rat. I think if I made him a dumb bird, he would have never known the difference, but I made him a smart bird and he didn't want to go back to being a dumb rat."

"Let's get on with this then. I don't care to stay this way forever," Barathol interjected. *"Let's go find your girl, kill the guys that took her and anything else that gets in our way and get back to Arundell in time for furlough. Now, how do you suppose we find her?"*

"If she still has my engagement present, I have a link to her. If they took it from her, I have a link to them and then to her."

"What if they don't want to tell you where she is?" Geldun asked.

"They'll tell me when I set their feet afire."

"Oh, all right, I just didn't take you for the torturing type, but that works fine for me."

The remainder of the morning was spent flapping about, attempting to learn the intricacies of flight. They discovered that while becoming airborne and flying in a straight line was not too difficult to learn, landing gracefully was more of a problem. After several tumbles through the sand, Geldun discovered how to brake to a near stop and shared the technique with the others. Once they had landing somewhat mastered, they took to the air and headed northwest towards Arundell. Thirteen hundred leagues, at sixty to seventy leagues a day, would take them three and a half weeks.

By mid-day, the summer sun at its zenith, the trio developed a serious thirst and hunger. The raven's physiology, though much better than a man's at shedding heat and conserving water, can still go only so far before replenishment is required. *"Let's land in the shade of those rocks over there,"* Aleron suggested to the others. Upon landing, Barathol asked, *"Do you turn us back now, so we can get to our food and water?"*

"Not quite," Aleron answered, *"I just need to be in contact with the ground for this next thing."* A golden glow surrounded the three for several seconds and then he asked, *"Anyone still tired, thirsty or hungry?"*

"No, as a matter of fact," Geldun answered.

"I feel empty, but not hungry or thirsty, for some reason," Barathol added.

"Good, then we can get going again. I don't know if there's any limit to how many times I can do this, but I'll use it as much as I can until we find out. And so, they continued on their way, until nightfall, when they found a tall outcropping on which to roost for the night.

✳✳✳

Gealton stayed up late in his office, as he often did these days. His daughter was still missing, though troops had combed the countryside for her since her disappearance. Ebareiza proved to be no help in the effort, so she was likely in Castia by this time. *I only hope Aleron has something up his sleeve. Hadaras spoke of visions of flying. I hope the lad figured that trick out by now, or there's no hope of saving her before she reaches Kolixtlan, or wherever they intend to take her.* The Steward knew that they likely intended to use her as a bargaining chip and no harm would come to her if he complied. He also knew that he could never jeopardize the welfare of the kingdom in the selfish protection of one of his offspring. A knock at the door prompted him to respond, "Yes, Forquin, is that you?"

"Yes, Your Eminence, one of your operatives to see you, Lord."

"Send him in."

"Your Eminence," the spy greeted him, as he entered, "I have news of your daughter."

Gealton shot up from behind his desk. "Enter and please sit." He gestured toward the empty chair opposite his desk. "Tell me what you know."

The man, who most would recognize as a minor functionary of the palace staff, took the seat, as the Steward returned to his."

"Milord, as you well know, Ebareiza has no elvish emissaries and our relationship is strained as well, so there has been little cooperation as to our investigation into your daughter's disappearance."

"Yes, go on."

"This is not the case with Castia and Coptia, however and they have been cooperating well, though until now, there has been no news. Tonight, we received a message from Kaas, through the elvish emissaries."

"What did they have to say?" the Steward asked, eagerly.

"A girl matching your daughter's description passed through the wall eleven days ago. She was in the company of two men. They were dressed nondescriptly and claimed to be merchants on a purchasing trip to Kaas. They were definitely either Sudeans or Ebareizans, and the men had the look of professional soldiers, not merchants. They have had ample time to make it to Kaas, but no group matching that description is known to have entered the city. Sudean merchants travelling without goods to exchange are rare enough to draw plenty of attention, since it means an influx of foreign currency, "new gold", so to speak."

"I understand. So, they never made it to Kaas, meaning they are likely on a straight course to Kolixtlan."

"Yes Lord, they should reach the border in about three weeks. Castian forces have undertaken the search, but the wilderness bordering Kolixtlan is difficult at best."

"Well, this is not the best news, for sure, but it is better than nothing at all. I want a message sent to Kaas and the elves as well, thanking them for their assistance. Also, I need a message sent to Lord Marshal Hadaras, at Swaincott, bidding him to come to the capital at his earliest convenience. Do not send it by royal courier. I wish for it to be unobtrusive, so use one of our people. Tell him that his grandson is on his way, and I would like for him to be here to greet him. Odds are good, that he already knows, but send the message anyway.

$$***$$

"Yes, Grandfather, I'm flying," Aleron said to Hadaras, as his friends dozed beside him.

"So, you finally braved changing yourself. Have you tried changing yourself back yet?"

"Yes, Grandfather, that was the very first thing I checked. So, Steward Gealton has not sent word to you about Ellie being kidnapped?"

"No lad, he probably didn't think it as important to inform me as it was you. He likely didn't realize that I could have gotten you the message many weeks earlier."

"I know, you could have told me when I was still in Corin, most likely and I could have set out across the Castian Sea and headed them off."

"True lad, but you would have done it as a deserter, without the official directive of the Steward. This is probably best."

"I understand, Grandfather, but I would have done it anyway, if it meant getting Ellie back safe."

"I know you would have, lad. Now get some rest, while you can, but keep your feelers out. There're more dangerous things than serpents and scorpions out in that desert."

"Thank you, Grandfather. Good night."

"Good night to you, my boy. I will be waiting for you in Arundell."

Chapter 37

Zorekday, Day 18, Haymaking Moon, 8765 Sudean Calendar

With the ship finally underway, Zormat was more content than he had been in ages. In a few short weeks, they would land on the shores of Mount Norwyyl, allowing them safe portage to access the icebound Northern Continent. They laid in three months' supply of dry goods, mostly fat, dried meats and fruit, on top of the usual ship's stores. His people would be waiting for them with guides, dogsled teams and cold weather clothing unobtainable here in the tropics. Temperatures would be brutally cold at the height of the polar winter and darkness would be absolute. He knew that the dogs and men would take him only as far as the shoreline of the continent, over seven hundred leagues across the ice. After that, he and his elves would be on their own to find the cave rumored to exist deep in the mountains of the interior.

A warm breeze blew in from the East, propelling them northward at a steady clip. Zormat knew the warmth would be short lived and enjoyed it for what it was. His own people were of the North and could easily bear the cold that was to come, but for now, they could enjoy the comfort a tropical breeze afforded. It would take at least a month and a half to reach their ship borne destination and then another three months by dogsled across the ice. After that, it might take another month to find what they were looking for. All told, they could be away for a year or more, *but after that, we will truly bring the fight to the Sudeans and whoever else stands in our way.* Now, all they needed to worry about was running the blockade at the Wabani Inlet.

THE HALFBLOOD KING

***

From her limited familiarity with Castian script, Eilowyn knew from the road signs that Kaas was to their east. They stayed in the foothills of the Blue Mountains, avoiding major roads and populated areas. After all this time, she was more accustomed to the saddle and they could ride further each day without rest and if she remembered her geography correctly, they would be entering Kolixtlani territory in another month. She prayed to the Allfather for help to arrive before that time.

Her captors were as talkative as ever. After two and a half months together, she still did not know their names. Stretch and Stubbs were the names they used for each other and were all she had to go by. She assumed they did this on purpose, to avoid implication in their crimes. If no one knew their names, or where they came from, it made it difficult to narrow any suspicions down to them.

The medallion Aleron gave her for their engagement still hung against her chest. He told her to always keep it with her and it would help keep her safe. Aleron's grandfather crafted it, and she suspected it contained some elvish magic. The crystal shone with an inner blue radiance, even in the brightest of light. She hoped that somehow, it would allow her love to find her over the thousands of leagues.

***

Hadaras looked out over Ball Harbor from the main deck, moments after boarding. The porters were busy stowing his bags in the cabin he rented for the trip to Arundell. Jessamine waved from the carriage they took from their cottage. He returned the gesture, and she wheeled the cart around, heading back out of town. Numerous men simply stopped what they were doing a stared at the dark-haired beauty making her way through the throng, earning several of them annoyed pokes and jabs from their wives. He wondered, as he prepared to go below decks to set his things in order, why Gealton had not sent word to him earlier. He could not have sent the message through the elvish ambassador, of course, as Hadaras' identity was still a secret, but why hadn't he sent a ground messenger by now? *I could have been there six weeks ago, my friend. Now I fear Aleron will need to penetrate all the way to Kolixtla to retrieve your daughter. Considering the boy's power, that could become an ugly scene very quickly.*

***

The trio of ravens flew on across the desert for the third straight day. As before, whenever they became tired or thirsty, they alighted on solid ground and Aleron used the golden healing power to rejuvenate them. Its efficacy showed no sign of abating and they used that to their advantage. Aleron began to believe that they should return to their natural forms before too long. He noticed that they were beginning to think more like ravens and less like men, the longer they maintained that form. It would not do for them to forget they were men and why they were on this journey. He decided that they would find a sheltered spot and spend the night as men.

As the day wore on into late afternoon, they saw a smudge of green on the horizon. As they drew closer, it became apparent that an unmapped oasis was before them. *"Good luck, lads, it looks like we found our place to camp for the night. Let's circle it a few times for good measure, before we land."*

"I don't like the looks of this, Al," Geldun commented, after they circled and flew over several times. *"What do you think, Barry? There are no tracks leading to this place and I can't believe the desert men don't know it exists.*

"He's right, Al. Those nomads know every square inch of this desert and they've settled every water source in it. Why would they leave this one out?

"It's probably just a poison spring, is all," Aleron offered, *"but we don't actually need the water, just a place to rest. Let's land and check it out.* Several old ruins existed, looking to have been abandoned centuries ago. They made for an ancient flagstone courtyard and landed, disturbing the rest of a large black scorpion that was sunning itself on the stones. It turned its attention to Aleron and Geldun, raising its claws and tail menacingly. Barathol swooped in behind it and neatly snipped off its stinger, before snapping it up and cracking it against the rocks. He then proceeded to rip it apart and gobble down the pieces.

"Hey, share some of that," Geldun complained, before lunging in and ripping off one juicy claw, cracking it with his bill before swallowing it down.

"There, no more empty feeling," Barathol declared happily.

"You know, we will have regular food, when we turn back to men," Aleron reminded them.

"Oh…yeah," Geldun replied.

"I don't care," Barathol retorted, *"That thing was tasty."*

Definitely thinking too much like ravens now, Aleron thought, but kept it to himself.

Later that evening, after a dinner of stew, made from reconstituted meat and vegetables, they settled their bedrolls around the fire. Finding that the water did indeed have a foul reek to it, they cleaned the utensils in the sand.

"I'll take the first watch," Aleron announced. "Three bells apiece, who wants second?"

"I'll take third," Geldun chimed in, leaving Barathol with second watch.

"Bastards!" was his only response to the results. Nobody ever wanted the middle watch.

"Gotta be quick there, big guy," Geldun quipped, earning him a backhand to the midriff.

"Yes, you do, little guy," he shot back, as Geldun fought to regain his breath.

Two hours into his watch, Aleron got the feeling that they were not alone. He maintained the trance state that Hadaras taught him, letting his senses feel for anything moving within a quarter league of the camp. The desert is remarkably alive at night, so there was plenty moving. What tipped him off was the sense of something quite large, moving out from the still water of the spring. A pair of red eyes appeared at the edge of the firelight and Aleron said, *"Good evening and who or what might you be?"*

"It's been a long time since I've tasted man meat," the other replied, moving closer to the firelight and revealing its horned reptilian head and long sinuous neck, followed by rather stubby clawed feet. It was a water wyrm, a sort of dragon. That explained the stench to the water, along with the abandonment of the oasis.

"You won't be tasting any this night either," Aleron assured it. *"Now go back to your lair and no harm will come to you."*

"You dare threaten me, puny mortal." This was pure posturing on the part of the dragon, since dragons are mortal, just very long lived, like elves.

In a flash of maroon energy, the serpent was punched through a mud brick wall and sent sprawling halfway across the oasis. Aleron's companions stirred slightly at the noise and then returned to their slumber.

"I told you, leave us be and no harm will come to you."

The wyrm would have none of this and, shaking off the blow, charged straight at Aleron. In a flash of white, the charging dragon suddenly veered into a charging gecko, barely larger than a grasshopper. As the world grew suddenly large around it, the gecko stopped, then in a panic, scurried off to find a place to hide.

Two hours later, as Barathol paced along the edge of the firelight to stay awake, he noticed a tiny gecko scurrying alongside him and hissing almost inaudibly, so he stomped on it.

Chapter 38

Sildaenday, Day 5, Squash Moon, 8765 Sudean Calendar

Three ravens alighted atop the southeast battlement of Arundell's Old Keep. In a shimmer of white light, the birds veered to the forms of three Sudean marines in full kit. A remnant of a bygone era, before the intense fortification of the outer walls of the city, this battlement was no longer guarded. Aleron and Eilowyn would occasionally come here for a bit of privacy and to enjoy the view, on the rare occasion he managed to steal her away from her bodyguards. It pained him to think that those two fine men were cut down defending his love and he was not there to help.

"Good, it's unlocked," he said, after checking the bulkhead accessing the stairs to the lower levels. They hurried down several flights of stairs. The old guard quarters were used for storage and minor offices, so they met no one before reaching the ground floor, where a guard stood by one of the entry doors to the main kitchen area. "Guard, we need to see the Steward, now!" Aleron announced, shocking the young man.

"Halt!" he yelled, lowering his pike to guard position. "Marines…Where in Zorek's name did you come from?"

"The roof, get us to the steward, now! It's an emergency." Aleron held his hand to stay Barathol, who snapped his own pike to guard. "Call for the sergeant of the guard. I don't expect you to leave your post, but we need to move quickly."

The guard screamed for the sergeant, who soon came running with two reinforcements in tow. Aleron recognized the face from a previous visit, though he could not place a name to it. "Sergeant Aleron," the sergeant of the guard said, upon recognizing him, "we were told to be on the lookout for you. The steward wanted to see you as soon as you arrived."

"They came from upstairs, not the door," the flustered guard stated.

"Well, that explains why we didn't get a runner from the gate then. Neither here nor there…I don't care how they got here; we just need to get them where they're needed. That will be all Private. Sergeant, Corporals, please follow me."

The sergeant led them through the kitchen and to the Stewards office, deep within the keep. "Tell the steward that Sergeant Aleron and his team are here to see him," he instructed the orderly manning the front office. As the orderly rose to announce their arrival, the sergeant of the guard turned to Aleron and said, placing a hand on his shoulder, "I know why you came. Bring her back and be safe. May all the gods watch over you."

Aleron nodded, replying, "Thank you."

With that, he signaled the other two guards to follow and proceeded back to his post.

The orderly called the three marines to enter the private office. In their well-worn and battle-scarred armor, they looked out of place in the opulent surroundings. Hadaras was seated beside the steward's desk and rose as Gealton did when the trio entered. "Greetings Aleron and company," Gealton offered, "and thank you for making such great haste to get here."

"Greetings, Lord Steward, Grandfather. We wanted to get here as fast as possible."

"You boys are all looking quite hale," Hadaras observed. "Barathol, you've grown, if that's possible. If I didn't know better, I would swear you have some westman in your blood."

"Thank you, Sir, I guess…"

Hadaras just laughed and asked, "So, how was your flight, lads?"

"Good, but long," Geldun offered, before anyone else could reply.

"I suspected you had something of the sort up your sleeve, lad," Gealton stated. "That's why I sent cash with the courier."

"Oh, about that, Milord, I only used a few coins to settle our tabs at the Thirsty Lizard," he said, dragging out the coin purse and making to hand it back to the Steward.

"Mine and Barry's, he means," Geldun corrected, at the raised eyebrows from the steward and Hadaras. Cape Town's Thirsty Lizard held quite the infamous reputation for the services available there, for those willing to pay for them. "Mister excitement here just sits down in the tavern, sipping ale, when we go to port."

"Keep the coin, lads," the STEWARD said, a look of relief washing over his face. "You may need it for something yet."

"Considering the time of Eilowyn's abduction and the sighting of her crossing into Castia several weeks back, I believe she will be in Kolixtla before you can reach her, even flying," Hadaras announced.

"Yes, it didn't occur to me that Hadaras could have spoken to you over distance, or I would have sent word to him months ago," Gealton said, before continuing, "As it was, you got word to him before my messenger arrived in Swaincott and he was already on his way here. I know you could likely use a good night's rest and some dinner, but what else do you think you need?"

"I believe it's time that I claim my sword, Lord Steward."

"What do you mean Al?" Barathol asked. "You have both swords, right there on your belt."

"He doesn't mean those swords, lad," Hadaras informed him. "Do you truly believe it is time?"

"Something tells me yes, Grandfather. I believe we will need the power for what is to come, and I feel that it is time that I claim my birthright."

"When?" was all that came from the Steward."

"I don't care to linger, after it is done," he answered. "Lads, do you feel an overwhelming need to spend the night, or may we proceed, with due haste?"

Geldun answered, "We know what you want to do, so let's get on with it. It's still early in the day."

"I agree," Barathol seconded, "but I wouldn't mind a decent meal before we roll out."

"Good, you can all join me for midday meal, and we will further discuss your plans," Gealton offered.

Shortly, the five were seated around the table in the steward's private dining and meeting room. After the last of the wait staff departed, closing the heavy wood door behind him, Hadaras stated, "You know, Aleron, together, we could construct something to focus and concentrate your power, without the need to reveal the secret the sword now holds."

"No, Grandfather, my dreams have been telling me, these past few weeks, that now is the time."

"And, your dreams have revealed many truths," Hadaras stated flatly. "If the Allfather deems that it is time, then we must heed the summons. I don't believe the Kolixtlanis realized what they would precipitate, once they stole your girl, Gealton."

"You're right, my friend," the Steward replied. "This will mean out and out war, when the truth comes to light."

"What is all this about birthrights and swords and wars?" Geldun asked the group.

"They don't know?" Gealton asked, looking between Hadaras and Aleron, then to Aleron's friends.

"We know he's a halfblood, Lord," Geldun stated.

"And, that he's a wizard," Barathol added, "but he just told us that a few weeks ago."

"What compelled you lads to follow him on this outrageous quest?"

"He's our best friend, Milord," Geldun answered, "and he needs help getting his lady back, your daughter, I mean, Lord," he finished, awkwardly.

"He would do the same for us," Barathol continued, "that is, if we had ladies and all."

"These are true friends you have here, Aleron and that is a rare commodity. You will find it to become more and more rare, the higher you go, my boy. Keep them close and don't ever forget where you came from," Gealton advised. "I believe that after this meal, all your questions will be answered, but not before." Hadaras nodded in agreement.

After the mid-day meal, and a change into clean uniforms, they made their way to the throne room. Barathol and Geldun had never seen the inside of the edifice and stared in awe at the sweeping architectural detail. A small contingent of palace guards was assembled in formation, along with several court scribes, to bear witness. Several citizens who had been touring the room gathered to see what was afoot and more came inside from the grounds as word spread. They approached the raised dais and Hadaras took Aleron and his friends to one side.

Gealton ascended the dais and proceeded to a spot, just to the right of the ancient granite seat. Turning to face the assembled crowd, he said, "Come forward, please, Aleron."

Aleron ascended the dais and strode past the Steward, proceeding up the platform behind the throne.

"Look at the sword!" a citizen shouted, "Look at the blasted sword!" The sapphire encrusted hilt of Andhanimwhid shone bright blue, even against the bright afternoon sun filtering through the high windows of the room.

Aleron reached the top of the platform and, turning to face the gathering, grasped the hilt, thumb side down. He felt the power course through his arm and into his body. Knowing now the feel of power, he could tell how much raw energy was housed in the blade and could sense the essence of all the rulers who held it in the past. Some of his being transferred to the artifact as well, just as it had for his predecessors. Thus, he became one with the sword and linked to four thousand years of his dynasty, from the last king, all the way back to the original Aleron. He drew the glowing sword from its granite sheath and turned it point skyward. The leaf shaped elvish blade shone with a bright blue radiance, filling the hall with a light overpowering the sun. Aleron then descended and came around to the front of the throne. He faced the gathering and flipped the sword hilt up, resting the tip against the stone floor and holding the hilt with both hands.

"Behold, citizens of Sudea," Gealton announced, "Aleron the Second, King of all Sudea!"

At that, Aleron sat upon the black granite throne, vacant for a thousand years, fully signifying his claim. Stunned silence prevailed, until Barathol began chanting, "Al-e-ron, Al-e-ron," which was echoed by Geldun and then by the soldiers in formation. Soon, the entire hall erupted in a raucous chant of "Al-e-ron, Al-e-ron."

Finally, Aleron rose from his seat and strode to the front of the dais. As the crowd became silent, he announced, with voice booming through the huge room, "Citizens of Sudea, I come to you in time of war, the like of which has not been seen since my namesake left you. I am a direct male-line descendant of that Aleron, as was my father, Valgier, though he knew not that he was anything but a common man. I am halfblood, through my mother, Audina, and descended of the royal house of Elvenholm. As such, I am the first direct link between our two houses. I look forward to leading my people in the difficult times to come, but first, I must leave you for a short time." In answer to the looks of dismay that began to form on many of the faces, he explained, "I must go now to Kolixtla to regain what was taken from us. I go to claim our queen, from the bondage of her captors!" News of Eilowyn's kidnapping was now common knowledge, so many in the crowd recognized who he was and understood, though none of them knew of his claim to the throne prior to that moment. With that, he raised Andhanimwhid high. Crackling blue lightning arced from the tip, filling the upper reaches of the hall. The crowd cheered fervently. When the cheers died down, he announced, "In my absence and as always before, your Steward shall rule in my stead. In addition, if he so chooses to accept the honor, I would name my grandfather, Lord Marshal Hadaras, known in past ages as Goromir, High Sorcerer of Elvenholm, as my chief military advisor."

Stunned silence overtook the hall once more, as Aleron again lowered the sword to point down. The utterance of the name "Goromir", in reference to a living being, much less a person in the same room, was more of a shock than the emergence of a new king. Even Aleron's companions stood slack jawed as Hadaras separated himself from them to ascend the dais. Genuflecting before Aleron, he said, "It will be an honor for me to once again serve the kingdom."

"Rise, Grandfather," Aleron directed, holding forth his hand. "You should bow to no one, not even me." Hadaras took the outstretched hand in his and stood. Then the three faced the assemblage, with Aleron in the center, Gealton to his right and Hadaras to his left. Aleron addressed the crowd once more, "People of Sudea, I fear that this war will see the Nameless One, the Adversary, loosed once more upon the world. Our newfound ally, Thallasia, reports of one, claiming to be Son of the Nameless God, who came to their shores. If he is as he says, he will seek to free his father and even return to him his weapon of power. Gird for war, my people." He turned away and moved for the door he had used so many years before, upon first learning of his destiny. Hadaras and Gealton fell in behind. Barathol and Gealton looked at one another, then hurried up the steps and to the back, after the others.

Upon entering the antechamber to the old Steward's office, Gealton stated, "That went remarkably well. Good speech, Your Highness."

"Please, Milord, don't call me that in private. I didn't even feel like that was me talking up there. As soon as I touched that sword, it was as if someone else took over."

"Well, you need to stop calling me, Lord, as well, so I guess we should just go with our names in private then?"

"That sounds good to me."

"That sword, my boy, contains the spark of every king that ever held it," Hadaras informed them. "It is not simply a reservoir of power, it is a source of compiled wisdom as well, like a book, with many authors. When you hold it, you are in communion with your ancestors and it may take you over, as it did just now."

"Well, that explains where that speech came from," Geldun offered. "I knew you weren't that smart."

An hour later, three ravens winged off to the north, with Hadaras and Gealton watching from the ancient battlements.

"I hope they find my girl, old friend," Gealton wished out loud. "I pray they find her, and all make it home safe."

"I as well, old friend, and I have faith in their abilities to do just that. What I pray for most, is that my boy practices some restraint."

"Why do you say that?"

"I hope that these years at war have not made him callous to the fact that there are innocents everywhere, even Kolixtla. I hope that he does not let his anger get the better of him."

"Is the lad that powerful?"

"In a word, yes. Considering the sheer force he wielded the day his power manifested, today, he could likely level a city."

"You're worried for his spirit as much as for his life?" Gealton surmised.

"Yes, now he has claimed the throne. Let us hope he does not ascend it a bloodthirsty tyrant."

"Let us hope and pray then."

Chapter 39

Shilwezday, Day 26, Squash Moon, 8765 Sudean Calendar

The ravens flew high above the jungle canopy of Kolixtlan, cultivated fields in sight on the horizon. They passed over many patches of settlement and cultivation, carved from the dense rainforest, on this journey, but the scene ahead seemed much more expansive than any they had encountered before. Soon, they found themselves over fields of maize and rice, orchards of citrus or banana, as well as crops none of them recognized. Livestock grazed upon open pastureland; the humped cattle of the tropics reminded the southerners of their first year as marines. After about one bell from when they first reached the fields, Aleron and his companions caught their first glimpse of the capital city Kolixtla and the Kolixtlani Sea beyond. They could see a complex of stepped pyramids, topped with temples, on the eastern edge of the city and the tall spires of the royal palace, towards the center of the city. Low, flat-roofed buildings, ranging from one to three stories, dominated the rest of the sprawling metropolis.

The trio memorized a map of the city and knew the approximate location of the government facilities. The original map was over four thousand years old, but the recreation they studied included recent intelligence, mainly gathered by Castian spies. Western Castians can easily pass for Kolixtlani in appearance and spies learn the up-to-date dialect from captives taken attempting to cross the borders. Smuggling is common along the borders of Kolixtlan and, many Kolixtlanis attempt to cross into Castia each year, to escape the oppressive regime and impoverished conditions of their homeland. Most immigrants gain asylum, as long as their story is verifiable, and authorities determine they are not spies. Castia imprisons or deports smugglers, though some enter into Castian Intelligence.   As emigration and smuggling are illegal in Kolixtlan, deportation is essentially a death sentence for any Kolixtlani sent back.

✳✳✳

Eilowyn waited in her "quarters", in a high tower at the Royal Palace. So far, they were treating her well enough, though heaviness filled her heart at the loss of Aleron's amulet. She remembered how two days prior, her captors delivered her to the Kolixtlani palace.

She was received by six female servants, supervised by one she assumed to be a priestess of some sort. They took her to the baths and directed her to disrobe and enter the steaming water. Eilowyn understood no Kolixtlani, but the pantomime from one of the attendants was sufficient to convey their intent. Not feeling as if she had any option but to comply, she undressed and made towards the bath. It was then that the priestess caught a glimpse of the blue quartz and silver amulet, screaming an oath in recognition. Two attendants grabbed her arms, pulling her to face the priestess, who unceremoniously, ripped the charm from Eilowyn's breast, breaking the fine silver chain. The priestess shouted instructions to the attendants and then wheeled about, leaving the bathhouse. Within minutes, a different priestess entered to take up the duty of supervising her bath and subsequent dressing. After they dressed, coifed and perfumed her, the attendants brought her into the presence of the king. As they halted before the throne, she genuflected, knowing that despite their rude treatment of her, propriety and graciousness on her part would likely irk them more than belligerence.

"Greetings, Princess. I hope your stay with us has been pleasant, so far," the king said in only slightly stilted Sudean. An elderly man, dressed in robes equally as sumptuous as the king's, stood off to his left.

"Yes, Your Grace, your staff has been most gracious in their treatment of me. However, I must tell you that as daughter of the Steward, I have no such lofty title as "Princess"."

"Very well, Lady Eilowyn, I applaud your modesty, but as the child of the most powerful individual in Sudea, your worth to us as a hostage more than equals that of any actual Princess the world over." He continued, saying, "Now, my High Priest informs me that you had in your possession a magical amulet. Would you mind explaining to us what purpose it served you?" The man to his left produced her amulet from beneath his robes. The chain repaired, it glowed from within, with a faint blue light.

"Your Grace, that was a gift from my betrothed," she explained.

"Are magical engagement gifts commonplace in your land?" the king inquired. "My friend here informs me that this artifact holds considerable power." The other man muttered something in Kolixtlani to the king. "He also assures me that you are no sorcerer. What sort of man is your betrothed?"

"My betrothed is but a soldier, Your Grace, from a minor noble family. He told me that he purchased it from an elvish craftsman, at no small price. He saved for many months to buy it for me. It is supposed to be warded to protect me and to draw him to me if I am ever lost to him."

"Elvish work, it obviously is, and it must have cost him tremendously, but I have trouble believing that the Steward's daughter should be promised to a common soldier. How is it that you father allowed this?"

"Your Grace, many, to include my father, believe him to be destined for greatness, possibly a generalship. By all accounts, he has dispatched hundreds of your fine fighting men, by his own hand and he is a fine strategist for one as young as he."

"Really, My Lady and do you believe your future husband, the fearsome warrior that he is, will come here to rescue you, here at the heart of my kingdom?"

"Your Grace, I do not believe that to be possible," she answered. "The charm was only intended for if we became separated, but still close at hand. There is no way he could make his way to me here, over such great distance." She truly believed this to be true, but that did not prevent her from hoping that she be mistaken.

"Anyhow, My Lady, my High Priest shall maintain possession of your little charm. It is not often that he has opportunity to examine artifacts of elvish make, plus, in case there is more to this charm than you allude to, it is best in his safekeeping," the king explained. "Besides, I have thoughts to wed you to one of my own sons. That would serve better to establish a tie between our nations than marrying you off to some common soldier. I seek an end to this unfortunate war between our countries."

Eilowyn's composure broke at that revelation, and she replied in a quavering voice, "I suppose I am at your mercy, Your Grace."

"Yes, you are, My Lady," he returned. Visibly beaming at her discomfort, the king continued, "That will be all for you today." To her attendants, he directed something in Kolixtlani and then they whisked her from the audience chamber and brought to her quarters here in the tower.

The following morning, she awoke to be taken, once again, to the bath, followed by the dressing room. She returned to her quarters for a simple meal of various fruits, some familiar, others not, accompanied by a cooked porridge of maize. After breaking her fast, two attendants arrived in the room, followed shortly by stooped, aged man, with long straight white hair and beard, carrying two leather bound volumes. Thus began her instruction in the language of Kolixtlan.

This morning began much the same as the one before. Apparently, the Kolixtlani are adamant about bathing daily. Finished with breakfast, she now waited on the arrival of her tutor.

***

Stubbs and Stretch wandered out from the market square of Kolixtla and into a back alley leading to their boarding house. Both wore the royal seal around their necks, allowing the foreigners to roam freely in a land normally closed to outsiders. Having spent two days resting in the capital, the hired kidnappers planned to take their leave of the city at next sunrise. Both carried a jug of the local cactus wine, which they swigged from periodically. "We gotta get some shuteye 'fore morning," Stubbs commented, "so let's find us some girls."

"Kinda early for them to be out," Stretch replied, "but we should be able to find an open brothel somewhere."

"We got a long road ahead, so we best take advantage of this city livin' while we can."

Three of the mangy local curs trooped out of a side alley, to mill about their feet. The smallest bounced and lunged, as if inviting them to play, so Stretch aimed a kick, which it deftly avoided. While the men were distracted, the largest of the three, a shaggy black mongrel, lunged for Stretch's throat. Stubbs moved for his sword, but the other two curs clamped onto his wrists, taking him to the ground kicking and screaming. Finished with Stretch, the large black dog lunged in to crush the shorter man's larynx in his bloodied muzzle and then backed off to replace one of the ones holding a wrist. Thus relieved, the rangy yellow dog moved to a place behind his head. Stubbs could only gurgle, struggling to breathe through his ruined throat, as the dog stared down into his eyes. He felt the layers of his mind peel away, as the thing he knew now could not be a dog, methodically picked through his memories, until it found that for which it searched. All at once, the curs released him and backed away, observing him curl into a ball, gurgling in a pitiful attempt to whimper, as he sank into madness.

"*His name is Cyrus, and his friend is Jerod, or was, that is,*" Aleron informed them as they trotted off, "*before Barry ripped out his throat. They came from Ebareiza, which explains how they passed for Sudeans. They dropped Ellie off to the priests at the royal palace two days ago.*"

"*What will happen to the one we left alive?*" asked Geldun.

"*I'm not sure. Maybe his mind will recover, eventually, if he lives through what Barry did to his throat.*"

"*I'll be right back,*" Barathol announced, before doubling back around the corner of the building from whence they came. The others waited for him to return a few moments later. "*Broke his neck…couldn't leave him like that,*" he explained on his return.

"*You're a better man than I,*" Aleron complimented. "*I was going to let him suffer.*"

"*We may be hard, Al, but I don't think we need to be cruel,*" Barathol replied.

"You're right, of course. It's just that I saw what he imagined doing to Ellie when I picked through his mind. I wanted him to suffer for that."

"Everyone has dark thoughts Al," Geldun interceded, *"but he didn't actually do anything to her, did he?"*

"No," Aleron admitted, *"he was a perfect gentleman toward her, aside from butchering her bodyguards and train."*

"Sounds like it was just business then, for them at least," Barathol offered.

"Yeah, but it gets kind of personal, when it happens to people you know."

Moments later, they were back in their corvid guise, flapping upwards for a better view of the city. *"I remember you saying that you use the magic around you,"* Geldun started, *"but what happens if there's no magic to be had?"*

"The only place I ever had trouble finding magic was deep in a cave," Aleron answered, *"and even then, it was only certain kinds and I still managed to scrape enough together to do what I needed to do. Why do you ask...worried about changing back?"*

"In a word, yes, I'd hate to be stuck as a raven with a fight at hand."

"I don't think we have anything to worry about." Aleron led them high above the rooftops, winging toward the tall spires of the royal palace. *"I can feel Ellie's amulet in that tower to the back right. I doubt she still has it, but whoever does may know where she is."*

They alighted upon the uppermost battlement of the tower Aleron singled out earlier. Similar to the situation in Arundell, this battlement was no longer manned since the city's fortifications were pushed to a wider perimeter than in ancient times. The three friends veered back to their proper forms, screened by the crenulated wall surrounding the uppermost level. "Where does our gear go when we shift?" Geldun inquired. "How come we don't end up naked?"

"I'm not sure," Aleron replied, in a whisper. "I just picture what I want, and the magic does the rest."

"Thanks for sharing that with us Al; now I feel much more secure about it," Barathol commented, facetiously.

They made for the bulkhead leading to the lower levels. "I can feel the amulet is just below this floor," Aleron announced. Aleron tried the door and discovered it to be locked from the inside. "Locked! Probably just a precaution, or else they're genuinely worried about someone scaling the walls to get inside. If that's the case, it doesn't say much for their confidence in the people."

"Remember the prisoners we've taken, Al?" Geldun reminded him, "every one a conscript, but the officers."

"Yeah, not a volunteer among them, if you can believe what they told the terps," Barathol added.

Aleron cast his senses to the hatch and soon the others heard a soft metallic clunk emanate from behind the door. He reached for the handle, as Barathol covered the opening with his pike. Geldun set himself to enter first, sword and buckler at the ready, as the hatchway opened, revealing a dimly lit stairwell. Aleron peered in, motioned him forward and then drew his twin cutlasses, in preparation to follow. Andhanimwhid remained strapped to his back, bulky and inconvenient in its full six feet. Barathol took up the rear and the three crept slowly down the stair. Upon reaching the bottom, the stopped to listen and then Geldun carefully checked both directions down the corridor. "Which way, Al," he asked.

"Left seems closer, he replied."

Geldun stepped to the center of the corridor and faced left. Aleron and Barathol took their places to his left and right, respectively. They could see the hallway curve to their right, obscuring what lay ahead. Doorways punctuated the wall to the outside, while the smooth granite wall to their right appeared unbroken. Aleron sensed a large chamber to that side and that the amulet lay within. *"Let's talk like this from here on out. I think we just have to find the doorway to this room on the right,"* he told them. *"Ellie's charm is in there somewhere."* Clouds of dust rose about their boots, as they quickly and silently made their way. Though the corridor showed little sign of traffic, theirs were not the only footprints. Tracks from soft boots, sporting oddly pointed toes, preceded them. Older tracks of the same sort, going in both directions and leading to many of the doors, could be seen as well.

The tower was large, but not overly so and they soon came to an ornate copper-clad door, etched with numerous glyphs and sigils. The signs seemed to vibrate and flow before their eyes, the unfamiliar symbols appearing to shift one to another. *"This is some strong stuff,"* Aleron commented, as he stepped forward to examine the door. *"Grandfather showed me living script once and it exhausted him to make even a short spell. This must have taken the maker months to complete."*

"What's living script," Barathol asked, *"and what does it do?"*

"Living script makes the strongest wards. Instead of relying on a single symbol, the ward can recite an entire spell, over and over again." He continued scrutinizing the symbols for a time, commenting, *"I can read a fair share of this, and I can tell that there's no way I can break this without the owner knowing about it."*

"Can you break it fast and dirty then?" Geldun offered. *"That may give us a fighting chance."*

"That I can do." Aleron held out his right hand, intending to draw off the chaotic red power, neutralizing the wards and then use it to break the hinges and lock. Instead, the door opened for them.

"You really must learn to shield your thoughts when you converse in that manner, my young sorcerer," High Priest Mahuizohm informed them, from the center of the large circular chamber. "You may as well have been shouting out in the corridor." The chamber was easily twenty yards across, with a domed ceiling supporting itself without any internal supports. The central part of the floor stood nearly a man's height lower than the doorway, forming a sunken circle, about ten yards across, with a black stone altar at the very center. Its obvious intent was an auditorium of some sort, as five rings of raised stone benches circled the presentation area. Additional furniture and benches, these littered with various works in progress, specimens, and artifacts, filled the central floor, indicating that someone had repurposed the chamber as a work area. The High Priest stood in front of the altar, facing the ramp leading up to the entrance. "Please enter my friend and your companions as well. There is no need for those weapons; let us converse as civilized men."

"We can converse priest, but we'll keep our weapons just the same." The men entered the chamber cautiously, looking up and around for possible traps, as they advanced.

"Very well, but this display is highly unnecessary. You come for the girl, I presume."

"Yes," Aleron answered. He could see the faint glow of Eilowyn's amulet on the altar, to the priest's side.

"Ah, what have we here? Is that what I think it is, strapped to your back? Andhanimwhid? So, a king has returned to the throne of Sudea. My apologies, Your Grace, I had no idea who I was addressing."

"I have no time for pleasantries, priest. Where is Lady Eilowyn?"

"Your Grace, we have all the time in the world for pleasantries. Neither your weapons nor your magic will avail you in this place." On that signal, numerous hidden alcoves opened in the wall surrounding the chamber, emitting soldiers armed with crossbows and various close quarters weapons. A quick glance behind them, revealed ranks armed men in position outside the door. Aleron and his companions found themselves surrounded and outnumbered, at least ten to one. Mahuizohm softly uttered something in Kolixtlani that Aleron did not catch, and he felt the power drain from his body. *"Tell your soldiers to hold fast, do not advance,"* he told whoever was in charge of the contingent and Aleron heard someone behind him relay the command.

"Stand down, but keep hold of your weapons," Aleron told the others. "He just told them to hold fast."

"I see that you understand much of our language, Your Grace, most unusual for a soldier, but then you're not just a soldier. You must sense the total draining of magical energy that just ensued. Wonderful stuff this Thallasian bloodstone is; we only discovered it because of the war. Prior to that, the Thallasian sorcerers kept it a closely guarded secret."

"I'm familiar with it, priest."

"Please, call me Mahuizohm. Unshielded, bloodstone draws all red magic to itself, but built into a device, it serves as a repository of power, like your sorcerers use the blue quartz. We have long known that we can be build blue quartz into a power trap as well, though it naturally works as a repository with no special treatment. For safety's sake, I have installed both types of traps in my study, as one can never tell who might attack."

Aleron glanced back at the pommel of the great sword on his back and was relieved to see it still glow with inner blue light, though he knew that if he attempted to draw on the power within, the traps would rob it from him. "Do you really think this will stop me Mahuizohm? I came for Eilowyn, and I intend to leave with her."

"Oh, that will not be possible, Your Grace; she is now officially betrothed to Prince Ehacatl, heir to Achcauhtli, king of Kolixtlan. It seems she did not believe you would come for her, so she chose instead to work toward a peace between our realms. If you like, the king has many beautiful daughters, and I am sure he would gladly marry one to the heir to the throne of Sudea. Thus joined, our alliance will be the most powerful the world has seen since the Great War."

"Still not interested." Aleron thought through his options. They could attempt to fight their way out, at ten to one odds, with the enemy holding the choke point. That would likely see them all dead. On the other hand, they could surrender and try to find a way out later. He did not doubt that Mahuizohm had some way to shield himself from the effects of a power trap, so rushing the priest was out. He glanced up to the ceiling, seeing the polished light tunnels from the rooftop providing diffuse natural lighting, when the idea came to him. He focused his concentration for a moment and his companions noticed the gasp of recognition from the suddenly wide-eyed High Priest. The chamber erupted with bright green luminescence, lasting a score of heartbeats. Small plants on one of the benches capriciously overflowed their pots, twining out onto the floor. Crocks on another bench bubbled and overflowed. The soldiers surrounding them grew withered and frail, several toppling as the armor became too much for their aged bodies to support. Mahuizohm, aged beyond comprehension, knelt by the altar, clutching his chest. Aleron strode down the ramp, toward the priest, swatting away two bolts launched by archers still in possession of the faculties to shoot. Other bolts flew wild and soldiers attempting to advance stumbled and fell, as old age took them. Geldun and Barathol mowed down those within reach and still on their feet and then turned their attention to the doorway. Fresh troops, not caught in the blaze, began their advance into Mahuizohm's study. Aleron reached the priest and placed one hand on his head. Mahuizohm's eyes glazed over as Aleron peeled back his mind like the layers of an onion. The High Priest collapsed when Aleron released his head and turned his attention back to the rest of the chamber. Snatching up the amulet from the altar, he placed it around his neck and advanced to assist his friends at the door. "Let me through!" he shouted, as he came up behind his friends. They held the entrance well, but being on the downhill side and outnumbered, it was doomed to not last. His friends stepped to the side, as he waded in, twin blades singing. A blast of blue flashed and crackled as soon as he cleared the door. Turning back to the others, he said, "All clear." Barathol and Geldun stepped over bodies into the corridor to see clouds of fine gray ash lazily settle to the floor, joining the older dust.

"That's a nice trick," Geldun commented.

"Yeah, that would have been handy in a few of the scrapes we've found ourselves in," Barathol added.

"Whoa!" Geldun exclaimed. "What happened to you? You look old as dirt." Geldun alluded to the fact that Aleron aged from channeling so much of the green energy at once, though he shielded himself from most of the effects. Green magic acts to facilitate growth, but for living things with a set lifespan, it eventually brings old age and death.

He glanced at the now rough skin of his exposed hands and replied, "Grandfather warned me about using that form, but I had little choice." Now that he had the time to think about it, his knees and back felt a bit stiffer than they used to. He noticed his companions bleeding from several minor wounds, so he reached out to them and placed a hand on each one's shoulder. Healing energy passed through him, into his friends and their bruises and lacerations faded and knitted together. All that remained of their wounds was a few smears of blood and faint pink lines. "Now my knees feel better."

"I feel great now, but you still look old," Barathol informed him.

Geldun nodded in agreement. "Fifty, at least."

Aleron looked to his weathered hands again and said, "Time to try something else." He concentrated once more, and a faint yellow-green glow bathed his form. His companions watched as his facial features reverted to those of a much younger man. "How about now?" he asked the pair.

"Much better," Geldun answered, "but you still seem older, just not old."

Aleron began to realize that the combination of green and yellow magic works to regenerate, but it would not reverse aging beyond healthy adulthood. "Well, we don't have time for anything else right now. I know where they are holding Ellie and it looks like it will be a fight to get her out. Let me cover up this mess; that will stall them for a little while." He returned to the doorway, kicked a stray arm to the inside and drew the door closed. The once flowing symbols now stood as raised letters, unmoving. With a slight gesture of his right hand, the bloodstains of the doorway dissolved in a spray of blue sparks. With another gesture, he reactivated the wards, and the script began morphing as it had when they arrived. Turning back to them, he said, "The stairwell is just around the bend, to the right, but we'll run a full circle first, to cover all these tracks. I'll take up the rear, this time, so let's go." They formed up and began to jog down the corridor, Geldun on the left, with Barathol slightly behind and to the right, covering his shield side with the pike. Aleron followed, with swords drawn and casting a curtain of blue energy behind them, incinerating everything they passed and leaving a smooth layer of fine, dusty ash behind. He had many things to think about, as they ran; Mahuizohm's mind held more than just Eilowyn's whereabouts.

Chapter 40

Shilwezday, Day 26, Squash Moon, 8765 Sudean Calendar

Zormat started from his meditation, Mahuizohm's anguish resounding in his mind like a clanging gong. Someone killed the priest and was none too gentle about it, shredding the man's mind in the process. An enemy of such power did not bode well for the cause of the One True God. They sailed the open sea again, having exited the Wabani Inlet, as the Adari referred to it, several days past. He could sense the power of Zadehmal now, drawing him north with visions of fire and ice. He was too close now to think of turning back. The Kolixtlani would have to sort this out for themselves. Once he had his father's weapon, he would free him and return his father's power to him. Then, he thought, none on Aertu could stand against them. *The time is close now Father, to bring the One True God back to his dominion.*

The ancient tutor left her and Eilowyn waited for the mid-day meal that followed her lesson. She felt refreshed by the cool breeze blowing through the open windows. Kolixtla is a bit warmer than Arundell, but a good sight cooler than the sweltering Cop-Castia border she recently passed through. Attendants soon returned with food. She noted that there seemed to be more and larger trays than in the days prior. The servants moved to the edge of the room just as two guards posted inside the doorway. An official stepped inside, shouted something in Kolixtlani about a prince, the rest she didn't catch and then stepped to the side and bowed deeply. The female attendants bowed as well and Eilowyn took this as a cue, leaving her chair and genuflecting in the manner of Sudean ladies. She noted trousers of purple silk, richly embroidered with silver thread, bloused over tall boots of soft red leather.

"Rise, please, my Princess!" the newcomer announced. "Bowing is for those below my station, not my future wife!" Bristling at the implication of his words, she looked up to see a tall and handsome man, with olive complexion. The oddly slanted eyes and high cheekbones punctuated by a proud aquiline nose, which appeared to have been broken at least once. He wore a short-sleeved gambeson of the same purple cloth and silver embroidery, belted at the waist and extending to mid-thigh. One of the curious, cleaver-like, Kolixtlani swords hung from the belt and his thick muscled arms sported splinted vambraces of fine leather and gold inlaid steel. The man was obviously a fighter and not some coddled prince. He barked something else in his native tongue, causing the servants and the official to recover and then the official proceeded to direct the servants about their business. "Allow me to introduce myself," he said, reaching out to help her rise. She took his hands graciously and he continued, "I am Prince Ehacatl, heir to the throne of Kolixtlan. Please, allow me to seat you." She let him lead her to her seat and push in her chair. She picked up the scent of fresh sweat on a clean body and horses, as if he only just finished exercising. He took the seat opposite her, and the servants immediately sprang into action, placing lap cloths, pouring drinks and delivering the first course. Noting the slight crinkle of her nose, he explained, "I must apologize, that I allowed my riding practice to extend too late to afford time to bathe."

"That is not at all a concern, my Lord Prince. I must say you have a strong command of my native tongue. I apologize that I cannot say the same for my mastery of yours."

"That is quite all right, my Princess. I realize that others do not consider our language important enough to teach. That is an unfortunate situation that I hope to see remedied in the near future. Those raised in the royal house are taught the languages of our neighbors, as a matter of course," he continued. "I must say, you are much lovelier than I even hoped."

"Thank you, Lord Prince," she replied, blushing at the compliment.

"Please, call me Ehacatl. May I have the privilege to address you by your given name?

"Yes, of course Eh...acatl," she stumbled slightly at the unfamiliar pronunciation. "I am called Eilowyn."

"Eilowyn...I like the sound of that. It is fitting for one beautiful as you are, like a jewel." The prince continued to compliment her, as they enjoyed the mid-day meal together. Despite her reservations at being captive and in love with another, she found it difficult to dislike this handsome, gracious warrior. He answered her questions about Kolixtlan and she, likewise, answered many of the questions he had about Sudea, carefully guarding anything that she thought useful against her people, but giving trivial information freely. She learned that he served as commander to an elite cavalry company that often engaged Sudean forces on the northern borders of the country.

"Perhaps you have met my betrothed?" she suggested. "He is a marine and has spent much time on that front. Tall, gold-brown hair and moustache, he wields two cutlasses, normally." She noted a glint of recognition in his expression and took some pleasure in that, but the prince said nothing to acknowledge her comment.

"I hope to convince you to accept a new life here in our fair kingdom, My Princess. Neither the king nor I will force you into an unwanted marriage. As a hostage, you are too valuable to ever trade away and your life here will be tedious, at best. As my princess and someday, my queen, you will be responsible for ending the hostilities between our peoples. For that you will be loved by all, and Kolixtlan will be at your feet."

✳✳✳

"This is likely to get ugly," Aleron said as they reentered the stairwell. "They know we're here now and it won't be long until the whole palace is on alert. As soon as those soldiers fail to return with us in tow, the alarm will go up."

"Do you think they'll find the bodies?" Geldun asked, as they sped up the gently curved staircase, toward the roof.

"Not for a while," he replied. "They will have to find a priest that knows the wards or is stronger than the one who set them. Either way, that will take some time."

They burst out through the bulkhead and onto the roof. Barathol uttered an oath, as he turned left in time to duck a sword strike. Geldun peeled right to engage a second guard. Aleron had opportunity to survey the situation as he exited the bulkhead and scanned the entire rooftop. A pair of guards placed themselves to either side of the opening, but the speed of the marine's exit provided enough surprise to delay their attacks on the trio. Barathol beat back his opponent, pushing until he rounded the bulkhead, forcing his adversary back-to-back with the other guard. Both guards carried short double-edged swords, widest at the chisel-pointed tip and tall skinny shields. The weapons, sandals, segmented cuirasses and pteruged skirts, leaving the legs bare, except for greaves, marked these men as foot soldiers. Kolixtlani cavalry wore boots, trousers, lamellar armor, and wielded longer swords of the same cleaver-like style. Geldun held his opponent at bay, neither gaining nor losing quarter. Mere moments sufficed for Aleron to take in the scene and deliver twin bolts of blue lightning from the tips of his cutlasses. The smell of charred flesh filled the air as the soldiers fell, the gaping wounds in their chests smoking at the edges. Barathol and Geldun stopped to catch their breaths and watched, as Aleron's eyes seemed to glaze over. The bulkhead faded into a cloud of white mist, too bright to look at directly. They shielded their eyes until the glare died down and when they were able to look again, they saw the stairwell plugged with a solid slab of shiny black stone.

"How did…Never mind," Geldun said, as Barathol stood goggle-eyed.

"Same thing as when I turn us to ravens," Aleron replied to Geldun's unfinished question. "Air is substance too, so I changed stone, wood, and some air into a slab of black glass a yard thick. It will be a while before they have easy access to this rooftop again. I got a good idea of where they have Ellie. See the tower to the center?" The others turned to where he pointed and voiced affirmation. Several hundred yards distant, a tall spire rose over one hundred feet above the red-tiled rooftops of the sprawling palace complex. "Let's go then," he stated, as they veered back into their raven disguises.

Flapping into the sky, they saw soldiers, priests, priestesses, and acolytes scurrying about in the courtyard below. Obviously, word of their arrival was out. Several runners moved out in different directions, including the tower that was the object of their attention. *We need to move fast, before they bundle her up and hide her somewhere else.*

✳✳✳

"*Your Highness,*" a messenger shouted, rushing to the doorway, and nearly plowing into the suddenly lowered pikes of the guards. Eilowyn could not understand much else of what the young soldier managed to get out between gasping to catch his breath. Something about an attack and she thought she caught the High Priest's name in there as well. Ehacatl leapt to his feet and shouted orders to the servants. She recognized her own name and something about safety or security among the shouts.

The official who had accompanied the prince sprang into action at Ehacatl's command and came to her, saying, "You must come with me, My Lady. The palace is under some sort of attack, and I must ensure your safety." He shouted orders in Kolixtlani, and her attendants joined him in escorting her off to a back room, centrally located, with no windows. It had the look of a well-appointed prison cell and Eilowyn guessed it to be just that, for important prisoners, like uncooperative hostages. A single small bed, one chair, a reading desk, and a footlocker made up the furnishings of the room. The two women guided her through the door by her elbows, while the official said, "You will be safe in here, My Lady, until we take care of this situation. He closed the door behind them and Eilowyn heard the muffled clank of the lock setting. She heard much shouting, accompanied by the stamp of numerous feet and the clank of weapons and armor, only somewhat muffled by the thick iron banded wooden door. The attendants continued to pull her toward the back of the room, away from the door. As they sat her in the lone chair, she sensed the noise subside, replaced by cold silence. The soldiers on the other side were waiting, patiently and quietly, for whatever might come.

✳✳✳

Well, we can't change back here now, can we? Geldun observed, as the ravens scrabbled for a hold on the steeply pitched tile roof.

And if we fly through a window, they'll likely kill us as we change, Barathol added.

We'll go in through the roof, Aleron replied. *Now look away this time, so I don't blind you again. We'll change back when we get somewhere with better footing. Ellie is somewhere in this upper level, so we need to go through the ceiling.* A portion of the terracotta roof tiles glowed bight white and then dissipated into mist. Aleron hopped into the dark attic space, followed by his companions. Something made him glance up to see several small sets of eyes glinting in the faint light afforded by the opening Aleron made. He croaked at the bats, but they only kept staring at the three birds that had no business disturbing their rest. *She's over here, I think,* he said, hopping across the open ceiling joists, *right under here I'm pretty sure.*

How can you tell? Barathol asked. *You have the amulet, not her.*

I bound the charm to Ellie and myself when I gave it to her. The spells I used connect us through the amulet, so it doesn't much matter which one of us has it, at least when we're close to one another. I'm sure of it; she's directly under me. Get separated and take a solid stance and then I'll change us back. With each of them occupying their own joist, Aleron caused them to veer into their natural forms. Unfortunately for Barathol, the form was that of a very large, heavy man in chain and plate. A sick expression crossed his features as his joist first creaked and then gave way, with a resounding crack. He fell through the ceiling in a hail of plaster, lath and dust. A woman screamed as Aleron leapt through the jagged hole his companion made. He saw Barathol roll through the debris and back to his feet. As Aleron landed, the butt of Barathol's glaive snapped out to catch the screaming woman in the left temple,

231

knocking her unconscious. *Not a sound, or you die,* Aleron commanded into the other Kolixtlani woman's mind, drawing one cutlass. A look of sheer terror came over her and she clamped her lips shut. Geldun swung to the floor right behind him as Eilowyn stood, knocking her chair over backwards, with a half stunned and half-elated expression on her face.

"Aleron, you came!" She shouted, as he crossed the room to gather her into his arms. She was unable to get another word out as he kissed her hard on the mouth. Finally, she pulled away, gasping, and said, "The door, it locks from the outside and that room is full of soldiers."

They could hear shouting in Kolixtlani from the other side of the door, along with the sound of a lock being cycled. Barathol had already taken position at the door, while Geldun held the conscious woman at the point of his sword. Aleron broke away, ran to the door, and placed his hands upon it. In a blinding flash, the doorway became one with the stone wall. A faint scream from the other side might have been from one whose hands suddenly became part of a solid stone wall. Turning, he strode straight to the attendant Geldun held captive. She cowered and started babbling when Aleron reached out to place a hand on her forehead. She went limp as soon as he touched her, and he caught her to ease her to the floor. He then went to the one Barathol had knocked unconscious and placed his hand upon her head as well. "You damn near killed her Barry," he said, before concentrating to guide healing energy into the injured woman. The yellow glow of it suffused her and then dissipated. Her breathing became stronger, and she rolled into a fetal position and a deep sleep. "Neither of them should wake up anytime soon."

"Eilowyn, My Princess, what is happening in there? Are you unharmed?" they could hear, heavily muffled, from a thickly accented voice on the other side of the wall.

"Prince Ehacatl, I presume?" he murmured to Eilowyn.

"Yes," she replied, "and how did you know?"

"The girl I put to sleep had it right on the surface of her mind, as if she was about to shout it out. Do you know him?"

"We just met. The king wants to marry me to him. He seems nice enough."

"So, you like him?"

Eilowyn's face took on an annoyed expression. "Yes, I like him. He's handsome, charming and has good manners, unlike some people I know, but I love you, you idiot."

"I hate to break up this little reunion," Geldun asserted, "but there's a mass of soldiers on the other side of that wall and we're sealed up in here. It's only a matter of time before they bust through the wall or figure out the ceiling thing."

232

"We'll just make a hole and fly out," Barathol offered.

"One problem with that," Geldun countered, "remember how long it took us to learn how to fly? Lady Eilowyn here hasn't had that opportunity yet. Al?"

"I may have overlooked that little detail," Aleron conceded.

"What are you all babbling about?" Eilowyn demanded. "You're making absolutely no sense! And how did you come through the ceiling anyway? This is the top story of the tower."

"I turned us into ravens, and we flew here," Aleron told her, "but now we have to figure a way out of here. Geldun's right, we don't have the time to teach you how to fly." A dull thud reverberated through the wall separating them from the Kolixtlani soldiers and it continued as a steady rhythmic pounding. Dust sifted from the joints of the stonework.

"What did I tell you," Geldun commented. "They're going to break down the wall."

"It looks like I'll have to blast a hole through the wall and take out as many as I can. Then we'll have to fight our way down to the ground floor."

"Sounds like a plan," Barathol replied, wryly. "I'll take the hundred on the left, like usual. You got the hundred on the right Gel?"

"Sure, just like usual."

"Aleron," Eilowyn interjected, "is there any way short of killing them all? They have not been unkind to me."

"They hired those men to kill your retinue and kidnap you. I'll kill them all if I can."

"Then why did you save her?" she asked, nodding toward the unconscious attendant.

"I...I don't know why I saved her. It just seemed like the right thing to do."

"I think he's a good man Aleron, just born on the wrong side. Try to find some restraint, please."

The pounding continued and some of the stones moved visibly. Soon the Kolixtlanis would be through the wall, and he would have to do something. "Cover your ears and look away," he commanded the others. A look of intense concentration came over him and thrusting his hands, palm forward, he caused the entire wall to flash bright white and then followed with a blast of purple from his palms. The back blast of the concussion drove him back a step and caused his companions to drop to their knees. His own ears were ringing, and he wished he had the opportunity to cover them as he instructed the others to do. As the dust settled and his companions recovered, they saw the entire wall absent, cleanly cut at the inside corners, from floor to ceiling. The room outside was littered with broken furniture and dinnerware. Wall hangings hung askew or dislodged altogether, and bodies lay everywhere, some still, some moving slightly and groaning. It looked to be a platoon of around forty foot soldiers, all rendered unconscious by the concussive blast he projected through the wall as he converted it from solid to gas. Barely a pane of glass remained in any of the window openings. He quickly identified the prince, in his fine horseman's garb and pulled him from the rubble. His sword arm was obviously dislocated and Aleron placed his hands on Ehacatl's chest and probed him for other injuries. Broken ribs and slight bleeding inside his skull were all he found.

"Al, let's go!" Geldun shouted. "There's sure to be more on the way."

"Just a moment Gel," he replied, as a golden glow enveloped the prince. The glow subsided and the prince's eyes fluttered open. Aleron projected, *Eilowyn is not for you,* into Ehacatl's mind, before putting him back to sleep. Meanwhile, Geldun kept watch on the doorway to the stairs, while Barathol wandered the room, knocking anyone who showed any trace of consciousness. "He will be fine Ellie, but we won't be if we don't get moving soon." She nodded affirmation and moved to follow him to the stair. "Barry, Gel, you form up the lead and I'll take rear guard. Ellie, stay right behind them and in front of me." They moved cautiously out of the room but found no opposition in the stairwell. Apparently, the soldiers intended to ambush them inside Eilowyn's quarters. They moved rapidly down the staircase, spiraling down the outer wall of the tower. Doors they passed on lower levels remained closed, but Aleron knew they would meet resistance somewhere, as there was no way the blast would go unnoticed. Quick glances out the windows they passed showed people gathering in the courtyard below, looking upwards. *I have Eilowyn back, but this is far from over.*

Chapter 41

Shilwezday, Day 26, Squash Moon, 8765 Sudean Calendar

Achcauhtli said, "Allow the messenger to enter." He sat upon his gilded throne, already troubled by the news of Mahuizohm's apparent disappearance, along with an entire platoon of garrison soldiers. He left word of something momentous about to occur, but since then, the High Priest communicated nothing and the doors to his laboratory remained locked and warded. None of the other priests had any knowledge of the wards Mahuizohm used to secure the room. He knew in his gut that they were under attack, and suspecting a connection to the Sudean Princess, he ordered soldiers to augment the tower guard and alert his son of the potential for danger. Now a messenger with more urgent news waited outside.

"Your Grace," the soldier hailed, as he bowed deeply, still breathing heavily from his sprint to the throne room.

"Rise and give me your news."

"Your Grace, there was some sort of blast at the top of the tower. Soldiers were dispatched immediately, Sire. We do not yet know what happened, or the extent of the damages.

"Ehacatl!" the king exclaimed, "my son!"

"Sire, what do you wish to do?" asked Matlal, the young Captain so pivotal in the first contact with the Arkans, who quickly became one of the king's advisors.

"I need to find my son," he replied, rising from his seat. "My armor, now!" Servants rushed to obey, while the king shed his royal robes.

"Your Grace, I can go with a contingent of the Royal Guard. There is no need to place yourself in danger," Matlal implored him. As the officer first to greet Zormat, his fortunes had risen, and he was now Captain of the King's Guard.

"That is my first-born son in that tower, Captain, I will go myself and you will accompany me. Don your armor Matlal and call up my escort." Servants arrived with the king's gambeson and armor, while Matlal sprinted to the guardroom to roust the king's escort and don his own armor.

***

They rushed down the stairs, keeping Eilowyn between them for her protection. Aleron knew the tower occupied the south corner of the keep and that they would likely have to fight their way out of the keep and across the entire palace grounds, to escape into the city. Once in the city, they would need to go underground. Mahuizohm's memories gave him extensive knowledge of the palace and the city, but the information remained somewhat jumbled in Aleron's mind. He hoped to be able to sort it out in time to make use of it in their escape. They were nearly to the bottom and had yet to meet any resistance. He knew the stairwell opened into a large hall, adjacent to the kitchens and there were sure to be people coming that way to investigate the blast. "This opens up into a hall where we'll probably find trouble. I'll take the lead and you protect Ellie. I know the way out; we'll try to go through the kitchens and out the back of the keep."

"Got it!" Geldun and Barathol replied, in unison.

As they exited the stairwell, a group of palace guards trotted across the open hall. Aleron shouted, "Hard right!" and they cut towards the kitchens. Shoving servants out of the way as they passed, Aleron led them on a winding path through the kitchens, toward a back service door. Barathol paused to upturn a large pot of sauce into the path of their pursuers. Two guards barred the exit, while cooks and scullions scurried to get out of the way. Aleron cut them down without a second glance and they burst out into the back corner of the courtyard. "We need to get to the outer wall as fast as we can. I'll make a hole and then seal it behind us." As he said it, they looked out to a sea of armored men pouring from blockhouses on the outer walls. More came from around the south corner of the keep. Aleron paused to quickly seal the exit behind them, but that would do nothing to stop the flood of soldiers entering the courtyard. He led them further into the open and raised a dome of blue energy to surround the group, just as he had seen Hadaras do, so many years before. Aleron could see no easy way out. Upwards of two hundred Kolixtlani infantry surrounded them, separated only by the dome of magical energy he maintained around them. The soldiers hung back warily after seeing what became of the first lance to probe the dome. He noted the throng parting to admit a group of red-robed individuals and commented, "This is not good."

"What, the fact that we're surrounded, with nowhere to go?" Geldun asked.

"No, the fact that the priests just showed up; looks like a dozen." Aleron felt the jarring sensation as the first volley of red energy crashed against the dome of blue. He sheathed his cutlasses and drew Andhanimwhid from the scabbard across his back. He felt the energy from the sword course through his body and the focus of his protective effort intensify.

"What are you planning Aleron?" Eilowyn asked. They could see the energy infuse him, causing his once gray eyes to shine blue.

"I plan to carve us a path out of this city," he replied, in a voice not entirely his own. As a second volley from the priests impacted, he adjusted his focus to capture the massive amount of chaotic magic. The hue of his protective dome took on a purple caste, as he incorporated the two forces into one.

✳✳✳

"Your Grace, the foreigners escaped through the kitchens to the courtyard, as we arrived to investigate the disturbance in the tower. They somehow sealed the door behind them so we could not pursue," The Lieutenant reported to Achcauhtli and Matlal, as they arrived at the hall adjacent the tower.

"What of the tower? Have you sent men to investigate? The prince was there when the blast occurred," Matlal inquired.

"Sir, the prince was found unconscious, but seemingly uninjured. Upon awakening, he immediately began supervising the evacuation of the wounded. Many soldiers were injured in the blast." Indeed, the first of the wounded were now making their way into the hall, some walking on their own or with assistance, while soldiers carried those still unconscious. They could see that several bled from the nose and ears.

"Your Grace, would you like to proceed to the tower?" Matlal offered.

"No, if Ehacatl is well, I will go to the courtyard to see these foreigners for myself. They should be cornered or captured by now and I wish to know where they came from and how they penetrated our defenses."

"As you wish, Sire," Matlal replied and to the king's escort he directed, "To the southwest exit! We will round the tower to the east courtyard." He preceded the king, while the escort took the flanks and rear guard, and they marched straightaway to the large double doorway. Guards stationed at the exit opened the ironclad doors before them and they stepped out into the bright sunlight and made a left flank to take them around to the east courtyard. They would march out in an orderly and stately fashion to confront these interlopers. The last sight for Matlal and his king was the wall of purple energy that swept them up and crushed them against the wall of the tower like insects.

Ehacatl felt the tower shake to its foundation as the last of the wounded left the upper chamber. "Hurry, get the men to safety!" he shouted, as plaster rained from the ceiling. The Prince had no idea what was happening, but he needed to get he and his men to safety before the tower came down around them.

Broken bodies littered the courtyard of the palace. The tower stood still, though pieces of stonework and roof tiles rained from the upper levels. Barathol was just trying to clear the spots from his vision when he turned to see Aleron lying on the ground, the great sword beside him now dark where it once shone with bright blue energy. Eilowyn stooped to crouch beside him and shake him by the shoulders, but there was no reaction. Barathol scanned the scene and saw a gap where the outer wall collapsed from the blast. He grabbed Aleron under the armpits, drew him upright and then slung him over his shoulder. With his left arm around Aleron's leg and the same hand grabbing the man's wrist, Barathol retrieved his glaive and said, "Eilowyn, grab that sword and stay on my left. Gel, you take point. We're going for that gap in the wall." He straightened under his load, and they sprinted to the wall. Eilowyn had to hike up her skirts to keep up. "Slow it down Gel; neither of us can move as fast as you can right now."

Geldun slowed the pace slightly and they reached the wall together. "It's all clear, so far," he stated, after poking his head past the gap. "We need to find a way to go underground and fast." He led the way across the open ground surrounding the palace walls and into a side alley. They saw a few individuals either unconscious or holding their heads. Apparently, the shock wave extended past the outer walls and into the city. Otherwise, they saw all the windows shuttered and the doors closed. They ran down the alley until he noticed what looked to be an open cellar door. "In here," he said as he ducked inside. The stairs led down to darkness and unknown, but it was their only option before the inevitable pursuit. He felt his way carefully, with Eilowyn close behind and Barathol lumbering behind her, breathing heavily under his burden. At the bottom of the stairwell, he found scant light from vent holes at the top of the wall. They were in what looked to be a storeroom. Whispering, "Set him down here and I'll secure the door," he sprinted back up the stairs and drew closed the door, locking the deadbolt before he went back down. "Where's Barry?" he whispered, upon his return.

"He went to look around," Eilowyn replied, softly, "to see if there's another way out of here."

"I found another stairway up, but it's bolted from the other side," Barathol announced, in as close to a whisper as he could manage. "I thought I could hear voices on the other side too."

"We need to hole up here for the time being," Eilowyn stated. "Help me get him somewhere comfortable."

The men went to work discretely moving crates and barrels around to open up a space in the back corner of the storeroom, while Eilowyn stood watch over Aleron. They returned to carry their friend to the area they cleared and laid him down on a pad built from empty grain sacks, with a sack of rice to cushion his head. Eilowyn followed behind with the sword, now dim in the presence of its owner, where it once shone with bright blue radiance. She thought she could see a faint glow, deep in the sapphires studding the pommel, but that was most likely the light from the vents. Barathol took the sword from her and replaced it in the gilded scabbard they had removed from Aleron's back.

Later, they found some dried meat and fruit, as well as many jugs of wine and Eilowyn stated, "This will do for now, but we need to find some water soon."

"Yeah, this stuff will dry us out like these figs, if we don't watch it," Barathol agreed. "The meat's salted too, so we should stick to the fruit and just enough wine to get it down."

"Sounds like we're under an inn or tavern," Geldun observed. The sounds of laughter and music filtered down through the floorboards.

"I can pick out a few phrases," Eilowyn declared. "It seems like they are all talking about the disaster at the palace, but they're all laughing about it. Must not be a soldier's tavern."

"Could go either way," Geldun declared. "Kolixtlani soldiers are mostly all conscripts anyway. Only the highborn officers have any authority."

"Uh oh, I think I heard something about the King. I think someone said he's dead." The raucous noise from above died down to a murmur. She noticed Aleron stirring and mumbling something in his sleep. "I think he's coming to." She knelt down beside him and brushed the hair from his face. "Aleron, wake up. It's Ellie. We're all safe, for now. Please wake up." Aleron mumbled something unintelligible and rolled to one side, settling himself more comfortably.

They waited several more hours. The level of noise increased after the subdued level that followed the news of the king's demise. Aleron bolted upright. "Wha…," escaped his lips before Eilowyn had the chance to silence him.

"Shhh…You need to be quiet, my love. We are hiding."

"Where…Oh my head! What happened?"

"We're holed up under a tavern of some sort," Barathol replied, "in Kolixtla."

"You did something that damn near knocked the palace down," Geldun added, "and then you passed out and the sword went dim."

At that announcement, Aleron's eyes went wide. "The sword, where is it?"

"Right here, by your right hand."

Aleron grabbed the hilt and said, "I don't feel anything, anything at all." He felt out further, beyond Andhanimwhid and exclaimed, "Nothing!"

"Quiet, or you'll get us all killed," Geldun whispered emphatically. "What are you babbling about?"

"I can't feel any magic at all, none at all."

"That's not good," Barathol commented, "not good at all." Geldun and Eilowyn looked at him and then turned their gaze to Aleron, as did Barathol. Aleron looked at each in turn, his eyes finally settling on Eilowyn, put his head in his hands and began to weep.

So ends The Halfblood King

the first volume of

The Chronicles of Aertu

Appendix A

Sudean Agricultural Calendar
Utilized for Daily Accounting in the Kingdom of Sudea

1	ALLFATHER'S MOON				
GURLACHDAY	SHILWEZDAY	CORBALLDAY	CARPATHDAY	SILDAENDAY	ZOREKDAY
1 NEW YEAR WINTER SOLSTICE	2	3	4	5	6
7	8	9	10	11	12
13	14	15	16	17	18
19	20	21	22	23	24
25	26	27	28	29	30

2	HUNGER MOON				
GURLACHDAY	SHILWEZDAY	CORBALLDAY	CARPATHDAY	SILDAENDAY	ZOREKDAY
1	2	3	4 FEAST OF FAELWE	5	6
7	8	9	10	11	12
13	14	15	16	17	18
19	20	21	22	23	24
25	26	27	28	29	30

3	BUDDING MOON				
GURLACHDAY	**SHILWEZDAY**	**CORBALLDAY**	**CARPATHDAY**	**SILDAENDAY**	**ZOREKDAY**
1	2	3	4	5 **FEAST OF LILLANE**	6
7	8	9	10	11	12
13	14	15	16	17	18
19	20	21	22	23	24
25	26	27	28	29	30

4	PLOWING MOON				
GURLACHDAY	**SHILWEZDAY**	**CORBALLDAY**	**CARPATHDAY**	**SILDAENDAY**	**ZOREKDAY**
1	2 **SPRING EQUINOX**	3	4	5	6
7	8	9	10	11	12
13	14	15	16	17	18
19	20	21	22	23	24
25	26	27	28	29	30

5	SOWING MOON				
GURLACHDAY	SHILWEZDAY	CORBALLDAY	CARPATHDAY	SILDAENDAY	ZOREKDAY
1	2 FEAST OF CERDAE	3	4	5	6
7	8	9	10	11	12
13	14	15	16	17	18
19	20	21	22	23	24
25	26	27	28	29	30

6	GROWING MOON				
GURLACHDAY	SHILWEZDAY	CORBALLDAY	CARPATHDAY	SILDAENDAY	ZOREKDAY
1	2	3	4	5	6 FEAST OF KORELLE
7	8	9	10	11	12
13	14	15	16	17	18
19	20	21	22	23	24
25	26	27	28	29	30

7	HAYMAKING MOON				
GURLACHDAY	SHILWEZDAY	CORBALLDAY	CARPATHDAY	SILDAENDAY	ZOREKDAY
1	2	3 ALERON'S BIRTHDAY YEAR 8745	4 SUMMER SOLSTICE	5	6
7	8	9	10	11	12
13	14	15	16	17	18
19	20	21	22	23	24
25	26	27	28	29	30

8	SQUASH MOON				
GURLACHDAY	SHILWEZDAY	CORBALLDAY	CARPATHDAY	SILDAENDAY	ZOREKDAY
1	2	3	4	5	6
7	8	9	10	11	12
13	14	15	16	17	18
19	20	21	22	23	24
25 SQUASH HARVEST FESTIVAL	26 SQUASH HARVEST FESTIVAL	27 SQUASH HARVEST FESTIVAL	28 SQUASH HARVEST FESTIVAL	29 SQUASH HARVEST FESTIVAL	30 SQUASH HARVEST FESTIVAL

9	HARVEST MOON				
GURLACHDAY	SHILWEZDAY	CORBALLDAY	CARPATHDAY	SILDAENDAY	ZOREKDAY
1	2	3	4	5	6
7	8	9	10	11	12
13	14	15	16	17	18
19	20	21	22	23	24
25 HARVEST FESTIVAL	26 HARVEST FESTIVAL	27 HARVEST FESTIVAL	28 HARVEST FESTIVAL	29 HARVEST FESTIVAL	30 HARVEST FESTIVAL

10	STORM MOON				
GURLACHDAY	SHILWEZDAY	CORBALLDAY	CARPATHDAY	SILDAENDAY	ZOREKDAY
1	2	3 FINAL BATTLE ANNIVERSARY	4	5 AUTUMN EQUINOX	6
7	8	9	10	11	12
13	14	15	16	17	18
19	20	21	22	23	24
25	26	27	28	29	30

11	FALLING LEAVES MOON				
GURLACHDAY	SHILWEZDAY	CORBALLDAY	CARPATHDAY	SILDAENDAY	ZOREKDAY
1	2	3 FEAST OF ANDULLE	4	5	6
7	8	9	10	11	12
13	14	15	16	17	18
19	20	21	22	23	24
25	26	27	28	29	30

12	ICE MOON				
GURLACHDAY	SHILWEZDAY	CORBALLDAY	CARPATHDAY	SILDAENDAY	ZOREKDAY
1	2	3	4	5	6
7 FEAST OF FINLE	8	9	10	11	12
13	14	15	16	17	18
19	20	21	22	23	24
25	26	27	28	29	30

YULE FESTIVAL WEEK					
ONEDAY	TWODAY	THREEDAY	FOURDAY	FIVEDAY	SIXDAY
1	2	3	4	5 FEAST OF ISELLE	6 ONCE EVERY FOUR YEARS

Appendix B

Comparative Timelines of Dwarves, Elves, and Men of Sudea

MAJOR EVENT	ELVISH CALENDAR	SUDEAN CALENDAR	DWARVISH CALENDAR
CREATION OF THE WORLD.	BILLIONS OF YEARS BRH (Before Recorded History)		
ELVES CREATED.	~6000 BRH	~7255 BRH	~5830 BRH
MEN, WESTMEN AND DWARVES CREATED.	~5000 BRH	~6255 BRH	~4830 BRH
DWARVES BEGIN WRITTEN RECORDS.	170 BRH	1425 BRH	YEAR 0
GODS APPEAR TO ELVES	YEAR 0	1255 BRH	170
DWARVES MIGRATE TO BLUE MOUNTAINS.	971	624 BRH	1141
GODS LEAVE ELVES, APPEARING TO MEN, WESTMEN AND DWARVES.	1255	YEAR 0	1425
GODS DEPART WORLD.	1755	500	1925
DWARVES BEGIN TO COLONIZE GREEN AND WHITE MOUNTAINS.	1760	505	1930
ELVES REACH CONTINENT.	1867	612	2037
GREEN MOUNTAIN KINGDOM OF DWARVES ESTABLISHED.	1990	735	2160
WHITE MOUNTAIN KINGDOM OF DWARVES ESTABLISHED.	2032	777	2202
SUDEA DECLARES INDEPENDENCE. ELVES WITHDRAW FROM CONTINENT.	3886	2631	4056
ADVERSARY RETURNS TO WORLD. ELVES RETURN TO CONTINENT.	4514	3259	4684
BEGIN THE GREAT WAR OF THE FREE PEOPLES AGAINST THE ADVERSARY.	6000	4745	6170
THE ADVERSARY DEFEATED, ENDING THE GREAT WAR. DEATH OF ALERON I.	6004	4749	6174
KING ALAGRIC IV OF SUDEA DIES WITH NO HEIR.	9000	7745	9170
WRITING OF SUDEAN HISTORY: YEAR 8000 EDITION.	9255	8000	9425
WRITING OF DWARVISH HISTORY: YEAR 10,000 EDITION.	9830	8575	10000
WRITING OF ELVISH HISTORY: YEAR 10,000 EDITION. BIRTH OF ALERON II.	10,000	8745	10,170

Appendix C

Historical Synopsis of Elves, Dwarves and Men of Sudea

Elvish History

At the beginning of time, the Allfather, creator of all things, begat the universe from incoherent matter. He created the multitudes of stars in the night sky. He beheld the beauty in what He had created from nothingness, but it gave him no comfort, for it still seemed cold and empty. The Creator fashioned beings like unto Himself, in the forms of male and female, for He remembered his Sisters as well as his Brothers and wished to create a family like unto the one from whence He came. These first children numbered fourteen in all and equally matched, consisting of seven male and seven female, not siblings, but each independent creations of the Allfather. This celestial family coexisted happily for uncounted ages, with only the stars as companions. They travelled widely, marveling at their father's creation. The male and female of his children chose partners, and with the Allfather's blessing, begat untold thousands of offspring over the course of the ages, like unto themselves, but of lesser stature. This was the natural state for these beings, and they did just as their Father had, before coming of age in his Mother's universe. These first children were not destined to stay forever in their Father's universe but would someday come of age and create their own to their own liking. Their offspring, begat of their Father's universe, however, would remain forever tied onto it.

As is the way of stars, some grew old and died. From their death were born new stars. It was at this age that the Allfather knew the time had arrived for the next stage of his creation. About one likely star, He congealed the formless gasses into balls of matter, glowing hot like steel from the crucible, spinning around the star. He did the same about many other stars and left them to cool for eons untold. One day, He returned, with his children and grandchildren in tow and said, "See all of you the many worlds I have made here unto this star. Only one of them will be suitable for our purposes next." He then led them to the third small rocky world from the star and said unto his children and grandchildren, "Behold that which is to be the fruit of my Creation."

His children did not yet understand, and one said unto his Father, "Why this one Father, for there are much larger and more beautiful worlds further out than this one. It is plain, dark and uninteresting with its steaming pools and black rocks."

"Ah my child, you do not yet understand our purpose. Though still rough yet, it will be as a jewel when we are finished. Let us go down and shape this rough new world to our liking."

The Allfather proceeded to separate the land from the sea. He brewed monumental storms over the seas and used the rain and winds to carve the highest mountains, wearing them flat and then raising new mountains in their place. Thus, was barren rock turned to soil over the course of untold ages. When at last it was ready, He said, "Come my children, let us bring life unto this fertile world we have before us."

"What is life, oh Father?" they asked in unison.

"I will show you now," He told them, as He took up water from the sea and bent his will to it. The first life sprang forth in His cupped palms. His children saw and were amazed, and He was glad for that but then admonished them, "My children, do not attempt to bring forth beings like unto yourselves into this world, for that is my prerogative. Make all forms of plant and beast but save for me the beings who will rule over them. My grandchildren, do not attempt to bring forth life as your parents do, for if you succeed, your creations will be flawed. Instead, it is your destiny to inhabit this world and others that we build, so that you may watch over them as caretakers."

With that instruction, the children of the Creator made all the life in the seas, then they made all the life on land. What had been barren rock and steaming pools, became green hills and valleys, white capped mountains, and crystal blue waters. The world had indeed become like unto a jewel.

At the point where the world had been populated with all manner of life, one of the children had become so enamored of their handiwork that he begged of the Creator, "Father, please, may I have this world as my own? I love it so and wish to watch over it and care for it for all the ages that are yet to be."

The Creator knew that this could not be so and saw through his son's plea to the covetousness that lay beneath the request. "Do not ask this of me, as it cannot be so. Your purpose is to create a universe of your own when you are grown. In due time, you will be able to create worlds and populate them, just as I have done. Do not thwart your own destiny, just to possess a portion of mine."

The errant child, much chagrined by his Father's reprimand, grumbled loudly to his brethren and their children over the unfairness of the Creator's decision. His brethren rebuked him as well for his insolence toward their Father, however, he swayed many of the grandchildren with his words and they became his followers. Secretly, he preached to his following of the unfairness of the Creator's prohibition on them to create living things. He taught to them the way to accomplish it and together they created all manner of despicable creatures, for it was true, as the Creator had said, that the creations of the grandchildren would be imperfect and flawed.

Soon enough, the others discovered that the beautiful world they had created was beset with foul creatures that crawled in dark places. The beasts were beset upon by biting things, parasites, and disease. The plants died from fungus, rot, and ravenous creatures. The Creator was not pleased with what He beheld and asked of his children, "Who among you is responsible for these foul creatures? They are a disgrace and a disfigurement upon our beautiful world." None spoke up to own to the wrongdoing. The Creator looked into the hearts of his children and when He came to the one who had disobeyed him said, "Do you think you can hide the truth from me, my disobedient son?"

"It was not I who disobeyed you, Father. I have always been your faithful servant," the son lied.

"Do you think I cannot look into your heart and see the truth? You add lies as well to your treason. I have seen now what you have done, and that you have drawn my children's children into your disobedience. Get thee gone from my sight, never to return and those of your following who refuse to repent." The disobedient son left the presence of his Father and his brethren, taking with him the grandchildren who would follow. Though many grandchildren repented, begged for forgiveness, and returned to the fold, most did not and followed the disobedient son. They took refuge in the spaces between the stars to bide their time, though many of the grandchildren remained in the world, hidden in dark places.

The other children then proclaimed, "Father, we must rid this world of all the vile things our brother has brought into being."

"That cannot be so," the Creator replied. "That which has been brought into being must not be destroyed out of hand and must be allowed to follow its natural course. We will give our creatures a means to defend against the creatures of your brother, who will now not be named. Our beautiful world will be marked by strife forever more."

Soon after, the Allfather discovered that the one who will not be named had done that which was unthinkable. He had created creatures after his own likeness, as was to be the sole prerogative of his Father. Like the creatures of his followers, these were fraught with imperfection, and he made many attempts, failing each time. Now, gruesome creatures of dim intelligence and evil disposition stalked the fringes of the world, wreaking havoc among the beauty of creation.

At the time that the Creator had divided the land from the sea, He had set aside a large island in the southwest sea. The disobedient son and his followers had never the opportunity to lay hands on this one piece of land, so it was devoid of his foul creatures. All was beautiful on the sparkling western isle, and it was here that the Creator brought forth the first of the world's creatures created in his own likeness, the first elves. Innocent and naked were these first of our people, and we wandered the island in that state for millennia. The mild climate of our homeland provided for us in abundance, and we wanted for nothing. We met many of the Creator's grandchildren during that time and they taught us many things about the nature of our fair island, but we knew not then the significance of these nature spirits.

One day, the first children of our Father appeared to us, and they frightened us in their magnificence. They told us, "Do not fear little brothers and sisters, for we mean you no harm and we have much to teach you," and teach us they did. They taught us to make tools and ornaments of metal, to hew stone and build with it and to domesticate the beasts and crops for which we had formerly hunted and foraged. We raised the first elvish cities and writing, and arithmetic came into being. The first line of elvish kings was established, and the cities became centers of learning. Our elder brethren taught us to forge swords, axes, lances, armor, and steel tipped arrows and taught us the elements of armed combat. We asked them why we would ever want to know how to fight, as we had never seen the need to fight among ourselves. They told us then of the history of creation as it is written in this very text. It was then that we learned why their number was uneven, with only six male and seven female. They told us that our destiny would take us from our lovely island to the brutal world to the east. There we would need to fight.

There came a day, one-thousand two-hundred and fifty-five years from the day we began accounting for time that our elder brethren took their leave of us. They told us of our brother races who came later, known as men, wandering the lands to the east across the sea and in need of their instruction. They warned us in parting to beware of the Adversary and his minions. Upon the conclusion of their instruction of men, our elder brethren were destined to leave this world and move on to others and finally to leave this universe to found their own. The Adversary, however, would never leave and would continue to gain strength as he matured, someday perhaps rivaling that of the Allfather. Thus, we were warned as our elder brethren left us for the world of men. There, they became known as gods, as men of that time lacked the sophistication to see them for what they truly were.

Many centuries passed. Our small boats gradually became larger, and we ventured further out to sea. Soon we developed seaworthy vessels able to cross the breadth of the ocean. Our lovely island was becoming crowded, and we decided to explore the lands to the east. At first, the sheer expanse of the western coastline of the continent daunted us. We landed our ships on the southwestern coast and encountered our first men. They were much different from us, being very dark and speaking a rude sounding language. They were friendly, however and it was soon apparent that they too had received some instruction from our elder brethren. They knew of steel, and they built small cities. They told us of larger, richer cities of their people far to the northeast, along the shores of a huge inland sea. We built our first colonies on this shore, as we were accepted by these people.

As we explored northward up the coast, we discovered that the men came in different races, unlike ourselves. The men further up the coast, past the towering mountains, which divided south from north, were not so dark and their hair was straight and black. Most did not greet us in a friendly manner. The jungle dwellers attacked us with stone tipped weapons, for they knew not of steel. As we moved north of the tropics, we passed another range of low mountains. The people inhabiting the land north of these mountains were a completely different race of men as those of the jungles to the south. These men were light-skinned, like us, but of a much more brutish appearance than any of the men we had met previously. These men were squatly built and immensely strong. Their faces possessed thick, beetled brows and receding chins. They had steel, however, and they greeted us in friendship. They spoke to us of their gods, and we recognized descriptions of our elder brethren, just as we had to the south. They became known in later days as westmen, to distinguish them from the other races of men, with whom they rarely mingled. They told us also, of another race of men to the east, which looked more like those we had encountered in the jungles, though of lighter complexion and more advanced in culture.

Yet another race, unknown to us previously, came to our attention. The men of the south encountered them as they explored the central mountains. They later migrated to the northeastern and southeastern coastal ranges. The men refer to them as dwarves and do not admit to them being men, nor do dwarves claim any kinship to men or westmen. They seem to live anywhere there are high mountains. In some ways they appear related to the westmen, however, they lack the receding chin, appearing more like a mix of westmen and men. They are shorter than either of the other two races, seldom exceeding five feet and stockier even than westmen. Dwarves are skilled miners and metal smiths, conducting huge excavations and living entirely underground. They are fierce defenders of their territory, and extremely suspicious of outsiders. Few foreigners have witnessed the splendor of their underground cities.

Our people established colonies in the far southern lands of the continent and the men there accepted us as their overlords, thusly they became separated from their brethren to the north of the Great Southeastern Desert, adopting aspects of our language and culture. The region became known as Sudea thereafter. This relationship ensued for over two-thousand years. Over that time, elves and men mingled their blood, even though elves could live many tens of centuries and men seldom lived as long as one. Elvish maids would take husbands among men, only to become widowed in their prime, often marrying several times in their lifetime. The same was true of the elvish masters who chose the same route. Heartbreak was commonplace among the elvish rulers of Sudea. Elvenholm sent pureblooded governors to preside over the colonies, often to the chagrin of the half-elf sons of former governors. Over time, the population of Sudea had become so mingled that the men lost, in much part, their dark complexions and looked similar to their elvish masters. Excepting half-elves, however, men did not inherit the longevity of their elvish forebears.

In the year 3886, by our reckoning, our colonies threatened open rebellion against the Crown of Elvenholm. The High Governor of the colonies neared the end of his life. With the support of his provincial governors, he declared that his half-elf son would rule after him. Since men multiply much faster than elves, the population of Sudea was far higher than that of Elvenholm. Additionally, the spread of elvish blood among men introduced the talent of sorcery to their number. The elvish King realized he would be unable to sustain a drawn-out war with the men and elves of Sudea, so he acquiesced and allowed them to go their separate way. Apart from the few who took an active role in the rebellion, the pureblood elves left Sudea and returned to Elvenholm.

By the year forty-five fourteen, elves became aware of the return of the Adversary to the world and once again, ships travelled to the shores of Sudea. We discovered there, a great kingdom of men, stretching from the west coast to the east coast and surrounding the Great Southeastern Desert and far eastern mountains on three sides. They were great maritime traders, sailing far up the eastern coast and into the inland sea to trade with the men of the far northeast and up the far northwest coast to trade with the westmen, as the inhabitants of that region became known. Their ruler was the grandson of the High Governor who had rebelled. They had retained and established a half-elf ruling class, by only allowing marriage among other half-blood families. Half-elves, though not as long lived as elves, often surpassed five centuries. Unfortunately quarter-elves and below tended towards the usual lifespan of men. The two kingdoms agreed to resume friendly relations and the Kingdom of Sudea agreed to help Elvenholm establish new colonies on the continent. Though difficult fighting ensued for several years, we pushed the fierce men of the coast, north of the Blue Mountains, into the deep jungle. Elves established colonies along the west coast, up unto the lands of the westmen.

Over the ages of our association with the lands outside our fair isle, we became acquainted with many other creatures and beings of which we knew not before. These were the children of the Adversary and his minions, their failed attempts to copy the fair creatures of the Creator and his faithful children. Foul beasts stalked the dark and lonely corners of the land. Trolls wandered the mountains and goblins haunted the forests. Cold, slimy creatures crawled the swamps. Worse than these were the minions of the Adversary who walked the land, just as the faithful grandchildren of the Creator did. These did always seek to bring havoc onto the fair creation of their sworn enemies. After the departure of the children of the Creator, the Adversary himself walked again across the land, setting himself as a god over ignorant tribes of men.

In the year six thousand, nearly fifteen centuries after our return to the continent, the Adversary brought war upon the lands of men and elves. The wild men of the jungle were long under his sway, and he brought three kingdoms of men under his control, as well. The war lasted four years, ending when the Adversary was vanquished by the Crown Prince of Elvenholm, who would become King Aelwynn. The final battle of the war took place on the shores of Lake Bul at the heart of the jungle, where the Adversary raised his black fortress, Immin Bul, as the seat of his power. King Aleron of Sudea perished in the fight with the Adversary, but his death allowed the prince to cleave the enemy's wrists with his great halberd, disarming him and then slashing his throat. The Adversary's minions were routed and driven from the field. The Adversary himself was bound to his dark throne with chains forged with high sorcery and his gates we sealed behind us, with wards indissoluble even for the ones who set them. So was the one who would usurp the dominion of his Father, imprisoned within his own unassailable stronghold, forever to wail in darkness. His weapon of cataclysmic power, the axe Zadehmal, proved indestructible, even to the hottest flame. Fearing to secure it in inhabited lands, lest it work to corrupt the denizens thereof, or to cast it into the sea, lest it find its way into the hands of a minion of the Adversary, it was spirited to the most desolate spot in all the world. None other than the High Sorcerer of Elvenholm, Goromir, shrouded the way to all who undertook the journey. It was he, who led the party to secure Zadehmal, and he alone knew the location of its hiding. Upon the journey's completion, Goromir put his affairs in order and disappeared forever into the high peaks of Elvenholm's Alban Mountains.

In the years that followed, elves, men, westmen and dwarves returned to life much as it had been in the years prior to the Great War. The minions of the Adversary still abounded in the world at large, though they lacked the common focus they enjoyed under their Master. The hobgoblins and half-trolls, bred from crosses with men in Immin Bul's heyday, multiplied. Their number was many times more cunning and dangerous than the original flawed creations of the Adversary. The Children of the Creator stayed always vigilant to incursions of these most foul creatures.

The Kingdom of Sudea began its slow decline. The halfblood line of its kings dwindled and eventually expired. Upon the demise of its last king, in the year nine thousand, the kingdom fractured, with a new kingdom established to the north and a steward minding the righteous throne of the lost line of kings. Over this time also, elves and men grew apart, most forgetting the indomitable alliance of the Great War. Westmen and dwarves kept to themselves as they always had. Now, in the ten-thousandth year of our kingdom, we have little contact with the other races of the world. Sudea, our once mighty ally among men, is but a shadow of its former glory, and the line of stewards still minds the realm in the absence of its king. However, the auguries have prophesied that a new age is upon us, and the fortunes of men will change, we know not for better or for worse.

Appendix C

Historical Synopsis of Elves, Dwarves and Men of Sudea

Dwarvish History

In the beginning, we dwarves lived among the westmen in the Iron Hills far to the north. They were similar, yet different from us at the same time. We preferred to shelter ourselves in caves year-round and seldom built shelters out of doors. The westmen took shelter in caves, in wintertime, but preferred to range across the land during the summer, chasing the herd beasts they hunted. Our people stayed in one place, making do with whatever game was available and storing food against leaner times. For many centuries, we knew only the westmen as our neighbors. They were half a head taller than we and lacked a chin, but otherwise looked much like us. We, each people, kept to ourselves for the most part. The day came, when we became aware of a new people, men, inhabiting the jungle to our south. They were a dark people, taller even than westmen, but fragile in appearance. They proved to be of vicious temperament, as if in compensation for their frailty. They hunted and ate, like animals, any stranger entering their territory, displaying the heads of their victims at the entrance to their lodgings. All those living on their northern borders feared their poison darts.

Because of our sensible, settled nature, we discovered the working of metal when others still fashioned tools of stone. First came copper, then bronze and finally steel. Bronze and steel tools enabled us to enlarge our dwellings and dig new dwellings where no caves existed. We became skilled miners, stone carvers and smiths. Soon, we found that our homeland could no longer support our numbers. Our hunters were forced to venture further and further afield, bringing us into conflict with our neighbors. Therefore, our Clan Chieftains met together as a single body, and came to a momentous decision; eight-hundred summers after we first began counting the years, our people embarked upon the thousand-league trek, which would bring them to the Blue Mountains, south of the Western Jungle. The journey lasted a full year, as we slogged through swamps and crossed wide rivers, hacking our way through the trackless jungle, pulling our carts behind us. We fought off marauding bands men the entire time and they learned to fear our swords and axes of bright steel. We lost many of our number to the cannibals of the jungle, they making no distinction between the helpless maiden or child and the able fighter. Finally, in what should have been the spring of the year eight-hundred one, we climbed out of the jungle, into the foothills of the Blue Mountains. We encountered few men in the foothills, but we pressed on for higher elevation, because we knew the men would come eventually. We found that we were still deep in the tropics, where seasons have no meaning and we settled in a fertile river valley, where the climate was as springtime was in our native land, high above the lands of men.

Our people prospered and multiplied, and we spread throughout the northwestern slopes of the Blue Mountains. At the northern part of the range, we were deep in the tropics and could settle at very high elevations, where the air grew quite thin. However, as we spread to the southwest of the range, we left the tropics and saw the return of the seasons. It was then that we discovered that the seasons inverted in the southern half of the world. What we had thought should be the months of summer, were in fact, the winter months. We had crossed the equator, but we grasped not the concept at the time, thinking that the world was flat like a plate. It was not until most recently, that the Sudeans sailed eastward from the inland sea, only to come, many months later, upon the western shores of the jungle, proving that the world was round. The southwest reaches of our mountains were dry and harsh, but they were rich in good iron, so they drew our people there as well. Soon we found our way through the mountains and settled the southeastern slopes as well. We dug deeply into the mountains in search of metals and precious stones. Our excavations expanded into cities, deep within the earth. We learned to tame the wild oxen and goats of our mountains, and as well, we began to till the fertile soil of our mountain valleys, clearing the great forests to grow barley and rye for bread and beer. Our people multiplied and spread throughout the Blue Mountains. The separate clans united to form two kingdoms, the Northern and the Southern, which in turn were tied together in bonds of kinship and mutual cooperation. It was thusly that we stood in the year fourteen twenty-five, when the gods of men and elves found us.

The Gods came to us in our mountain holds and we greeted them cordially, for they spoke to us in our own language. It soon became apparent that these were beings much like the nature spirits we had already encountered, but of greater magnitude. We did not worship the nature spirits as some among men and westmen had, so we were not inclined to worship these new arrivals either. They told us as much, saying that they did not require our worship and that we should venerate only their Father, the Creator of all things. They said that they would soon leave our world, to go on to build their own worlds, as their Father had done. They came only to instruct the peoples of the world in those things that they needed to prosper. The peoples of men and westmen were still living in savagery at this time and we knew not of the elves, who were civilized, but had not yet come to these shores. The Gods saw that we had already learned much of what they had come to teach us. They helped us to refine our methods, but spent much more time among men and westmen, as they had much further to go in becoming civilized. One of their number, however, Gurlach, was intrigued by our people and spent much more time among us than the others did. He is known among the other peoples, as the God of the Forge, for it was he who was tasked by his father to teach the working of metals. Since we were already accomplished smiths in our own right, he was able to teach us much more advanced methods than he could to the other peoples. He taught us to work metals unknown to the rest of the world, in crucibles sealed from the outside air, over fires of unimagined intensity. Dwarves learned to work metals lighter than steel, but many times tougher, and to make incredibly tough steel that would never rust, or steel that could withstand the heat of a typical forge without deforming. It is because of this relationship and our thankfulness, that dwarves venerate Gurlach alone among the gods, along with the Creator.

The gods departed our lands exactly five-hundred years after their arrival, in the year nineteen twenty-five. We were saddened for Gurlach to leave us, but he said it must be that way. He warned us of the likely coming of the Adversary, who only awaited their departure to begin his quest for dominion over our world. He told us also of two new mountain ranges far to the east, as yet unsettled by men. In the year nineteen thirty, we mounted expeditions to colonize the White Mountains of the northeast coast and the Green Mountains of the southeast coast. The men of the east, living on the shores of the inland sea, were long friendly to our people and let us pass unmolested. The mountains, on the other hand, we found to be infested with trolls and other foulsome creatures. The creatures of darkness had multiplied in the empty lands, which we had not allowed to happen in the Blue Mountains. Two brigades of warriors were sent from the twin kingdoms, one to each range, to clear the way for the colonists. By nineteen forty, the task was complete to our satisfaction in the Green Mountains and a thriving colony was established there. The task proved much more formidable in the White Mountains, however. That range stretched far to the north. The trolls of the far north grew larger and more ferocious than their southern cousins. Though we established a strong colony in the south of the range by nineteen forty, it took an additional twenty years of vicious fighting to subdue the northern trolls sufficiently to allow our expansion in that direction.

By twenty-one sixty, the Green Mountain colony had advanced to the point of self-sufficiency and an independent kingdom established under members of the Southern Kingdom's ruling family. Soon afterward, in twenty-two hundred two, was the White Mountain Kingdom established, under a branch of the Northern Kingdom's ruling house. Thus, the White Mountain dwarves share stronger kinship with the Northern Blue Mountain dwarves, while the Green Mountain dwarves are more closely connected to the Southern Blue Mountain dwarves. Due to their separation by five-hundred miles of open sea and our dwarvish mistrust of boats, the Green Mountain and White Mountain kingdoms have not grown closely together, though they are closer geographically to each other, than either is to their parents. This does not mean, however, that there are no bonds between them, as all dwarves the world over are bound through kinship to one another. We have accounted for our lineage since we were but few in numbers, living in the Iron Hills and have retained that record now for ten-thousand years.

The world remained relatively peaceful, with the exception of some minor wars among men, several of them caused by elves, for nearly two and a half millennia. We kept the wild men of the jungle at bay and had generally good relations with our other neighbors among men. As ever, we labored to keep the dark creatures that haunted our mountains at bay. Our first contact with elves occurred in twenty forty-one. They were tall and much fairer in complexion than men were, more like unto us in that respect. They seemed to us a strange people, aloof in their dealings with others, projecting always an air of superiority. They were indeed far more advanced than men were, but upon comparison, our calendar was one-hundred seventy years older. In addition, they, like men, lived in savagery until the Gods came to teach among them. They claim to be the elder race of our world, or so the Gods told them, but they have no concrete evidence to support that claim. They do possess uncanny powers of perception and sorcery and so they seem to share some kinship with the Nature Spirits or the Gods. Aside from anything that may be true of the elves, dwarves were the only race of this world to rise from savagery by our own wits. We stayed out of the wars of men and elves that occurred over the ages, letting them settle their own scores among themselves, that is, until the coming of the Adversary.

259

Sometime after the year five thousand, we began hearing rumors of a new sinister power moving in the world. He roamed among men, swaying many to his cause, especially those primitives who had rejected the Gods and continued to worship the unsavory spirits inhabiting the dark corners of the world. When he came to us, we had been warned already of his coming, and we rejected his overtures. What needed we, power and dominion over the other races? We had dominion over our mountains and that was enough. In sixty-one seventy, outright war broke out with the Adversary, involving every kingdom of this world. Suspecting, rightly, that our extensive tunneling connected the northern and southern Blue Mountains and thus provided a direct route from his jungle stronghold to the southern lands of men, his forces attacked the Northern Kingdom. He had early brought the men of the Jungle under his sway, arming them with weapons of steel. Along with them, he had also the men of Kolixtlan and goblins and trolls he had bred by the thousands. We held the Blue Mountains from him, thus doing our part for our allies among the free peoples of the world. Our kin in the White Mountains marched upon the men of the Thallasian Coast that had also come under his control. The Southern Blue Mountain and Green Mountain kingdoms provided troops, and superior weapons to the armies of men who fought the Nameless God. We finally defeated the Adversary in sixty-one seventy-four, scattering his minions, and the sorcerers of elves and men imprisoned him within his own fortress at Immin Bul. Our dear friend among men, King Aleron of Sudea, lost his life in the final battle, as did many of his kinsmen. His line lasted another three millennia before dying out just over eight centuries ago, but his kingdom never regained the splendor it had in the days before the Great War, when it was the mightiest of the kingdoms of men.

Our lives returned to much as they were before the war. We kept to ourselves, as we always did. The elves retreated to their coastal lands and their island in the west, meddling no longer in the affairs of men. Men, as they always had before, began once again to squabble among themselves in petty conflict. Westmen, always peaceful, returned to their placid, pastoral existence in their northwestern lands. Therefore, it stands, in our ten-thousandth year that the free peoples of the world, who once united against a common enemy, are again fragmented, and concerned only with their own affairs.

Appendix C

Historical Synopsis of Elves, Dwarves and Men of Sudea

Sudean History

In days past, our forefathers walked the land in savagery. We wore clothing of animal skins and hunted the forests and plains with spears and arrows tipped in stone. We made war among ourselves, for we knew not of government. We lived by hunting and foraging, for we knew not how to farm. We wandered in this fashion for uncounted ages, for we knew not writing, or the counting of years. We encountered spirits in the lands of our birth, and we learned much of the ways of nature from them. We learned as well that not all of these spirits were to be trusted. Some were tricksters, or worse and often meant us harm. Many among us worshipped the spirits and raised them up as gods and goddesses, for we knew not then their true nature, that they were the grandchildren of the Creator.

There came a day that a new set of beings came into our midst. These newcomers were far more powerful than the spirits of nature to which we were accustomed. Many among us accepted them as gods. Though they never revealed their true nature to us, they told us of a greater god, the Allfather, Creator of all. Our new deities numbered thirteen in all, six gods and seven goddesses. We knew not at that time the reason behind the uneven number. They taught us many things, the smelting of metals, rearing of livestock and the growing of crops. Our numbers multiplied and our rude villages became towering cities of stone. For exactly five-hundred years, the gods walked among us, and then they left, telling the people that they must depart, never to return. There was much weeping upon the departure of our gods, and we continued in their worship, hoping futilely that we could convince them to return. During our time with the gods, our people spread from the hot jungles of our ancestral homeland, into the empty lands to the south. The few scattered bands of men we encountered there quickly became assimilated into our own numbers and our kingdom stretched from the mountains and sea of the north to the frozen wastes of the south, and from the west coast to the east. Men even ventured into the forbidding wastes of the Great Southeastern Desert, taming the camel and becoming one with that harsh land.

During the year of six-hundred twelve, a new race arrived on our southwestern shores. They were tall and fair of skin, many having blond hair, as of yet unknown among our people, for we were a dark race at that time. We knew them as elves, and we accepted them as overlords unto us. They revealed to us that they too had been pupils under tutelage of our gods, but for far longer than we had. They would reveal unto us the true nature of our gods as creations of the Allfather and the nature spirits as their children in turn. They would also reveal unto us the reason for the gods' uneven pairing and the nature of the Adversary, he being otherwise unnamed and the one missing from their number. The seat of our kingdom lay over one-thousand leagues to the northeast, at Cop, on the shores of the inland sea. Our king chose not to accept the overlordship of our elven friends and brought war upon us southern men who had. The elves possessed powers of sorcery akin to those of the spirits of nature and used their powers to forge magical weapons for their allies among men. The forces of our former king were defeated in the year six-hundred twenty-one and the Province of Sudea established, being all the land west of the Great Southeastern Desert and south of the parallel marked by the capitol of the dwarvish Green Mountain Kingdom. For over two millennia, our people prospered, and our numbers multiplied. The blood of the elves mingled with our own, even spreading into the populations north of our borders. Over time, Sudeans came to resemble their elven masters more than they did their northern cousins. With the spread of elvish blood among men, also came the emergence of sorcerers among men.

In the year twenty-six thirty-one, in order to avoid outright rebellion, the Kingdom of Sudea was established, its capital at Arundell, freeing us from thralldom to Elvenholm and the elven king. The provincial High Governor was declared king of Sudea, with his half-elf son as heir apparent to the throne. The halfblood caste was established and members of halfblood families were forbidden to marry among the families of lesser men, else they lose their status in the ruling caste. The halfbloods lived not as long as those of pure elvish blood, but their lifespans far exceeding those of men. 628 years passed with no contact between the Western Isle of Elvenholm and the lands of men.

During the first six centuries of our independence, Sudea's men prospered and multiplied. We pushed our borders far to the north, taking western Coptia, coming even to the mountains of the dwarves. We claimed the Great Southeastern Desert and controlled the entire east coast of Elmenia unto the inlet to the inland sea, though we never gained dominion over the Elmenian highlanders, and the desert men gave us but loose allegiance. We took what we had learned of ships from the elves and improved upon it. Our people became great mariners, the greatest the world had ever known. Sailors travelled both coasts, even braving the ice-ridden seas of the far north to navigate the waters of the northern inlet that divides the lands of the west from those of the east. Sudean ships made their way even to the northern slopes of the impassable mountains dividing our lands from those to the north, trading with the strange people of Kolixtlan, o the coastal jungle. Our tongue became the language of trade for merchants the world over and in many lands, it became as commonplace as the native tongue. Our armorers, rather than being common smiths, were sorcerer-smiths, forging terrible weapons of immense power, as had the elvish smiths of old. As our civilization approached its zenith, the elves returned to our western shores.

In the year thirty-two fifty-one, elvish ships once again landed on our shores, making the thirteen-hundred league journey from their homeport across open seas. We found that we could still understand their tongue, as it had only been two generations of our kings since our peoples parted. They told us that a great evil was afoot in the world and that elves and men would need to stand together against it, lest it gain control over all of creation. We agreed to ally ourselves with them, as we knew the gods were departed, never to return. We helped the elves to establish two colonies northwest of our kingdom, along the coast. We pushed the crude savages of the jungle back from the coast, deeper into the forest. They were men who had shunned the wisdom of the gods, as they were already thrall to the evil spirits abounding in their homeland. They knew not of steel, for they had rejected the gods, so we brushed them aside. For nearly fifteen centuries, our kingdom and the elvish provinces coexisted in peace, as the elves slowly expanded their borders eastward, heavily fortifying against incursions of the wild jungle tribes. During this period, our kingdom became the most powerful of all the kingdoms of men. Combined with the might of the elvish kingdom, we were a force unstoppable.

Throughout these years, our traders received reports of the Adversary moving among the lands of men, claiming to herald the return of the old gods. Always, our statesmen were at work, convincing the foreign kings of his fraud, intending only to enslave the world under his dark dominion. He found a ready ear among the already corrupt savages of the jungle tribes and from there was eventually able to sway the mysterious central kingdom, Kolixtlan, to his ends.

Next to fall, was the kingdom of Adar, west of the Great Northeastern Desert and our ships were no longer welcome to ply the northern inlet to the great bay beyond. Rumors abounded of neighboring peoples being waylaid and carried off by raiders loyal to the Adversary, bound for slavery, or worse, offered up during inhuman sacrifices to their new god. Those few who escaped told of flat-topped pyramids in Kolixtlan, capped by bloody stone altars, where the hearts were cut, still beating, from the living victims. It was as though the heart of our land was rotten and the rot was slowly spreading outward. Eventually he managed to bring the Thallasians of the northeast coast under his sway and our ships no longer found safe harbor there. The Adversary also began to gather sorcerers to his kingdom, recruiting them with promises of wealth and power and using their greed as an avenue to poison their minds fully. The weaponry and tactics of the jungle men became more advanced under their new master and incursions against the elves became frequent. During these raids, males were killed outright, but females were abducted whenever possible. We wondered at the sinister designs of the enemy, until the day that one elf maiden escaped her captors. She feigned drowning and made her way out the inlet, washing up on the shores of the westmen. They rescued her and nursed her back to health, at which time she told her harrowing tale. She and the other elf maidens were penned up as animals. The sorcerers of the Adversary daily visited them. None left the pens unless they became pregnant, then they were moved and not seen again. The Adversary's plan was now made clear, to breed Halfblood sorcerers of his own, twisting them to his own designs. She told of other, more ghastly things as well. Maidens of both men and westmen and even some few dwarf maidens were penned up alongside the elves. Goblins and other monsters regularly visited these. Many did not survive the abuses of their captors, but some did, becoming pregnant and leaving the pens. Obviously, the Adversary was trying to perfect his dark creations by breeding them to the children of the Creator. Our hearts became darkened at the thought of what new monsters he would unleash upon the world.

In the year forty-seven forty-five, also the year six thousand by the elvish calendar, the Adversary chose to attack. He had massed his forces, secreting them in the depths of the western jungle. It was springtime in our lands when the enemy attacked the elvish colonies, attempting to push them into the sea. He also made war with the westmen of Sunjib. The Blue Mountains dividing us from the north are impassable, except at the coasts and through the tunnels of the dwarves, so he made war also upon the dwarves and Castia on the inland sea. Ships from the Thallasian Coast harried our shores. In the end, the Adversary spread his forces too thin, fighting on too many fronts. Our forces landed armies on the west coast to bolster the elvish defense. Soon the armies of Elvenholm joined us. Our forces combined with the armies of the westmen, Sultea, Mittea and Waban joining their Sunjibi brethren. We pushed the Adversary deep into the jungle. The dwarves held the mountains. Castia, aided from the south by Coptia and from the east by Chu, pushed back against Kolixtlan, crushing them, and tearing down their temples. Our navy destroyed the ships of Thallasia, while Chebek horsemen subjugated the land. The lightning cavalry of the Taliks swarmed across Adar, laying that kingdom to waste. By forty-seven forty-nine, deep in the jungle, we discovered a great lake, Lake Bul, possibly the largest in the world. On the shores of this lake, the Adversary built his towering fortress of seamless obsidian, Immin Bul, surrounded by a sprawling city. The forest was cleared for many miles from the shores of the lake for fields, tilled by slave labor, to feed his armies. The battle fought at the walls of the Adversary's city was the bloodiest of the entire war. Multitudes of foul creatures issued forth from the gates, trolls and goblins by the thousands and monsters of diverse types. Then the Adversary himself strode out upon the field of battle. His personal retinue consisted of 100 dark halfblood sorcerers. Accompanying him as well were goblins and trolls of types never before seen by the eyes of men and elves. The goblins being larger and stronger than those we had fought previously and the trolls smaller, faster, and far more cunning. We believed these to be the product of his breeding his creatures to men. They bore magical weapons, like unto our own, but charged with dark, malicious power. The Adversary wielded a great axe, its blade glowing red with malevolent energy. Simple men at arms quaked in fear in his terrible presence, but the elven warriors and halfblood knights pressed on. Eventually the armies of men and westmen rallied at the sight of the courageous Sudeans and elves, turning the tide against the enemy. The westmen, being fierce warriors, many times stronger than men, crushed the hosts of goblins in their path. Our sorcerers focused their will and the dark sorcerers fell by the score, as magical energy crackled in the air about both groups. Finally, King Aleron of Sudea and Crown Prince Aelwynn of Elvenholm stood shoulder to shoulder, facing the Dark Lord in all his terrible majesty. The prince of elves held his massive halberd, while the king of men wielded his greatsword, fully as long as a man is tall. Both weapons glowed with cold blue radiance, as the greatest sorcerer of Elvenholm had forged them, for the sole purpose of defeating the Dark Lord. The Adversary proclaimed, "Behold, Zadehmal, Cleaver of Souls, the instrument of your undoing." Aleron and Aelwynn said nothing in reply, their faces set in grim determination. Blows rained and were parried, sparking like lightning when blue nimbus met red. The king of men swung low, his great blade cleaving the greave of the Adversary, sinking deeply into his calf. Howling in pain, the Dark Lord swung his axe overhand. The king, his blade jammed in the thick steel, was unable to parry the blow and was split asunder by the great axe. Unable to save his comrade, the Prince of Elves swung his halberd, cleaving the Adversary's arms, above the wrists. The great red axe tumbled to the ground, as the Dark Lord screamed, the stumps of his arms spurting black blood. The halberd swung once again, chopping through the gorget protecting the Adversary's throat. The Dark Lord toppled, his lifeblood pouring out on the muddy ground.

With the fall of the Adversary, his army faltered and broke under our assault. The elves brought forth chains forged of high sorcery and bound the Adversary hand and foot. It being understood that no one, save the Creator, had the power to actually kill a god, the Dark Lord would need be imprisoned for all eternity. They dragged him to his black fortress and even into his own throne room, resplendent in gold, silver, and electrum. The elvish sorcerers chained him to his massive seat of obsidian, guarding his locks with diverse powerful wards. Even as they finished, they saw that the flesh had already grown over the stumps of his arms and his throat had knit itself together. The Adversary was far from dead and was only now sleeping, regaining his strength. The gates of the dark fortress were barred and locked with sigils of great power. None would be able to break the bonds securing the Dark Lord in his imprisonment, save that they held more power than that of the combined sorcerers of Elvenholm and Sudea.

The king of Sudea was burned upon a massive pyre, as is the custom of our people and our dead were cared for in a like manner. His greatsword was born back to his heir in Sudea, to serve as the symbol of the royal office from that time on. The other men and westmen reclaimed their dead and treated them, as was the manner of each their own people. The dead of the elves were born away by their people, to be burned in Elvenholm, across the sea. The dead of the enemy were left to rot where they lay. The Adversary was left imprisoned in his own hall, in his indestructible fortress of solid black obsidian. It is said that his howls of rage echo through the depths of the western jungle to this very day. The elvish Prince and his chief sorcerer Goromir took up the great red ax of the Adversary. A furnace was erected, and they cast the massive weapon into the white-hot coals, as the bellows were pumped and still more charcoal layered atop it. Clean yellow flame roared from the chimney, as the furnace burned itself out. Once cool enough to approach, the furnace was opened and there the axe sat, totally unscathed. It was cool enough even to touch, though its blade glowed red as fresh blood. It was plain to them that this weapon would not be unmade by mortal hands. Some said that it should be cast into the sea, but wiser heads prevailed, reasoning that this was a thing of great power and could possibly find its way even from the depths of the sea. They sensed that the Adversary had tied much of his being into the weapon, and it may still be subject to his will. Because of this, they ruled against safeguarding it anywhere in the lands of elves or men, else it may work to sway them to its master's purpose. The elves took up the cursed blade and bore it into hiding, saying only that it would be safely hidden away in a dark corner of the world, where no living beings tread. Beldan, the young prince of Sudea, yet only ten years of age, received the sword of his father. In his hand, its blade shone with the same blue radiance it had when in the hand of the king, signifying that he was the rightful heir to the rule of Sudea. From that time after, it became known as Andhanimwhid, Sign of the King. He took the sword, its glowing blade forged from a fallen star by Goromir, the greatest sorcerer of the elves and sunk it into the stone of the back of his granite throne. Only the hilt, bound in bright electrum and set with glittering sapphires, remained above the surface of the rock. None other but the rightful heir could ever remove the sword, thus providing a sign to verify future claims. The young prince was crowned king of Sudea in the summer of forty-seven fifty and ruled more than five centuries.

In the years following the cataclysmic war, the world went about rebuilding itself. The men of the jungle returned to savagery and the kingdoms of men attempted to return to their normal state. The golden age that was prior to the domination of a quarter of the world by the Adversary was past. The three kingdoms that fell under His sway maintained their enmity toward the other kingdoms of men. The Kolixtlan Sea, to the south of the northern inlet, remained closed to us, all its shores unfriendly. Pirates sailed out of the harbors of Thallasia, harassing all shipping. The halfblood families of Sudea were decimated, unable to maintain their viability. The royal line weakened as the noble families slowly dwindled. The prohibition against intermarriage between halfbloods and common men was lifted, and the purity of the strain diluted. Soon, our kings lived no longer than the average commoner, though the sword would still release for the rightful king and a faint blue nimbus remained to indicate his right to rule.

In the year seventy-seven forty-nine, exactly three-thousand years after the defeat of the Adversary and the death of the king at his hand, Alagric IV, the last king of Sudea, died leaving no heir. Many pretenders to the title came forth, bearing their credentials, but none could draw Andhanimwhid from its granite scabbard. The line of Stewards was established to oversee the affairs of the kingdom and no king has sat upon the throne of Sudea for nearly a millennium.

Ten years after the death of Alagric IV, civil war broke out among our people. After five years of bloody strife, a pretender established himself as king over our northern lands of Ebareiza, though he had no rightful claim to the title and our border became once more, the parallel defined by the dwarvish capitol. Thus weakened, we soon lost control of the Elmenian coast, the men there recognizing no king. Though still claimed as part of the kingdom, the desert men stopped paying tax and instead, charge our caravans to pass. Thus, it stands, six-thousand years after the founding of our fair kingdom; our borders are reduced to nearly the same extent as then.

Printed in Great Britain
by Amazon

4d3649f4-9fad-4490-855a-350230f64bddR01